# DARK SACRIFICE

## BOOK THREE
### OF THE
## HIDDEN HERITAGE SERIES

## TARA WINTERS

PUBLISHED BY WINTERMOON PUBLISHING

Copyright © Tara Winters, 2015

Visit Tara Winters' official website at www.tarawinters.com for the latest news, book details, and other information

Date of first printing: November 2015

Editing by: Sue Ducharme of Textworks
Cover Design: www.coveryourdreams.net
eBook formatting: Guido Henkel, www.guidohenkel.com

*To Paula and Joe: Beta readers and Strategists!*

*The Ultimate Sacrifice for knowledge is not in the pain but in the loss of innocence.*
—Odin

# CHAPTER ONE

DARK HOLLOW.

Even the name gave him the creeps. Kayle straightened his back and cast a steely glance toward the curtain of fading sunlight that slid through the heavy overgrowth. Kayle's gaze shifted to the long black bag laying on the granite out-cropping nestled among the dense foliage.

With its old legends, Dark Hollow was certainly morbid enough to host such a macabre package.

"You're done then?"

Kayle nodded and turned to the detective waiting patiently behind him. Sergeant Donaldson of the Porta Negra Police Department leaned against his unmarked car; the fading sunlight glinted off his dark sunglasses as he waited for Kayle's attention to shift back to the present.

"Yes, I got everyone. It took me some time to reach all of the Boston FBI, but I think that I was able to get to those who saw the body. Everyone else can be allowed to believe that the discovery of the body in Dark Hollow was just a hoax."

The sergeant glanced back at the black body bag lying in the shadows. "Well, I would rather have to deal with a hoax than the real thing. So you are taking her back to her family tonight? Back to…that place…" His voice trailed off.

A slight smile crept across Kayle's stony visage. "Yes, she will return with me to 'that place.' The less you know about it the better."

The detective agreed. "And you are sure I won't have anything else to worry about? No other fairies posing as FBI or crazy-ass dragons coming from that place?"

"They are Faye, not fairies. And we don't have any dragons." Kayle inhaled deeply. "At least we didn't when I left. Who knows now?"

Detective Donaldson laughed. "Well, I wish you safe travels." He glanced over again as the gloom began to hug the long, dark body bag, "Please send my condolences to her family. Whoever she is."

"I will." Kayle exhaled. "Watch over Tabitha and Doni's family. I do not anticipate any trouble, but I am not sure if this might escalate."

"I thought you said that you reinforced this…" the detective wiggled his fingers in air quotes, "'magic net'—or whatever it was that was supposed to keep out clowns like our fake FBI fairy."

"I did reinforce it, but he was able to slip under while Doni and I were away. Of course, it keeps magical folk like myself out, but that does not mean that humans cannot come and go," Kayle cautioned.

"Why humans? I thought that the magic people would present most of the problem."

"That should be so. But if the magic are not allowed on the island, it would make sense that anyone looking to stir up more mischief might seek to use humans," Kayle commented.

"You know, when you started telling me all this bullshit, I was kind of under the impression that your plan was to clean this up. Now you are telling me we may have more to worry about?" Detective Donaldson walked toward the door of his unmarked car.

Kayle extended his hand in farewell. "You think that if I hadn't shared this with you, you wouldn't have come up with something else to worry about? The offer is still open. I can still wipe your memories, as I did with the others."

Donaldson shook Kayle's hand and responded with a wry grin. "What, and miss out on the ongoing saga? Besides, with the tourist season in full swing I just didn't have enough to worry about. I was hoping you could dish out some new excitement to keep me up at night."

"Take care, my friend."

Kayle turned to head back toward the portal, his thoughts already focused on his return to Caska.


As the sun began to set behind the Caskan mountains, Doni gazed out the door. She wrapped the robe tighter around her slim waist before she lifted her cup of tea and stepped onto the balcony. The humid air was still warm after the sticky day, but after a cool shower, the darkening skies now gave the evening a cool, misty feel. Her nerves began to settle. She intentionally made her mind blank to allow the calm from the expanding pink skies to seep into her soul and soothe the turmoil there.

The door below slammed, and heavy footfalls echoed as they made their way up the stone stairs toward her circular chamber.

So much for peace.

"Doni?" Kayle's voice sounded harsh.

"Out here."

He joined her, his gray eyes taking in the steaming mug and her long robe. "Early to retire, isn't it?"

"Perhaps I am not retiring but returning from a shower, lover. And hello to you too," she snipped.

He took the mug from her hands and swallowed a mouthful of the hot tea. As he choked down the burning fluid, she lifted a sardonic brow at him. "It's hot, by the way."

He growled in response and walked back into the cool room, stripping off his shirt. Without further comment, he stepped into the adjoining chamber. Doni heard the hiss of water. She wandered into the room and picked up his discarded shirt and pants.

"Is everything settled?" she asked.

Kayle's face was lifted to the spray; he turned to let the water stream down his hair. Doni leaned against the sink and quietly sipped her tea while he released a long, drawn-out sigh. "Yeah, she is back," he said quietly. "The DesChamps family was waiting for me on my return from Dark Hollow."

Doni remained silent. He gave her a moment to grieve before he quietly spoke. "You should have been there. She was your best friend."

Doni nodded.

"She gave her life to see you safely away." A soft sob escaped Doni; Kayle's gaze did not relent. "You owed her at least that much."

"I know, dammit! I know!" Doni cried. She swept out of the room with a swirl of her long robe.

Kayle's voice followed her. "I cannot keep cleaning up your messes!"

Kayle finished his shower. He dried off and slipped into a comfortable pair of pants and fresh shirt as he joined her on the balcony. "You know I am right."

Doni lifted a delicate shoulder but did not respond. They stood in silence, each lost in thought. Doni stared off into the distance. The sunset had become the deep violet onset of night, and she gritted her teeth with the strain of the ongoing task.

"I spoke to Tabitha."

Kayle glanced over in surprise. "Did you? And? Has she left Antoine's care? Were you able to get her away?"

Doni shook her head. "No. Since you departed, things have deteriorated. Antoine is keeping her prisoner. In fact, he has gifted her to Luc DesChamps in return for his loyalty."

"What?"

"And Luc has apparently killed Katie Hennessy, on Antoine's orders. My father has been moved to Antoine's estate, and Cole is also a prisoner, but I have not heard how he is. I cannot contact him as I do Tabitha," Doni reported. As she lifted the cup for another sip of tea, her fingers tightened to white claws.

Kayle exhaled. "Luc DesChamps? Killed Katie? I have not met the man, but knowing Marcus and Bertòn as I do, I cannot believe that he would do such a thing. Who told you this? Tabitha?"

"Yes."

"How did you speak with her? I assume you did not go back into the viper's nest."

"I drew her out with separation, much like Larissa did when she was at Bertòn's home," Doni replied.

"And she was able to maintain it?"

"Kayle." Doni placed a hand on his arm. "You would not have known she was not physically there."

Kayle's brows knit. "How can that be? Any Faye doing a separation has a hazy shape at best. Larissa is one of the best I have ever seen, and even she is not fully substantial."

"I have spoken to the elders. The ability was lost to us many generations ago. When the Faye opted to discontinue breeding with the Caskan and humans, it was thought we needed to strengthen our bloodlines to regain former abilities. We lost so many abilities when we let the inferior blood of the Caskans and humans leech into our lines."

Kayle smiled mockingly. "Inferior? Doni, you have lived among the humans all your life. After a short time here, you are now becoming an elitist?"

Doni brushed him off with an irritated wave of her hand. "I am speaking of blood purity only when it comes to the magic that we Faye carry. Obviously, as I grew up human, I harbor no prejudice."

"I see. So when you discussed this with the elders, what was their response? Did they understand Tabitha's bloodlines?" Kayle asked pointedly.

Doni answered slowly. "If you are asking if I was truthful about her true parentage, I was. I never told Antoine that she and Cole were his children."

"But you never told him they were not," Kayle countered.

"How could I? You know how perilous my situation was there. You know I was in fear for my life and for the lives of my children. For God's sake, Kayle, you were the one who came to train me and help me get out. You were there in my darkest hours. You saw the marks on my body from his style of love. Did you honestly think I would have told him about us?" Doni demanded.

"But even now, Tabitha does not know the truth. You let this lie become reality to all, including your children," Kayle snarled.

"I never told them Antoine was their father!"

"You never told them that he was not! Now, he has them both."

"While he believes they are of his blood, they are far safer than they would be if he knew the truth." Doni shot back.

Kayle leaned forward, his eyes shards of steel, as he released the words between clenched teeth. "You could have told Tabitha many times in the past eighteen years. For the love of the One God, Doni, she grew up knowing me. She lived three miles from my house. I saw her every day. You could have informed her, and then we could have told her about our world and why we ran from it. She would not now be a prisoner of that madman."

Doni stepped back as though she'd been struck and stared at him. "Are you serious? How could I have told her? After so many years, how could I suddenly just blurt out the truth? One day suddenly say, 'Hey, honey, how was your day? By the way, you know that fisherman, Kayle? Well, it's a funny thing...'"

He slammed his fist on the railing. "Dammit, Doni, it could have been that simple. It could have been as simple as starting that conversation. I watched her for eighteen years, and I could not reach out and talk to her or even ask her about herself without looking like some kind of pedophile. I am her father, Goddammit, and if you had the sense to have had that discussion with her, I may have been able to help her. Now she is in the hands of that madman. And he has handed her over to a man who killed on his order and allowed him to rape your daughter. This could have been avoided."

Doni spun around. "How dare you! This is no game! We are talking about telling our daughter she came from a different world. How do you tell a child she has magical abilities? That her parents are not even human? What would she think? She needed to find her own way in our world!"

"That is not *our* world. We don't belong there anymore than Tabitha does." Kayle hissed.

"She does. She grew up in that world, and she can make a life for herself there. No impending war, no parent who would hold her prisoner for her healing..."

"Doni, by all that is holy, she is a full-blooded Faye, with abilities that we have barely scratched. She cannot remain in that world with those abilities." The fight faded from Kayle's voice. "You knew she would come here. You left her that damn note."

"How could I have known she would come here? How could I have guessed that she would find the portal?"

"Because Antoine's spies were watching her. They were waiting for you to leave and let the net weaken. I told you to stop coming over. What were you thinking, leaving her that note? What did you think would happen?" Kayle demanded.

Doni shook her head. "I thought that after I left that small detail, I would tell her when I returned." She slid her hands into her long white hair and let her fingers run through the silken strands as she stared out at the scenery. "I could not bear to have her think I had been committed yet again."

Kayle turned from her, realizing the game she played with his emotions. With her full arsenal of wiles, she knew how to get beneath his anger. "Damn your pride, Doni. Tabitha's life may be forfeit for your selfish ends."

Doni let her hair drop and glanced back at him. "Pride? My daughter grew up thinking her mother was nothing more than a fragile little egg who would break apart as soon as things got difficult."

Kayle turned back to her. "No, I think Tabitha thinks her mother is a frightened mouse who runs every time things get tough."

"I thought this was what you wanted, for me to tell her the truth!"

"Yes! Back before she showed up in Caska! You knew she was here when she arrived in Calais. You could have met her and turned her back, yet you let her fall into his clutches," Kayle accused. "Now how many lives will be lost trying to get her out again?"

"No lives need be lost. She can get herself out of there, as I did."

Kayle's short laugh was caustic. "If you recall, you had a full-blood Faye to assist and train you. Tabitha is there on her own."

Doni turned to him and placed a gentle hand on his arm. "Kayle, I am trying to tell you that she is even stronger than I am. She can get out. And when she does, she will be that much more powerful. When she returns home, she can hone those powers. And then she will be unstoppable."

"Unstoppable? Exactly what is your plan for her?" Kayle asked suspiciously. He lifted her delicate hand, observing the well-manicured fingers resting in his work-roughened hand.

"That she be able to face any who would again threaten the life she chooses," Doni whispered. "And she can, with a full-blooded Faye trainer to help her. To train her as he trained me."

"Don't you think it might be too late for that?"

"Kayle, the past is the past. I know you do not agree with what I decided, but it is done. Now we must get her home. After you return with her, you can teach her to control her powers so she can make a life for herself in a safer world."

"Safer? Have you seen the news lately?"

Doni shrugged. "Let us find some dinner and speak to the elders. I think you will find their theories interesting."

# CHAPTER TWO

THE DOOR SLAMMED. ANTOINE LOOKED FROM TABITHA'S departure to Dylan, perplexed. "Did she just order me to *'bite her'*?"

Dylan shrugged. "I suspect it was more of a local colloquialism than an actual invitation."

"Bite me?" Antoine shook his head. "Surely they can express themselves better than that?"

"I assume you have noticed that her temper seems to get the better of her. It would be useful to remember she has a tendency to respond emotionally." Dylan rose from the chair. "Other than watching you infuriate my sister yet again, is there any reason for my attendance?"

Antoine also stood. "You will join us for dinner tomorrow? I require your assistance to make sure she behaves herself."

"I thought watching over our little hellcat was Luc's job?" Dylan's voice dripped with sarcasm.

"I wonder at his ability to get back in her good graces. He does not seem willing to take her without her consent," Antoine commented. "I was under the impression she rather liked him."

Dylan coughed out a dry, sardonic laugh. "You overestimate the female ability to forgive. Give him time, he is a patient hunter. He will bed her in time."

Antoine grunted. "And our friend in the basement? How are the accommodations?"

"It rests there quietly and seems content, until I take it out to feed. It is becoming more solid and more...shall we say cognizant?" Dylan responded.

"Cognizant? How so?"

Dylan exhaled. "I guess it would be best described as aware. As though it recognizes more of what is going on around it and is paying attention. I wonder if it is as impassive as we believe."

Antoine stared at the younger man before stepping around his desk, a packet of papers tucked beneath one arm. "Let's hope we do not find out. Just make sure you can keep it under control. If that gets loose on the estate, the consequences would be innumerable."

Tabitha leaned against the door, her ear pressed to listen to Antoine and Dylan, her hand resting on the guard's chest. When she had stormed from her father's office, she had shoved the ever-present guard up against the wall and signaled him to be silent. When he prepared to speak, she'd hissed a threat and then pressed her ear against the door of her father's office.

*Basement?* She thought. *Is that where Dylan keeps the creature?*

Behind her, the guard made a sound, and she let out a sharp "Shhh!"

"But...."

Tabitha pressed her hand harder against his chest. As she strained to hear the conversation through the door, she felt warm breath on her cheek.

"If you are trying to hide, I can still see you."

She leaped with a startled cry and spun to see Luc grinning at her. "Buffoon!"

He shrugged. "You would have gotten further by just casting a thought to overhear them," Luc commented.

"I was not listening, I simply..." She floundered to find an excuse.

"Caught your earring in the door on the way out?" Luc offered.

"Go to hell," she snapped. She stalked away from Antoine's office, moving with determination toward the main hallway, her sheepish guard close behind.

Luc watched her go and lifted a single shoulder in resignation. "I think I am already there," he whispered to himself.


Tabitha stalked through the hall. "What is in the basement?" She demanded.

Her guard glanced behind him and trotted to keep up. "The basement? Well, nothing, just empty rooms and offices. And they are off limits to you."

"Your instructions are to simply follow me," Tabitha growled back. "Can you take me to see my brother?"

"Didn't you just see him?"

"Not Dylan, the other one. Cole."

The guard nodded and pointed down the stairs. "This way."

Tabitha waited in the sitting area for Cole, impatience gnawing at her belly. She had not seen him since they had been in the room in the basement. The thought of that night still gave her chills: the explosion of the gun and the sight of Luc staggering back, the bullet hole gaping in his chest, had sent waves of nausea pulsing through her.

"Tabitha?"

Cole finally emerged, and with a cry, Tabitha launched herself into her brother's arms.

"Cole! Are you all right? Is Lena okay?" The words tumbled from her mouth as she clung to him as her tears slipped down his shoulder.

"Shhh... Yes, yes, Tabitha," Cole soothed. He gently pushed her back to look at her. He leaned down and took in her tear-stained face; his fingers traced the purple bruise blossoming on her cheek. "Are you all right?"

Her answer was a hiccup. Not trusting words, she nodded her head.

"Antoine?" Cole asked, gesturing to the bruise.

"Yes. He seems to think it is the only way I will listen to him."

Cole shook his head and turned to the pot of javé swinging from the hook in the fireplace. He took down a mug and filled it for her. "Sit."

She accepted the mug and sank to the arm of the couch; he leaned back in the opposite corner.

"How is Lena?"

"She is frightened, but she will be fine. Tell me, how are you? What happened after Dylan carried you from the room?"

Tabitha shrugged. "I woke later that night, feeling as though I had been beaten."

"You had." Cole pointed out quietly.

"Well, I went to see our father in the morning, and he explained the facts of this world," she responded as she absently rubbed the black swelling on her jaw. Her cheeks burned as she whispered the next words. "He has gifted me to Luc for his loyalty."

Cole nodded. "Well, at least you are safe for now."

"Safe? How long will it be until I have to—" she stammered. "He made it perfectly clear that if Luc does not swear fealty to him, he will give me to someone else."

"Luc won't let that happen," Cole assured her.

Tabitha leaped from the couch. "Luc? Seriously? He has turned into nothing but an opportunistic little snake! He brought Grandfather here!"

Cole stood. "He saved Lena's life."

"And he killed Katie!" Tabitha shrieked.

Cole lifted his hands in supplication. "Calm down, Tabitha. Listen, however you may feel, we have to figure out how to get you away from here."

"Cole, I saw our mother. I spoke to her."

Cole was surprised. "And? Can she help?"

"She is working on something, but she needs our help."

"Our help? What does she want?"

Tabitha perched on the corner of the couch. "She showed me the black elves, Cole. I saw what they do, and… well, they killed Viho and the men who were with him."

Cole dropped his head forward as a curse slipped from his lips. "You saw this?"

"Mom was able to bring me with her back in time to show me. Dylan controls the thing," Tabitha told him. "With a stick or wand-type thing."

"Wand? Stick?"

She nodded. "I saw it respond to the stick when Dylan waved it. Whatever it is, he can control it by waving this thing at it."

"What is it? What is it made of?"

She shook her head. "That is what Mom needs to know. She wants me to try and find out."

"Are you serious?" Cole exploded. "She cannot ask you to try and find that out! We have to get you out of here!"

"Yes, but in the meantime, I need to see what I can discover."

"No. It is too dangerous," Cole answered.

"Cole, Antoine won't hurt me. I am a healer. He needs me," Tabitha argued.

"Oh no?" Cole lifted a finger to her jaw. "I think we both know that he will. He may not kill you, but he can hurt you."

"I will be careful."

"No, Tabitha. I cannot help you. We are locked in these rooms. Food is brought in. I can't get out." Cole stood with a growl and kicked the low table out of his way.

"Cole, can you separate?" she asked.

"You mean from my physical body?" She nodded. "No. I can't. I do not seem to have the Faye abilities."

"But we are twins. Wouldn't we have the same abilities?"

Cole shook his head. "We are the first twins I have ever heard of. I don't know if we get the same abilities or not, but I know I can't do some of the things that you seem to be able to do."

"Well, can you make yourself invisible? Move around without anyone seeing you?"

"Seeing? Maybe. Sensing? No," Cole admitted. "But I was not exactly the best student of abilities. I always did what I had to do, but I was not particularly interested in working that hard to learn about my abilities."

"Hmm… Well, it looks like I am going to have to get creative," Tabitha admitted. Her thoughts were already churning. She stood. "I will be back later."

"Wait," a soft voice called from the inner bedroom. Tabitha and Cole both turned to see Lena standing at the doorway, her arms hugging her slender body. "If you want to know more about the black elves, there is a woman in the village who might be able to help you."

Tabitha took a step forward, but Lena stepped back into the darkened doorway. Cole shook his head. "Who? I can't remember anyone."

"The woman who runs the historical center. Teira Dun-Hem? You know her." Lena huddled in the shadows, her voice barely above a whisper. Tabitha could sense more than see her melt back into the darkness; her words floated out to them from the depth of the dark room. "She has done a lot of research on black elves. She can help you."

Cole sighed and turned back to draw Tabitha against him. "Be careful."

# CHAPTER THREE

TABITHA STIRRED FROM HER SLEEP WHEN SHE FELT LUC'S body slip into bed beside her. She stirred briefly and despite her anger, her drowsy mind drew comfort from the fact that he was back, and with a sigh she fell back to sleep.

When Tabitha awoke, she stretched, working the kinks from her muscles, before she felt a stirring in the bed beside her. She had forgotten she was not alone. In a panic, she huddled back to her side of the bed.

She ducked her head and felt more than saw his attention focus on her. She kept her eyes tightly closed, the blankets tugged high to her chin, and she willed Luc to simply leave. The moments stretched. With a start, she realized that there was a mild brushing against her shielded mind. Luc was trying to speak to her, but she remained tightly shuttered. The memory of their past intimacy brought stinging tears to her eyes. She huddled deeper beneath the covers and ignored his attempt to draw her out. When no further movement ensued, she slowly lifted her head, wondering what he was doing.

He lay beside her, his chest bare, the blankets snug around his hips. His blue eyes were intent as he regarded her, and she struggled to tear her gaze from his. He reached out with his hand; a finger stroked her cheek, tracing the purple bruise that ran from her cheekbone to her jaw.

"Leave me alone," she whispered.

He did not answer, but his finger dropped to the blankets, drawing her hands from her protective cover. He gently pressed her back onto the bed. As he leaned over her, still no word spoken, Tabitha released a surprised cry. He dipped his head toward her. Tabitha closed her eyes and turned her head away, avoiding the kiss she was so sure was coming.

To her surprise, his mouth dropped to her throat, his lips leaving a trail of fire along her neck as he nuzzled up toward her jaw. He traced her jawline, and his mouth stopped next to her ear, his words barely above a whisper.

"Katie is alive. She is hidden. She has not yet had her baby, but her time is approaching rapidly. The days are numbered. You have very little time to learn to shape shift. Use the bird as your guide."

With that, he turned from her and rolled off the bed. Tabitha lay still, her mouth frozen in an *O* as he walked around the bed to the bathroom, wearing his dark bed pants. She was still lying in shock when she heard the water running in the other room.

Katie was alive? How could that be? Hadn't he said she was dead? Or had he? She struggled to remember his exact words to Antoine. And use the bird as her guide? Goddammit, if only she had let him through her shields, she may have been able to ask him what the hell he was talking about. Apparently, he was concerned about being overheard and so had masked his comments behind an intimate nuzzle.

She lifted her fingers to her neck, the warmth of his mouth still playing havoc with her nerves. What does this mean? Katie is alive? Luc had not killed her? Had he been playing her false, or was he involved in a more elaborate game?

The door opened and he emerged, a towel wrapped about his slim hips. He ran a hand through his wet hair, pushing it from his face. She felt her face get hot; she sat up, huddled beneath the blankets. He was nearly naked and seemingly oblivious to her. He wandered over and poked through some of the drawers and cabinets, hunting for the clothes that they had moved for him. She was about to speak when he dropped his clothes on the side of the bed. With her face burning, she averted her eyes just in time as the towel hit the floor.

"What... What did you mean—?"

"Not now," he growled low.

"Ears?"

"Yeah," he snapped before he wandered back into the bathroom. He emerged, fully dressed and seeming in complete control, cool and aloof. His hair was dry, which amazed her. He had only walked in there a few minutes ago and his hair had been wet. Without a word or a glance, he left the room, leaving her startled, sitting up in bed, staring at the crow across the room.

Tabitha rose and showered, reviewing Luc's whispered instructions. The sun seemed brighter as she emerged from the shower, the possibilities for the day more optimistic. Was there the slightest glimmer of hope that he had not betrayed her? Was he even now working on a solution?

Wearing a tightly wrapped towel, she slipped into the bedroom and hunted for clothes. A brief knock at the door startled her. Forgetting the towel still wrapped around her, she rushed to open it. She hoped it would be Luc and that they would be able to speak, but it was Jules with a breakfast tray.

"Getting a bit lazy with all this free time?" he quipped as he put the tray down.

"Jules! Where have you been?" she demanded, tugging the towel closer about her.

"Why, working here, of course. And I hear that you have done little more than get into more mischief!" he exclaimed. He walked through the bedroom, tugging the curtains open and opening the balcony doors to the fresh breeze.

"Jules, I am not dressed," Tabitha complained as she tugged a corner off a fruit tart.

"Who can see you, up here on the fourth floor?" he retorted as he lifted Luc's damp towel and wandered into the bathroom to gather the clothes. "You two have not yet consummated your relationship, I see."

Tabitha rolled her eyes. She tugged her underclothes on while Jules was in the bathroom. "Seriously, Jules? I am not going to sleep with anyone just because my father demands that I do. That is ridiculous." She chose pants and a comfortable top from the closet.

Jules returned and discreetly turned away while she finished dressing. "Have you forgotten the rules already? He has given you to Luc. If Luc fails to take the proffered gift, Antoine will find another who values it."

"Well, he has to give us some time. We have done little more than fight since this whole thing transpired," Tabitha argued. Jules shrugged as he straightened the bed. Tabitha nibbled on some fruit, her mind working. "Jules, can I ask you something?"

"Of course."

"How do you know if you have shape-changer ability or dryad blood or water sprite blood? How do the different talents manifest themselves?"

"Well, usually that is something one learns from parents. In a standard adoption, the parents' abilities are well documented, so children will know what potential talents they may possess," he explained as he poured her a cup from the steaming pot of javé.

Tabitha nodded. "And if one does not know the parents' talents?"

"Well, that is a trial-and-error situation," Jules remarked. "Anything else I can get for you?"

She shook her head. "No, I think it best that I lay low and try to get some rest."

Jules nodded. "I agree. I think a little boredom and inactivity will do you, as well as those assigned to watch you, a world of good. Please let the guard know if you need anything or if you would like to see your grandfather."

Jules's strong hint drew a quick smile from her. "Yes, I think I will go see my grandfather this morning. I can ask him more about my family's abilities."

Jules grinned. "Indeed. Learning about one's heritage is always an excellent way to spend some time."


Later that day, Tabitha bounced back on the settee and watched the crow with steely eyes. Her grandfather had been able to tell her that because she was part Faye, she would have abilities found in all of the Caskan tribes, but he explained that each individual had their own flair and knack for learning certain abilities. Generally speaking, users had to attempt to experience various shape shifts to determine which they might have a strong propensity for mastering.

She spent the better part of an hour studying the crow from every angle. She tentatively opened the cage, allowing him to hop out onto her lap and make his way up to her shoulder. She let him hop to the floor, enticed by some of her leftover lunch. As he pecked at the food, she caressed his lean body and ran her hands along his wings, studying their curves and the muscles he used to hop, flap, walk, and eat. As she watched him explore the room, she began hiding morsels of food. She watched attentively as he walked to where she'd tossed a bit. She placed pieces on the settee and bed and watched as he flapped his wings and lifted himself a couple of feet to reach the food there. His injured wing kept him from actually flying, but he could use his wings to elevate a couple of feet before he settled back on the floor.

She was thankful for his apparently constant hunger; it allowed her to watch him as he cocked his head, pounced on morsels of food, and captured bits she threw toward his talons. She could have been mistaken, but she felt like the dark bird was enjoying their play as much as she was.


Jules returned to remind Tabitha that she had been invited to join her father and his guests for dinner that evening. The invitation, Jules reminded her, was not to be ignored. Tabitha shrugged and went to sit on the bed, intent on the bird, until Jules turned from the closet with a deep blue dress over his arm.

"Jules, are you serious? I am not wearing that! It is dinner. Can't I just go in what I am wearing?"

Jules huffed and gently laid the dress on the bed. He indicated the shower with his chin. Tabitha groaned and stood, glaring at Jules. "This is really not necessary."

"You could wait for Monsieur DesChamps to return if you would prefer? He will need to shower and change as well." His tone was surly. He glared at her as he turned to leave. "Can I assume you will be safely escorted to dinner, or must I return?"

Tabitha grumbled as she rose and headed for the shower. "Yes, I will get safely to dinner."

Tabitha spent the next hour taking a long, hot shower and then winding her hair into some semblance of order. She slipped into the deep-blue dress. With a glance around, she found one of the shoes that Jules had selected for her. She had pulled the second shoe from under the bed and was trying to slide her foot into it when Luc entered the room.

"You are attending the dinner tonight?" Luc asked as he tugged open a closet and swung some clothes out. Tabitha nodded, and he scooped up his clothes. "Let me grab a quick shower, then I will walk you down."

She bristled with irritation at the reference to her alleged inability to walk to dinner. But the truth was, she had no intention of wandering into the dining room alone. At least Luc would be something of a buffer between her, Dylan, and her father. She hoped Luc and she could find a moment alone to speak.

He had dropped the fact that Katie was alive in her lap and taken off for the day, leaving her to cool her heels without more information. Why had Luc lied to her father? Why had he let her think he had killed Katie?

Tabitha wandered into the sitting area and poured herself a glass of fruit beverage from the sideboard. The fire popped cheerfully, and she lowered herself in front of it, not seeking the warmth as much as the comfort of the glowing flames. It surprised her that the estate kept fireplaces going through the warm summer months, but Jules had explained that the pipes running in back of the fire kept water hot and easily accessible, and the abundant dark fuel they burned kept the estate's interior dry. Apparently there were some challenges to using dirt to insulate the homes. When he had started to explain the dynamics of the humidity factors, she had begged him to stop.

The shower stopped, and she heard drawers opening and closing in the bedroom as Luc changed for dinner.

*Luc?*

*Wow. You lowered your shields? To what do I owe this?*

*Oh, shut up. You know damn well that after telling me this morning about Katie—*

*Not now.*

*But, Luc, who can hear us?*

He stepped into the room and shook his head, lifting a finger to his lips. *Be patient. Let me teach you to focus on me alone when you use our link. Until then, we need to be cautious.*

*Well, teach me now!*

*We are expected downstairs.*

*I still hate you.*

She saw the slow roll of his eyes as he extended a hand to her. *Why am I not surprised?*

Dinner progressed at a glacial pace. Tabitha grew restless with the endless parade of courses. She had long since tired of eating and was little more than pecking at her dinner as the conversation flowed around her. She was the sole woman at the table, surrounded by her father, Luc, and Dylan, as well as Antoine's advisory council. Tonight they were hosting the newest delegate from the Plain's tribes and his small entourage. After meeting them all when she entered, she found herself mostly ignored. She took her seat next to Luc; to her chagrin, Dylan sat on her other side.

After two hours of endless droning discussion, Tabitha was seriously considering excusing herself with a headache or some other imaginary ailment when the newest Plains delegate pushed his plate away and addressed Antoine.

"Viho sends his regards from his home and apologized for his hasty departure. He filled me in on the negotiations thus far and seemed pleased with the progress."

Tabitha felt herself freeze at the mention of Viho's name; her fork clattered to her plate. Viho had been murdered by the black elf, under Dylan's direction. Her attention perked up as she wondered how he was communicating to Ituha.

Antoine lifted a hand. "Of course, Ituha, we can review everything we were able to accomplish before he had to depart. I trust his family is well? I was concerned when I had heard they were ill."

"Yes, all are well! I had not heard his wife had fallen ill and was surprised that I was not aware until I got here. My earlier communication from him alluded to some lag in the negotiation process," Ituha commented. His sharp, dark eyes watched his host.

Tabitha held her breath as the vision her mother had shared with her spun before her eyes. In her peripheral vision, she noticed Dylan's hands as he continued eating, periodically reaching for his glass, appearing unfazed by the discussion. Tabitha fought to keep breathing; panic began to simmer along her nerves. She placed her hands in her lap, gripping them fiercely, willing herself to be calm.

How could Dylan sit there so calmly as they discussed Viho? She had watched him as he callously directed the black elf back into its cage after he had let it loose to kill Viho and his men. She had seen the four bodies lying there, left to rot under the night sky as Dylan left with the beast in its cage. How had this emissary received word from Viho about negotiations that never took place? Before she had been caught by her father on that fateful night, Viho had admitted to Luc and her that he had grown tired of being ignored by Antoine and was heading north to enlist the assistance of Marcus.

*Calm...* Luc's voice in her head was a soft reminder.

Luc didn't know. He had caught the lie, no doubt, but he believed Viho was en route to meet with Marcus and Bertòn. She had not shared what she had discovered from her mother with him. She had not been speaking to him when she saw her mother. Their relationship had little improved since, but the realization that he had not killed Katie at least gave her reason to pause and listen to him.

*Luc, there is something I have to tell you.*

Luc did not respond or even glance up at her comment, but Dylan swiveled his head around to look at her. "All is well, sister?"

Tabitha nodded and noted that all eyes had turned to her. "Yes, I just do not feel well."

She saw a flicker of annoyance cross Antoine's face. He gestured curtly toward the balcony. "Perhaps you should get some air, my dear."

Tabitha ground her teeth at the foolishness of their father-daughter act. "Yes, perhaps it would be best."

She rose. Luc stood, as though to accompany her, but Antoine waved him down. "She will be fine until you are finished here."

Tabitha noticed Luc's jaw tighten, but he nodded and sat back down. Tabitha excused herself and wandered out to the balcony. She gulped the evening air to calm her raging nerves. Her stomach roiled in agitation, and she placed a hand on it, praying she would not be sick. She stepped over to the wall, looking out over the grounds of the estate as she willed herself to be calm.

The lie that had been blatantly laid out before her had shaken her. Had Ituha lied about getting word from Viho, or had her father or even Dylan falsified information and led Ituha to believe that Viho had returned home? Did her father even realize Viho was dead? On his land? Her mother had assured her that Larissa would take the bodies back to their families; soon they would know what had transpired.

Wouldn't they?

The horrors unfolding around her seemed to be multiplying. She was not sure how much longer she could keep herself together. The pieces of this elaborate puzzle were not fitting; every time she reached for one, it blew apart.

She was not sure how long she stood out there before Luc joined her.

"You will have to come back in sooner or later."

"I have to speak to you," she murmured.

"I gathered that, but now is not the time," Luc snapped. *You need to keep our link a secret. Dylan could detect you trying to speak to me at dinner.*

*This can't wait!*

*It has to. We cannot stay out here not speaking without them becoming suspicious.*

"You are feeling better?" he asked aloud.

"Yes," she stammered, taken aback at the change in the discussion. *Can you teach me now? To use the link so others cannot detect?* "It must have been something I ate."

*No, not right now. Whatever is so important will have to wait until a more opportune time.*

*Maybe not...*

Tabitha turned to face him. Before he could fathom what she intended, she reached up and drew his mouth down to hers. His startled response turned more amenable as she lifted onto her toes to better match his mouth to hers.

*They lied about Viho.*

She could sense his surprise; he paused ever so slightly to look down at her, his mouth still slightly open. *I am aware of that. The question is whether or not Viho actually sent the—*

*Viho is dead,* she responded, settling her arms around his neck.

He stepped back in shock. "What?"

She groaned and tugged him back to her and attacked his mouth again, hoping the kiss would provide sufficient distraction from their linked discussion. *I saw it. My mother showed me. Dylan had them killed by a black elf that he controls, and they left the bodies there. I saw them, Luc.*

She gripped him harder, sliding her arms tighter around his neck. It took a moment for the information sink in. She could feel his hands rest on her hips as the shock wore off. Her mouth played with his as she allowed the familiar sensation of his lips calm her and prayed he would respond in the same way. All she could do was keep kissing him as he tried to sort through this latest development.

His hands tightened around her back, and he drew her tighter against him. *So Viho and his men never made it north.*

*No, and we do not know whose side Ituha is on. We don't know if he is playing along or being played,* Tabitha responded, enjoying the feel of his tongue sliding and playing with hers, despite the gravity of the discussion.

*We have to talk,* Luc agreed, but she could already feel his body tightening and knew that his thoughts were turning toward more intimate avenues.

She slid her arms from his neck and stepped back ever so slightly. His breath was coming in rapid gasps, and she let her lips lightly play along his. *Can you get me into the village? There is someone there I must speak to. Maybe if we can get out of here for a few hours, we can talk openly.*

*I am not sure, but this seems to be working for me.*

*I am sure.* She slid her hands between them and stepped out of his arms toward the doors. *But I am afraid our discussions would rapidly deteriorate. Besides, you still have some explaining to do.*

He crooked a half smile. *I had better find a reason to get you into town.*

Tabitha stepped back into the dining room. Dinner had finished, and the men were milling about, talking in small groups. Her father glanced over and nodded at her with a smile. He gestured for her to join him. She heard Luc enter behind her, but his attention was quickly captured by a group of the senior advisors.

"Feeling better?" Antoine asked with an arch grin.

"Yes, thank you. I just needed some air."

"Ah, yes. And I noticed that Monsieur DesChamps was kind enough to share some of his with you."

Dylan released a booming laugh. Tabitha felt her cheeks redden as the group all turned in her direction with knowing grins.

"If you will excuse me, I believe I will retire." She stepped away from the group with as much dignity as she could muster, but the eruption of laughter after some comment made her cringe. Resisting the urge to look over at Luc, she quickly departed the room and, with a guard in tow, hurried to her suite.

# CHAPTER FOUR

TABITHA STRUGGLED AS THE DAYS PASSED. LUC WAS LITTLE more than a shadow who slid into bed late and was gone when she rose in the morning. After their brief discussion, he had seemed intent upon finding out more about what she had told him, but they had barely spoken since, and in the few waking moments when she saw him, he shook his head quickly and ducked back out of the room.

Frustration welled within her as she sat on the floor of their bedroom, tearing apart her lunch to share with the crow. She could not help but wonder if she had been mistaken to share the little knowledge she had. His assertion that Katie was not dead had sent her spiraling from pure hatred to indecisive wavering to hope. She was desperate to pin him down and get to the bottom of what had transpired.

Had he betrayed her? What game was he playing? Did the players even know that they were part of a greater manipulation being directed by Luc?

What if he was telling her father right now that she had spoken to Doni? Would he do that? Where did his loyalty lie? She groaned as she put her head back against the chaise and tossed another bit of food toward D'Noir. The crow tottered over to it and gulped the morsel down before turning back to look for more.

She tore her thoughts from Luc and continued intensely studying the bird, as she had been doing for most of the day. Tabitha absorbed each facet of his physique. She regarded him as he sat on his perch, as he walked and hopped and made attempts to fly. She sent tentative thoughts to the bird and tried to wrap her senses around his, but she'd had little more success than seeing the room from his perspective. More often than not, she ended up seeing her own face staring at him, creased in intense concentration. She might receive an impression of vague interest in her presence, which would quickly be replaced by some more interesting sparkly object.

After hours of what she now thought of as "bird time," she needed a break. She rose and threw open the door, startling another new guard, and asked to be escorted to her grandfather's room.

Her grandfather was, as always, pleased to see her. She sat across from him and curled her legs under her, listening as he told her about growing up as a healer in secret.

Throughout his youth, he had been hidden away, as many of his kind were, his talents known only to a few. He met people in need of healing in the back rooms of taverns and dark corners of barns. It was never a matter of cost but a matter of need. As word spread of the presence of a healer, authorities began to investigate, and he would have to go underground and hide again.

Roane cackled at the absurdity of having to hide and heal those in need. "But that is," he said with a sad shake of his head, "how the world is at times. It does not always make sense, and logic does not always prevail over passion."

He met the love of his life when he healed her of a terminal disease that had plagued her since childhood. She fell for him immediately and followed him, begging to be an assistant and aid him in helping others. He had refused; certain that such a young, beautiful woman was more captivated because he had saved her than truly enamored. Almost two years passed before he returned to that village; curiosity drove him to check on his young patient. He found Daera, grown up and even more beautiful than he remembered.

They wed within a week. The couple lived like traveling young gypsies, staying in villages only long enough to heal anyone in need, sliding away in the night before word spread. When she became pregnant, they decided to find a village to settle in and start their family. He set up a simple medical practice, using his healing ability to quietly assist his doctoring. Few suspected but those that did had the good sense not to mention such a thing, fearing that they would lose their healer.

Their lives together were happy with the exception of the miscarriages and losses they suffered trying to have a child.

"Couldn't you heal her or save them?" Tabitha asked.

He shook his head. "I will tell you a sad lesson, my dear. Healing is meant to be a balm, soothing sickness and knitting bones. Healing will not change what is meant to be. Our babies died silently without warning in my wife's womb. On two occasions, we were lucky enough that they were born, but we lost them silently in the night, in their sleep. A healer is only reactive; we cannot determine what and when something will happen. I could not save them; it was the will of the One God."

Tabitha nodded. "Did any survive besides my mother? How did she come to be in my world?"

Roane sighed as sadness slowly overtook him. "We went many years without a pregnancy, but we were happy nonetheless. I must confess that I spent many a day trying to determine what it was that was keeping Daera from carrying a child and the children who were born from surviving. I was not able to understand that missing link, even though I studied many successful and unsuccessful pregnancies and many babies.

"We were getting older, your grandmother and I, and had just about given up hope when she became pregnant again. We were in our later years, so we were quite surprised." He smiled. "Our beautiful daughter came into this world on a beautiful summer day."

"June thirtieth?" Tabitha asked.

He nodded. "By your calendar, yes."

"And how did she come to be in our world?"

"My wife almost died in childbirth, but I was able to save her at the near expense of myself. I was in my medical office. After Doniella was born, Daera began to hemorrhage and became hysterical. It took everything in my power to save her. I was at the limit of my energy and became disoriented. An elite member of our parliament was passing through our village. His wife was also pregnant, although her child was stillborn. I saved his wife but not the child.

"My wife was my usual blood source when I expended too much energy, but she was close to death and still hemorrhaging. I could not take from her. So I tried to hide. I felt as though I was staring down a long tunnel and could see the rooms around me, but only from a distant vantage point. I had trouble breathing, and I felt as though my heart was going to pound its way out of my chest. I knew full well that I looked like death. My wife had told me that when I got that bad, my face was gray and my eyes glassy. She told me I had frightened her the first time she saw me with my fangs. She grew accustomed to it, but I knew I had to gather my strength before anyone saw me."

He drew a deep breath and Tabitha knew he was reliving the past. She held her breath. He continued. "The gentleman, one of the chancellors, arrived to visit his wife. He entered her room as I was trying to make my way to one of the back offices; I planned to lock myself in and sleep until my energy returned. He saw me and was convinced that I was going to kill his wife. There was no talking to the man, and I was in no condition to defend myself. Daera was still too weak to even rise from her bed.

"He left with his wife and went to the local authorities. The governor at the time was a gentleman by the name of Brodie Montfort, the man who would become your other grandfather."

"Antoine's father?" Tabitha was shocked. "Then what happened?"

"Thankfully, I had friends who helped us leave before the authorities could reach us. I am ashamed to say that I took blood from many friends to gather the strength to run. They were true friends, and gracious, but as you know, we are in an intimate and vulnerable place when we require replenishment. I did not like being in that state, and I liked even less that the last time many of those people saw me I displayed the fangs that I used to draw blood from their wrists."

He coughed lightly. Tabitha helped him sit up to clear his lungs. She fetched a cloth to wipe his mouth. "Are you all right? Shall I come back after you have rested?"

He shook his head and struggled for a deep breath. "I grow weary so very easily. I wish it were otherwise, but age is catching up with me. But back to that night, the chancellor returned with the authorities. The Lord Regent, your grandfather, deemed that not only was I to be placed under arrest but my daughter would be given to the chancellor as payment for the death of his child. I knew my baby was a healer, I could already sense it. I could not turn her over to that man. I knew what her life would become if I gave her to him.

"Daera and I ran for as long as we could. We were fugitives and found few places open to us. As the word spread, the story grew, as stories have a tendency to do. Those who would have hid us refused after they heard I had killed a baby for its blood. The tales of my blood lust and fangs also grew, until I was a legend and a horror. There are stories about me haunting the freshly dead at burial grounds for their blood, and oh, it goes on.

"We were able to find temporary refuge in Calais. A man I knew, once a very close friend, agreed to hide my wife and daughter in safety. He promised to take them to a place where no one knew them or had even heard of healers. In my desperation, I agreed to his terms."

Tabitha held her breath. "What were the terms?"

"My wife, whom he had always desired, was to travel to that place as his wife, to avoid detection." He gave a long sigh and wiped at his tears. "I agreed. I did not know what else to do. I had no choice. I loved them more than anything in the world. I would have turned myself in to the Lord Regent if I thought it would save them, but that was not the case. So he took my Daera and my little girl to another place, another world, with no magic, no healers."

"And no Faye," Tabitha whispered.

"And no Faye. My wife had to have her beautiful ears 'fixed,' as did my daughter. My Daera had to take another man as her husband in order to make a life in your world." Roane's voice was low, and the pain from those troubling years reflected in his eyes.

"But how did my mother end up living with Trude? And what happened to Daera?" Tabitha asked.

"I found out later that Trude was already that man's wife in your world. They were newly married; he was older than she. He was a talented portal-seeker and built himself a life selling goods from your world here and taking goods from here to sell there. Of course, as a Caskan, he was also magical in your world. I believe he made himself a fortune by telling people their own darn thoughts or some-such foolishness."

Tabitha was stunned. "Trude's husband was a Caskan?"

Roane nodded. "And with two wives. I understand that they had to pretend that my Daera was Trude's niece, but the truth is, he used them both." The old man hissed out his aggravation. "Had I known what I was sending my Daera to, I would never have agreed."

"Why didn't you just go with her?"

"He wouldn't take us all. He said he wouldn't be able to smuggle the three of us over there. I didn't know any better. Truth be told, I was desperate to save them. I wanted to at least know that Daera remained with Doniella. I could live with that arrangement if I knew they had each other. It would have killed my Daera if they had found us here and took our baby. I think that he believed that Doniella might be a healer and planned in the long term to make a fortune with her when she was old enough," Roane spat.

"And what happened to Daera?"

"She died," Roane said softly. "I wasn't there. Doniella was with this man's wife, posing as her niece. Trude loved her, I knew that, and Doniella grew to love this Trude, or whatever she called herself. I never forgave Martin for taking my wife for his own ends. I have lived with that bitter taste, but the truth is, if not for him, they would have taken our baby from us. I believe, despite it all, that I did the right thing."

"My God! Trude was married to a Caskan! And her husband took a second wife. So that is where she got all the money when he died. Wow." Tabitha shook her head in disbelief. "I cannot believe this! And to think she played stupid all those times when I asked her about my mother and what happened! That is crazy!"

Roane agreed. "We all believed that the less you knew, the safer you'd be. We all thought it best. No one quite believed you would have the abilities you do."

"My abilities?"

He nodded. "You are quite powerful. It worries us to send you back without further training. But it seems it cannot be helped. You must get away from him. You must not be kept here, a prisoner."

Tabitha's voice dropped to a whisper. "I know. I know. It is just not that easy. I am watched all the time. When a guard is not on my heels, Luc is with me. I don't know how I am going to get away. When I do, how will I find a portal back?"

He squeezed her hand before his head dropped back to the pillows. "Concentrate on honing your abilities; an opportunity will present itself. Just be ready when it does. Do not hesitate for any of our sakes."

"You need to rest." She stood. "I love you." She kissed his head and stepped back from the bed. As she was closing the door she heard his tired voice say he loved her too. She stopped for a moment and rested her forehead against the door to his room, tears glistening in her eyes. It was the first time she could recall anyone in her life except Callie telling her that they loved her.


Tabitha sat staring at the crow as he pecked his way through a bowl of torn bread pieces. "You know, when you are finally able to fly again, you will be too fat to get off the ground."

She crossed her legs, resting her elbows on her knees and cupping her chin.

*I cannot seem to find a way to connect. What am I missing?*

She extended her thoughts one more time and let herself just stare at the apparently ravenous bird. She was tired; the new knowledge about her mother and grandmother's trials had been emotionally exhausting.

The bird pecked up a piece of bread he had pushed off the side of the plate.

"Yeah, don't miss anything. You might not eat for another couple of minutes," she said. He hopped onto the small plate, knocking pieces of food to the sides. He then began to reach for bread he had knocked askew.

She shook her head. "If you poop on that plate, I am going to cook you and eat you."

D'Noir ignored her and continued scavenging the bread pieces. Tabitha let her thoughts wander back to her grand-father's tale, to the reality that her grandmother had not been Trude's sister but her uncle's illegal second wife. She combed her memories for the stories she had heard about her uncle, who had died in some inexplicable way. Callie had once whispered that she had overheard Trude and Aunt Ellen arguing. They mentioned that there had been some investigation into his death, but neither ever shed any light on it. Tabitha did recall having been taunted as a child about her aunt—something about her knocking off her rich old husband. No one had ever filled her in on the rumors, and she had not pursued them. Enough was being whispered about her; she had no time or energy to track down every allegation about her aunt that was whispered within the small island community.

It was just so strange; her uncle was a Caskan and her grandmother a Faye. So many connections seemed to twist and entwine but led her nowhere. Tabitha let her mind drift. She slowly lowered her shields, attempting to sink into the bird's consciousness. She reached out slightly. All she could perceive was the bird's persistent focus on his next morsel of food. As she slowly let herself sink into the bird's mind, she saw herself through his eyes, sitting, gazing at him. A sudden caw from the bird startled her out of his mind.

"You just ate a whole roll and all the stuff that was in it. Seriously, all you can think about is mooching more food?"

*You're trying too hard.* Luc's voice echoed in her mind. It had been so long since they had reached out to each other that she was too surprised to respond. *Don't try to get into his consciousness. You want to go deeper.*

She was not sure she wanted to respond, but she was frustrated with her lack of progress. *What do you mean? And how did you reach me?*

*You finally dropped your shields.*

*Oh. Okay. What do you mean by that? Go deeper? I don't understand.*

*Will you let me show you? When I get back. Also, let me show you how to focus your thoughts so that it is not so apparent that we are communicating.*

She felt her face redden at the slight but swallowed her irritation. *Fine. When are you coming?*

*I can be there shortly. Will you have dinner with me?*

*I just need you to show me what I am missing... I don't really need anything more than that from you.* Her response was curt.

*Fine. Then I will be there after I have dinner... elsewhere.*

The connection broke, and Tabitha lifted her shields quickly.

"Fine," she blurted to the bird. "Whatever. Take your time. And don't subject me to more of your lying presence. Go have dinner with my father or Dylan."

The bird ignored her. He shoved the plate aside with his head, looking for pieces of bread he might have missed.

# CHAPTER FIVE

AFTER HER DINNER ARRIVED, TABITHA SAT IN THE CHAISE by the fire, looking out the balcony at the darkening sky. She draped one leg over an arm of the chair; the crow was perched on the other arm of the chaise, its eyes closed, seeming to nap. She was still irritated, unsure if she were angrier with Luc or herself as she imagined him enjoying a meal with her father and Dylan. Her thoughts shifted; she pictured Luc standing by the windows, chatting with some beautiful political affiliate of her father's. She had to quell a pang of jealousy. She could not suppress the frustrations over her isolation. Yet he was out with people, no doubt entertaining any number of women who would be clamoring for his attention, the handsome favorite of the lord regent. No doubt his status brought him numerous invitations.

She fumed, trying to ignore the anger that gnawed at her belly. It could not be jealousy; after all, she'd wanted nothing to do with him since he had compromised her trust. And she definitely wanted no part of his company. She considered having her guard bring her to her grandfather, but night approached, and she should not disturb his rest. She wished she could visit with Gwyn, but she had been very busy and had limited time for Tabitha, although she had slipped a slender vial into Tabitha's hand with whispered instructions to take a small sip every morning.

Tabitha rose and went to the window, wondering at her own frustration. She did not want to admit that the isolation was getting to her. She wanted to be out, seeing people, but not the people in this damn house. She wanted to be back with a friend or two in random crowds. This solitary confinement was maddening.

She was becoming frazzled over her inability to figure out how to crack the shape-changing puzzle, and that damn bird did little more than eat half or more of her food and then caw for more. He had taken to following her around the room and, on occasion, pecking and cawing at the bathroom door. It was starting to drive her a little insane.

And Luc... His aloofness was really grating on her. He had a hell of a nerve, after what he'd done, to be distant. As though this was all her fault. He had barely attempted an apology or even the slightest attempt at any reconciliation. Her heart had nearly stopped beating when he had rolled over on top of her the other morning, only to whisper sweet instructions in her ear and then revert back to his stoic presence, barely attempting to explain or even bullshit her about why he had turned on her. In favor of giving her father the benefit of the doubt?

"I don't get it," she complained to D'Noir. The bird had disposed of any pretense of propriety and was, at the moment, standing in the center of her dinner plate, yanking apart a piece of chicken. "Want me to cut that up for you or are you good?"

In response, the glossy black bird drew the piece of chicken from the bone; it snapped into his face. "Nice. I am not so sure I want to delve into that mind."

She gave up for the night and decided to have a bath while she waited for Luc's return. She swept the balcony doors open to fully to capture the sweet late-summer breeze that picked up after dark and stoked the fire into crackling brilliance. She propped open both of the bathroom doors to capture the breeze and dimmed all the lights. The luminous fire lent the bathroom a warm, golden glow. She opened the tub faucets and filled a glass with the sparkling honey liquid they were so fond of here. She was not sure what was in it, but she liked the flavor. It had a tendency to relax her, and right now, she needed all the help she could get.

She lit a candle or two in the bathroom. As the tub was filling, she wandered out to the balcony and placed her hands on the railing, deeply inhaling the warm night air. She could taste the salt from the ocean so far away. The slight tang made her homesick for her island home. She wanted to hear the waves crash and listen to the lonely cry of the gulls and taste the briny salty air. She missed the tightening of her face in the salty spray and the glimmer of the moonlight dancing across the black carpet of ocean, hiding a multitude of sea life. She was so homesick she wanted to cry; she needed Callie to talk her down from her crazy ledge and Aunt Ellen's calming influence and warm hugs when the world seemed to crash in on her. She even missed Trude; no one had called her a single foul name since she had been here.

She turned from the dark landscape that she had failed to notice, lost in her thoughts. She wanted nothing more than to stop thinking and just let her mind rest. She went back inside, slipped out of her clothes, and twisted her hair into a knot on her head. The bathwater was steaming. Tabitha placed her glass beside the tub and slid into the hot water, under the layer of warm white bubbles, and let her body soak. The heat drew the tension from her body. She rested her head against the back of the tub, her eyes shut, wishing she had some music to take her into a deeper meditative state.

She sipped from the tall glass of the honey drink and let the soothing powers of the drink relax her. She was actually considering dozing in the warm and soothing cocoon she had hidden herself in when she heard the hall door open and shut. She didn't even bother opening her eyes; it was too early to be Luc. It must be Jules.

"Jules, will you be a doll and refill my glass for me?" she called, letting her hand drape lazily over the edge of the tub.

There was no answer. She let her gaze drift toward the door. "Jules?"

"Sorry to disappoint you." The silky voice sent a warm shiver through her body. She saw Luc leaning against the doorway, a smile curving his lips.

"Hmm. You're back early," she remarked.

"I told you I would be back after dinner so we could continue our discussion," he replied. Pushing himself away from the wall, he wandered into the room and stopped to lean on the side of the tub, one elegant leg dangling and swinging when he sat. "Had you left your shields down, I would have forewarned you."

Tabitha sank deeper into the tub, thankful for the foamy white bubbles covering her. "I was sure you would find more captivating company than me and my... What was that my father called it? Oh yes, my damned sharp tongue."

"You deny it?" he questioned, his finger dipping into the water to swirl a tiny whirl of water.

She sat up, alarmed that his toying with the water might disturb her frothy protection. "Only to a select few."

"Ahh, and I am just lucky enough to number on that list, along with your father and Dylan?"

"Yes," she responded, taking a sip from her glass and letting the last of the liquid tickle her mouth. She watched him over the edge of the tub. "Will you refill me?"

He reached out, his fingers brushing hers as he took the empty glass. "It seems the least I can do."

She laughed softly as he left the room and tried desperately to recover from his presence. When he returned carrying two glasses, she had regained some of her languid demeanor. She took the glass from him, avoiding contact with his hand, and nodded her thanks.

"You look quite comfortable," he remarked. "I am tempted to join you."

Her eyes flew open. Luc laughed at her alarmed expression, toasting her with his glass.

"What is in this anyway?" she asked, taking another sip from her glass. "Is it alcohol?"

"Alcohol?"

"Uhm… fermented?"

"No, it is mixed with lavender and chamomile, honey, and assorted flowers." He glanced at the glass with a melancholy cast to his eyes. "You know, this is made by Sybille."

"Is it?" Tabitha was surprised. "Her little business has a long reach."

"She is quite entrepreneurial and humble. One would not know that her products are sought far and wide," he commented, a hint of pride in his voice.

"And she makes them all herself?"

He shook his head. "No, you saw her experimenting with new lines."

"So, back to our discussion from earlier tonight..."

He shook his head slowly and indicated she should lower her shields.

*I don't know if we are being listened to or watched.* She allowed his voice in her head. *What I want you to do is imagine looking at me. Focus your eyes on mine.*

She did and was captured in the charismatic gaze of his blue eyes.

He continued. *This line of sight, my eyes to yours, imagine a line between us that only we can see. Normally, when we communicate, you cast your thoughts out. As I am the only one linked to you, I am the recipient. When others are around, they will not know what you are saying, but the energy that you put into casting the thought spills out. They can sense that. I want you to focus on me and only me.*

Her eyes were still locked in his, and she swallowed. Did he have any idea what locking into his gaze did to her? Did he feel the same thing, or was this simply an educational venture?

*Now, speak to me. Tell me something. Focus only on me. Direct your thought only to me.*

Her mouth was dry; she wondered what the hell to say. *I am directing this to you and only you.*

*Good. Try again.*

Her eyes were wide and uncertain, the silver framed with long dark lashes held the deep blue of his. She tried to quell her fear and confusion to maintain the eye contact. She wanted to release him, but she was too proud to back down.

*Tabitha, speak to me. Only me.*

*I am trying. Is this better?*

He smiled. *Yes.*

She released his gaze and looked away. *Will you allow me some privacy?*

"Of course." He left the bathroom, closing the double doors behind him. Tabitha sank into the tub in anguish.

How had this happened? How had she lost her edge, her advantage? He had been able to knock her off kilter. She had held the rage, but now she needed him to show her how to crack the mystery of shaping the crow. She needed his help to get away from this house. Her feelings for him kept her swinging between anger and dejection, adding to her confusion. She wanted to scrub her skin and wipe herself free of him, tear him from her soul and her heart. She wanted to eradicate him from her life and her bloodstream, yet every time she saw him her heart set a new pounding pace. Her mouth was unable to speak, and her mind tumbled in confusion.

She slid out of the water, which had cooled while they spoke. She toweled herself off and wrapped the warm towel around her tightly. She had not brought a change of clothes in with her as she had not expected him back for hours. She spied the robe hanging on the hook behind the door, and she dropped the towel and grabbed it. She wrapped the long robe around her slim hips, tugged her hair from its knot, and grabbed a comb to sweep the tangles from the long, dark mass.

She stopped in front of the mirror, watching the raven hair tumble down her shoulders. In the mirror, her eyes were huge and wide, uncertain. Luc had the ability to knock loose her confident stance. She had to admit she was not sure she was able to handle him as she had once thought she could. He had the upper hand. She had to dredge up her courage to walk out there, to let him help her but maintain her distance.

*You can do this,* she told her reflection. *You can do this!*

She lifted her chin and opened the doors. She swept out into the room, cool and confident.

Luc stood by the balcony, staring out into the night; he turned as she entered.

"You ready?" he asked.

She drew in a deep breath. Her confidence seeped through her feet into the carpet.

*Oh no... I am so not ready to deal with him,* she thought in despair.


Tabitha stepped over to join him at the balcony. He lifted a decanter and refilled her glass. "You look like you need more of this."

"Is it supposed to relax you?" she asked, taking a sip of the sparkling honey drink.

"It is," he replied as he topped off each glass. "Among other things."

She took another sip and glanced up questioningly. "Other things? What other things?"

"It is supposed to be an aphrodisiac," he commented.

She stopped the glass midway to her lips and lowered it. He laughed and gently placed a finger under the stem of the glass and nudged it back to her lips. "It is only a rumor, but I think the relaxing properties far outweigh any chance of you finding that you can't keep your hands off me."

She snorted. "Hardly."

*I think is best we keep switching back and forth between verbal and linked communiqués.*

*You really think we are being watched, listened to?* She glanced back into the room, wary of prying eyes.

*I don't know, but I cannot shake the feeling. I wouldn't put it past him to get updates on the state of our relationship,* Luc replied.

Tabitha nodded and wandered over to the chaise. She flipped open D'Noir's cage door, and he hopped out, nosing her fingers and the floor around her. "You are just insatiable."

*What I want you to do is sink beyond the crow's present state, beyond the "here and now" of his consciousness and absorb the instinctive, inherent, and learned behaviors,* Luc instructed. *You are not looking for his immediate state of being but the behavior he was born with, the abilities that he has learned: to fly, to use his wings and the air around him. Most of that you will learn, but first you need to gather information about his early flying and how he flies now. It is not a thought process but a learned ability. You need that information, or else you will leap off the fourth floor balcony and try to learn to fly on your descent. Remember, you do not have the instincts that he was born with, so you must locate them within him.*

Tabitha knelt before the bird. He hopped to her trustingly. She reached out her thoughts and tried to find his instinctive thoughts, something that would trigger how he had learned to fly, but all she could find were memories of flight, trees, the sky, and, of course, food.

She sat back on her heels in frustration. *I don't understand!*

Luc knelt beside her and reached out. *Just wait. Let me try. Open your mind to me and let me help you.*

She backed away from him. *No, I can't.*

*You have no choice. No one else can help you. You are down to a matter of days...*

Tabitha stood and walked away from him. *Don't ask me to do that.*

Luc leaned his head against the chaise with a long sigh. *Tabitha, I know what you are feeling, but...*

"But? But what?" she spat, her voice cutting through the silence. "Trust you anyway? You know, I have to ask, what exactly makes you think that I can just disregard my instincts and trust you? I already did that. Quite frankly, it hasn't turned out so great for me."

"Or you can remain completely angry and impossible and huddle in your self-pity. That seems like a great plan!" He lifted an arm in frustration. "At some point, you have to move past this."

"No, actually I don't. I have spent the better part of my life trying to maintain some semblance of normalcy and to do that, I have kept people at a distance. I have no intention of just.."

"Tabitha!" he interrupted, rising from the floor. "This is not about maintaining emotional distance." He completed his comment mentally. *This is about the limiting of your physi-*

*cal freedom and any future you may have. If you huddle down and do nothing, you won't have any choices open to you again.*

"I understand that, but for chrissakes, Luc, stop asking for what I cannot give you!" She cried.

"I haven't asked for anything except your trust!" He shouted back.

"And I just cannot give you that. You had that, and you threw it away." She paced the floor, lifting her hands in supplication, "I don't understand you! You tell me I have to leave and then you turn me in and turn my grandfather over to my father! You tell him I am a healer. You have played into his hands. You can't possibly expect me to trust you, to let you in!"

Luc shook his head. "And you have thrown that in my face, I know. I thought I was doing the right thing, and I still do. I brought your grandfather to safety. I waited to try and sort out the facts before I went off and joined Marcus's war. I cannot in good conscience put more lives at risk with assumptions."

*You could have gotten me out of here and you—*

*I did not put you in jeopardy! You did!* He snapped. *You did! You went down those stairs—I tried to stop you. All I did was get your grandfather out of there before he could have been used as a negotiating tool by your father against you.*

*Did you expect me to leave Cole? Did you think my escape was more important than my brother's life?* She sneered back at him.

*A brother you only met as of a few weeks ago! Yes, and if you were to ask him, he would have agreed! He should have given his life to see you safely away,* Luc argued. *As your father's prisoner, your healing ability will be sold to the highest bidder. Only those who can afford it will have the right to be healed—only those who swear fealty to your father will be eligible. With you gone—*

*Gone! To another world. I am no good to anyone there! What the hell good is it to you to have a healer when you have no access to me when I go home? Your people are no better off! I don't understand you!*

He groaned in frustration. *You are the last of the healers. The line ends likely with you. We don't know if your brothers can sire a healer. We think they might be able to and your father is banking on it. They learned with Katie that they can sire a child, but we do not know if it is possible for a human to carry a healer. The only healers to be born in generations were born from Faye healers. Your mother had three children, and only one carries the ability. You, though were born from a Caskan mix.*

*Don't you see? If your brothers cannot sire a healer, then you are the last and my world's last hope of saving itself.*

*Here, you will never be seen again except when your father parades you out to perform for him. Your children would be prisoners. Is that what you want?*

She spun around, her eyes blazing. *Of course I don't! But you are insinuating that people should actually lay down their lives in order for me to escape! I mean, what does it matter to your people if my father has me or I am in my world? You'll still have no one with the ability to heal. You'll be no better off.*

He lifted a hand. *Except that your father is gathering an enormous amount of power and support from what he will be able to offer people. Katie's child was supposed to go to a regent in the south; her daughter cannot conceive. How much support would she be willing to throw behind him after he gives her daughter a child: her grandchild? And what of the people you would be asked to heal? What would anyone give to cure a loved one or save themselves when they are incurable? What price would they pay? What if it were as simple as their support and fealty to your father?*

*In that case, I would be more valuable to you dead than as my father's prisoner,* she whispered back.

"Yes, you would," he responded, his voice low and his eyes averted.

She sighed. "Well, that makes for an interesting thought. So back to not trusting you, I guess. Trust you or die?"

"Lives are at stake: yours, mine, our families. No one is safe," he commented slowly. "So, tell me, I have put my trust in you. Why should I? If you escape, my life is forfeit. If you anger your father, my life is forfeit. A word from your father and I can be dragged out and replaced with someone else until he finds someone you will accept. Let me tell you, the inclination to just go home has occurred to me."

"Yet you stay?" she replied, her voice hesitant, almost afraid of what he would say.

"I can't leave." He dragged his hand through his hair and sighed explosively. "One God, but I can't walk away from you."

Tabitha stepped back, confusion reigning through her mind. "Luc…"

He lifted a hand and turned his back to her. "Tabitha, I can't keep away from you. I know what this is going to do to me in the end, and the truth is, I wouldn't have done it otherwise, knowing what I will face when you leave."

Before she could utter a word, he turned and left the room, quietly shutting the door behind him.

# CHAPTER SIX

LATER THAT NIGHT TABITHA LAY IN BED, STARING AT the ceiling. Sleep was impossible as her inner dialogue became a battlefield of opposing thoughts. The hours ticked by; Luc did not return. She could not even begin to imagine where he was, but images of him finding peace elsewhere harried at her nerves.

What exactly had he told her? What had he admitted before he walked out of the room? She played their fight over and over in her mind and could not find any terms or concessions. Luc had betrayed her. He had left her a prisoner in order to preserve himself.

And then he had pulled her grandfather out and brought him to safety. But her father would not have hurt him. Why did he have to move him? She snarled in frustration and rolled over, burying her face in the pillows. Inadvertently, she had grabbed one of Luc's pillows, and as she inhaled, his scent filled her mind. Tears stung her eyes.

"What am I supposed to think?" she groaned.

The recent days passed through her mind in a slow parade of discussions. The truth was, she was no closer to finding out about the black elves, shape shifting, or getting Katie out of this than she had been before. She shook her head and flung herself onto her back, continuing to stare at the ceiling.

D'Noir rustled in his cage. She exhaled sharply at the thought of trying her hand at that again; even with the information Luc had given her. She couldn't exactly leave the room, so she was in no position to go seeking any hidden black elves.

Or could she?

She had separated before. She had done it before under the skilled direction of the Faye; first back at Bertòn's house and then to meet her mother on the night she had shown her the black elf. Her mother had been the one to shift her into the shape of an owl but the talent had been hers. Hadn't it? She had nothing to lose by trying.

Once she slipped out of her body, she would still be seen as the separation left her with a gauzy shape; so separating would not help her unless she could do it invisibly. Could she? Was such a thing possible?

She lay back and closed her eyes, willing herself to relax. *How do I separate from my physical body?* She stilled her mind and let her thoughts drift to where she wanted to be. She imagined rising from the bed and stepping over to the balcony, but her muscles did not respond.

She drifted and focused on imagining leaving her body on the bed and lifting herself, moving without using a muscle. She remembered snippets from different suggestions people had given her: Sybille instructing her to focus on a meditative tide, Luc instructing her to focus. Bertòn's words echoed through her mind; he had given her advice before she left his house with Jules.

"Tabitha, you have incredible abilities, but you need to remain cautious about their use. When it comes time to flex the muscle, do it slowly and carefully—your powers will respond. Just give them due respect. Remember, focus your will, and your powers will react. They are, after all, yours to control. Just pay heed and keep them in your control."

"The power is mine to use. The power is mine to control, just direct it…" she murmured. As she cleared her mind, she let her body relax; her muscles seemed to melt onto the bed. She turned her head slightly and was amazed to find herself floating above her own body. Weightless and stunned, she let out a cry. She dropped back into her body with what felt like a thud.

She kept her eyes closed and relaxed again. Her breathing remained calm and steady. She focused on rising from the bed without stirring a muscle. For a moment, she felt as though she were falling asleep, but the lightness that seemed to infuse her reminded her to lift herself.

As she felt herself float above the bed, her eyes opened slowly. With slow and determined focus, she crawled off the bed and stood, looking down at her unmoving body. She looked in wonder at her hand, translucent, with a slightly gray haze. She turned and walked to the mirror and observed herself; a gauzy ghost-like visage stared back at her.

*Okay, one more trick*, she thought. She focused on losing the haze and just letting her form drift into nothing but her own thought. She imagined twisting a dial and watching her outline gradually disappear. Her mouth froze in a shocked gasp as she watched her own image dissipate in the mirror.

With a last glance at her sleeping body, she moved toward the door. She reached for the doorknob and almost laughed as her hand drifted through it. She walked through the door in amusement, considering the fact that she had approached the door at all. With that thought, she drifted through the wall into the hall.

She paused when she approached the guard. He did not respond at all when she walked out of the wall and past him. To be on the safe side, she opted to use less-traveled stairways and stick to the shadows. Of course, whether anyone could sense her or not was another question. The guard had not noticed her, but she had not given him any reason to extend his senses.

The stairs in the back hall came into sight, and she picked up her pace. Although she seemed to have mastered this new talent, she was not about the push her luck. As she descended toward the basement, she realized that she did not have to mentally take every step; she could just leap forward toward the bottom of the stairs. It was not as though she landed or made any impact; she was more or less floating.

As she turned to the stairwell of the second floor, it occurred to her that she did not have to use the stairs; she need only send herself to the basement. After that revelation, she descended rapidly through the floors, stopping at the lowest level. She paused. Even without a body, the darkness that hugged the walls and surrounded the basement sent her heart fluttering.

She sucked in a figurative breath and began moving down the hall. She had not taken into consideration the enormity of the estate. She had envisioned simply wandering into the basement and finding the black elf hidden down there. She had not thought through the task of searching the whole basement. As she approached the easternmost wall of the estate, she turned and observed the long, dark hall behind her.

"Well, better get started."

The endless rooms, twisting corridors, meeting areas, and suites seemed to go on forever. Tabitha felt her strength waning as the effort of maintaining herself out of her body began to take a toll. Room after room, dark seating areas and endless storage areas, unfolded as she methodically continued her search.

She reached the back of the estate with its open rooms and felt some relief from the endless darkness that clung to the rest of the basement. She meandered past an enormous stretch of packed sand laid in a huge ring. Three of the walls were circled with a dark wood railing, porches rolling along the edge like a viewing area. The sign at the entrance proclaimed it to be the practice yard. Tabitha noted the long row of targets and dummies along the dark outer circle. The image gave her the creeps. She hurried past the empty arena toward another set of unlit corridors. Before plunging back into the dark, she glanced up to see the moon fading slowly toward the hills. The night was dwindling; she had better finish and get back.

She was on the verge of quitting when she noticed a single gloomy long hall, a set of double doors tucked deep at the end. She glanced behind her at the moonlit halls that beckoned but turned to slip down the dark hall. As she approached, she saw thick chains wrapped around the door handles. Disregarding the locks and chains, she slipped through the door and found a large empty chamber. Another set of double doors on the far wall beckoned ominously. She felt the hairs on her arms rise, and she knew she was in the right place. With a slight smile, she wondered if her arm hairs had actually risen on her body, back in their—

*Oh God, what if Luc has returned? What if he's found me lying there?* She paused for a moment and realized that she would just have to deal with whatever she found when she returned.

Her resolve once again strengthened, she slipped through the heavy doors into a dark room. She could not ascertain the actual dimensions because the corners of the room were hidden in the gloom, but a large gray shape dominating one corner caught her attention. As she approached, she made out a large cage with gray metal bars. The same gray metal covered the floor and ceiling of the enclosure. In the dark depths, she observed a single wooden chair. Its occupant, wearing a long dark hooded robe, slowly unfolded as she approached.

*Whatever it is cannot possibly see me, right?*

She slowly moved toward the cage. As she approached, the shape within moved toward the front of its cell. She stopped a few feet from the gray bars; the creature stopped as well. The dark robe implied a human shape, but the hood was up, and she could not see within the depths. She glanced about quickly and extended her senses to ensure that they were alone in the room. Then she lifted her palm and willed a glow to illuminate her surroundings. The light gave off a golden ring of illumination within her immediate area. The creature reared back, away from the glow. She stepped forward cautiously and lifted her hand toward the shape within the gray cage. The movement within stopped and the being turned its head. Within the hood was a white mask, with human-like contours and shape; the gaping mouth hole and blank eye sockets were dark and vacant.

The creature stood motionless and turned expressionlessly in her direction. Tabitha had no idea if the creature could see her or not but she could almost feel its intensity as it stood still, apparently waiting.

She had no idea what to do next. She was tempted to try and feel the metal, but the slow approach of the creature as it moved toward her halted her. She watched in mute fascination as it lifted a cloaked arm and extended it through the bars toward her. The sleeve fell away from a long, smoky arm; skeletal fingers reached for her. She gasped and retreated another step.

Obviously the creature could either see or sense her. The pale fog-like texture she had noticed when it killed Viho and his men now had texture and mass.

"Oh my God, you are becoming a solid creature," she whispered.

The creature lunged toward her, pressing against the bars. Tabitha screamed and fell back. Suddenly she found herself on her bed.

The sight of those limbs reaching for her shook her to the core. Her arms and legs vibrated, and her head spun at the intensity of the experience. She inhaled deeply and rose to find something to drink. Luc's side of the bed was empty, but she refused to spend time wondering where he was.

Her fingers shook as she poured a glass of water; she held the glass with both hands as she lifted it to her mouth.

*Now what?*

The moon had slipped behind the horizon, but the sky had not yet begun to lighten. Fatigue washed over her, and she stumbled back to the bed. She used the last of her strength to wrap herself in the blankets before she succumbed to sleep.

The late morning sunlight was streaming through the balcony doors when Tabitha woke. She blinked as the bright light pierced her eyes and slowly lifted her head. She shot a glance at the still untouched opposite side of the bed before rolling off the bed with a groan. Her body felt weary and her mind was foggy; she felt herself stagger as she made her way into the bathroom. She brushed her teeth and moaned at the sight of her disheveled hair and the purple circles beneath her eyes in the mirror above the sink.

In the shower, the hot water streaming down her back and hair felt refreshing. Energy slowly seeped into her muscles as she turned and let the steaming water pour across her face to drive away the cobwebs still clinging to her mind. When she stepped out of the shower, the scent of hot javé tickled her nose, and she wrapped herself in a towel before going to grab a cup.

Breakfast was waiting for her in the sitting room. As the scents wafted to her nose, she realized that for the first time in days, she was starving. She carried a plate of fruit into the bedroom with her, where she found clothes for the day and considered what her next steps would be.

She had to get out of the suite. She needed to get into town, and she could not wait any longer for Luc to get her there. She would have to find this woman that Lena had suggested: Teira DunHem.

But how? And how could she get a message to her mother about finding the black elf? She glanced at the crow and wondered if she should not try to get out by separating. If she did, where would she go? What would she do?

She bit into a ripe piece of fruit and heard the outer door slam.

"Tabitha?"

She leaped up. "Luc?"

He strode into the room, looking not at all disheveled. Not at all like he had spent the night elsewhere—not at all like he had been agonizing about her and their relationship.

"You are dressed. Good, we have an errand in town."

Slightly taken aback, she had to reel in her automatic tirade to let his words sink in. "Errand?"

"Yes. In town." He lifted a well-shaped brow at her. When she did not respond, he raised his hands. "Can we go?"

"Uh… Yes, let me grab some shoes." She grabbed a last sip of her javé before she went in search of her shoes. Slipping them on her feet, she could not help but comment. "You did not return last night."

"No."

She glanced up at him, but he looked away. At his lack of response, she felt her heart sink into her already-tumultuous belly, but she rose and nodded. The prospect of getting out of the estate was much too attractive to let melancholy ruin it.

Luc spoke quietly to the ever-present guard before leading her down the front staircase. Tabitha glanced behind her and smiled when she saw the guard remain behind. "What pull do you have to get me away unguarded? I thought I would go to my deathbed with one of my father's minions right behind me."

"I am your guard," Luc responded softly.

"Ah. Going to make sure I don't make a run for it?"

"If need be."

She grumbled a muted curse, but he ignored her as he shoved open the doors to the outside. Sunlight lit the estate's front lawn, and Tabitha inhaled deeply of the outdoors. It felt like forever since she had just been outside. The prospect of running away, free, and shaking the whole place off was very enticing.

"Don't even think about it," Luc growled.

"What? I didn't say anything," she responded, but she could barely contain the impish grin that curved her lips.

"I could see it all over your face. You are very expressive." He directed her toward the lane that led to an arched line of high-reaching trees. "Don't make me chase you across the lawn within sight of the estate. I don't need to give Dylan any more fuel and accentuate my apparent incompetence."

"Oh, is the poor boy getting picked on?"

Luc glanced over at her with exasperation and shook his head. He inhaled deeply as they made their way toward the shaded lane.

"We are not journeying or anything exotic?"

He shook his head. "I could use a walk, and I assume you could as well."

She nodded. "So what is this errand?"

"We are going into the village to see the child of one of your father's advisors. Your father has offered your services," Luc responded.

"And you agreed?" Tabitha stopped. "You agreed to take me? I have no intention of healing anyone for him. He may hold me prisoner, but I am not going to start healing on his command."

Luc turned to her. "Sometimes, Tabitha, you take the opportunity to get to where you need to be. You said you needed to get to the village to talk to someone. Do you think your father has any intention of letting me take you anywhere unless for a specific task? Do you honestly think he would risk that? Do you think we are not being watched, even now?"

Tabitha glanced around them. "And can they hear us?"

Luc shook his head and slid his hand to the small of her back to direct her to keep walking. "If we stay in any one place long enough, I suspect they would be able to eavesdrop, but as it is, if we keep moving, they will not be able to listen."

"So we can talk freely?"

"This will probably be the best opportunity we will have."

She stopped and turned to face him. "Why did you tell me that you had killed Katie?"

"I didn't tell you that I had killed her. I…" he waved his hand back and forth, "let your father believe she and the baby had died."

"I thought you said Caskans cannot lie," She accused.

"Well, we cannot. Our emotions are so readable that when we lie, it can be detected." He shrugged. "It is why we must choose our words carefully. I told your father that the child did not make it. I didn't lie; the child had not made it…yet. It still had not arrived. When he asked about Katie, I simply told him that many women die in childbirth, that it was bound to happen anyway. I never told him that I had killed her or that the child had been born; he assumed they had both happened."

"Why would you do that? Place yourself in that kind of jeopardy?" Tabitha demanded. "I feel like you are spinning this all to confuse me."

Luc smiled and shook his head. "You only see the net result, don't you? You can't look beyond your belief that because things did not go the way you wanted them to, I must have had my own plan. Either I work for your father or I don't. I am either on your side or I am not."

"You let him take me, and then you took my grandfather to him. Oh, and then you told him I was a healer. We may have been able to salvage that situation if you had not told him I was a healer. How did you hide your scars, anyway?"

"I am a shape changer. I can alter appearance," he responded almost absently. Then he turned back to her. "Did you expect me to take on all of your father's men? Did you think I could leap down there and fight my way through and carry you to safety?"

"I don't know what I expected, but I didn't expect you to take off and then show up when I was tied up in that damn basement," she argued, her anger returning.

"We are back to this again? I left you? Tabitha… I did what I thought was the—"

"I know! I know! You did what you thought was right, and that played right into my father's hands! I thought we were fighting the same enemy, and then you go and join the other side! What the hell? Now what? You are going to convince me that you are still on my side but have been careful to maintain your allegiance with my father? You yourself said that lives are at stake." She walked several feet away, wanting to put some distance and space between them. "Seems to me that you are playing both sides. Quite frankly, I am not sure that I can afford to trust you."

Luc stared at her and then snorted in derision. "You have no option. There is no one else, and you have got to get the hell out of there. I told your father that Katie was dead so we could smuggle her to safety. We have no idea if the child she is carrying is or could possibly be a healer."

"And if it is not?"

"It does not matter. She has to get out of here, and her child as well. If it is a healer, then all the better."

"Why?"

He inhaled deeply. "It would mean that a healer can be born to a human parent. You are proof that a child can be born to a Faye and Caskan mix. That gives us some hope for our future. But if the child is in your father's hands, we lose some of that leverage because he will use that knowledge and that child to boost his own legacy."

"So if we can get Katie out, what will you do with her?"

"Whatever she wants. She can remain here in Caska or she can return to your world. It should be her decision, not your father's," Luc responded. "Of course, your father took that decision out of her hands and opted to end her life when she became less than pliable." Luc leaned back against a slender tree and crossed his arms. As the sunlight dappled through the leafy green covering, shadows played across his body.

"So you would not make her stay or make her child stay?"

Luc sighed. "We do not all have an opportunistic agenda."

"Don't you mean deadly?"

He nodded. "So I hid Katie from him. I moved your grandfather to protect him."

"You moved him into my father's home. How will we remove him now?" she shouted. "You should have—"

Luc lifted his eyes toward the sky and groaned. "Will you stop second-guessing what I should have done, for the love of the One God! I tried to move him to a safe house, but I was caught!"

Tabitha stopped and gaped at him. "What?"

"I told you, I was caught. I had no choice but to let them think I was taking your grandfather to your father's house for his safety."

"And they believed you?"

"Obviously. Otherwise, I would be dead," he responded.

"And still you stayed?" she whispered. "Why?"

"I told you, there is a lot at stake here: my home, my family, my people. Quite frankly, your father needs to be stopped before he controls all the commerce, trade, and information between the regions," Luc explained. "There is much more involved than your freedom. That is critical, but it is not the only thing that is happening. It is as though your appearance simply sparked the chain of events."

"So this has all been building up?"

He nodded and picked up a small handful of rocks to toss against a slender tree. "Yes."

"And what now?"

"We get you out of here." He focused on the simple act of throwing rocks against the tree trunk.

She lowered herself onto a fallen log and watched him, debating the validity of his words. Could she believe him? Had he actually not betrayed her? "So now my father trusts you?"

Luc stopped throwing, appearing to be fascinated by the rocks remaining in his hand. He did not respond immediately. When he lifted his gaze to her, she could see the concern embedded deep within the blue depths. "He has given me the benefit of the doubt, but don't let that fool you. That little test of his in the basement was as much a warning to me as it was a test of your healing abilities. He would have me taken out and killed without a second thought. If he thinks for a moment that I will not be useful when it comes to you, I will be gone. So as long as he believes that you will eventually forgive me and I can be useful in swaying you to his cause, I have value."

"You took an awfully big risk."

"I did."

"Was it worth it?"

He smiled. "We will see. So far, I am having my doubts."

She crossed her ankles and watched him carefully. "So you need me as much as I need you?"

"We are in this together."

"And if something else happens to put us in danger, will you abandon me again?"

"I did not abandon you in the first place," Luc commented softly. "I almost killed two of your father's men in an effort to get to you. I almost lost my life and your grandfather's to try and salvage something of that. Had your father known I was upstairs with you, we would not be having this discussion."

"So what now?"

"We go into the village, we heal your father's advisor's daughter, and we stop and do a couple of things in town," he replied.

"A couple of things?"

"Yes." He extended a hand to her. "A couple of harmless errands designed to give you a feel for the area, the region, and our culture."

She hesitated before taking his hand and letting him pull her up. "Harmless errands?"

He nodded; she noticed he did not release her hand. "You will have to trust me on this one."

"I am not sure I am ready to give you that." Her comment was a little sharper than she intended.

"No, I don't expect you would." His comment was dry, and Tabitha snapped her head up to face him. Before she could respond, he glanced back at her. "You didn't even give me a chance. You were so quick to lose all faith in me and believe the very worst."

Tabitha stepped back as though struck and stared at him. Her anger flared. "Are you trying to blame me? Should I have blindly assumed that everything you did was in my best interest?"

He stepped toward her. For the first time, she saw a flash of anger in his eyes. "Yes, Tabitha, that is what I expected. I thought we had more. I thought we had a foundation of trust, that you'd assume that what I did was the right thing, for you and the larger situation." He shook his head and ran his hands through his hair, clearly frustrated. "Do you know how I feel about you? Do you have any idea what I have been through to try and get you away from here? Tabitha, you judged and convicted me without even listening to my side."

Tabitha felt her rage bubble over, and her fists clenched. *He has the audacity to try and make this all about me. He betrayed me... He did!*

He turned and released an explosive sigh. "I am not him, Tabitha. I am not Greg."

He walked away. All of Tabitha's rage seemed to drain out of her body. She felt her breath leave her, and her stomach constricted as though she had been hit. Luc kept walking, and Tabitha felt more alone than she had in her whole life. The truth stared at her. She realized she had painted Luc with the same brush she used for Greg. She assumed that because she could not be honest, because she withheld a part of herself, they had the right to treat her as though she were less than worthy of every ounce of their respect.

She had assumed Luc was out for his own gain. He could not possibly be doing all of this for her, right? People just did not place themselves in jeopardy for her safety and her protection.

She had kept herself carefully hidden behind high walls, and now, here she stood, alone in the prison she had built. Luc had tried to scale the wall. But the first time he slipped, she had shoved him down. She had stood at the top of the wall and dared him to try to reach her. She had not even tried to find a rope. She had been waiting for him to slip so she could put him in the category of people who lied to her, cheated on her, and treated her as though she deserved to be alone behind those walls, where it was safe.

Luc kept striding farther from her; she watched him go.

Of course he would leave. Everyone went. If you trusted them, they would hurt you. It was safer to stay behind the walls.

Was being safe supposed to hurt so much?

A sob broke from her lips, and the walls around her began to crumble. Tears flowed faster, and Luc's shape began to blur. It was a split second before she realized she was running, racing after him as the released dam of tears poured down her face.

"Luc!"

He turned. She put all of her might into those last steps and threw herself into his arms. She felt him stagger back a step as she clung to his neck, sobs racking her body. His arms encircled her, and she cried harder. She had not driven him away. He was right there, holding her.

# CHAPTER SEVEN

THE SUN SEEMED WARMER THAN SHE REMEMBERED AND the air sweeter. After what seemed like a river of tears had cascaded over Luc's shoulders, Tabitha's tears had finally dried. She leaned against his damp shirt, listening to the strong and steady beat of his heart beneath her cheek.

"I am sorry." She was almost afraid to lift her face and see what expression haunted his eyes.

"You better be," he murmured. She tightened her grip around his waist.

She tilted her head back to look at him. The blue of his eyes mirrored the summer sky, dazzling her. "Were you going to leave me?"

He smiled and slowly shook his head. "No, I would not have left you. I thought giving you some space might help. I was not sure if I should expect anger, apathy, or a projectile aimed at my back."

She slid her fingers through his hair. "Will you forgive me?"

He lowered his mouth to tease her lips. "Will you trust me?" He countered.

She nodded. "Yes."

She opened her mouth to his gentle probing. The warmth that simmered through her body became searing heat. His hands tightened around her. Tabitha held nothing back when she responded to his passionate kiss. Hot lava flowed through her bloodstream as the last of her barriers dissolved. The taste of his mouth and the intense sensation of his long body pressed against hers sent her mind reeling. Her fingers slid through his hair; his hands ran along her body, touching, molding and igniting her.

He slowly lifted his mouth from hers, his breath ragged. His eyes smoldered. She tugged his mouth down to hers for one last taste and then released him.

"We should go," he murmured against her throat.

She smiled and dropped her face against his shoulder. "We do not find the best make-out spots, do we?"

He chuckled and slowly released her. "We are expected in town. When we get that over with, perhaps we can have some dinner together and talk about a more suitable place to make out next time."

She laughed and started walking next to him, her hand clenched in his. "Are you asking me on a date?"

"A date? After all we have been through?"

"Well... You know, you have never actually asked me out."

"I see." He laughed. "And should I ask your father for permission?"

She groaned. "I am not sure that I want to know what his response would be."

They wound their way through the canopied lane. Soon the trees gave way to a wide-open avenue that stretched before them, leading into the heart of the village. Tabitha studied the village laid out beneath them and tried to figure out where she had entered when she went to Gwyn's cottage. Luc pointed out the route that snaked in from the forest behind the estate. As he stood behind her, pointing over her shoulder, his mouth near her ear, indicating where she would have emerged from the woods, she lost track of what he was saying and leaned into his chest.

She heard the soft rumble of his laugh through his chest. "You are not even listening to me, are you?"

She shook her head. "Nope, just taking full advantage of your arms around me."

He reluctantly withdrew his embrace and tugged her hand forward to continue walking into town. She was in a blissful trance from his kiss and the subsequent occasional kiss stolen along the walk as they approached town. It took her a few moments to realize his demeanor had changed. His shoulders tensed, and he released her hand. She glanced up; his jaw was set, his eyes scanning as they approached the edge of the village.

"Let's get the advisor's child taken care of first. I don't want to have that hanging over my head," Luc said.

"Why is one of my father's advisors living in the village? I thought they all had apartments at the estate?"

They approached a warm and cozy bungalow tucked at the end of a long lane. "Most do, but some refuse, preferring to have a separate domicile. Your father, of course, prefers them to be close at hand," Luc responded.

"This is it?"

Luc nodded and opened the gate, directing her toward the front door. A young woman answered his knock; her dark hair was pulled severely back from her face, revealing deep lines around her dark eyes.

"Yes?"

"The lord regent has sent his daughter to see your child." Luc's voice had taken on an edge that Tabitha had never heard before.

The woman's eyes shot back and forth between them. After a hesitant nod, she stepped back from the door and allowed them to enter.

*When you heal the child, do not exert yourself. It is imperative that you remain in control and that she does not see your blood need,* Luc cautioned.

Tabitha hid her surprise and followed them through the entryway into a formal sitting room. The woman turned suspicious eyes to them. "Can you see the child here?"

Tabitha nodded, amazed that the woman used such a cool form of address when speaking about her child. The woman disappeared upstairs and returned, holding a small girl, possibly a year or eighteen months old. She placed the child gently on the low table in the sitting area.

Tabitha approached and lifted a tentative hand. "May I?"

The woman's eyes moved rapidly from her to Luc and then back again. With a slow swallow, she stepped back. Tabitha placed a gentle hand on the child's belly and looked into the dark eyes that returned her gaze. The child's eyes began to well as she looked for her mother.

"Would you put her to sleep, please?" Tabitha asked.

The woman gently placed her hands on the child's forehead with a slight surge of energy. The child's eyes drooped and closed. The woman stepped quickly back from the table. With a flash of insight, Tabitha realized the woman was terrified.

*Why is she afraid of me?* Tabitha asked Luc.

Luc had taken up position by the door, his arms crossed across his chest. She glanced back and could not shake the impression that he was guarding her.

*She knows the rumors and legends about healers. I suspect she is not exactly thrilled with you being here. I suggest that you do what you have to do so we can get out of here.*

Tabitha nodded and then pushed her concerns aside as she focused on the tiny bundle in front of her. The child was tiny, her limbs long and thin. Tabitha wondered if she were older than she appeared but so small due to whatever ailed her. She dropped to her knees next to the table and placed her hands on either side of the child. Her fingers began to warm and glow. Tabitha's eyelids immediately dropped; her surroundings slipped away as the healing energy engulfed her.

Her mind's eyes noted the dark swirling of the illness that plagued the little girl. The healing glow slid through the child to begin the process of sweeping the darkness from her organs. Tabitha lost track of time as she sent the glow to gnaw away at the sickness. It was not exactly like healing Cyra back in Calais; this corruption seemed to cling, glued to the child's organs. She watched as slowly, the glow chipped away and released small, dark pieces from the delicate organs.

After what seemed like an eternity, she felt the glowing healing sweep the last of the darkness from the child. The glow began to fade. As Tabitha felt her surroundings begin to come back into focus, she felt the familiar weakness overtake her limbs. Her head drooped. She tried to draw in a deep breath, but her lungs felt as though they were being squeezed. The little girl was whisked from beneath her hands. Luc's hands were suddenly there, supporting her and lifting her to her feet. Tabitha felt her legs give out, and he hefted her into his arms. The effort to lift her head was momentous, but she opened her eyes as Luc's voice, sharp and commanding, issued instructions to the woman. She was surprised to hear the woman respond in a high and hysterical tone. Then Luc strode from the house with Tabitha in his arms.

She tried to speak, but her lips felt as though they were swollen shut. Her head again drooped over his arm. She heard a sharp banging and more voices but had no idea what was being said.

The darkness was slowly slipping around any last vestiges of consciousness when she felt her head lifted. The thud of a heartbeat rang in her ears. Her teeth plunged, and the salty fluid pouring down her throat felt like liquid energy as it hit her belly and then quickly ran its course to her icy outer limbs.

Conscious thought began to return; she became aware of her surroundings. She quickly disengaged from Luc's throat. She dropped her face against his shoulder. Her stomach threatened to expel the blood she had consumed. Luc's hand slid to her midsection. She felt the calming warmth he exuded, and the gripping in her belly slowly eased. As she began to focus, she realized that he was sitting on a sofa. She was in his lap, her legs over his, her arms around his neck.

She slowly lifted her head to find him looking down at her, concern in his eyes.

*Are you all right?*

She nodded and began to get her bearings. She released her arms from around his neck and realized she had no idea where they were. The room was completely unfamiliar. She started when she saw a young woman sitting on a low table, watching her. Golden hair tumbled over her petite shoulders. Her blue eyes were watching the interaction between the two of them intensely.

"Is she all right?" the woman asked Luc.

Tabitha felt Luc nod as he lifted her off his lap onto the sofa beside him. Questions were on her lips before she noticed the small rivulet of blood on Luc's neck. She lifted a glowing finger and healed his wound, noting that the twin scars remained behind.

"Where am I?"

"My house," the blond woman responded. She proffered a cup of water. "I am Colene. Luc brought you here to settle you back among the living."

Tabitha drained the water from the cup. "Thanks."

"Colene has been kind enough to assist us," Luc explained. "I came here before the advisor's wife became hysterical. It seems she was wondering if you were going to demand blood from her or the baby in exchange. Thankfully, you kept your mouth shut so she didn't see your fangs. I told her you were just weak."

"I got to see them though." Colene grinned, and her blue eyes twinkled before she winked. "It was my first healing."

Tabitha felt her mouth curve into slight smile. "Thank you for letting us in."

Colene shrugged and took the empty cup from her. "I have a tendency to take in Luc's baggage. Every time I open the door, he needs something else."

Tabitha glanced back and forth between them, unsure about the reference.

Luc chuckled. "Colene is hosting a houseguest of ours."

"Houseguest?"

Colene grinned. "Yes, someone who was hoping you would stop by. Want to come and say hi?"

"Who is it?" Tabitha asked. Her legs quivered, but energy began seeping back into them as she stood. "Wait, is Katie here?"

Colene turned and beckoned Tabitha to follow her down the hall. "She is. She has been asking for you."

Tabitha followed the young woman, aware of the sharp contrast behind her own raven locks and the tumble of blond hair cascading down her host's back. Colene stopped at the first door on the left, turned the handle, and let the door slip open. She stepped aside to allow Tabitha to enter. Katie lay sprawled on the bed. Her ungainly belly swelled from the bed, her limbs surrounding it. She glanced up as Tabitha entered. With a happy cry, Katie struggled to flop her way off the bed.

Tabitha stopped to watch this process with a grin. After Katie had backed off the bed and finally turned to her, her stance slightly unsteady, Tabitha could only laugh out loud. "Very gracefully done!"

"Yeah, well... Wait until you are carrying a huge bowling ball in your belly and see how graceful you are!" Katie retorted as she tottered over to enclose Tabitha in a huge hug.

"You are okay," Tabitha sighed into her friend's shoulder.

"Yeah, I am okay," Katie replied. "Thanks to your man. God, he is so cute!"

Tabitha laughed. "Yes, he is, but you have other things on your mind!"

Katie giggled. "Hey, I won't be this big forever! You just wait. I might give you a run for him!"

Tabitha nodded. "I am just so glad to see you are doing well. Any idea when the baby is due?"

"Any day now. I am not dreading it now that people are trying to get me away. I won't have to give this one over if I don't want to." Katie rubbed her swollen belly as she spoke.

Tabitha shook her head. "No, you won't, assuming we can get you out of here."

Katie lifted a shoulder as though that was inconsequential. "Well, I would not have had a chance if not for your friends. Luc tells me that he has a plan."

Tabitha smiled. "I am sure he does."

"In the meantime, I have been teaching Miz DeSkin to play whist. I will tell you what, I am going to kick her ass again tonight!"

Tabitha glanced over and saw that Colene and Luc were deep in conversation in the hall. Colene glanced over at the mention of her name and smiled at Katie. With a shake of his head Luc indicated that it was time for them to head out. She and Katie shared a last hug before she and Luc headed for the front door. Colene escorted them and waved them off as they headed down the walk.

Luc glanced down at her. "You feeling all right? Energy back?"

Tabitha nodded. "Almost. Where to now?"

Luc led her down the lane toward the village green. "I thought some time at the historical society might help you garner an appreciation for the history of our world and the different races."

"Seriously?" Tabitha asked, leaning on his arm slightly as the shaking in her limbs subsided. *Will I be able to speak to Teira DunHem? Lena said she is the one who knows about black elves.*

*That is the plan.*

They entered a main thoroughfare, where Tabitha got her first sight of the busy village during a bustling day. It was not as busy as Porta Negra, with its throngs of tourists, but crowds of people surged through the narrow streets. The shops were busy. People strode along the streets with a focused purpose that Tabitha recognized from an ordinary workday back on the island.

Luc glanced back behind them and ushered her toward a squat building off the circular village green. The cool interior was dark; it took a moment for Tabitha's eyes to adjust. Luc walked to the desk as Tabitha glanced around at the walls covered with shelves filled with books and dusty scrolls. Dust sprinkled the air and spun through the sunlight streaming through the dingy windows. For a moment, she grew nostalgic for Porta Negra's old town library, its familiar scent of books and old memories sifting through the air, each begging to be held, to whisper secrets and tales to anyone willing to listen.

"Tabitha?"

She shook herself back to the present and turned to see a young woman standing next to Luc, an open and warm smile on her face. Her light hair was caught in a ponytail, and her warm light eyes were lit with amusement. Tabitha realized she had quickly assessed the woman to be human, based on her open and friendly expression.

"Yes. Are you Teira DunHem?"

"I am! I understand you are looking for me?"

Luc spoke before Tabitha could respond. "We were advised to seek you out. Tabitha is new to the area. Antoine was hoping you could share some of the history of Windrift. He was hoping his daughter could learn more about the history of his governance."

Teira smiled and indicated that they should follow her toward the back of the building. "Of course. I would be happy to tell you about Windrift, and all of Chandolyn. You are aware that the governance of Chandolyn reaches from the southern border of St. Mikel all the way down to the border of Borgue. Of course, Windrift is the capital and our lord regent's seat," she explained as they followed her. A large window with crosshatched wood framing cast a checkerboard effect across a massive desk.

Teira indicated that they should sit there. She offered them some hot tea from a porcelain pot. Luc shook his head, but Tabitha accepted the hot mug as she settled into a wood chair.

Teira pushed some papers to the side of the desk and glanced between them. "So, the history of Chandolyn…"

Luc glanced back toward the front of the building, checking that they were alone, before letting his voice drop. "Specifically, black elves."

Teira stopped pouring tea into her mug and absently set down the pot. "Black elves?"

He nodded. Tabitha watched as Teira's expression quickly changed from pleasantly engaged to alarmed to excited. "You want to learn about black elves?"

"Yes. What can you tell us? We understand you to be the resident expert." Luc leaned forward. "Of course, we would prefer this discussion to be discreet."

Her grin widened as she sank into her seat. "Oh, I can tell you everything I know about black elves. Of course, what there is to tell is limited. All we have are the Faye legends and historical accounts that were handed down from one generation to the next. Obviously, there is no one left who was alive during the Black Years."

"Black Years?" Tabitha asked.

Teira's frown was fleeting; she hid it behind a sunny nod. "Yes, the Black Years. You know, the period when the Faye were decimated by the coming of the black elves."

Tabitha quickly nodded as she realized that Teira did not understand that she was not only new to Windrift but to their history. "So the only information you have are the writings about former legends? Who wrote it down? And when?"

"Well, the most comprehensive of the works was from a human historian by the name of Edgar Lee Donn. It was his life's work to study the Black Years and pull together the list of legends that had been passed down. Those tales were passed down by the Caskan storytellers and the Faye had scrolls detailing the events leading to and during that timeframe. Of course, only the Faye can read the Faye language, so we have had to rely on the tales. Our closest estimation is that it occurred about seven hundred years ago, and... here, let me show you."

She rustled through the papers on her desk and stood to quickly thumb through a pile in one corner. She tugged free one sheet and placed it on the table before them. The sheet was worn and faded, the writing a spidery scrawl. A hand-drawn graph was in the center, surrounded by arrows and comments. Tabitha and Luc leaned in to see better; Teira turned the page to face them.

"Here, the graph depicts the timeframe when the invasion took place. You can see that it really was only a short period of time. The X-axis indicates the months, and the Y-axis details the estimated number of lives lost in each month. You can see that the whole event spanned about eighteen months. In less than a year and a half, the Faye lost almost eighty percent of their total population. And a great deal of the local flora and fauna were lost as well. The tales told of miles and miles of lifeless land." Teira pushed the graph back onto its pile.

"Eighty percent? What does that translate to in the number of lives lost?" Luc asked.

Teira shrugged and sat back against the back of her seat. "We don't really know. There was no census back then. The Faye did not account for their population numbers. Edgar was able to have a couple of the scrolls translated by some Faye. Those suggested somewhere around two to three million."

Tabitha sat deep in thought, combing through the medieval history lessons from her senior year. "Seven hundred years ago? Late thirteenth century? Was it possible that the black elves could have been exiled into another world?"

Teira nodded, pointing to a number of scrolls behind her. "I have a number of the Faye scrolls, but we are unable to read them. From what I have been able to gather from Edgar's work and the little I can actually understand from my own studies, the black elves' departure was rather sudden. Within about twenty years, the portals from the other world began to open. Edgar theorized that the Faye had opened them to repopulate this world with birds and animals. Consequently, humans also entered through the portals. As you know, the first humans that were brought over formed the basis for the Caskan race when they intermarried with the Faye."

"But we don't know if the Faye were able to fight or destroy the black elves," Luc prompted.

Teira shook her head. "No, there isn't anything about that in his writings, with the exception of a couple of references to a substance that was discovered that the black elves could not tolerate. There was nothing about where or how they found it."

Teira rose and walked over to a bookcase behind Luc; she tugged a small book free and gave it to him. "This is a copy of some of Edgar's writings. Most people think his theories are nothing but a bunch of nonsense, but in his time he was the most educated about the legends and tales. If anyone could have developed a basis for the theories, it would have been him." She sat back down and picked up her mug. The room was quiet while she took a sip of the hot liquid.

Tabitha rose and stretched, letting the information sink in. "So no one can read the Faye language? I was not aware that they had their own language." Teira glanced at her in surprise, and Luc put his face in his hands with a barely audible groan: obviously she'd taken another misstep. "Well, I mean, I knew they had their own language, but I've never seen their writing." Tabitha tried to salvage what was surely an idiotic comment. "It is not like it is that common, right?"

*Will you please stop babbling and change the subject?* Luc grumbled in her mind.

"So why do you think that people think that Edgar Von what's-his-name's theories are nonsense?" Tabitha asked as she lifted a dusty scroll from the stack behind Teira's chair.

Teira's eyes showed her concern as she watched Tabitha tug and then unroll the delicate scroll. She lifted a hand in caution but dropped it. "Edgar Lee Donn was his name, and as you are aware…" She paused, obviously wondering if Tabitha was in fact aware. "—that not everyone believes that the black elves were ever more than a legend. Many believe a sickness wiped them out. A lot of people believe that the humans brought the sickness because they began to acclimate to this world around the Black Years. We believe it was shortly after the black elves, but the timelines are a bit fuzzy. We are talking about trying to pin down history based on tales passed by word of mouth."

Tabitha was looking intently at the scroll in her hands, turning it over to reveal the writing as she spoke. "Well, it does correspond timing-wise to the Black Plague, but that occurred mostly in Europe and the Mediterranean. I have heard that the humans who were initially sucked over were Native Americans."

As she stared at the words on the scroll before her, she did not notice the lengthening silence. She scanned the lines and unrolled the scroll, her brows furrowing as the strange writing unfolded before her.

*You seriously did not just say that, right?* Luc's voice was exasperated. *How would you like to try and recover now?*

She glanced up to see the two of them staring at her. Luc's expression was clearly infuriated, but Teira's eyes were wide. Teira was the first to speak. "The Black Plague? The Native Americans? Are those things of the other world?"

"Oh." Tabitha hesitated, realizing what she had said. The scroll had captured her attention, and she had not been paying attention to what escaped her mouth. With a slightly foolish grin, she commented, "I am studying alternative cultures. I know a lot about the world the humans come from. I learned it at school. With Luc. We go to school together. It is where we met. Of course, he is not studying alternative cultures..."

*Please stop.* Luc begged.

Teira nodded and glanced between them, her smile slightly frozen. Luc returned her smile and changed the subject. "So, you are able to pinpoint that the Black Years lasted less than two years and they coincided with the increase in the human population. Tell me more about the information that you have—"

Tabitha's attention returned to the scroll. "Wait. What does this mean? This line here..." She put the scroll down on the desk and pointed to a tightly written line about halfway down the dusty document. "It says..." She leaned closer to read the line, but it appeared that the writing were undulating, as though underwater. "This is the oddest thing. It is hard to read. Why is that? Is it the ink or…"

She glanced up to find Teira and Luc staring at her with mouths slightly agape. "What?"

*What did I say now?*

Before Luc could answer, Teira slowly leaned in to where Tabitha pointed. "You can read that?"

Tabitha nodded and glanced between them. "Well, yeah. I mean, it's a little wiggly, but it is right here, plain as day."

Teira shook her head. Her voice croaked slightly. "It is Faye writing. Only a full-blooded Faye can read it."

Tabitha glanced between her and Luc. "You…umm… can't read this?"

Both shook their heads.

Luc lifted the scroll gently from her hands and looked closer. "I can't make out a word. In Faye writing, the letters shift and change. Even if you speak the language, you would not be able to read a Faye document."

Tabitha sighed and glanced sheepishly at Teira. "I am half Faye."

"Tabitha, as rare as the half-Faye are, even they usually cannot read the language. You have to be a full Faye to be able to read it," Teira responded.

Luc glanced over. "What do you see?"

Tabitha glanced back down at the scroll in her hands and perused the words before her. As archaic as the language seemed to be, the words looked as familiar as any of the books in her own home back on Porta Negra. She saw the letters as being from her own familiar alphabet.

"I can read it. It looks like regular writing to me. What do the letters look like to you?" she responded, handing the scroll back to Teira.

"They look like a different language. The letters are not familiar, which is why it is difficult to decipher, even knowing a little of the Faye language. But the thing is, when I look at the scrolls, the letters change every time, and I am unable to figure it out in time. Every time I open one, the letters look different. So unless you are a Faye and can read through the spell, there is no way to decrypt it," Teira stated. She delicately took the scroll from Tabitha's fingers and rolled it tightly. "Why don't you tell me why you are here asking about black elves? There has not been any word of black elves in more than seven hundred years. Why the interest now?"

Tabitha opened her mouth to respond, but Luc lifted a hand. "Teira, we suspect that the drought in the central plains may be caused by a return of the black elves."

Teira shifted her focus from one to the other before she replied. "Why would you suspect such a thing?"

Tabitha responded. "Because I have seen one."

The room went deadly silent again. Teira slowly lowered herself back in her seat. "What? Do you know what this means? Does the regent know?"

*I am not sure you should have let that information out just yet.*

*If she is going to help us, she needs to know.* Tabitha turned back to Teira and said, "I don't know. I think he does, but I just don't know."

Before they could respond, a young girl burst into the library. "Luc?"

"Here, Jylian. What is it?" Luc stood, and the girl threaded her way through the stacks of books toward them. She could not have been more than thirteen. Her limbs were still teenage gangly. Her light hair hung in a long ponytail down her back. "Colene sent me to get you. You have to come quick."

Tabitha leaped up. "Is it Katie?"

The girl shook her head and, with a wave, headed off toward the entrance of the library. "Quick!"

# CHAPTER EIGHT

LUC SPED AFTER THE GIRL OUT THE FRONT DOOR. AFTER A moment's hesitation, Tabitha dashed after them. The young girl's steps were sure and light as she threaded her way through the streets. Tabitha ran with a single-minded focus on Luc's back in front of her. As they turned a corner onto a tree-lined lane, she halted abruptly, recognizing Gwyn's cottage tucked among the shade trees. Luc and Jylian had slipped around the side of Gwyn's cottage; Tabitha raced after them before she lost sight of them.

She emerged to find herself on the trail she recognized as leading to her father's estate. Luc and Jylian had just joined Colene at the base of the trail. She wore a pair of gleaming knives strapped on each hip by a single, worn leather belt that rested low on her hips. Her expression was dark and somber, her mouth set in a deep scowl. Colene gently placed a hand on Jylian's arm and with a quick word sent her back into town.

"What is it?" Luc demanded.

Colene's eyes dropped before she turned her face away, drawing a deep breath between closed teeth. Her words were clipped. "Follow me."

She led them up the path but then veered sharply off into the underbrush; her steps were sure and rapid. Tabitha felt fear building in the pit of her belly as they traveled farther into the woods. The sun was slowly dipping behind the trees; the gloom seemed to cling to the tree trunks like dark moss. The leaves whispered in a hollow breath that sent icy shivers down Tabitha's spine. The thought occurred to her to race back and wait for Luc beside Gwyn's cozy fireplace, a hot cup of tea in her hands.

*Luc?*

He didn't respond and kept following Colene as she deftly climbed over a rocky outcropping. He turned to help Tabitha, but she shook her head, determined not to cower in the face of whatever they were approaching.

The woods were silent. The body lay in the dead leaves; her silver hair was ragged, twisted dried leaves interspersed among the gray strands. Breath escaped Tabitha in a long moan as she recognized Gwyn's face, ashen and still.

"Oh God!" She felt her lungs constrict, and a deep pain filled her, as though she had been struck. "No!"

Tabitha crept to Gwyn's side, her fingers already reaching for her, willing healing energy toward her. She fell to her knees, but the warmth never began. She felt Luc behind her, drawing her back.

*You can't, Tabitha. She is gone.*

*No no no no no...* Tabitha gently swept the soft strands of hair back from Gwyn's brow. Her skin was cold. The grayish tinge in her face made her almost unrecognizable. Tabitha placed her hands on the woman's chest and tried again and again to start the healing energy, but her fingers remained cold against Gwyn's body.

*Oh, Gwyn... Why you?* Tabitha felt tears splashing down on her hands as she knelt beside her friend in hollow disbelief. She gently lifted Gwyn's hands and folded them upon her chest. Ragged sobs racked her as she tried to find a way out of the sadness that seemed to swallow her. Even as Tabitha tried to sweep the debris from Gwyn's shoulders and sweater, she could not help but see the dirt encrusted beneath Gwyn's nails, as though she had been clawing through dirt in an effort to escape whatever had chased her. Dark smudges were callously drawn across her ashen cheeks beneath the once merry blue eyes that now stared blankly at the sky. Tabitha gently placed a finger across her friend's eyes to close them, but they refused to remain shut. The grimace of pain or perhaps fear on her mouth would not be erased.

Tabitha's sobs began to abate to soft hiccups, and the small sounds of the world around her began to creep back into her awareness. It was a moment before she realized that the birds were chirping. The soft buzz of the summer bugs rose in a sharp cacophony through the gloomy woods.

She could hear the harsh hiss of Colene's rage as she spat out her ire over the offense. Luc's response was a dark and dangerous rumble. She could not make out his words, but she recognized the anger that brewed beneath the tone.

"Luc, when was she found?" Tabitha's voice was a harsh rasp even to her own ears.

"Jylian found her and came to get me. I sent her to find Luc. Her friend Enna has gone to fetch my husband and the sheriff. They should be here shortly," Colene responded.

"The birds," Tabitha whispered. "The bugs... They were not making any noise before."

Luc and Colene exchanged glances, and Colene shrugged a shoulder. "I didn't notice."

Tabitha drew her teary gaze from Gwyn and glanced up at the two of them. "I didn't either, until they started singing and buzzing again." She let Luc help her rise to her feet. "I don't know if it means anything, but I was told that the black elves initially eradicated insects, small animals, and birds before they started taking larger lives."

Colene looked thunderstruck. "Black elves? What do you mean, black elves? You think that is what happened to Gwyn?"

Tabitha nodded. "I think that the reason the woods were so silent is because one was still close by. I think that Dylan had not yet had a chance to bring it back, and that was why the woods were so still."

*Well, I guess we have given up on using caution regarding information about the black elf,* Luc murmured to her.

*These people have every right to know what my father has up there,* Tabitha snapped back, her sadness blooming into a simmering rage.

"Dylan? You mean Dylan Tefers?" Colene demanded, her hands automatically grabbing the hilts of her twin knives.

Luc exhaled. "This is not the time to discuss it but yes, Dylan Tefers, and yes, a black elf. Let's keep this between us for the moment, until we can decide how we can best handle this information."

*Why are you angry with me? Why shouldn't they know?*

*Because we don't need a full-scale panic. We need to get this information out to people so they can safely get away from it. If people start running away in droves, that will force your father's*

*hand. The One God only knows what he would do then. You can-
not send people into a frenzy based upon something your mother
showed you in a past regression.*

Luc's response was terse, and Tabitha felt herself bristle.

As he reached an arm around Tabitha's waist, Luc turned
to Colene. "I want to take Tabitha back to the estate. I will
meet you back in the village after you have brought Gwyn
and help you with the arrangements."

"No, wait!" Tabitha argued. "I don't want to go back! I
want to help."

Luc shook his head and led her away from the wooded
dell that held Gwyn's body. "You need to get back. Someone has to tell Cole."


Many hours later, Tabitha was in her suite, waiting for Luc
to return. Her head pounded, and her eyes still stung from
the tears she had shed when she had told Cole about Gwyn.
He had taken the news as poorly as she had expected, breaking down in sobs.

"How? How did this happen?" he had demanded time
and again.

Tabitha simply told him she didn't know. Gwyn had
been found dead in the woods. There were no wounds or
signs of any beating or blows.

He had finally stopped asking, and Tabitha had swallowed the truth like a bitter pill. Luc's words of caution returned to her. He had advised her to not tell Cole about the
other strange circumstances until they knew what had killed
Gwyn. She had argued, but Luc had pointed out that as certain as Tabitha felt, they had no actual proof that Gwyn had
been killed by the black elf.

Cole had railed at the door, demanding to speak to their father as soon as possible. The guard promised to get the message to the regent, and Cole had then collapsed on the couch, uncommunicative. Tabitha had gently touched his hand as she left, but he remained motionless.

Now she sat in front of a small fire in the sitting room, sipping a cup of tea. Her stomach complained of hunger, but she ignored it. Images of Gwyn's body lying in the dead leaves danced over and over in her mind. Why had Gwyn had to die? Did she know something?

Had she seen something? Gwyn had access to the entire estate. Might she have wandered into the basement? Had she been killed because she had found Dylan's pet?

She heard Luc's voice outside the door before he slowly swung it open and entered, his head down. His shoulders slumped in fatigue as he closed the door behind him. He did not immediately see her sitting in the shadows on the sofa, but she saw his smile when he glanced over and saw her, legs curled under her, a blanket across her lap and a teacup gripped in her fingers.

"You're awake."

"I was not looking forward to facing the nightmares waiting for me."

"Have you spoken to your father?"

She shook her head and slid over to allow him room to sit. "No, not a word. I assume he knows?"

Luc nodded. "He came into the village when he got word. He brought Cole with him."

"Cole?"

"Cole was the closest thing she had to family. I don't think Gwyn had any blood relatives. Your father granted Cole the right to prepare her for her funeral." Luc took the hot cup from her hands and took a slow swallow.

"I am surprised. I did not expect that he would let Cole go."

Luc shrugged, handed her the cup, and leaned his head against the sofa with a long sigh. "What can Cole do? Your father still has Lena locked away. He knows Cole won't leave without her."

Tabitha felt the warm sting of tears behind her eyes once again and buried her nose in her teacup. After deeply inhaling the steam, she glanced over to see Luc's eyes were closed. "What will Cole do? To prepare her? How do you honor your dead?"

Luc released a long, drawn-out breath and lifted his head. "There are differences depending on the region, which I imagine is much like in your world. We do it as they do in the north. Tonight, her body will be cleansed with water and lavender oil. She will be dressed in her best clothes for the viewing. The dead lay for three days in their home. They are never left alone. People come by to pay their respects. Before sundown on the third day, we build a funeral pyre. The smoke from the fire will help carry them to their final resting place. The southern lands bury their dead. I believe the Plains tribes usually bury theirs as well, although there is some ritual with the bones that I don't know much about."

"And Cole is preparing her?"

"Yes."

"Will I be allowed to pay my respects?" She asked.

"I will bring you down when you are ready," he replied.

A growl of frustration rose in her throat at the reminder about her restricted freedom. "I am so tired of this. I just want to do whatever I feel like doing. I hate that he has me locked up here like a prisoner."

Luc watched her warily. "Make no mistake about it, Tabitha. You are a prisoner. You are his prisoner. Your healing ability is what keeps you alive."

"I don't have to like it."

"No, you don't. But don't forget that you are at his mercy," Luc said.

"For now."

He let a small half-smile curl his mouth at that, but the smile never reached his eyes. He took her cup from her and wandered over to the pot bubbling gently over the fire. He gestured toward it, and she nodded.

"It is tea, not javé."

He refilled her cup and turned to pull another cup from the rack for himself. She watched the flames of the fire curl around the dark fuel. She began to imagine a funeral pyre. The log in her fireplace became a long, dark body, the flames running along it like the caress of a lover's hands. The fire was a living thing, engulfing the body, devouring the fragile remnants and all other evidence of the life that had been there to welcome her at her birth, the life that had hid her brother and kept him safe, the connection she had needed to finally begin to pull the fragments of her own history into some semblance of order.

Her eyes stung, and her nose began to run as her emotions began to overtake her again.

*Tabitha?*

She glanced over at Luc.

*Why don't you tell me about your mother's visit and what she showed you? You have not given me much detail. I want to know exactly what she showed you when Viho died.*

She sighed and tugged herself away from the emotions that were threatening to send her into tears yet again.

*It feels like it was years ago when I spoke to her. She woke me from my sleep and had me separate. I did not know whose mind was controlling me, so I used Bertón's technique to escape it... When I came to my senses, I was standing on the balcony railing, and I fell.*

She drew in a deep breath at the memory of her plunge; she felt a shiver run through her body.

*I was falling, and I screamed out to her, and she changed me into an owl. I shape changed.*

Luc sat up. *You were able to shape an owl?*

*She told me she had done it for me so I could meet her. I don't know how it happened.*

*But if you were able to do it once, you can do it again? You have the ability?* Luc was watching her closely.

*She told me she had forced me into the shape. I don't know if I could do it again since I didn't do it that time.* She saw the gleam in his eyes and knew he was already working on the next phase of whatever plan he was cooking up. *When I met her, she told me that when I left I was to take Katie with me. I told her you had killed her. I was furious with her for not getting me out before she admitted that she could not take me out but she was working on a plan.*

Luc nodded. *And then when she showed you Viho?*

*My mother took me back in time to a clearing. Dylan was there, and the black elf. When we got there, she told me that Dylan could not see me because it was in the past. They were already dead when we were there. I could see the gray mist floating over the bodies, and then the thing itself began to solidify. My mother told me that every time it fed, it became more solid and more aware of its surroundings. Luc, I swear that the thing could see me. I felt like it was staring at me, and it seemed to turn its head whenever we moved.*

Luc tapped his fingers on the edge of the sofa, his thoughts intense. *What else can you tell me about it?*

*When it was done, Dylan told it to get in the cage. He waved some gray wand-like thing at it, and it did what he directed.*

*Wand? You are not falling back on your world's beliefs that we fly around and use wands?* He snorted in disgust.

*Well, that is what it looked like to me. He waved this stick-thing at the monster and it got into its cage, and they left,* she replied, stung by his derision. *My mother told me she was working on a plan to get me out of here but that in the meantime I needed to find out how Dylan was controlling the thing.*

Luc's eyes were intent on the fire. *So you saw the black elf through a past regression with your mother, but we don't know anything else. We have no proof that the thing is here or that.*

"It's in the basement," Tabitha blurted out before she remembered to use their link.

"What?" Luc's eyes snapped toward her, his mouth agape. *How do you know that?*

*I saw it. I separated one night and went down to the basement. I saw it. Even though I was invisible, it knew I was there. It lunged for me.*

Luc stared at her, his face a mask of amazement and anger. He rose from the couch and turned to her. *Why didn't you tell me? What do you mean, you separated and you were invisible? What the hell, Tabitha?*

Tabitha leaped up. *I don't have to tell you everything. If you remember correctly, until this afternoon I was not exactly speaking to you. There was no way I was going to tell you something like that. I thought you were working for my father.*

Luc clenched his teeth and ran his hands over his face, clearly frustrated. *All right. All right. Is there anything else you haven't told me? Anything else I need to know?*

As she became calmer, she abruptly recalled that her mother had shared the identity of the woman in Dark Hollow. The mysterious body that had been discovered in that glade back in her own world was in fact Luc's mother. He had told her that he believed his mother had died of a fever when he was a small child. Her mother had admitted that Luc's mother had helped her escape that fateful night eighteen years ago and had lost her life doing it.

She glanced over at him. His jaw was still set in anger, with dark circles under his eyes. She realized he was probably running on sheer adrenaline at this point. He had been going night and day. How could she possibly admit to Luc that his mother had died saving her mother? Would he even believe her? Tabitha swallowed the memory, not yet ready to begin to unravel that part of the story. It seemed like more than she could emotionally bear.

She shook her head. *No, I don't think so.*

*This whole rescue plan will be a lot easier to keep together if you can remember to share information with me. I have to go out.*

*What? Now? After what happened? Where are you going?*

He turned on his heel and headed into the bedroom. Tabitha raced after him.

*I have to update the others.*

*What others?*

*Tabitha, you are going to have to trust me on this.* He flung the balcony doors open. Before he could step out, she grabbed his arm.

*Tell me. You can't keep me in the dark. I have to know what is going on and who is helping you. You cannot possibly expect me to trust you when every time we speak you disappear.*

Luc turned to face her and took her by the shoulders, the look in his eyes grave. *The less you know, the safer it is for everyone.*

She tugged free of his grasp. *How dare you demand that I trust you when you don't even trust me with the simplest information! I am sitting here like a... like ...* She glanced around wildly. *Like a damn crow in a cage!*

He spun her around to face him, cupping her chin in his hand, but she jerked her head back, shards of rage shooting from her eyes. He slid a hand behind her neck and wrapped the other around her waist, but she wiggled free.

*You are not going to avoid this by kissing me!*

*Who said anything about kissing you?* He grinned as he reached for her again, but she dodged his hand and slipped under his arm.

*I mean it, Luc! I was honest with you. Now it is only fair that you tell what is happening and whom you meet when you disappear.*

She whirled in fury but he was quicker. She found herself trapped when he slid his arms around her waist and drew her to him. She struggled, but the feel of his hands around her middle as he drew her against him threatened her focus. She found herself leaning into his embrace.

*Damn you!*

He chuckled against her hair and turned her to face him, his hand still locked behind her back. *I do not tell you not because I don't trust you but because a highly trained Caskan could compromise you. I won't put lives in danger until I am certain that no one can pull the information from you.*

The warmth drained out of the embrace, quickly replaced by emptiness as she faced her inadequate abilities. She dropped her head, nodded, and attempted to break out of his embrace, but he only tightened his arms.

"Tabitha. Look at me."

She shook her head and refused to look up at him.

"Tabitha..." He lifted her chin so that her eyes met his. She bit her lip to keep her pain from flashing in her eyes, but he would not let her look away. *This is not about you not being trusted. You are the center of all of this. It is your life and your freedom that we all fight for. You have to trust us to do that for you.*

*You are right. I don't want anyone at risk because I could let information slip—*

*Tabitha, there are so many moving parts to this right now that I can hardly keep my mind around what is happening. The less you know, the less you have to lie to your father. I don't want them trying to get information from you. It is for your protection as well. There are potential avenues in this plan that depend on your surprise. The less you know, the better.*

She pulled her chin free and let her head drop against his chest. The comfort in his words melted the sadness. Her emotions faded into fatigue.

*When will you be back?*

She felt his shoulder lift in a half shrug. *I don't know. I have to get away from the perimeter. I promise to be back as soon as I can.*

She lifted her head and slid her hands behind his neck. She tugged his mouth down to hers. She felt his body tighten against her as he hugged her closer. She pressed herself against him and tilted her head to better taste the warm passion of his kiss. He leaned back against the railing, his hands tracing her back and her hips as he molded her to his body. She gently slid back. He gave a groan of desire, his mouth following hers as she leaned farther from him.

She slipped from his embrace, her mouth curving into a saucy smile. *Sorry, you have things to do, remember? I think I will go curl up in bed and let my imagination run a little wild with me—*

She squeaked in surprise. She was pushed up against the balcony door, pressed against the glass, his mouth attacking hers with ferocious passion. Tabitha felt her bones melt and her muscles lose all will. Only the feel of his body and the taste of his mouth had any root in her reality.

He released her as suddenly as he had grabbed her and stepped back, sending her a sensual grin of his own. *Oh, don't think for a minute that I forgot your promise.*

She stared at him, her lips swollen from the searing kiss, her body throbbing for him. *What promise?*

He winked, and with a leap he was up on the railing, thrusting himself off into the night sky. The hawk circled above her head. *The one about a better make-out spot.*

With a powerful sweep of his wings, he disappeared into the night.

# CHAPTER NINE

TABITHA AWOKE DURING THE NIGHT WHEN LUC FELL into bed beside her. She groped for him and felt his arms slip around her. She slid closer to him, sleep still clinging to her and felt his body sink into exhausted sleep. Satisfied that he was back, she dropped back to sleep with a contented sigh.

The sound of running water woke her, and she glanced over to see the bed beside her was empty. Her vision was blurry as she stumbled out of the bed and made her way to the dangling pot of hot javé. She slipped D'Noir's cage door open on her way to the balcony. The warm summer breeze slipped over her nightshirt and slid playfully along her bare legs. Luc stepped out onto the balcony behind her and slid his arms around her waist. She leaned back, enjoying the warmth of his bare chest against her.

*You were back late.*

He murmured an unintelligible response as he dropped a kiss on her neck. She passed him the cup of javé to share and enjoyed the quiet minutes of just standing with him, wishing that life were this simple. He leaned over in search of a more substantial kiss, but she put her hand up between them and shoved him back.

*I haven't brushed my teeth yet.*

He grunted as he released her and returned to the bed-room. He was tugging a shirt from the closet when she came in from the balcony. She cast an admiring eye at his lean belly and muscular shoulders as she watched him shrug into it.

"I have an early meeting with your father this morning." His voice was rough with fatigue.

"When will you return?"

"Do you want to go to see Gwyn this afternoon?"

She swallowed back the flood of tears that threatened to engulf her as the peace of the morning evaporated. The truth of her surroundings clicked back into place. Tabitha felt the strangling bonds of every insurmountable obstacle drag her back to reality. She groaned. With little more than a nod, she turned toward the shower.

Luc was gone when she emerged. She quietly dressed for the day. She found a tray waiting for her in the sitting area, and she sat to sullenly pick at the food. D'Noir toddled over to inspect the breakfast options. Dark thoughts clouded her mind as she recounted the last day's events to herself. Cole's descent into depression over Gwyn's death had been ex-pected. Tabitha felt pangs of guilt as she wondered if any of this would have been avoided if she had never come into this world in search of her mother. Sadness played heavily among her emotions, like the deep notes of a cello throb-bing and echoing through her body.

Had anyone told her grandfather? The question twisted her belly in knots, and she shoved the tray away. Even as she tried to convince herself that someone had surely told him, she knew that as the only relative he had available, it was her responsibility to go and find out.

She knocked on the door and asked the guard to take her to see her grandfather. Her voice sounded hollow and soft in her ears, and she barely recognized the quiet, sullen girl who followed the guard through the halls. It had not taken much to break her, she thought as she stared at the floor passing beneath her feet. It was not so long ago that her surly attitude and defiant stance with her guards had been her right. But now she could not shake the feeling that her actions had led Gwyn to her death. Somehow, her father had wanted to teach her that he could strike when he chose, that those closest to her would suffer if she continued her tirades against his rules.

"Tabitha?"

She stopped in her tracks. Her father's voice sent cold chills down her spine. She lifted her eyes and saw him approaching.

"I was on my way to see you."

She lifted a brow. "Really? Why?"

"Please sit." He gestured toward a small sitting area tucked beneath a large, sunny window. "Join me."

"I was going to visit my grandfather," she mumbled as she lowered herself in a seat across from him.

"I have been to see him." Antoine stared at his hands, clasped between his knees. "He took the news poorly."

"You told him?"

"I did," he sighed. "I did not want to be the one to carry such sorrowful news to him, but I felt it best that it came from me."

Tabitha choked back the tears and acid words she wanted to fling at her father. She did not respond. Instead, she turned her head, hoping that Antoine had said all he wanted to say.

"I wanted to offer you my condolences. Although I am aware you did not know Gwyn for long, I know you were close. I know how difficult this is for you." Antoine's voice carried warm tones of condolence, and Tabitha was on the verge of believing him.

Before she could stifle them, the words tumbled out. "Why Gwyn? Why did she die?"

Antoine's eyes lifted. For a moment, she could almost believe she saw sadness and grief etched in their dark depths, highlighted by the gray circles beneath them. But she flared her nostrils, refusing to accept that he could possibly feel anything except some form of triumph.

His released a breath in a deep sigh. "Who am I to answer such a question? How can anyone ever understand the—"

As anger swelled her chest, she hissed in rage. "Don't you dare sit there and get philosophical on me. You know damn well why she died, and I will never forget that. I will never forgive you for this. Every one of my loved ones you lay a hand on will drive me farther from you. Don't think for a second that I have any intention of doing as you demand just because you threaten to harm those I love."

Antoine looked genuinely shocked. "You think I had some hand in her death? To prove a point to you?'

Tabitha stood and glared at him. "You threatened me with her death, along with those of my grandfather, Cole, and those back home I love."

Antoine also stood. "I can assure you, Tabitha, that when you force me to follow through on that threat, you will be well aware of the consequences of your actions."

"So her death was a coincidence?" she snapped.

"If it were not, you would have been well aware of that fact." He lifted a finger toward her face and leaned in. "Do not force me to prove this statement."

Tabitha quailed a little, but she kept her eyes on his, refusing to let him observe her fear. "I have done nothing wrong. I have given you no reason to harm those I love."

Antoine started to smile before sadness crept back into his expression. Weariness seemed to emanate from him. "I had nothing to do with Gwyn's death. I wanted to offer you my condolences."

"I have someplace to be," Tabitha growled. She turned and gestured to the guard.


Tabitha made her way back to the suite, her silent guard following. The morning had passed in a long trail of tears. Her grandfather had taken Gwyn's death hard, and his tears left Tabitha drained and hollow. She longed for a few moments to curl on her bed and just wallow. She wanted to visit Cole, but her emotional energy had evaporated from watching her family struggle with heartache and captivity.

Captivity.

The truth of her circumstances hit home again as the guard closed the door behind her with a definitive click. She wanted to scream and pound her fists against the wood, but that would accomplish nothing.

Where was her mother? She had told Tabitha that she had no way to contact her but with the situation dwindling into hopelessness, she had hoped Doniella would find some way to contact her, some way to get her out of this place.

Luc returned later, and after a brief, mostly taciturn lunch, they headed into the village. Silence wrapped around them as they walked down the shady lane. Had it only been a day? Was it only yesterday that she had walked down this dusty road with Luc, crying, admitting, and then forgiving, before they had found Gwyn? Now pain seared through her as she wondered how she would face Gwyn's body. How would she eliminate the memory of the older woman's body lying in the moss and dead leaves, staring sightlessly at the sky?

Gwyn's house came into view. Tabitha reached for Luc's hands, clinging to the illusion that she could absorb sanity from his contact.

"You don't have to do this," Luc murmured.

"Actually, I do," she replied. "I could run away and ignore it all, but that is what my mother would do, and I will be damned if I am going to escape like she did."

He nodded. Heads bowed, they walked around the cottage to the back entrance. A small line of people quietly waited to enter, and they took their place at the end. Tabitha overheard snippets of conversations about Gwyn and how dearly she would be missed, but she turned away, shutting out the murmurs. She could not listen. She did not want to acknowledge that Gwyn was gone.

As more people moved inside the cottage, the line shrank. Soon they entered. Tabitha was struck by the emotional memories of her previous visit: facing her father, the crack of his blow to her jaw, her life spinning out of control as she was tied and escorted from the house, a prisoner.

*Calm...* Luc's voice was gentle in her mind.

*Luc, I can't. I don't think I can do this!* She turned to bury her face in his chest, but she heard a quiet snort of cynicism behind her that snapped her away from him.

She turned to find Dylan watching them with a leering twist to his lips, leaning against a low table at the far wall. He stood straight and made his way toward them.

*Luc, I am going to kill him... I promise you!* She snarled.

*Not today, you aren't.* Luc propelled her in the opposite direction and moved behind her to intercept Dylan. Tabitha's attention was immediately caught by the low platform holding Gwyn's body. She felt an involuntary breath escape, and the fight drained from her.

The platform was draped with deep blue fabric; flowers of every color were arranged around the edges. A few bystanders glanced curiously at her but then turned back to their quiet discussions. Cole sat by the fireplace, staring into the flames with dead eyes.

"Cole..."

He glanced up and then rose to envelope Tabitha in his arms. His shoulders shook as he buried his head against her hair. He choked back a quiet sob as they clung to one another. Tabitha felt her pain slowly ease. She could not have said how long they stood there before Cole slowly released her. He turned his head and swiped at his red-rimmed eyes with the back of his hand.

"You all right?"

He grunted and lifted a shoulder. "I guess. I mean, it is not like I have any option, right?" He gestured to Dylan across the room, in deep conversation with Luc that appeared to be none too friendly. "My gatekeeper is over there to make sure I don't take off."

"Cole, we will get through this. I promise you, I will find a way to get you and Lena out of there." Tabitha felt her own doubt even as the words left her lips. She was making promises she was not sure she could keep.

Cole looked down at her. "What the hell happened to her, Tabitha? What killed Gwyn? There wasn't a mark on her body, except for a bruise or two, and those she could have gotten from a fall."

Tabitha shook her head and glanced over to make sure Dylan was not close. "I can't talk here. I will come see you after. Then we can talk."

Cole glanced behind her at Gwyn's body. "I'll be with her until the pyre."

"Pyre?"

"Yes. Tomorrow night we'll put her to rest."

"Oh."

"Can you check on Lena? I hate leaving her alone, but I can't—" His voice broke, and he turned back toward the fire, his shoulders shaking as grief overtook him.

"I'll check on Lena when we get back, I promise."

He nodded and lifted his chin, his eyes on the ceiling, trying to pull himself together. "Will you be here tomorrow night?"

Tabitha nodded. She squeezed his hand one last time before she made her way around the platform. She kissed her fingertips and gently placed them on Gwyn's forehead before turning toward Luc.

Dylan and Luc were still in a heated discussion when Tabitha approached. Dylan's eyes snapped over to Tabitha as she stepped between them, and his mouth curled in a derisive grin. Just as his mouth was opening to make a comment, she swung her fist with every ounce of her strength and caught him in the jaw. Dylan staggered back against the wall. Luc, his lip quivering part in shock, part amused, grabbed Tabitha by the arms and half carried her toward the front door.

Dylan held his jaw, his eyes wide and stunned. "What the hell was that for?"

Tabitha sneered. "You know very well what that was for."

Dylan's eyes narrowed, but Luc pulled her through the door before he could respond. "What are you doing?"

"I couldn't help it, Luc! I know he killed her! I know he set that monster on her. I am going to kill him!" Fury intermingled with pain as she sobbed.

Luc tugged her arm and led her away from the cottage. "You keep making dangerous enemies."

"What more can he do to me?"

When Luc stopped, she slowed her steps.

"You don't think what happened to Gwyn is enough of an example of what he can do?"

She opened her mouth and shut it.

"Tabitha, he is not playing games. He is a very dangerous enemy."

"You goad him and bait him at every opportunity," she retorted.

"To get his focus off you. We have a very long rivalry. Now with you in the middle of it, it has turned dark. Don't get me wrong. I never feel safe around him, but I know he will lash out if you embarrass him. He takes himself very seriously," Luc cautioned.

"I think his little ego will survive my tantrum," Tabitha said with more confidence than she felt.

Luc shook his head slowly. "He will get you back for that. Maybe not today or tomorrow, but he will not forget."

"I could not control myself. Gwyn was lying there, and I know he did it. I didn't plan it. I just could not help it," Tabitha groaned.

"I know. It is what scares me. As you discover more and witness more as you search for that black elf, you are not going to be able to remain impassive. You need to be able to go along with them until we can get you away from here—safely." Luc walked on, and she fell into step beside him. "I will drop you off at the historical society. Teira told me she would be there. The two of you can see if you can find more information in those documents. I have to run an errand for your father. I will be back for you."

Tabitha nodded and let him lead her over to the rounded building they had visited yesterday. With a brief kiss, he left her at the entrance. Feeling slightly lost and forlorn, she turned and entered the building. As her eyes adjusted to the dark interior, she searched for a sign of Teira. Seeing no one, she wandered through the stacks of books toward the long table at the back of the building. Her thoughts were dark and distant as she rounded a tall stack of books. She stopped short, her gaze caught at the table.

Teira sat with her head slumped to the side, her eyes shut, her long ponytail lying listlessly along her shoulder. A cat sat on a chair at the edge of the table, watching Tabitha with deep green eyes.

"Teira?"

The cat continued to stare at her; a familiar tug at her memory caused her to pause. She leaned forward, staring at the cat: it could not possibly be the same cat, the stray from behind the café in Porta Negra. How could it suddenly appear here? *Impossible.*

The cat stretched up on its haunches and was suddenly replaced by her dark-haired kidnapper from Porta Negra. He sat in the chair, observing her with a calm regard.

"*You!*" Tabitha cried.

"Well, pretty lady, we meet again." As he stood, Tabitha backed against the bookrack behind her.

"How did you get here?" Tabitha demanded as she searched for the fastest exit route. Before he could respond, she sent out a frantic call to Luc. The deafening sound of her internal scream of his name echoed in mind. She clutched her skull between her hands. "Hey! That hurt!"

"Well, stop using your link. Why don't we talk for a few moments before you call for help?"

"You tried to kidnap me! Twice!" Tabitha spat at him, shaking her head to lessen the dull ringing that remained after her call to Luc was blocked.

"I did not mean you harm. I only wished to speak with you." The dark-haired man sat back down, regarding her with calm and impassive eyes.

"With a gun? Is that your idea of opening up a dialogue?"

"Please sit. I promise you no harm if you will just give me a few minutes of your time."

"What have you done to Teira?"

"She is only asleep, I assure you."

"What is it you want from me?"

"I have told you, I only wish to speak to you. I promise no harm, and you will be free to go once we have spoken." His voice was silky; Tabitha felt like prey waiting for the predator to swoop in.

"I am not free to leave now?" Fear took root in her belly, and she took a step back.

He smiled. "Not if I choose not to let you go. Of course, that is only because you are unaware that you have the ability to break my hold."

Tabitha nodded and glanced toward the doorway, wondering if her call to Luc had escaped.

Following her glance to the potential escape route, he continued. "This does not have to be difficult, unless you make it so. You could simply sit and speak with me." His voice took on a darker edge, and his eyes slipped over to Teira before coming back to rest on Tabitha.

Tabitha understood the implied threat. She slid into the chair in front of her. "How did you get away from Luc's family?"

"I am of the Faye. The Caskan cannot detain me should I wish to leave."

"What is so important that you tried to kidnap m? Twice? With a gun, I might add."

"You have not been the most approachable person. You were hidden beneath that net on the island. When you left, which was seldom, you were all too often followed by that Faye protector of yours," he answered.

"Faye protector? My mother?"

He eyed her with a narrowed, curious glint. "No, not your mother."

"Are you telling me there was another Faye on the island?" Her curiosity was increasing, despite the inherent threat of the man across the table.

"You don't know?"

She shook her head.

He nodded gracefully and began. "Let me start at the beginning. My name is Darko Heinriks. I am of the Northern Faye. I was sent to the world of the others in search of a healer who was rumored to be hiding there.

"Upon my arrival, I found the island to be under the protection of the Eastern Faye. I was unable to gain access. I did my best to understand the nature of the healer and was surprised to find she was a young girl. As I learned more from interviewing people familiar with the island, I found that her tale was quite unique. Your mother, it seems, had made her way back to Caska to give birth to a healer before she later returned. The reasons behind her departure and return were unknown, but I was able to ascertain that there were not one but two healers living on that island."

Tabitha felt annoyance brimming. "You are not telling me anything I do not know. Who is the second Faye?"

"Another of the Eastern Faye. I assume you are unaware of his identity?"

Tabitha nodded.

The man's lips curled into a small smile. "Interesting. And the scrolls, you can read them?"

"Yes. Can you?"

"I am full Faye, so yes, I can," he told her. "My people live in the far northern territory. We have not had a healer in many generations. My goal was to discover the healer and then try and entice you back with me."

"Entice? That was some enticement. You knocked me out the first time I met you and then pulled a gun on me the second," Tabitha replied. "When I had met you, you promised to tell me about my father, so you must have known about him?"

"Oh, I did. Or so I thought. After you eluded me, I returned and did further research about your mother. Interesting that you ended up here. And you can read the scrolls. Do you know what that means?"

She lifted a shoulder. "Well, Teira tells me that only a full Faye can read the language. Does that mean that my father is Faye?"

"It would appear as much. You are quite an enigma. A full Faye," he commented.

"Does my father know he is Faye?" Tabitha wondered. "That would make Dylan and Cole also Faye."

Darko's expression changed in response to her logic. "Interesting assumption. Here you are in Caska, with Antoine. Is it your intention to remain here?"

"Why would I answer any question you ask me? You admitted that I could break free whenever I want. Why should I tell you anything?" Tabitha responded tartly. She began to extend her thoughts, exploring the web he had cast to surround them. As he further explained, justifying his attempts to abduct her, she ignored him and ran an inquiring thought along the boundary he had cast. The edge over the three of them seemed domelike; it had bounced her call to Luc back and would repel anyone from entering or leaving.

"So you are from the Northern Faye? You wanted to steal a healer to bring home for your people," she commented. "You tell me to listen to you and say you will tell me something fantastic besides the implication that my father is a Faye."

He nodded. "Teira tells me that you have seen a black elf. Where did you see it?"

She released a brief, dry laugh. "Any more questions?"

"I don't think you understand the gravity of the situation here."

"Oh, I understand it all too well. I just have no intention of sharing any information with you." She continued inspecting the constricting net, letting her mind run along it without touching it, concerned about alerting him. The construction of the barrier seemed fairly simple; it would bounce back any magic extended to it from inside or out. He did not seem to be struggling to maintain it as he continued to try to convince her to trust him. "Why would Teira tell you that I thought I saw a black elf?"

"She is human and, as such, can be persuaded to trust and divulge information without even being aware that she is being manipulated."

"Like mental rape?"

He recoiled at the comment. "Why would you say such a thing? Not at all like rape. I cannot believe you would even suggest such a thing."

She grinned. "Oh, sorry. You come in here, mess with her mind so she thinks you are trustworthy, all the while telling you anything you want to know without her even realizing you are putting the thoughts in her head," Tabitha snapped. "Yes, like mental rape."

He shook his head at her logic. "Why would you insist upon twisting this? She is only human, after all. I never harmed her. I simply calmed her into the belief that I could be trusted and allowed her to tell me what I needed to know."

"But you can't be trusted."

"Can anyone? Tell me about the black elf."

"Break the barrier, release Teira, let me go, and go find it yourself," Tabitha growled as she identified the pattern in his blockade. She could see the configuration behind the net he had cast, and with a tweak of her mind, she broke it. She became aware of the walls coming down.

She released a cocky smile before she stood and sent a call to Luc before commenting to Darko. "Release Teira and get out."

To her surprise, Darko's mouth curved into a slow smile. "That took you longer than I thought it would."

"Longer? You are kidding me, right?" she sneered.

"With your power, you should have been able to do it quicker, yes. But I must remember that you are untrained," he responded calmly. Before she could growl a curse, he leaned back and crossed his arms. "So if you could figure out how to break my enclosure, why did you feel the need to call your friend? Is he, a Caskan, going to save you against a full Faye?"

"You cannot take both of us."

"I don't have to. You won't fight me anymore than he will." He gestured at Teira's slumped form. "You know the risk. And besides, I have information. I want to help. And quite frankly, it is in his best interests, as well as yours, to hear me out."

"What information?"

He gestured to the seat in front of her. "I have information that your mother seeks."

Tabitha did not bother to sit. "My mother?" She felt her curiosity stir again. "Why don't you tell me what is so important that you have come to me three times?"

He leaned forward and indicated the rolled scrolls on the table in front of Teira. "There is a great deal of information about the black elves within these, but the answer is not among them. Tell me what you know of the black elves. What did you see? Where did you see one?"

She shook her head and could not help but laugh. "Why would I tell you any of this?"

"The Eastern Faye are well aware that your father has a black elf in his possession and is using it to terrorize the local villages. The problem, however, lies in the fact that not only do they not know how it is being controlled, they do not know how to eradicate it. We have some information.

We believe that the answer is a substance that comes from your world. The research during the initial infestation seems to have been completed in your world," he explained.

Tabitha recalled that Teira had mentioned "a substance" in relation to the black elves during their first meeting. Had she mentioned where it had originated? "In my world?"

"Yes, during my mission to find out about the healers on your island, I also tried to research what might have been written about the black elves, but the trail went cold. When I returned, the emergence of a possible black elf in Caska shifted my priorities to tracking the source of those rumors. " He slipped a piece of parchment out of a deep jacket pocket and unfolded it. "You have heard of Edgar Lee Donn?"

She nodded. "Teira told me he researched black elves."

"Yes. Well, he was able to collect most of the existing information regarding the invasion. His writings encompass a wealth of the Faye information. Of course, the scrolls offer much more about the daily interactions with the battle." Darko glanced toward the door and slid the parchment over to her. "I have been reviewing the scrolls while I waited for you. There is additional information about them that I believe you will find useful. This seems to hold the key."

Tabitha leaned over the table and took the parchment. She opened it and then looked at him, puzzled. "What is this?"

He shrugged. "I don't know. It was one of the last entries in Edgar Lee Donn's writing before he returned to the world of the others. I was hoping you might recognize it."

She shook her head and pushed the parchment with its odd symbol back to him. "I've never seen it before."

"Will you tell me about when you saw the black elf?" The smugness had left his face. "You understand that the presence of a black elf affects all of us in this world. The species nearly destroyed us the last time they came. We cannot allow our world to be decimated again."

After hesitating briefly, she recounted the vision her mother had shown her, as well as her own experience with the black elf when she was searching the basement of her father's estate.

"You separated?"

"Yes."

"And you were able to control your intensity?"

She nodded. Then she felt tension expand in her chest as she remembered Luc's warning about sharing too much about one's abilities. "I think I've told you enough."

He stood. "You have been very gracious to share your knowledge. My people will be indebted."

"Before you leave, I must ask," she entreated. "You were in the shape of a cat when I entered. You looked just like a cat I encountered back home."

His chuckle cut her off. "You recognized me? I was indeed the same animal. As I told you before, the net kept me from crossing to your island, but I discovered I was able to cross in my alter shape. Of course, once I arrived, I was unable to alter back until I left the island. I had been watching you for some time. The test seemed a little extreme, but I was convinced that if you had the healing ability, you would not hesitate to save your young friend."

"If I had the ability? What if I had not?"

"Then I would most certainly have cut my mission short, no?" He passed the page with the mysterious symbol back to her and pointed at it. "This symbol holds the key to the black elves. Can you help us?"

Tabitha took the page from him. "I don't know. If I can, I need to get away from here in order to do so. You are making a big assumption that I will be returning home."

Darko leaned toward Tabitha. "It is not an assumption at all. You are well aware that you must leave Antoine's home or forever be in his control," and with that last comment, he disappeared.

Suddenly, Teira sat upright, her eyes blinking as she woke.

"Tabitha? How long have you been here? Where did Darko go?"

# CHAPTER TEN

"YOU TOLD HIM WHAT?" LUC EXCLAIMED WITH EXAS-
peration as they walked back toward the estate.

Tabitha waved off his irritation. "I told him about the
black elf."

"You are very free with that information. I think you
need to be more cautious instead of telling just anyone. If
your father or Dylan become aware of your knowledge,
there is no telling what they will do," Luc cautioned.

Tabitha shifted the long leather tube from one shoulder
to the other. Teira had slipped the scrolls into the protective tube and asked Tabitha to read them and later share the
information they contained. Luc took the tube from her and
tossed it over his shoulder, clearly still irritated.

Tabitha lifted a shoulder in response. "I am already his
prisoner and under his control. What else can he do to me?"

Luc stopped and stared at her. His voice carried a sharp
edge. "Have you forgotten about Gwyn? How many other
funeral pyres will we attend before you take his threats seriously?"

Tabitha felt his sharp words reopen the wound in her
chest. "He promised me he had nothing to do with her
death."

Luc shook his head in disbelief. "And your father would never lie to you?"

"Just stop! Darko told me what he knew about the dark elves. He told me why he had been on the island and what he wanted with me. The least I could do was tell him what I knew," she snapped, stung.

"No, the least you could have done was tell him nothing. You don't know if what he told you was true," Luc retorted.

"If we are going to figure out what to do about the black elves, we need every bit of information we can find," Tabitha rationalized.

"Even if it involves someone who tried to kidnap you?"

Tabitha strode forward, ignoring the snarl in his voice. "You worry too much."

She could almost hear disbelief oozing from him, and she turned with a mischievous grin.

They soon entered the estate grounds. As they approached the stairs, the guard informed Luc that Antoine was waiting to speak with him. Luc turned to give Tabitha a quick kiss. She murmured that she was going to check on Lena before settling down with the scrolls.

"Dinner?" he asked as he turned to leave.

As she mounted the stairs to go to their suite, she hissed over her shoulder, "Only if we are alone. I am not joining my father and Dylan."


Hours later, Tabitha, her feet drawn under her, transcribed what she was reading from the scrolls. She had completed the first one, which was relatively short. This next scroll was longer. She paused from transcribing to read the next passages.

The creature will draw the energy of the living things it encounters. It begins with relatively small life forms, such as grass and insects, and quickly escalates to larger life forms as its strength increases. The form will begin to solidify as its demand for sustenance increases. As the creature becomes denser, it requires higher levels of energetic beings to sustain its existence as well as to increase in size.

When the being has increased its needs to Faye level, absorption will increase. The being will begin to display signs of a higher level of cognitive awareness. The being will begin to adopt anthropoid characteristics and will mimic actions of those around it.

It has been theorized that once the entity has begun to recognize the larger life form, it may opt to adapt to that life form's native surroundings, making it unidentifiable to others of the same species. This method of hunting has been dubbed cannibalized integration. The creature will be adopted as a member of the pod. Once integrated, the creature uses the pack with which it has surrounded itself as a food source.


Tabitha lowered the scroll. She read the passage again. What is this saying? The creature solidifies upon further feeding, that much she knew. Eventually it would get to a point where it became a solid life form, indistinguishable from another of the same species? She remembered watching through her mother's vision as the smoky image mimicked Dylan's gestures.

The thought was horrifying. If she interpreted this right, the black elf would be able to pass among humans and use the population as its food source, gaining power with every feeding. She read on, looking for more clues about their integration. She scribbled the words as she read them and reviewed her writing over and over. She read and transcribed scroll after scroll, leaving them on the floor in a rolled heap as she poured through the next documents.

She had no idea how much time had elapsed when she raised her bleary eyes to see Luc's blue ones staring down at her.

"I take it you have been busy?"

She shook her head, feeling as though she were swimming up through the depths of a long sleep. She glanced around the room. "What time is it?"

He smiled. "Late."

"Did you have dinner?"

"Yes. I called to you but got no answer. I assume you worked through?"

She nodded, her head still buzzing with the archaic dialect and the words written so long ago. "You called me?"

"Yes, I tried to reach out to you. I just asked the guard to bring you some dinner. Tell me what has captivated your attention so much that even our link eluded your attention."

She shook her head and looked down at the pages of notes she had taken from the dozen of scrolls she had read. "My God, Luc. You have no idea what theses things are capable of."

He settled himself across from her, his long arm resting across the back of the chair and a cup of javé in his hand. "Tell me."

She began to describe the process: an initial invasion by a single "scout" organism would lead to the arrival of more if the first was a success. The species' intention was to take over and live as long as possible on the existing living species, eventually annihilating them. There was no malicious intent, no domination; drawing the life energy from every species, starting with the smallest before including the most complex, was simply a survival strategy. They would acclimate to the local climate and surroundings and eventually assume the form of the most complex of the native species. Once they integrated with the top of the food chain, they would become a member of that society and, one by one, consume the members of the civilization.

The guard knocked on the door and delivered a plate of hot food. Tabitha gobbled bites of food and chewed and paced as she told Luc everything she had learned about the creature living in the basement.

"Luc, the Faye wondered if the people whose life energy was absorbed might remain in the creature's consciousness." She absently chewed a corner of a roll as she considered the concept. "What could that mean? Would it be possible to get them back?"

He shrugged. "And if we could? What then? What would happen if we could get Gwyn or Viho back now? Their bodies are gone, Tabitha. If we find a way to kill the creature, we release them," Luc said.

"Release them? So you think they might be trapped within the creature?" The thought sent shivers through her body. She put the plate down, her mouth dry.

"We don't know. Likely we never will know," he responded. He stood. "It's late, and it's been a long day. Let's get some sleep."

She nodded and slid the scrolls back into their tube. Her thoughts swirled with the information she had learned from the centuries-old writings. When she slipped into their room, the lights were off and the curtains drawn. D'Noir sent a quiet caw of greeting as she passed him; she dropped a few crumbs from her dinner to the bird. She collected her nightclothes and went to wash. The information from the ancient scrolls troubled her, and she reviewed what she was learning as she brushed her teeth and drew a brush through her hair.

Luc was already in bed, shirtless, staring up at the ceiling, his eyes troubled, as his brows furrowed in concern. Tabitha climbed on the bed next to him and leaned over, folding her arms across his chest, her chin on her hands, gazing at his handsome features.

"Penny for your thoughts," she whispered.

As his gaze shifted to meet hers, he grunted, his eyes warming as he returned her smile. "I wish I were thinking about anything except this torrid mess snaking around us."

He lifted a hand and stroked her cheek, his thumb running along her lower lip. His eyes took on a husky glint. "I am caught between wanting to get to the bottom of this and take you out of here and wishing we could stay forever. Once we discover a way to get you safely back to a portal, you will leave."

She leaned her head into his palm, enjoying his slow and sensual touch. "You could come with me."

He didn't respond at first, and she did not have the courage to lift her eyes to his. She already knew his answer but prayed for a moment that he would change his mind. He placed his thumb under her chin and lifted it so she faced him. "Come here."

She leaned to lower her lips to his. They lay together, mouths fused in a passionate kiss. Tabitha lay on top of Luc, the sensation of his long, muscular body beneath her sent her heart pounding and her blood to a slow simmer. His hands slid from her hair to her back and along her hips to cup her bottom as he slowly rolled her beneath him, capturing her in an intimate embrace. A long moan slipped from her lips as he nuzzled her neck and slid the straps of her top from her shoulders to expose her to his exploration.

Her hands slid along his shoulders and over his back, but before she could continue, he pulled back.

"Luc?" Her voice was raw with need. "What's wrong?"

His breath ragged, he shook his head slowly and pulled back from her. "I can't, Tabitha. As much as I want you, I can't do this on his terms. It has to be on our own."

She stroked his cheek and turned his face back to her. "I want you. I want only you, and not because it is what he wants from us."

He shook his head. "When you are free from here and you are not relying on me to help you escape... Until then, I just can't do this. I feel like I am your only option."

She smiled sadly and leaned her cheek against his shoulder. "I don't feel that way about you. I don't feel obligated to do this."

"I know. But I want to know that you won't regret being with me. I can't take advantage of what your father has done to you."

He reached down for another long kiss. She slid her hands into his hair and wrapped herself around his body, pressing him close to her. She felt his response; his arms tightened around her, drawing her closer.

"That does not mean we don't have any options—" she murmured against his lips.

Tabitha jogged down the staircase toward the front door. She was looking forward to heading back into town and getting free of the estate, which despite its size had started to suffocate her. The tube of scrolls knocked against her backside as she descended, but her thoughts were far from the information she had transcribed. The memories of the night before still warmed her, and even the ever-present guard on her heels could not dampen her mood. A shiver slid along her torso at the memory of Luc's touch and his mouth during their passionate interlude.

"Tabitha!" Dylan's sharp voice cut through her pleasant reminiscences with a cold shot of reality that stole the warmth from her limbs. She stopped and turned to see him coming down the hall toward her with a purposeful stride.

"Where are you going?"

"What business is it of yours? I have a guard, I don't answer to you," she snapped.

"I need your guard for a few minutes. Your outing will have to wait." He brushed past her and indicated that the guard should follow him. "I assume you can find your way back to your suite without too much trouble?" She ground her teeth in frustration, her fists balled at his rudeness. He turned back to her, a sneer twisting his mouth. "Unless you need to be accompanied?"

She heard the bang of the front door after Dylan and the guard left. Her anger dissipating, she ran to the window and watched them stride down the front lawn of the estate. She was unguarded and Dylan was heading away from the estate. She knew she did not have long. This might possibly be her only opportunity.

She turned and raced back up the steps, taking them two at a time, as she made her way up to the fourth floor. She grabbed the stair railing and propelled her way down the hall toward the suites in the eastern wing. She hurried past her own suite and made her way toward her father's personal apartments. Just past Antoine's rooms, she stopped one of the household staff for directions. The woman pointed toward a suite near the end of the hall. Tabitha made her way to the door and knocked quickly, not expecting any response; she let her mind unlock the door and slid through the narrowly opened door into Dylan's apartments, pulling the door quietly closed behind her. She clasped her arms around her torso as she entered his suite, praying she would not have to venture into his bedroom. The setup was similar to the one she shared with Luc but more disheveled and with a definitively more masculine slant to the decor.

Now that she was here, she had to admit that the task of searching Dylan's private suite was a bit daunting. The desk seemed the most likely place to start. Papers, scrolls, and Dylan's personal things cluttered the desktop. She tried to keep things in their original order as she searched.

Would he leave the gray creature controller just lying around? She began searching through the drawers for any

relevant bit of information or the wand itself. She was leaning over, searching the bottom drawer, when a soft thud
from the bedroom caused her to freeze.

She had seen Dylan leave; impossible that he could have
returned that fast. A second click from behind the closed
door convinced her that someone was indeed in that room.
She inhaled deeply and was backing toward the exit when
the door to the bedroom swung open.

Tabitha froze. So did Lena, Cole's girlfriend. Seconds
ticked by. Tabitha's mouth felt frozen closed. Neither of
them moved.

"What are you doing here?" Lena finally hissed.

Tabitha sank into the chair behind her, her hand on her
heart. "You scared me half to death! What do you mean,
why am I here? Why are *you* here?"

Lena averted her haunted eyes and remained silent except for a soft gasp. As the shock of discovery wore off, Tabitha looked closer at Cole's girlfriend and noticed the red
welts on her wrists and the bruises on her throat. "Lena, did
Dylan give you those?"

Lena slid her wrists behind her back and entered the sitting area. "A guard will be here any minute to bring me
back to my rooms. What are you doing in here? Do you
know what he will do if he catches you here?"

"Does Cole know?"

She shook her head, her dark eyes huge in her pale face,
as she lowered herself into the chair behind her. "I can't tell
him. It would destroy him. He would kill Dylan."

"That might not be such a bad thing," Tabitha murmured. "A guard is coming?"

"Yes, to take me back. They cannot see you here."

Tabitha agreed. "Listen, before they take you, can you tell me if you have ever seen a long gray stick, about this long?"

Lena glanced at the bedroom door and nodded, indicating Tabitha should follow her into the room. With quick, nervous steps, Lena skirted the bed, where rumpled bed sheets were twisted and strewn over the mattress, some hanging off the sides. Tabitha averted her eyes from the sight, not wanting to imagine what had been happening here.

Lena went over to a set of shelves tucked into the wall and drew out a box. Her dark hair brushed her cheeks; Tabitha saw a deep blush on her throat as she tugged the cover off the box, carefully holding the lid up to hide the contents from Tabitha. She removed a narrow cylinder, about a foot long and no more than an inch or two in diameter. She slammed the cover shut and shoved the box back in its place.

"If he accuses me of stealing it, I will admit that you took it," Lena's snapped as she handed it to Tabitha.

A knock at the door made them both jump. Lena scurried past Tabitha without a glance and went to answer the door. Tabitha felt herself tense a moment too late when the threat of discovery became all too evident, but she heard Lena's soft voice and a man's response before the door shut behind them.

Tabitha turned her attention to the tube in her hand. She removed the cap and emptied the contents into her palm. The long silver wand slid out, as well as a single page torn from book. The page was very old and yellowed, and the paper felt dry and fragile in her hands. She saw faded gray writing scrawled on the page. Her eyes scanned the writing, it was hard to read and the language antiquated, but Tabitha could make out the words. She learned that the substance of the wand could control the black elf and contain it but not kill it. The spidery scrawl was followed by the name: Donald Greene and a symbol.

Is this Edgar Lee Donn's writing? And what did this mean?

She slid the paper and the wand back into the tube and replaced the cap. Before she could reconsider, she slid the small cylinder into the tube holding the scrolls, left the bedroom, and pulled the outer door open a crack. The hallway was empty, thankfully, and she slid from the door, shutting it silently behind her before she raced to her own suite, her heart pounding.

Her door clicked behind her as she rested her back against it. Her suite had been picked up and the windows opened to catch the morning breeze. Tabitha let the scroll tube slip off her shoulder and wandered out toward the balcony. Now that she had found the tool that Dylan used to control the creature, what was she supposed to do with it?

A knock at the door interrupted her musings.

"Tabitha? Open the door. It is Colene."

Tabitha opened the door and let the tiny blond woman in. "Colene, is everything all right? Is it Katie?"

Colene shut the door behind her and shook her head. "All is fine. Katie is doing well. Her time is coming quickly—should be any day now."

Tabitha waved her to a seat. "Good, I have been thinking about her."

"Can we talk here?"

"Yes, Luc showed me how to protect a room so we won't be overheard."

Tabitha gestured to the pot of javé. Colene agreed and Tabitha walked to the fireplace to pour her a mug from the pot hanging there. She handed the woman a cup of the steaming brew.

"I have a message from your mother."

"My mother? She was in touch with you?"

"Yes. She wants me to tell you that it might still be a few days anyway before they can get you out. We are waiting for a few people to arrive to help."

"Is that all she said?"

Colene nodded. "We need to keep this brief."

"Will you be able to get a message to her?" Tabitha's eyes were already on the cylinder propped against the chair. "Or a thing?"

"Yes, I should be able to get something to her. What do you need? It's not something huge, is it? If I can smuggle it out of here, I can get it to her. I am not sure where she is, but I know who to contact to locate her."

Tabitha grabbed the cylinder off the floor. She opened the top and slid the smaller case out. "This tube contains the scrolls for Teira. Can you get them back to her? My transcription notes are tucked in there as well." Tabitha held the smaller tube toward Colene. "My mother needs to have this."

"What is it? Will she know?"

Tabitha slid the cap off and let the paper and the wand drop into her palm. "This is what Dylan uses to control the black elf. I don't know what is in it or why the creature responds to it, but it does. Tell my mother that and show her the note."

"I will take Teira her scrolls and get this to your mother." She tucked the smaller cylinder back into the larger tube. "Are you all right? You took this from Dylan?"

"I can only pray he either does not realize it is gone or that he won't figure out who took it before I can get out of here."

"All right. Be safe." With that, the young woman was gone.

Tabitha stood alone in her suite, her stomach in knots as she tried not to think about Dylan's reaction to his missing wand.


The evening air stirred up a dust cloud along the edge of the field. Tabitha watched the tiny spinning vortex whirl across the dry earth. The sun was setting, and a violet net of twilight dropped across the crowd gathered around the wooden platform that held Gwyn's body. Tabitha stood next to Luc, taking comfort from his presence, all too aware of the eyes that watched them.

Her father and Dylan stood together across from them, their faces somber. The legion of people hovering by her father and offering comfort made her stomach twist in disgust. Dylan's eyes met hers with a dark glint. His direct challenge lacked his customary sarcasm. She ignored his glare. Her eyes sought Cole, who stood on Luc's other side, his eyes red in his downcast face. Lena stood next to him, her fingers clutched around his arm and her eyes wary. She glanced up, met Tabitha's gaze, and averted her eyes immediately.

The crowd had gathered at Gwyn's house in preparation for following Gwyn's body as the platform was borne to the wooden structure in the field. Tabitha averted her eyes away from the woods where Gwyn's body had been found. She concentrated on the uneven ground before her as the long entourage made its silent trek in the waning sunlight.

The shadows of the surrounding forests reached toward the circle of mourners as the sun relinquished its position before dipping behind the trees. A single voice rose as a portly woman, her long gray ponytail tied behind her neck, an intricately embroidered sash hanging from her neck, faced the crowd from the head of Gwyn's platform. Arms outstretched, she projected her words over the crowd. The language was unknown to her, but Tabitha was for once glad she could not understand. She knew the message all too well; the fact that she did not have to hear it almost made the reason bearable.

As the woman was finalizing her benediction, a slender bald man approached, carrying between his gloved hands a large crock that issued a pillar of smoke from its center. He placed the crock at the woman's feet. As he bent down, Tabitha noticed that four long sticks with thick, greasy-looking bulbs on their ends rode in a quiver on his back. He withdrew them and lifted his face toward the crowd with an expectant look. The woman nodded to the crowd. Dylan, Cole, Luc, and Jules walked forward; each took a stick. The woman removed the cover from the crock, allowing the fire within to swell. Each man took turns, dipping the bulbous tips into the flame. Their sticks flaming, each stood at a corner of the wooden structure as the woman lifted her voice in a long and beautiful song. Tabitha's throat constricted. She focused on Luc, standing at his designated corner, his face somber. The wind lifted his hair in a playful tug.

The woman bowed her head and the crowd followed suit. Tabitha did not recognize the words being murmured so she used her own words as she prayed that Gwyn had found peace. The thought that her soul could be trapped within the creature twisted Tabitha's gut; for the first time in many years, she sent a heartfelt prayer to the heavens.

The silence in the now-dark field spread. With a final word, each of the four men dropped their torches into the piles of kindling at each corner, setting the corners ablaze. They fitted the torches into holders; the flames leaped toward the raised platform. The fire began to lick greedily at the dry wood. The crackling and spitting heat pushed the crowd back. The flames caught, and the platform was engulfed in a bright and searing blaze. Tabitha watched the dark shape of Gwyn's body through the dancing flames. The crowd was silent as the fire swelled into a tall behemoth, fiery arms stretching toward the dark sky, casting long trails of smoke to the heavens.

The wood hissed and the fire's deep and thunderous voice raged, drowning out the surrounding tears and gentle sobs. Tabitha remained stalwart and still, not letting Dylan or Antoine see her tears. The smoke pricked her eyes; the pungent odor of the fire and ash stung her nostrils. She could not have said how long she stood there, mesmerized by the inferno as it chewed its way through the wood platform. The flames entranced her and left her empty as her grief leaked out through the tears she could not suppress.

Her thoughts were dark. She felt as though her sense of self had been stripped from her bones. Her ever-present guard and the constant threat of abuse were wearing her down. She knew without a doubt that if she did not escape soon, she would go mad.

# CHAPTER ELEVEN

THE FLAMES HAD SIMMERED DOWN TO A TAME AND GENTLE burn, and the crowd was beginning to disperse. Tabitha noticed that many people tossed small tokens into the flames as they turned to leave.

She turned to Luc. "What are they doing?"

"They are sending gifts with Gwyn to heaven. It could be a favorite flower or a few words or a poem. The smoke is said to accompany her to the Great Spirit. Their gifts are farewells that she will have with her as she sets up her home in her new world." He put his hand on the small of her back. "Are you ready?"

They left with the dwindling crowd as darkness crept across the village. Tabitha felt a longing ache as they passed Gwyn's house, wondering what would become of it now. As Tabitha and Luc made their way through the village, the crowds around them melted away as groups separated toward their homes. By the time they reached the wide lane leading out of the village toward the estate, they were walking alone.

Silence engulfed them. Tabitha felt relieved that Luc did not seem to want to talk either. The darkness was like a cool and gentle blanket. The evening breeze blew her hair from her shoulders, and she inhaled deeply, wanting to clear the smell of the fire from her nostrils. The estate loomed ahead, jutting up from the ground, blocking the starry sky, its glowing windows indicative of the life carrying on in the house. Tabitha swallowed back a bitter taste as she realized anew that Gwyn's opportunity to sit before one of those glowing windows was gone forever.

As they climbed the stairs toward their suite, Luc murmured that he would join her shortly. Tabitha nodded and proceeded up to the fourth floor, her steps dragging as the pent-up emotions of the day stirred deep within her, fighting to be released in a torrent of tears. She noted the guard had fallen into step behind her as she climbed. As he took up his post outside her room, she slid the door shut.

Her clothes carried the scent of the fire into the room. The strong acidic smell seemed to have lodged in her skin and her hair; she could not escape it. She found herself choking back a muffled sob as she ran through the sitting area into their bedroom. She tore her shirt off and hurried around the bed. Her skirt and undergarments fell on the floor with dull thumps. As she threw open the bathroom doors and ran to the shower, her breath came in rapid gasps. Her fingers grasped at the spigot as tears blurred her vision.

Hot water pumped through the showerhead and Tabitha stepped beneath it, plunging her hair under the strong spray. A low howl of pain emerged from deep within her. She massaged shampoo through her hair and scrubbed her skin with soap, trying to get rid of the smell. She felt as though she had let Gwyn down and now carried the scent of her death on her skin, in her hair; it was still stuck in her nose. Water ran into her mouth, and she coughed and gagged, struggling with the sobs that racked her body. She

fought for breath as pain ripped through her chest and propelled the tears from her eyes.

Gwyn was gone.

She finally gave up and leaned against the cool marble
stall wall. She rested her head on her arms and let the tears
fall as the hot water poured down her back. She was not
aware Luc had arrived until she felt his hands tugging her
arms. She turned and threw her arms around his neck, sobbing against his chest, letting the pain and the agony pour
out as the water sluiced down them both. She was hiccup-
ping after the last of her torrent when she felt his hands
rinsing the shampoo from her hair.

His hands were gentle. He lightly kissed her temple as he
massaged the soap from her hair and then stroked her back.
She clung to him, letting the hot water block out the rest of
the world, leaving them alone with their pain. Tabitha lifted
her face to Luc's and brushed the streaming strands of raven
hair away from his face. Her hands on either side of his face,
she pulled his mouth down to her lips and drank deeply. His
mouth slanted across hers, their bodies pressed close under
the steaming shower.

She could not have guessed how long they stood there,
tasting and teasing each other's mouths, their hands caressing and exploring each other's bodies. She barely noticed
when he shut off the water. They staggered toward the bedroom, their bodies close, their mouths fused with passion
that bubbled up from their cores, erupting along their bodies.

Tabitha was aware of the softness of the bed as they fell
together, hearts hammering, their mouths hungry for the
taste of their desire. Her blood pounded in her ears as she
opened her mouth to his exploring, tugging him closer and

sliding her hands into his thick hair. His hands slipped along her body, down her back to her hips. She could not get enough of his kiss; she grew giddy with the sweet heat of his embrace. She slid her hands along his shoulders, down his waist, thrilled at the sensation of his warm skin and taut muscles beneath her fingers.

Their breaths came in hot gasps of passionate urgency. Tabitha pressed her body against his, wanting to feel every muscle, every inch of him against her.

Luc drew back. Their eyes met. Luc did not move. His eyes were hot with desire, his chest pumping after their intense contact. But still he held, waiting for her decision. She slid her hands along his chest, admiring the feel of muscle and his flat belly.

She met the startling blue of his eyes. Her breath was little more than a whisper. "Please, Luc."

He groaned. She gave a startled giggle as he rolled her over beneath him, his mouth once again claiming hers, his fingers searching, caressing, and touching every inch of her.

Tabitha opened herself to him, drawing him in, slowly letting go of fear and resolve, until the only thing left was a deep warmth that seemed to emanate from her soul. The feel of his body and the taste of his mouth became her only reality; every other thought slid from her mind. Only Luc remained. Her body responded to his touch. Then she felt a tremor pass through his body as they gave into sheer physical elation.

Later, Tabitha lay nestled beside him, her hands caressing his chest, her head resting on his shoulder. One hand gently caressed her bare bottom. She lifted her head and rested it on her hand, gazing up at him. He glanced down. A lazy smile shaped his lips.

"Now what?" she asked quietly.

Luc stretched beneath her and reached with his other hand to fondle a breast. "Well, if you give me a few minutes…"

Her laugh was low and sexy. "I meant with us. What will happen? How will we… I mean… What will we do?"

He rolled her onto her back as his hands continued their exploration. *Will you trust me?*

*You ask me that right now? After what just happened?* She commented, amused.

*What I mean is, can you trust me to try to get you away? I can't tell you what is going to happen, and I can't give you any details. Just trust me.* He was emphatic. No trace of humor showed in his eyes. In fact, they were dark with concern as he studied her face.

She nodded and slid her hand into his hair, tugging his mouth back to hers. All thought of escape and danger left her mind as she gave herself to him, her body responding to his touch with a fierce passion that left them breathless.

The night waned as the entwined couple, finally sated, fell asleep. D'Noir quietly cawed once as he hopped into his cage and onto his perch. The moon crept over the landscape. Pale gray light played along the bed, bathing Luc and Tabitha in a silvery glow.

Shadows crept across the room. Luc felt a gentle nudge in his mind and then another one, harder and more insistent. He slowly swam awake, Tabitha's naked body was stretched out against him, and a soft breeze from the balcony swept over their bodies. He rolled toward her, and she snuggled against him, burrowing her head against his chest and wrapping a lazy leg over his.

*Wake up and get out here, or I will be forced to come up and get you.* Tristyn's voice cut through Luc's pleasant half-doze.

He groaned inwardly. *You have got to be kidding.*

*Come on, lover boy, let's go. Come out here. I need to speak to you.*

*In the morning,* Luc snapped.

*Let's go! Come on, we've got work to do!*

Luc sighed and disengaged from Tabitha's limbs. She moaned softly and reached out for him. He leaned down and kissed her, sending a thought to return her to sleep. He slid into his pants and grabbed his shirt off the floor with a muffled curse. He glanced back at the bed and cursed Tristyn again as his eyes ran over Tabitha, the sheets wrapped around her loosely, a long, well-shaped leg peeking out from under one corner, her arms resting on his now-abandoned pillow, the slightest swell of one breast barely visible beneath the top of the sheet. Her face looked peaceful, unlike some of the other nights they had lain together. But tonight she lay warm and resting, his at last, and damn Tristyn wanted to talk.

Luc leaped onto the railing and changed as he dropped over the side, letting the strong wings of his hawk shape catch his fall. Powerful thrusts pushed him forward, and the cool night air swept the last dredges of sleep from his mind. He reached out and searched for Tristyn, his eyes, now adjusted for the dark, sought the familiar dark shape, no doubt sitting on his haunches, his tongue hanging from his mouth in a familiar mocking pant.

He sensed him just off the side of the estate and headed in that direction, to the depths of the woods. Luc dropped from the sky in a quick swoop. As expected, Tristyn sat, waiting patiently, his dark eyes sparkling with amusement as his cousin dropped into the clearing, changing back into his own shape and landing softly before him. Tristyn leaped into his own shape and sat on the large rock behind him.

"You have no shoes on," Tristyn commented drily.

"And you sleep with shoes? I got up and dressed quickly. I do not mean to stay here long," Luc stated.

"Dressed?"

Luc lifted his eyes toward the sky with a deep growl. "Yes, dressed! I don't sleep fully clothed. What the hell? Do we have to discuss my wardrobe or can we discuss why you are here?"

"Only if it pertains to your state of dress in regards to sleeping with the subject of our discussion," Tristyn persisted, humor emanating from him at his cousin's discomfort.

"What is so important that you could not wait?" Luc demanded, trying to change the subject.

Tristyn stood, and some of his humor evaporated. "You took her."

Luc sighed. "As if this has any bearing—"

"It does. It has every bearing," Tristyn interrupted. "What did you tell her?"

Luc shrugged. "Does it matter? I mean, as long as we can get her to leave?"

Tristyn nodded sadly. "So you told her you loved her?"

"What makes you think I love her?" Luc snapped, stepping back and grabbing a fallen branch and swinging it absently, with a parry.

"It matters. We all are at risk here. This plan has one chance to succeed, and your lady is the most pivotal part," Tristyn countered.

Luc could not argue that his cousin, as well as his wife and however many others were also hidden around the perimeter of the estate, had put their lives at risk. "I did." He sighed. "It will make this all the more difficult."

Tristyn shrugged. "Perhaps not. This development will give you a day or two of confidence with the lord regent. It may buy us the extra time we need. Will she be able to shape shift when we need her to?"

"I don't know, Tristyn. I have been coaching her. Now, with Gwyn's funeral over, she needs to get working on it. Her mother was able to shape her to an owl in order to meet her, but that was during a separating. I am not sure if Tabitha can do it on her own. I don't think she knows how much power she has."

"And how powerful is she?" Tristyn asked.

Luc lifted his shoulders. "I just don't know. I honestly cannot gauge it. She has learned to shield quite well. Unfortunately, unless she drops her shields, I have no opportunity to see her potential."

Tristyn let a slight smirk curl his lip, but the suggestion emanating from him was unmistakable. "You are telling me you two were intimate and her shields were not down?"

Luc snorted. "Do you think I was honestly scanning her magical abilities?"

"You should have taken the opportunity. Any information that you might have—"

"Enough!" Luc roared.

Tristyn held up a hand against his cousin's anger. "All right. I am just saying that this seduction will play well into our plans. Had you the foresight to take advantage of her preoccupation to learn a little more about what she is capable of, it might have been advantageous."

Luc's eyes were cold and hard, but Tristyn stood his ground, staring at the rage he had evoked behind that icy stare. Luc held his temper with an effort but lifted a finger toward his cousin's eyes. "Do not even think that what I did was something I put forethought into. I did not plan a seduction so that she played into our plan better."

"No?" Tristyn's voice carried a taunting edge. "Than what do you call it? If you are telling me you don't love her, than it was a calculated seduction."

Luc saw where his cousin was going with his reasoning, and his rage dissipated into guilt. "I love her. The last thing on my mind last night was her abilities—or anything else except just loving her."

"I know," Tristyn said simply. "It is best you realize that before we start this, because your actions will be as crucial as her reactions."

"I know."

"And she may not listen to you. You may not have the chance to explain." Tristyn cocked his head and spoke frankly. "I hope you thought this through. Had you simply let things lie without this additional level of involvement, she would have run and they would have followed her. She would have let you help her elude them. But now you may have to herd her where we need her to go. If she is as angry, as I know my wife would be, she may not do what you want."

Luc nodded. "I know. I wish I could say that my motives were anything but selfish, but I am not so sure they were not."

"And now you'll send her home after that added level of involvement. You do have a tendency to complicate things." Tristyn shook his head.

"Antoine will know the minute Tabitha breaks the perimeter. He will send everything he has after her. Dylan will be the first on her heels."

"And yours."

"And mine," Luc agreed. "Dylan and I have been vying for Antoine's attention; he has grown resentful of my apparent place within Antoine's confidence. I also grow concerned that he is jealous of Tabitha's involvement with future plans."

"Why is that? He must recognize that she is under lock and guard, not exactly a threat to him," Tristyn observed.

"But I came into his world, where he was Antoine's heir apparent. And not only does Antoine play us against one another, he encourages the competition. Tie that to Tabitha's high status in Antoine's eyes and that, as of now, I am Tabitha's mate. I am trying to convince Antoine to promise me to her, but he will not allow any further relationship until he is more confident that I will not only swear fealty but assist him in winning over Marcus."

"And now that you have broken down his daughter's resolve, perhaps he will see you as more prepared to take another leap," Tristyn suggested.

Luc released a long exhale. "If she suspected I was with her last night to further myself politically, I am not sure I would get away quite so unscathed. Of course, now Dylan will be more apt to want to have me replaced."

"He is encouraging Antoine to replace you?"

Luc nodded. "Any number of eligible men are vying for his attention with his promise of a good word to Antoine about his daughter's hand. Dylan made it well known that I was not able to...umm...encourage her to be with me."

"Delicately stated. So now that she has succumbed to your charms? How will Dylan react?" Tristyn asked.

"I don't know. It will take some of the momentum out of his argument. Assuming, of course, that Antoine sees her and discovers that she has given in to me," Luc said, trying to hold down his shame over speaking about their intimacy with such callousness.

Tristyn nodded. "And now we are down to the final couple of days. You need to continue this dangerous game."

A slight breeze stirred; leaves shuffled. The men tensed, sensing a presence nearby. They stilled and extended their senses.

"It is Alena." Tristyn mentally reached out to draw her to them.

She slipped into the clearing, her soft boots making barely a sound. She smiled when she saw Luc and slid into her husband's waiting embrace. "I was hoping to find you two."

Tristyn replied, "Have you any news?"

Her smile diminished. "Rumor has it that Dylan might be planning something."

Luc frowned. "Something? Like what? And why wasn't I aware?"

"Well, it seems you departed with Tabitha. Dylan spent a lot of time at Antoine's ear, trying to convince him of some plan. I served them dinner. He was most certainly trying to monopolize Antoine's attention. I suspect that Dylan was taking advantage of your absence."

Tristyn shook his head in wonder. "It makes no sense for them to be planning anything offensive. I mean, they are still trying to deflect attention from the last attack. To plan another attack now would be insanity."

Alena glanced at her husband. "You think that we are dealing with total sanity here? Dylan is desperate to gain the advantage over Luc, and the only way he knows how to do it is with his own special brand of violence."

Luc considered. "I cannot imagine that Antoine would do anything but keep Dylan on a tight leash right now. He cannot afford a mistake."

Tristyn looked at his wife. "So you know nothing more than that?"

Alena shook her head. "Dylan left with one of the serving girls not long after dinner. He has a propensity for bragging in bed. I will talk to her in the morning and see if he had anything to say."

Luc shook his head at her and grinned. "How is it that within only a few days of working here, you have garnered so much trust?"

Alena laughed and tossed her head. "You have to know how to gain trust. A talent you seem to be sorely lacking!"

Tristyn chuckled. "Not anymore."

Luc groaned. Alena glanced at him with an impish grin. "Ahh, so you have made amends and negotiated your way back into our young lady's good graces?"

Tristyn leaned forward and whispered dramatic, "It seems it is not only her good graces he has negotiated himself into."

Luc lifted a hand in surrender. "You win. I am going back now. Let me know if you hear any news."

Alena smirked at him. "I will, but I suspect the news in the halls tomorrow will be that Antoine's new favorite has apparently won the heart of more than one member of the family."

Luc shook his head. Without further comment, he leaped and changed shape, driving himself up toward the balcony.

As he banked back toward the familiar doorway, the still-open doors beckoned him and his thoughts turned toward the warmth of Tabitha's naked body and their bed.

He never saw the arrow that sped through the darkness. With a piercing cry, he fell, and darkness engulfed him as he plunged toward the ground.

# CHAPTER TWELVE

TABITHA WOKE WITH A LONG SENSUOUS STRETCH, HER body pleasantly sore. She smiled as the events of last night played through her mind. When she reached out and found the bed beside her empty, the sheets cool, she sat up. With a small pout, she glanced toward the bathroom.

"Luc?"

No answer. Hmm. *Luc?*

A slight chill swept across her body. She rose, grabbed her robe off the floor, and wrapped it around her. The balcony doors stood wide open; she glanced out to see if he were out there.

*Nope.*

*Bathroom?*

*Nope.*

"Huh." She wandered out to the sitting area outside their bedroom. No sign of Luc. She returned to the bedroom, noticing for the first time that his clothes were gone. At some point during the night, he had risen and dressed. But the clothes he had left wearing were clothes he normally only wore in the privacy of their suite. He was usually quite meticulous and took care in his dress. If he had been summoned for some emergency or to meet her father, he would have dressed in more appropriate clothing.

She vaguely remembered him kissing her during the night before she had fallen back to sleep. The tiny bite of concern nagged at her mind, blossoming quickly into genuine panic.

*Luc?*

If he were with her father, he would respond, even if only to let her know when he would be done. She walked back to the balcony and glanced out at the beautiful summer morning. Nothing seemed amiss, but there was no sign of him.

*Where the hell is he?*

*All right... all right. Don't panic.* She paced the floor, ticking off possibilities. *I know he would not have slept with me and then turned tail and run for home. If he is anywhere nearby, he would have heard me calling him.*

*Unless he cannot respond.*

She dashed that line of thought and put herself back on track. *No jumping to conclusions. I am sure he is just busy. He has been summoned—something must have happened. He will either be back shortly or send word. I am sure he cannot respond to me because he is afraid that our link will be detected.*

A rap on the door made her jump. She spun around and rushed to yank it open. It was Jules's turn to be startled when she seemed to leap to a stop before him, her robe hastily tied, her wealth of hair in wild disarray around her shoulders.

The anticipation died on her face when she recognized Jules. "Oh, it's you."

"Yes, it is! It's very pleasant to see you as well. What a lovely morning." His voice dripped sarcasm as he strode into the room and placed a breakfast tray on the table by the chaise. "Will Monsieur DesChamps be joining you for breakfast this morning? It seems he rose later than is his usual habit—"

"You don't know where he is?"

"Should I?" Jules inquired, lifting one brow at her. "I understood he retired early last night and has not yet left."

"He didn't leave? The guard said he has not left? Are you sure? Is it the same one who was on duty all night?" She demanded, panic erupting despite her intention to remain calm.

Jules shook his head, perplexed. "Yes, it is the same guard. He was just waiting for his replacement before retiring." He gave her a long look of consternation. "Have you two fought again?" He stopped and regarded her with interest. A slow smile curled his mouth. "Ahh. Well, well."

Tabitha could have spit in frustration. "Stop that!"

Jules's expression lost some of its delight as a shadow crossed his face. "He didn't force you, did he? Regardless of what your father may think, I will not condone—"

She groaned in frustration. "No! He did not force me! We were, well, we were fine. But I woke up to find him gone. The guard said no one left the room. Jules, he must have..." She glanced out at the balcony. "He must have left in hawk shape. He would not have done that unless he was trying to avoid detection."

Jules followed her gaze. "How long has he been gone?"

Tabitha shook her head. "I don't know. I have only been awake for a short time, and he was gone when I woke up.

He would have woken me if he thought he would be gone for too long."

Jules nodded. "So we must let your father believe that he is still with you, to give him time to return."

"Jules, we have to find him."

"I will see what I can find out. Stay put, and don't let anyone see you." He gave her a quick glance, scanning her slender body, clad only in the robe. "Don't dress. It's best if anyone comes looking for Luc that you remain in the robe. Turn on the shower and shut the bathroom door. Let them think he is showering and that you two were otherwise occupied this morning."

Tabitha blushed but nodded. She shut the door tightly behind Jules after he left. She ignored the breakfast tray and went to the balcony, scanning the sky for some sign of her wayward hawk.


An hour crept by. Tabitha had gone from pacing the floor to climbing the walls as time dragged on with no sign of Luc. The quiet tap at the door startled her. She raced to the bathroom, flipped on the shower, and shut the door behind her. She took a deep breath and walked to the door with as much calm and poise as she could muster. She had to remember that she was supposed to have recently risen from the bed with her lover.

She opened the door. A young tawny-haired woman stood holding a handful of sheets and towels.

"Oh. Oh. Uhm, could you leave those out here for now? I mean, we were just... Well, we are not quite ready yet... still not dressed." She waved weakly toward the bathroom. "He's taking a shower."

She stared at the floor, a rosy flush on her cheeks, blushing after the stammering mess she had just uttered. *Of course he is in the shower, you fool, the damn water is running.*

The young woman pushed past her into the room and caught the door with her heel, tugging it out of Tabitha's hand and slamming it behind her. Tabitha lifted her head, shocked at the behavior. The servant dropped the pile of towels on the chaise and turned to her.

"Alena!" Tabitha had never been so glad to see anyone. She threw herself into the other woman's arms, stifling a frightened sob. "Tell me you know where Luc is!"

Alena shook her head sadly as she gripped Tabitha's shoulders. "I don't, but I do know where he was."

"Where?"

"He left you last night to come down and speak to Tristyn and myself."

"Tristyn? He is here as well? When did you get here?" Tabitha asked, trying to settle her nerves.

"Tristyn was out in the forest and called to Luc to meet him. Luc was, not surprisingly, less than enthused," Alena said with a bawdy little smirk.

"So he flew down?" Tabitha asked, ignoring the obvious reference to their intimate evening.

"Yes. It was a maybe an hour before dawn. Tristyn called him, and Luc came down, and we discussed the next steps and what I had heard."

"So where is he now?"

Alena lifted a shoulder. "I was with Tristyn when Luc left. He flew off to return to you. The last we saw he was heading up over the treetops. Are you sure he didn't come back and leave later, maybe to meet early with Antoine?"

It was Tabitha's turn to shake her head. "He was gone when I woke. It is possible he came back and went out again without me seeing him, but the guard posted at the door said that no one left all night. If he left, it would have been via the balcony."

Alena swore and lowered herself to the chaise to sit on top of the pile of towels she had placed there. "Antoine thinks Luc is still in here with you. Jules has suggested to him that you two had an entertaining evening. We're not going to be able to keep this deception up for long. Antoine is going to ask you where Luc is."

"So what do we do? We have to locate Luc... I haven't been able to even find a trace of him, and he is not responding to me." Tabitha felt her heart squeeze; her fears were being confirmed.

"In the brief time I have been here, I have heard of the competition between Luc and Dylan. Dylan, it seems, is already trying to gather support." Alena said.

"Luc told me that he has to watch his back."

"I don't doubt it. Your brother is a dangerous man," Alena stated. "I think that we had better get you out of here and look for Luc. Our story should be that you are heartbroken because you two shared intimacies last night and then Luc left before you woke. You were feeling used."

"What? Go to my father?"

Alena nodded. "If you don't, he will come to you asking where Luc is. Already, he is asking Jules to bring Luc to him. He has already missed some meetings this morning. If we delay any longer, he will think you are covering for Luc."

"But what about the guard reporting that no one left the room?"

"Leave that for your father to figure out. All you need to say is that you woke and he was gone, and you have been crying since, feeling like he used you." Alena rose. "I have to get going. It looks like I have some searching to do."

"And you will let me know?"

"Yes. Your father has to think that you gave yourself to Luc, who is the only man for you. If he thinks for a second that you are less than heartbroken over Luc's absence, he will have another suitor up here before you know it," Alena warned. "And the less you know, the better. Your father has to trust that you are not involved in any scheme, or you will never be allowed your freedom."

"Okay."

Alena smiled and hugged her quickly. "We will find him."

Tabitha swallowed the lump in her throat as Alena shut the door behind her. She slipped out of the robe and went to shower, hoping against hope that Luc would fly back into the room, tired but safe.


She followed Jules down the hallway toward her father's offices, letting the strain and fear show plainly on her face. Jules left her at the door with a wan smile. Tabitha lifted her chin as she entered the room. Her father was behind his massive desk. To her chagrin, Dylan leaned nonchalantly against the back of a chaise.

Antoine glanced up and cocked his head as she entered, studying her. Tabitha felt the heat rise to her face. Dylan's responding grin told her he was enjoying her discomfort.

"So, you and Monsieur DesChamps had a pleasant evening," Antoine drawled.

"Do you know where he is?" Tabitha snapped.

Antoine slowly shook his head. "I was going to ask the same question of you. It seems he departed sometime in the early morning hours, from what Jules told me, and has not been seen since. Where do you think he may have gone?"

Tabitha shook her head and let the tears that pricked her eyes slowly slide down her cheeks. As shameful as it was to cry in front of her father and gloating brother, she needed to uphold her side of this sham until they could locate Luc. "I don't know."

"Did you fight?"

"No."

"Ahh… And then?"

She shrugged, averting her gaze. "I woke and he was gone."

"Does he shape shift?"

Tabitha hesitated. Should she admit to knowing? Did her father already know? Dylan's gaze was ruthless as he observed her.

Before she could respond, Dylan spoke up. "His family usually shapes the wolf. Does Luc have another shape?"

She shrugged. "I don't know."

Antoine leaned back with a *harrumph*. "And you—do you have any such tendency?"

Tabitha allowed her eyes to grow wide in amazement, "Me? Shape?" She snorted. "I wouldn't even know where to start."

"Of course." Her father rose, commenting drily, "Yet you have a tendency to find ways to skirt the normal thought process and learning curve."

"Well, this is all new to me. I am just learning," she protested, but he waved a hand at her.

"I need to speak to him. I think it safe to assume he had some reason to leave you. Did you please him?" Antoine's directness left her speechless. The rosiness already in her cheeks expanded to a whole new shade of red at the question.

Dylan saved her from answering by throwing in his own interpretation. "I think it safe to say that our little girl may have not known... seeing as this was a fairly new experience for her."

Tabitha's embarrassment turned to seething rage at her brother. She fought the urge to leap at him, claws extended toward that insidious smirk.

Antoine lifted his hands toward Dylan, indicating that he should refrain from his needling. Dylan pursed his lips in agreement, but it seemed he could not help but watch her with a knowing leer.

Tabitha stated primly, "Are we done?"

"Will you join us for lunch?" her father invited.

"I will most certainly not. Have you forgotten that you gave me to a man as a gift? I am being kept prisoner here," she retorted hotly.

Antoine looked surprised. "You are not happy with Monsieur DesChamps? I thought you were pleased with him."

"Regardless of the state of our relationship, you still had no right to force us to share a bed. You could have let our relationship follow its own course," she snapped.

"Of course, a lady likes to be courted. Well, in our world, courtship comes after a couple has deemed they are a sexual match. Judging by his actions, I have to wonder if you did not fulfill your part. Apparently he went away without so much as a word," Antoine responded. "I would suggest we give him a day or two to return before we reevaluate your relationship. I have many other options."

Tabitha filled with rage but stifled her outburst. She had no intention of defending her sexual prowess in this room with these two buffoons. The last thing she wanted to consider while Luc was missing was her father parading a new line of men before her. With a final snarled curse, she turned on her heel and headed back to her room.


Later that afternoon, Tabitha sat huddled in her chaise, exhausted from worrying about Luc and trying to figure out how to sink below the damn bird's consciousness. She was tired and could not squeeze another lucid thought from her brain, but the constant inactivity was making her crazy. She was beginning to hate the room and could not for the life of her imagine spending the night in that bed without Luc.

She needed to do something. But what? Where could she even begin to look for him? She could not begin a search around the estate, indoors or out, with a guard at her heels. She wished Alena would return, or Jules, or anyone. She had no idea how to find them, or Tristyn, for that matter.

What if Luc was out there, hurt? Or captured? Or dead? Was it possible he was still alive but unable to contact her?

With a growl and another curse, she rose and grabbed her soft boots. She tugged each one on as she headed to the outer door. She yanked it open and startled the guard stationed outside her room.

"I want to see my grandfather. Let's go," she stated before she marched down the hall. The guard fell into step behind her and followed silently, which infuriated her even more. She knew the way to her grandfather's rooms by now and found him tired and struggling to stay awake. Soon Tabitha opted to return to her rooms in the hope that Jules or Alena would return with some news. Tristyn, who was also linked to Luc, was out there looking. It was possible they had found him and word had not reached her yet.

In an effort to keep from screaming as she headed back to her suite, she silently repeated this possibility over and over. She was deep in thought, reviewing every possible scenario she could imagine, when she rounded a corner too quickly and came close to colliding with Dylan. She felt her face redden and averted her eyes. With a mumbled apology, she tried to brush past him.

It was apparently not to be that easy. She could have screamed in frustration when he grabbed at her arm. "What is your hurry, Sister Sweet?"

"Oh, let me go. What is wrong with you anyway?" She yanked her arm free of his grip.

"Just trying to catch up with you. I went to your rooms to pay a little visit and was told that you were visiting our grandfather," he replied pleasantly. "How is our old relation doing, anyway? Enjoying his new accommodations?"

"Why don't you go visit him for yourself?" she suggested, turning to leave.

"What's your hurry?" Dylan called after her. "I thought we might be able to chat about your lover."

Tabitha stopped and turned slowly to face him, cold dread building in her belly. "Luc? You know where he is?"

Dylan indicated a dark door with his chin. "I might. Or I might not."

"Where is he?" she snapped, considering violence if he didn't start telling her what he knew.

"Come with me. I will show you," Dylan said. He reached for her arm.

She ignored his hand and gestured for him to proceed. Trepidation crawled through her, but her options were limited. This was the first and only clue she had to Luc's whereabouts. The fact that it was Dylan who had found him sent shivers of dismay racing up and down her spine.

Dylan led her into a small library and shut the door behind them, leaving the guard behind.

Tabitha stopped short and stood with her hands on hips. "Well?"

"Before I give you any information about him... or his condition..."

Tabitha felt her stomach drop at the insinuation.

"I must ask if you happen to know about an item of mine that has disappeared."

She felt the blood drain from her face. "I don't know what you are talking about."

"A certain item went missing. Your imprint was found on my door lock. That help your memory at all?"

She struggled to lie but the words would not come. She couldn't think fast enough to get herself out of the situation.

He continued. "Let me show you how your lover is doing, and then maybe we can discuss a trade?"

He lifted a round mirror from the desk and concentrated on the surface. Tabitha could sense the power emitting from him. The mirror's face began to swirl with a billowing fog.

"Show me." Her voice came out as a croak.

Dylan grinned and turned to the mirror, his expression triumphant as he gave the mirror to her.

Tabitha felt her belly clench as she took the mirror in her hands. Warmth coursed through it as Dylan maintained the image for her. The fog began to dissipate, and a warm yellow glow slowly emerged. She squinted, trying to discern the developing image. It sharpened to reveal a long body lying on a low table. The light flickered over his features. Tabitha gasped at the swollen eyes, the distended cheekbone, and the deeply bruised swelling on Luc's face.

Dylan shifted the mirror so the blossoming purple swelling over Luc's ribs came into view. A long gash ran the length of his leg, which seemed to be resting at an odd angle.

"You bastard," she breathed.

"I want what you stole from me. Once I have that, you can have him. Assuming he lives, of course."

Tabitha's breath came in rapid gulps as she tried to still the rage that was shaking her limbs. Dylan held out a hand to her. "And if you go to our father about this, I will make sure that your lover's throat is slit before anyone can find him." Dylan's voice dropped to a low and deadly hiss. "I will give you until tomorrow night to return my object. I will send for you and we can make a trade."

She maintained her composure as best she could and turned to glare at her brother. Without a word, she yanked the door open and left, trying to calm her boiling emotions. If she had remained in that room with her pompous brother, she might well have strangled him.

She made her way back to her room and shut the door with a click. She could not react. She could not move. She wanted to scream, to cry, to howl her rage. She needed to get the wand back from her mother.

*Colene*. She would find Colene, and they would get it back. But Antoine would not let her go to the village, and sending a message might endanger Colene and her family as well. She glanced over at D'Noir. Her only hope was to leave here undetected.

# CHAPTER THIRTEEN

TABITHA STARED AT THE CLOSED DOOR AND INHALED deeply. There was no time left. *This is it. I have to commit to doing this or I will fail.*

She grabbed a plate of the food and sat on the floor in front of the open balcony doors. She broke off pieces of her dinner, ate some, and shared some with her glossy-winged friend. While she chewed and the bird nibbled at the bits she offered, she let her mind slowly sink into the bird's consciousness. She relaxed and just let her mind drift through its mind; she watched the room from his perspective and let his sharpened senses simply flow through her mind. Gradually, she became less aware of her physical self as she absorbed the bird's memories and instincts.

She could not have said how long she sat in that relaxed stage. Taking advantage of the peaceful, unemotional state she had achieved, without further thought she threw her concentration into pouring herself into the form of the bird she had constructed in her mind. The wings were long, black, and glossy. She saw each individual feather, the deep ebony eyes, and the slope of his head down to his back. She let herself become the image she had made, imagining herself with the tiny sticklike legs and wide feet, the long beak and wide, graceful wings. She imagined extending her arms and letting the soft sweep of her glossy wings move the air around her. She felt her head tilt as she cocked an ebony eye at her surroundings. Now she inhaled the deep smells all around her, as well as the woodsy scents enticingly being carried in from the warm summer breeze.

She slowly opened her eyes to find herself staring up at the chaise, her head cocked as she tried to see the chair seat. She turned. The entire room before her was at floor level. She made a tentative hop forward. The unaccustomed weight shift as she tried to balance on the two insubstantial legs beneath her belly dropped her forward. Her wings flapped as she tried to use human hands to catch herself, but she ended up staring down at the carpet, beak first, her elegant black tail feathers pointing toward the ceiling.

She gasped and tried to right herself but found herself stumbling drunkenly to the right until she leaned against the chaise leg to try to adjust her inner balance to accommodate her new shape. With a startled caw, she pushed herself back from the chair leg and again tried to hop forward. This time, she ignored her human instincts and concentrated on the crow instincts she had absorbed from D'Noir. She took a tentative hop, and then another. Tabitha was delighted to find that she could now navigate using small movements.

She glanced over, her head cocked to the side, to see D'Noir watching her attentively. He hopped over, staring at her, and Tabitha cawed her amusement. He faced her and fluffed up his feathers. Extending his neck, he partially spread his wings and bobbed his head, emitting a brief cackled song.

She returned a startled caw at what she now understood was a mating ritual. *You are not seriously hitting on me?*

D'Noir gave up when she ignored his display.

Tabitha focused on attempting more serious maneuvers. She flapped her wings and tried to take short leaps but felt as though she were in her human body. Flapping her arms and leaping, she accomplished little more than knocking things off a side table while she fluttered around the room. She knew she must calm her mind, let go of her human instincts, and mentally plug herself into the bird's memories. She felt her shoulders shift as she rotated her wings to sweep the air beneath her instead of flapping wildly. With a cry, she elevated off the ground and propelled herself a few feet toward the bed. She was so surprised and amazed that she released her bird form. With a strangled yelp, Tabitha fell across the bed in human shape, her arms extended and legs tucked up behind her. Before she could reconcile which shape she was in, she rolled off the side of the bed and hit the floor with a firm *thud.*

"Nicely done," she grumbled from the floor. D'Noir flapped over to her and stood beside her head. "I know you were impressed with that," she snapped at the bird.

She practiced for the next hour. Flight slowly took shape. She knew she would not need to be able to travel very far, only to town; she'd meet Colene and then fly up to her balcony. That was her immediate focus for the shape shift. Her mind concentrated on that need. She would think about what was next later. For now, one thing at a time.

When the hour had nearly ticked past, Tabitha decided the time had come. It was now or never. As long as she did not panic or think too much, she was confident she could control herself long enough to get to the village. Her guard would believe she was still in her room; she would not set off the perimeter alarm.

She tugged a colorful throw pillow from the sitting room onto the balcony and set it in the corner so she could easily notice the patterned pillow when she returned and be certain it was her balcony. She climbed over the railing to sit astride the top rung, hooking her heels into the support rungs. She had seen Luc leap and then shape as he fell, almost instantaneously, but the fear of dropping and the ensuing panic might sabotage her ability to concentrate. She pulled her feet up under her and squatted on the railing; she closed her eyes and poured her thoughts into the bird shape she formed in her mind. The air felt different, the scents sharper. Her balance on the railing became effortless as she settled her weight on her bird feet.

Wings extended, she slowly leaned out over the railing, rolling her shoulders, feeling the air cup beneath her wings. As she flapped her wings, she could feel herself lift with the current. She could barely detect the moment her feet left the railing. The power in her crow wings drove her toward the sky. The evening air flowed through her nostrils, the scents from the woods below teasing her senses. The sensation of being a crow was the most beautiful she had ever felt. For the first time in her life, she truly appreciated her abilities.

She flapped slowly, trying to let her crow instincts shape her movements rather than using her human mind to drive her actions. She kept her thoughts quiet and just let the physical sensation of flying be her guide. She turned to soar over the estate and began to make her way to the village. As she flew, she raked her memory for details about leaving Colene's house with Luc. What direction had they taken?

She flew toward the town center, intending to find Colene's home starting from the historical society; the round building would be easily identifiable. Once there, she circled over it and tried to recall the direction she and Luc had taken from Colene's house. The lanes all looked the same from her height but she headed in what she thought was the general direction. The cool wind in her face and the warm surge of air beneath her wings felt amazing.

A familiar shape caught her attention. Her sharp crow vision recognized Alena and Colene heading toward the cottage. Tabitha let her altitude drop; she circled and gently dipped toward the cottage's front yard. The lanterns along the lane were slowly lighting in the shrinking daylight. She decided to land in the front yard as Alena and Colene turned toward the cottage.

Tabitha had watched Luc land gracefully on his feet as he soared in for a landing, and she felt sure she could do the same. She let herself sink lower as she flew behind Alena and Colene and approached the fence along the house. She decided she would swoop over the fence and change as she was landing. The problem was that she did not take into account that human legs and the additional height were factors. As she cleared the railing, shaping back into her own form, her feet tangled in the top rung of the fence. She fell flat on her face in the dirt, the breath knocked out of her in a whoosh.

As she tried to unsnarl her legs from the fence and stand, Alena burst into laughter. Tabitha indignantly brushed dirt from her face and clothes. "All right. Enough. It was not that funny."

Alena tried to comment, but tears ran down her face. She collapsed on the stoop of the little cottage and buried her head in her arms, her shoulders still shaking. Once she had composed herself, she lifted her head and wiped her eyes, chuckling. "I am sorry, Tabitha. I just could not help myself."

Colene's shoulders shook and a muffled cough escaped her as she turned to unlock the front door. She regained her composure, but the deep lines around her mouth and dimples gave her away as she lifted a brow at Tabitha. "You were looking for us?"

Tabitha nodded and the levity left her face. "Luc is hurt. Dylan has him."

"What?" Alena stood, alarmed, and Colene spun from the door, shock registering on her face.

"Dylan has him. I have until tomorrow to return the wand to him. I don't know how badly Luc is hurt or if he is going to survive until tomorrow." Tabitha's voice quivered as her tears choked her.

Colene glanced quickly at Alena. "The wand is already gone."

"We have to get it back! Does my mother have it? Can we contact her?" Tabitha demanded as desperation gripped her chest.

Alena looked deep in thought. "All right, we need a quick plan. Colene, get word to the Faye. They need to know what is going on."

"How will you contact them? Can I help?" Tabitha desperately inquired.

Alena shook her head. "Tabitha, I think it is time we get you out of here. Leave rescuing Luc to us. I think we have risked enough. Now that you can shape, we have some time before they are aware you are gone—"

"No." Tabitha's voice was flat. "I am not leaving—Luc is hurt. I will help get him out of there. He has risked everything for me. I won't leave him."

Alena's eyes narrowed as she regarded Tabitha. After a moment's consideration, she nodded. "All right. Let's go inside. Tell me everything you know."

Tabitha followed the two women into the house. Colene immediately excused herself to send a message to the Faye. Tabitha sat on the edge of a chair, facing Alena, and told her everything she could remember about the weeks in her father's estate.

"You saw the black elf in the basement? How did you do that?" Alena asked.

"I separated. No one could see me, but it could sense my presence. It knew I was there."

"Could you do it again? Separate so no one can see you?"

"You want me to search for Luc?" Tabitha asked.

Alena nodded. "Let's head back to the estate. I will stay with you. If you can find him, you can tell me where he is."

Alena went in search of Colene to tell her their intentions before they left to walk back to the estate. Alena took the lead and Tabitha followed her through cobbled pathways lined with shrubs. The winding avenue took them past other small, neatly kept cottages with well-tended gardens and flowerbeds dotting their yards. Some had little fences; others had trellises with winding, fragrant flowers peeking from among the leaves. The village was quiet and well kept. Tabitha could almost forget their stressful circumstances as they meandered through the scenic lanes.

"It is so beautiful down here," she commented quietly to Alena.

"It is. Your father has designed a lovely home for these people. The initial impressions of people who come to view the village are that it is ideal here, with a lot of opportunity. The prices are reasonable. I think people believe they can make a life for themselves here, but the easy access to credit and the high taxes on everyday items cause people to run up debt. Your father provides counselors to assist them. Of course, the ideas they present to people for dealing with debt run from servitude to giving up a baby."

Tabitha shook her head, horrified. "So why don't they leave?"

"These 'human villages' have become commonplace in your father's governance. And of course, the idea has spread through the south as well. He has a lot of support through-out the south, and he has taught the other regents these tac-tics," Alena explained.

"I don't understand. Are you telling me that the people here are all human? Why aren't there Caskans as well?"

"Well, a couple of reasons: the Caskans do not have the travel restrictions that apply to humans. We are, after all, less than ten percent of the population. And as difficult as it is for us to conceive and bear children, that is something fairly new to the human population. The past generations of humans did not share the same issue, so we were a growing population. And of course, the intermarriage of Caskan and humans produced fewer humans." Alena spoke quietly as they skirted a young couple.

"You mean half-Caskan and half-human?"

"No. If children have Caskan blood, they either have the talent or they do not. They are considered full Caskan; the power is seldom diluted by the human blood. If they have abilities, they are Caskan, and if they do not, they are human," Alena explained. "So the human population has also been diminishing. Of course, Antoine's directive for intermarriage has also slowed the expansion of the human population."

"Directive for intermarriage?" Tabitha asked.

"Yes. You have not heard? He wants more Caskans to marry and procreate with the humans, producing more Caskans. Future generations will have fewer human babies that way. He is discouraging human marriage. Many suspect he will outlaw it totally at some point." Alena gave a dry, humorless laugh. "I understand he hates to have to give away human babies to his friends. He much prefers to be able to give away Caskans."

Tabitha groaned. "That is horrible! Then why is he bringing in human women from my world?"

"Well, the first offspring they produce will be human. Antoine will take a child anyway he can get it. But the second will be Caskan if he continues to encourage Caskan men to seduce and impregnate human women," Alena explained with a disgusted expression. "Of course, the human women from your world do not have the same issue with getting pregnant and carrying to term that we have here." Alena glanced at the young woman at her side. "Your father promotes several initiatives with implications across our territory like his adoption and housing programs for the humans. He has influenced leaders to the south of us, and they are adopting his tactics."

"Doesn't anyone see this as wrong?" Tabitha asked.

Alena shrugged. "Tabitha, if your father were to explain all this, the spin would be very much different. In fact, given time, I have no doubt that he could convince you that this was all fine, that there was no issue whatsoever. I really think he would be able to convince you that his way of trying to shape his realm is simply governing in the best interest of the people."

Tabitha crossed her arms in front of her chest, her expression incredulous. "How could he possibly spin this as positive?"

"Let me give you some examples: Caskans outnumber humans nine to one. As such, our world is tailored to the Caskan lifestyle. Homes can be maintained with power; traveling is done via journeying or shape shifting. Humans are at a disadvantage because they are such a small, diminishing part of the population. New technology and research is for the Caskan people; it's not directed at finding ways to improve human lives. So your father has developed human villages where the homes are closer, reducing the need for the humans to travel or transport goods great distances. He has devised an adoption service for humans who cannot afford children, to offer their children a chance for a better life. He provides employment opportunities and affordable housing for humans who struggle to find work versus Caskans who have magic at their disposal." Alena finished her statement with a sad shake of her head. "He has positioned himself as a champion of the human population, but he is simply preying on them, using their own fears to gain their trust so he can take from them. You don't hear that he encourages his guards and soldiers to find human women within the villages and impregnate them. Of course, should these single women become with child, how would they continue to work and support themselves? Many end up giving their children up because they cannot afford to have a child and work for your father. There have been initiatives for affordable childcare but these initiatives are quickly struck down. It is as though your father wants these people to have no other option."

"Is this the way of your world? Is it like this all over?" Tabitha asked quietly.

Alena shook her head. "No, these things have transpired since Antoine's father time and then Antoine's subsequent election. But your father is a compelling speaker. He can convince people that what he says is true and that what he is doing is benefiting the community. People trust him." Alena shook her head slowly. "And his ideas have slowly taken hold in the southern regions. I understand that those in the far south, down in Borgue and Southern Borgue, do not subscribe to this approach, but Antoine carries his own realm and the territories between Borgue and St. Mikel. You know, it was that initial plan that originally drew Dylan up here. He is actually the adopted son of Polan Tefers, your father's advisor. She was here several weeks ago but has left to return to Fallomar. Dylan came under your father's influence while he was studying. He is widely considered the heir apparent to your father's legacy."

"Dylan? I am not surprised. He is, after all, his eldest son and as ruthless, if not more so from what I can tell."

Alena replied, "From the information I have been able to dig up on him, Dylan was not always quite this brutal. Under your father's careful tutoring, he has released some inner demons. He and Luc were very close friends at one time, but I think Luc learned quickly that Dylan could be very cruel. Antoine keeps him close, but I am not sure that even Antoine knows what Dylan would be capable of should he be let loose. Should he ever succeed Antoine, he could possibly be a very dangerous overlord."

"St. Mikel is governed by Marcus?" Tabitha clarified.

Alena nodded, "Yes, Marcus governs St. Mikel. He does not believe in Antoine's views or politics, but he has to be careful. His allies lie far to the south, and we have limited access to them. Of course, in the midst of this chaos, the Plains people are starving, and Antoine's region lies between the Plains tribes and St. Mikel. News of the Plains tribes attacking outlying villages has reached us, but we believe Antoine's people are perpetrating these attacks to create panic in an attempt to unite the region against a common enemy."

Tabitha felt compelled to ask, "What proof do you have?"

"Not much besides what people have relayed. Let's face it, we are in a dilemma as we try to distinguish the truth. We are proceeding on people's opinions and what they have heard." Alena's voice lost some fire as she admitted, "We are starting a civil war with rumors."

# CHAPTER FOURTEEN

TABITHA AND ALENA MADE THEIR WAY THROUGH THE darkened town back toward the estate. Alena walked with a surety and confidence that Tabitha could not muster.

"We are approaching the house. Can you revert to your other shape? I will meet you in your suite." Alena peeked around a corner, waiting for foot traffic to ease before turning to Tabitha. "Change shape. Let's go."

Tabitha closed her eyes and focused on her bird shape. She imagined each of D'Noir's details and focused her energy, shifting her attention to pouring herself into that visualized crow. When she opened her eyes, she perceived the world from a different angle; she was staring at Alena's soft boots. Alena patted her shoulder, and Tabitha flapped her wings with a squawk of protest.

"You cannot be serious. You have got to get the taking-off thing down. If you need me to fling you in the air to begin flying, we are in trouble." Alena lifted her and, with a whisper of caution, sent Tabitha winging into the evening air.

Tabitha pumped her wings and gained altitude to soar over the estate toward their suite. Although the darkening sky elongated the shadows, with her sharper crow vision, she spotted the patterned pillow she had left on the balcony. She alighted gently on the balcony, changing as she landed. Her momentum carried her across the balcony a few steps before she was able to catch herself.

Her spirits were optimistic now that she had the glimmer of a plan. She stepped into the suite and headed into the sitting area to wait for Alena. A tray of food had been left. She was ravenous, despite her gnawing concern over Luc's welfare and was eating when Alena entered the suite.

"You ready?"

Tabitha stuffed a piece of some orange vegetable into her mouth and nodded. "Let's go into the other room. I need to be able to lie down and relax to do this."

"Did you recognize anything around Luc when Dylan showed him to you? Walls? Anything?"

Tabitha shook her head. "I was so intent on Luc that I didn't even notice."

"This is a large estate. It may take you hours to search the whole thing. If we could narrow it down, you might be able to get a better idea of where he might be," Alena commented.

Tabitha nodded, dark thoughts of where Dylan might have hidden Luc nagging at her. "I have an idea. There is one place that is sealed off and locked up tightly. My father won't go down there. Dylan as much as told me that Antoine does not know Luc is hurt and being held hostage."

"Okay. What can I do to help?" Alena asked.

"Just wait. Once I know if Luc is where I think he is, you can get him out before I have to meet Dylan," Tabitha replied as she settled on the bed.

With a deep breath, she closed her eyes and focused on separating from her body. Stress and pressure pumped through her veins, and her anxiety made focusing difficult. Once or twice, she felt herself become weightless, but the instant she tried to move, she dropped back in her body, her heart pounding. Her aggravation and frustration mounted.

Tabitha sucked air through her clenched teeth and willed herself to relax. She recalled taking a yoga class back on the island; the instructor's recommendations came back to her. She tried clearing her head, focusing only on her breath as it slipped in and out of her nose, letting her body relax one small area at a time until she felt the tension slipping down her body, out through her toes. Nothing disturbed her focus. She soon felt herself slipping off of the bed; she turned and saw herself lying relaxed on the bed behind her. Alena lifted wide eyes to Tabitha's hazy outline standing over her inert body. Tabitha noticed the other woman's eyes widen as she began to evaporate before Alena's eyes. After a glance at the mirror to ensure that she was not visible, Tabitha headed toward the basement.

She was not sure she wanted to find Luc where she thought Dylan might be keeping him. If he was indeed locked in that chamber with the black elf, Dylan's promise of a simple exchange took on a whole new threat. But if Luc was not there, she would need to search the entire estate. As she made her way toward the basement, the floors slipped by as though she were in an elevator.

She followed some twists and turns along the dark corridors and tried to locate the long hallway and locked double doors. Her energy began to wane as she meandered through the basement. Every footstep she heard sent her heart racing, even though she knew no one could see her. When she spotted the correct hallway, she almost broke into a sweat at the idea of facing that dark creature again.

The doors remained locked. Although it seemed quiet, a guard sat outside the doors. Dylan would not have left Luc unattended, on the off chance that Tabitha found him or Luc was strong enough to escape.

Tabitha slid past the guard through the locked doors. Once inside, she lifted a hand to illuminate the room around her. She could barely drag her eyes from the gray cage in the corner of the room. She could sense more than hear the creature shift when her arrival caught its attention. The glow from her palm was bright enough that she could watch the creature as it floated to the bars; in the midst of the dark robes the white mask glowed eerily. The blank eyeholes faced her direction, and Tabitha shivered despite being nothing more than a ghost herself.

She tore her eyes from the dark creature, and with a cry she noticed a shape lying on a low cot against the wall. She recognized his dark hair, matted against his head. He lay motionless, the shallow rise and fall of his chest the only indication that he lived.

"Oh, Luc..." she sighed as she approached the cot. She tried to reach out to him, to see if any conscious thoughts were close to the surface, but her probe returned, blank.

She longed to heal him. She extended her phantom hands toward him, but no healing energy warmed them. Tabitha hated leaving him, but she knew she could not do much for him until she was in a more solid form than spirit. She glanced back at the dark creature. It stood quietly at the bars, the ebony eye holes eyes staring back at her.

She let herself fall back into her body. Alena was watching her intently when she opened her eyes.

"I found him."

"Is he all right?"

"No, but he is alive. That is all I can guarantee." Tabitha sat up and let the world slip back into alignment around her.

"I assumed he was alive when I saw your hands glow." Alena gestured to Tabitha's now cool fingers.

"They did?"

Alena nodded. "You weren't gone long; is he being kept where you thought he was?"

"Yes, he is in the same room with the black elf, which is in its cage. I can't help but think that Dylan has some evil intent, holding Luc there." Tabitha fought against her increasing panic and rose to find something to drink. She described as best she could the location of the corridor. Alena stood and headed for the door.

"Stay here while I get Tristyn. Let's see if we can get Luc out of there before Dylan comes for you."

Tabitha's mind was heavy with worry over Luc's injuries; she curled up on the bed and let the tears flow.


The morning sun beaming through the balcony doors woke Tabitha. She rolled out of bed with a groan. The night had been long and restless, bouts of crying intermingled with exhausted sleep plagued by nightmares about Luc. A hot shower began to help, but the memory of Luc joining her there after Gwyn's funeral turned the pleasure torturous. She dressed and paced through the suite; no word from Alena, Tristyn, or even Jules arrived.

Had they retrieved the wand from her mother? Was her mother involved in some elaborate plan to free them all? Had anyone rescued Luc? Was he still alive? She glanced at the bed and debated the merits of separating to go check on him. She decided she might need the energy it required later when Dylan sought her out to make the trade.

A serving man she did not recognize delivered her breakfast; he left without a word. She chewed absently on some food and sipped at a steaming cup of javé, waiting for what seemed an eternity for a word from anyone. Time ticked by. She paced, wondering what she could possibly say to Dylan when the time came for the exchange. She had just made up her mind to fly to Colene's house when a knock at the door made her jump from her chair.

She had never before seen the guard who waited for her. He tersely requested that she follow him. She had not done anything that Dylan had demanded, and now she was walking into the enemy's lair without a single weapon at her disposal. She had no idea what would happen when she showed up without the wand.

Her thoughts were interrupted by a commotion on the stairs. She and the guard were pressed to the edge of the staircase as a group of her father's personal guards ran by. She glanced over, but her guard seemed unfazed. He gestured for her to follow him and continued along the corridors and then down the next flight of stairs as more guards raced past them with a sense of urgency.

Obviously something was going on. Tabitha doubted it was in response to Luc's disappearance; her father had not checked in with her again to see if she had heard from Luc. On the next level, there was more agitation, and additional guards ran past, sometimes in pairs.

Any hope that she would not be meeting with Dylan was quickly dashed when the guard proceeded toward the basement. She began to sweat as she followed him through the twisting maze of basement halls. He finally stopped and indicated that she should continue down the last hall toward the locked double doors.

Tabitha felt a stab of dread as she made her way down the familiar hall. The doors opened as she approached. The darkened room awaiting her was like a yawning mouth eager to swallow her. She knew that once she entered that room, she would not leave unscathed.

Footsteps sounded behind her and she turned to see Cole and Lena at the end of the hallway; the guard pointed down the corridor, toward where she waited. Relief flooded through her; she felt a glimmer of hope that maybe they had a plan for how they would all get out of this. She waited for them to join her. Hope began to fade when Cole approached her, confusion evident on his face.

"Tabitha. What is going on here? Why were we brought to the basement?"

"Oh God, Cole, why did he send you?" Tabitha groaned. "I take it you don't have any information about what is happening."

He shook his head. "Haven't spoken to anyone since the funeral," Cole told her. Lena's anguished expression caught Tabitha's attention.

"Lena? Do you know something?" Tabitha demanded.

Lena looked horrified and shook her head before turning away from her.

Cole stared at Tabitha in amazement. "What would she know?"

Tabitha was on the verge of telling him but held her tongue instead. "She will have to answer that question."

Deep suspicions echoed through Tabitha as she turned toward the open doors. This would not end well, of that Tabitha was fairly certain. Dylan obviously had some reason for gathering Luc, Cole, and Lena here.

As Tabitha passed through the doorway, her eyes slowly adjusted to the darkened chamber. She saw Dylan comfortably sprawled in a chair in a dark corner of the room, twisting a silver stick between his fingers as he watched the trio enter. His eyes never left hers as he twisted the wand back and forth in his hands.

"Look familiar?"

Tabitha swallowed and felt her confidence slip another notch. She had lost more negotiation ground; he apparently had a second rod. She had not considered that possibility.

Three guards were positioned near the door. Tabitha's eyes swept over to where the cot rested against the opposite wall, a sheet draped over the body lying on it. She strained to see Luc's features in the shadows, but all she could make out was the draping over his body.

Cole pressed closer to her. "What is he talking about?"

Tabitha shook her head and glanced over at Lena. The girl's eyes were wide with horror as she stared at the black-cloaked creature moving into view within its enclosure as if to watch the unfolding drama.

Dylan continued. "So what I need to know is, who did you give the original controller to? And what did you tell them?"

Tabitha shook her head and opened her mouth, but she had no idea how to talk her way out of this. Luc's injuries complicated any chance they had to escape. Her complete lack of anything remotely close to a plan did not help.

Dylan stood and stepped toward the three of them. He glanced between Tabitha and the cot and shook his head sadly. "I know you don't have it. But I don't know when you got rid of it or who you gave it to. Who knows about this?"

Cole stepped forward, pointing at the gray bars in the corner, his eyes squinting against the gloom. "What is that thing? In there?" His eyes darted between Tabitha and Dylan. "Can you please explain why we are here and what it is that you think that Tabitha has?"

Dylan nodded. "Fair enough. Maybe you can talk some sense into her. Let me enlighten you. First, Tabitha has stolen from me a certain item that I need to keep the weapon at my disposal from claiming the life of her lover. Seeing as she stole it and has not been able to get it back, I see no reason to keep my end of the bargain."

Tabitha shouldered her way past Cole with a snarl on her face. "You know damn well that I have every intention of telling our father what it is you are doing down here. If you kill Luc, he will not be pleased that you are harming his advisors to satisfy your own sense of justice. I will also tell him that Viho was killed by you and I saw it."

Dylan's face flashed his surprise; his brows rose. "How could you have seen that? You do have a tendency to get around, don't you?"

"You know, I think I will leave that little bit of information out. You can just try to figure it out. No matter what you do down here, you will need to release me at some point, and I have every intention of telling our father—"

"Stop!" Dylan roared at her. "He is not 'our father'! He is nothing to you! You didn't even know he existed until a few weeks ago, so why don't you just stop throwing his name around like you are the favored child." His face twisted.

Tabitha stepped back. Rage mottled Dylan's complexion, and his eyes seemed to burn with a deep, intense hatred when he snarled at her. "You think you are so special? You seem to think you are the little princess who shows up without warning expecting to be adored? Just because Antoine favors you, it does not make you anything more than a political pawn, his chance to gain some leverage." He waved an arm toward the immobile figure on the cot. "He is nothing more than a way to get into the North's good graces. Our mother left us behind and took her precious little girl away with her. Now you are back and think that everyone should just bow down to you."

Tabitha glared at him in outrage. "You call being locked up, given to a man as a reward, and beaten being treated like a princess? I am a prisoner. I cannot even walk the halls without a guard following me."

Dylan turned his head, his shoulders tense with fury. "Things were much better before you showed up. I have worked with Antoine for years and gained his respect. Now you show up and are suddenly the answer to all of his prayers. You are nothing. He would not even notice if you went missing along with your lover over there. He is already looking for another likely candidate to try and bring you under control."

"You bastard! Luc should not die because he threatens you!"

Dylan's laugh was caustic. "Threatens? Luc? Hardly. But I would not mind getting you out of the way. I should just send you back to Mother. You are, after all, the favorite, aren't you? She didn't try to get me back, and she abandoned your twin here. But you—oh, she had to sneak her precious baby girl away and hide her in safety."

Cole watched this play out in amazement. "What is wrong with you two?"

"He is acting like a jealous little ass!"

"She is a self-centered princess!" Dylan shouted. "And I am tired of everyone fawning over her!"

"Fawning? I am locked in a room, and my father has hit me…twice!"

"It is what you deserved." Dylan scowled. "You think that because Antoine's blood runs through your veins that you are above everything? Our 'mother'"—he sneered the word as if it were burning his tongue—"took you away to hide you and bring you up like a human! A *human*! What could she have been thinking?"

Realization began to dawn on her that Dylan was not entirely rational. She took a step back. Dylan was unaware that she had pulled back and continued his tirade. She glanced over to find Cole's confused eyes on her. He lifted a shoulder in question, and she shook her head. She didn't know where this was heading either, but she realized that needling Dylan's anger any further would not help any of them.

Dylan finally stopped speaking, wiping angry spittle from his chin as he turned from them, the tension in his body obvious as he stiffly headed toward the cage. Without further explanation, he lifted the latch. The door swung open. The creature did not hesitate before slipping past the bars into the room. It waited, still and deadly.

"Dylan, what are you doing?" Tabitha whispered.

The creature now had Cole's full attention. He stared at the being, horrified, and pushed Lena behind his back. "By the One God, is that what I think it is?"

Dylan was regaining his composure, but his eyes still burned with a deep intensity that scared Tabitha more than any raging tirade could. "Do you know the people they gave me to?" Dylan asked.

Tabitha glanced at Cole in confusion, but Cole's eyes were riveted on the creature. He shook his head in response to Dylan's question; his eyes never left the dark shape.

Dylan released a low snort as he stepped between them and the creature, "Of course you do not. I was given away before you were born. I was the first offering to advance our father's career. He sold his first son to the highest bidder." The creature did not move; Dylan's slow pacing between them continued. "The one who could offer Antoine the biggest career advancement won the prize."

He shook his head slowly and gave Tabitha a sidelong glance. "You, she whisked away to be with her, to raise as her daughter. You have the audacity to complain about Antoine hitting you? You don't know anything about being beaten. Those were love taps compared to what I endured. Love taps! You don't know the half of what being beaten is like."

He stopped pacing, his eyes on the floor. Tabitha held her breath, awaiting his next move. In a sudden motion, he lifted his silver wand toward the creature. It reared back, its movements noiseless and graceful, but fear at the threat of the silver substance was evident in its response. Dylan laughed as the creature reacted. When he lifted the stick again, as though to strike, the creature lifted an arm in defense. The robe sleeve fell away. The once-bony appendage that Tabitha had seen before was now a ghostly white transparent arm, gleaming bone shining within.

"My God, it is becoming more solid," Tabitha gasped.

Cole opened his mouth. Lena hid behind him, her face buried against his back, her shoulders shaking.

Dylan snapped his head around to her. "Becoming?"

Tabitha's heart sank as she realized she had made a grave misstep.

Dylan approached her, waving the creature to the side of him. His voice was a deadly whisper. "Becoming? You saw it before?"

"I... Uh, no... It is just that it is solid, and they are only mist when they come over, so..." Tabitha stammered through dry lips, fear enveloping her.

Dylan stood before her and placed the tip of the silver stick under her chin. He lifted it so her eyes met his. His tone was conversational, even pleasant. "Why don't you tell me everything? It might save lives here tonight."

Tabitha could not tug her eyes free from his. She moved her mouth once or twice, wordlessly. Dylan watched her as she struggled to find words, any words that would salvage this situation.

"Yes?"

Panicked, she trembled and sweat broke out over her skin. The truth eluded her.

"Do you need some prompting?"

"Dylan," she began. "I, umm, came down here. I found it while I was searching for Luc."

"Liar."

"No, I told you, I came down here..."

"And I say you *lie*!" he shouted in her face. "Do you want to know how I know? Because you did not leave an imprint on the door as you did at my suite. Because he—" he stabbed his free hand toward the still form on the cot. "Is still here. You are a healer. Had you been here, you would have healed him!"

He shoved the baton into her chin and pushed her head back. She cried out and stumbled backward. Dylan reached behind Cole for Lena's arm, but Cole shoved him. Dylan lifted a hand. Two of the guards came forward and grabbed Cole, each holding an arm. Cole fought, screaming for them to release him, but the guards twisted his arms painfully behind his back.

Dylan's grip on Lena was gentle as he drew her to him, his mouth twisted in a smile. "Come with me, my sweet."

"Lena!" Cole shouted.

"Dylan! Stop! I will tell you! Just stop! Leave her alone!" Tabitha begged, but the third guard had come up behind her and now pressed her arms to her sides in an iron grip. "Dylan! Leave her alone!"

Dylan glanced between them, mock astonishment on his face. "What do you think I would do with her?"

He wrapped an arm around her and stroked the side of her face with his free hand. Lena shrank back, and Dylan's smile widened. "No, you don't know what they do to little boys in their power. But I am the one with the power now, aren't I? I hold the power, and as my partner there gets stronger, I will be the one with the power. Then no one can ever hurt me. I will be the one who does the hurting, won't I, Lena?"

Cole shouted again, but Dylan appeared to be lost in his own world as he brushed Lena's cheek and then her arm with gentle caresses.

"Lena!" Cole's voice was growing hoarse. "Leave her alone! I am going to kill you!"

Tabitha begged and pleaded, but Dylan ignored them as he continued to murmur, his eyes intent on Lena, his hands gently stroking her. He cupped her chin, and his grip tightened as she tried to pull away, a sob breaking her lips, tears spilling from her terrified eyes. His smile was almost sad as he kissed her lips and murmured against them, his words drowned out by Cole's ragged cries, as his struggles against his captors grew more intense. Dylan seemed unaware.

Dylan's eyes suddenly focused, as though he'd snapped back into himself. He once again turned his smile back toward them. "We are going to miss Lena, aren't we, Cole? A little something we shared and both enjoyed."

Cole fell to his knees. He spat his fury at Dylan, shock and revulsion written in his eyes as he stared at them.

"You didn't know? She never told you?" Dylan asked. "I would have thought she would have mentioned me."

Lena's face crumbled with humiliation; she avoided Cole's eyes.

"Lena," Cole begged.

"I am sorry, so sorry." Her voice was barely a whisper, her eyes avoiding his.

Dylan turned back to Tabitha. "This one is a warning."

With that, he shoved Lena away from him, toward the waiting creature. Lena stumbled and fell to the floor, her sobs louder. She lifted her head in terror, and the creature was suddenly on her. The dark robes engulfed her, and she collapsed to the floor. As Cole howled, the guards pressed him to the floor. Tabitha felt her strength leave her, and she slid to her knees.

# CHAPTER FIFTEEN

As Tabitha knelt, her arms still secured by the guard, Cole's harsh sobs were the only sound. She bowed her head. She could not bear to lift her eyes and see the lifeless body on the floor. She had assumed that Dylan would torment them, but she was unprepared for the level of menace he had reached. She had thought on some level that he was playing the same dangerous game, but he had slipped into a much darker place that she had not been prepared for.

When the creature rose from the lifeless body at its feet, Tabitha lifted her head at the gentle rustle of the robes. Lena lay on her side. Her hair hid her face. Tabitha was relieved to not have to see her lifeless eyes or the final terror on her face. Cole lay on the floor; both guards were still holding him, but his struggles had ceased.

Dylan approached Tabitha. Sobs wracked her body as she knelt on the floor before him. He lifted the silver baton and once again tilted her chin up until their eyes met. "How did you know about the creature?"

She hesitated.

"Luc could be next," Dylan said dispassionately.

"I saw it when you killed Viho. I separated from my body and was searching for an escape." Her whisper was flat.

"You separated?"

She nodded.

"You can do that?"

She nodded.

"Why didn't I see you?"

"I can make myself unseen."

"I don't believe you." His voice was not as confident. He studied her. "A Caskan cannot separate, or even a half-Faye."

She shrugged as much as the guard's grip on her arms would allow. "I know I can do it. I don't know enough about our capabilities to argue with you."

"Show me."

She shook her head. "I am not sure I can. I need to focus and relax, and I am a little tense right now."

"Show me, or your lover is the next victim."

"I can't. I can't! I have to focus!"

"Then he dies now." Dylan spun away from her.

"Dylan! *No!* Please! Let me try!" she begged, but Dylan's pace did not slow.

The silver wand flashed. He pointed at the cot, and the creature moved with a soundless swirl of dark robes. Tabitha shouted again, her voice hoarse, her tears flowing in earnest as the creature moved closer to the cot. Tabitha's vision blurred as she again cried out for Dylan to stop the creature. She tried to focus her abilities on the cot to move it, to stop the creature—anything—but the dark robes advanced on the still form lying beneath the white sheet.

The air in the room whirled up and spun around them as Tabitha threw everything she had against the dark form approaching Luc. Voices were lost in the maelstrom she created. The guard behind her had shielded himself against anything she could throw at him, so she knelt, tears pouring from her eyes, the wind whipping her hair as she howled out her pain.

The creature knelt over the cot; the dark robes seemed to engulf the body lying there. She could make out a bare foot. Luc must have jolted as the dark elf leaned over him. The foot did not move when the robes gently collapsed onto the still form.

Tabitha's head dropped as she sobbed, tears splashing onto the stone floor beneath her knees. Pain ripped through her heart. Her guts felt as though they had been torn out, leaving nothing more than a gaping hole. She threw back her head in a long anguished cry and let the agony of Luc's death tear her apart. She tried over and over to reach out to him through their link, but nothing returned to her except a silent echo.

She was barely aware of being hoisted to her feet or the hands that gripped her arms. The guard held her while Dylan agitatedly strode back and forth. Cole was also dragged to his feet, and the two of them stood side by side, heads low, as Dylan cursed.

When Dylan stopped pacing, Tabitha's soft sniffles were the only sounds before the soft rustle of the dark robes caught their attention. Tabitha gulped back her sobs and lifted teary eyes to the still-present danger of the black elf as it began to rise from the cot. Tabitha's breath caught as the robes slid from a gleaming, fully formed human body, the bright white of the bone structure was still visible through the slightly translucent skin and muscle, like a jellyfish in the murky depths. It shifted its gleaming skull toward Dylan and stood fully erect, the dark eye sockets perusing the room from the depths of the still gauzy skull.

"This is not good," Cole murmured from between dry lips.

Dylan turned to them with an almost gleeful grin and lifted his arm, as though presenting them with a gift. "Beautiful, isn't it? Do you know what this means? Do you have any idea?"

Tabitha tried to jumpstart her brain into action and remember what she had read about the black elves. The Faye had theorized that black elves would solidify and incorporate into their host communities, but based on the gauzy appearance of the creature, she could not fathom how it would ever look and act like a person.

Dylan continued to smirk as he watched his siblings' disbelief. "I can see that neither of you understand what is happening here."

"You mean that you have just had our loved ones murdered?" Tabitha croaked.

"For a greater good! All for a greater good! Their sacrifices will strengthen the weapon meant to align all of our territories into one land! We can dictate the terms and make sure that all Caskan and humans are treated with the distinction that they deserve!" Dylan assured them.

"By whose rules?" Tabitha spat. "Antoine's? Yours? Who decides what is best for everyone?"

"Why, the one with the most powerful weapon, of course," Dylan sneered. Tabitha stepped back, realizing that she was not out of danger. "And your friends have provided all the extra energy needed to reach the level I require to take over."

Tabitha shook her head. Suddenly all emotional energy drained from her, and she felt as though she were ready to collapse. "What else do you need from us, Dylan? You have taken everything."

"I told you at the beginning. I need to know where the other rod has gone and who else knows about the black elf," Dylan reminded her. "I cannot take the final step without knowing who else may be aware of the black elf. Of course, I have to imagine they would not understand the implications, but I do need to ensure that when I harness the power, no one will be able to put shackles on me."

Cole shook his head and glanced over at Tabitha. He spoke softly as Dylan continued his diatribe. "Do you understand what he is talking about? Do you realize what he is planning?"

Tabitha shook her head, her brain still muddled with pain. She was almost beyond the point of caring. "I don't care. I just want to get out of here."

Cole sighed and glanced over at the still forms on the floor. "We can't let their sacrifice be in vain. We cannot let him have that final control. Everyone we know and love will be destroyed when Antoine uses Dylan to bring all of the territories under his heel."

Dylan's attention was captured by a guard entering the room wearing an intense scowl. He approached Dylan and imparted a whispered message. Tabitha wondered if it had something to do with the guards she had seen running through the halls as she was being brought down to the basement. Something else was happening on the estate, and it seemed that Dylan was just learning what it was.

Dylan swore and glared over at the two of them. He stopped in front of Tabitha. "Did you have anything to do with this?"

She stared at him in confusion. "With what?"

"What have you done with the old bastard? Where is our grandfather?"

Both Tabitha and Cole exchanged shocked looks. Tabitha lifted a shoulder and shook her head. Dylan's hand swept back and, with a snap, a backhand slap caught her across the face, forcing her head back against the chest of the guard holding her. The metallic taste of blood filled her mouth, and shards of light swam and spun before her eyes. Dylan's footsteps echoed as he stalked away from her toward the cot. She was unable to comprehend what he was doing.

The muffled shouts in her head began to clear as she recognized Dylan's cries. "No no no no! What have you done?"

When her guard suddenly released her, Tabitha was amazed to see the floor rising to meet her. Her hands stopped her face from smashing into the hard surface at the last moment, the room careened around her as shouts filled the air. With an effort, she turned her head to see Dylan lifting the sheet from the cot, his face filled with rage. He pointed at her, his face contorted. He jammed the gray rod in her direction, and the creature turned its head toward her.

She groaned and struggled to lift herself amid fresh shouting. The guard who had whispered to Dylan opened the door to leave, only to have the door pulled from his hands. Cole suddenly erupted into action. The guards holding him seemed to be dragged back. Tabitha felt herself hefted to her feet by strong arms that then drew her against a solid wall of chest. The familiar scent and the feel of those arms around her snapped her back to reality. A beloved voice cut through her hazy mind.

*Tabitha, hold onto me. I am getting you out of here.*

"Luc?"

She threw her arms around him and clung to him, relief pouring through her as tears streamed down her face. Her eyes began to focus, and she lifted them to see Luc standing over her, his arms locked, holding her up.

*You're not dead.*

"Not yet," he responded with a small chuckle. He began backing toward the door. The room had erupted in a battle scene; Alena seemed to be covering their retreat. As her vision began to clear, Tabitha felt the cold steel of Luc's sword against her side, held at the ready, as he dragged her toward the door. Cole and Tristyn, as well as three or four others she did not recognize, were battling the guards while Dylan shouted orders, his silver rod at the ready. He tugged a pistol from his waistband.

Tabitha cried out. Cole and Dylan were shouting, their words drowned when a shot rang out. The fighting slowed as both sides turned to stare in amazement. Cole looked down at the hole in his upper arm and turned back to Dylan with a snarl.

"Step back!" Dylan roared. He turned toward the creature and, with a last grin at Cole, he began racing toward the creature standing still in the shadows. Cole, apparently knowing what he intended, shouted and ran to intercept him. The silver rod flew in the air as the two crashed to the floor.

"Cole! No!" Tabitha shouted. The truth behind Dylan's intentions suddenly dawned on her. "Luc! We have to stop them!"

Luc hauled her toward the door. "We have to get you out of here while we can! Cole has enough help."

"No, Luc, you don't understand! Dylan is going to—"

Before she could finish her statement, Cole had hefted Dylan off of him. As Dylan slid across the floor, Cole leaped toward the waiting creature. Tabitha let out a howl. Luc's grip tightened to keep her from running back. As if in slow motion, Cole jumped on the creature. The creature wrapped him in an embrace as the two tumbled down to the floor. Cole hit the floor with a sharp thud and lay still. The creature seemed to disappear.

"Oh God, what has happened?" Tabitha murmured against Luc.

The guards fought on, and Tabitha saw Tristyn spin as he shouted to Luc to get her out of the room.

Dylan dove for the silver wand and lifted it as he rose, turning toward where Cole lay on the floor in a still heap.

"What have you done?" Dylan screamed. Tabitha found herself being dragged toward the door.

The fighting resumed in earnest. Tabitha clung to Luc's chest as he thrust his sword with one hand to defend them against an attacker. Alena fought viciously, protecting them as they made their way toward the exit. More guards swarmed into the room, temporarily blocking the door, but more Tristyn's enforcement followed, shoving their way through the ranks to engage in the battle.

*Quickly—we have to get out of here! When I give the word, run for the door!*

Before they could make their escape, Cole slowly began to stand. The fighting began to abate as both sides stopped to stare in amazement as Cole rose. There was no sign of the creature. Tabitha gasped when she saw Cole's bright eyes glow with a silvery light that seemed to spread along his skin down his body, until his whole body shimmered with pale luminosity.

Cole turned his face toward her. Tabitha abruptly realized that the creature had not disappeared but had been absorbed into Cole's body. They were now one, fused, sharing a single host body.

Dylan stood, his hands shaking in rage, as he stared at the new development. He gripped the gray baton, his teeth bared in an angry grimace.

Cole took this in, the bright eyes slowly moving from the silver wand to Dylan and then over to Tabitha. His head moved slowly as he perused the room, resting for a moment on Lena's quiet body and then sliding over to the body on the cot. Tabitha followed his gaze. She could see little more than a bare foot and a hand lying off to the side under the sheet that Dylan had tossed back over the body.

Cole turned his eyes to Tabitha; she felt a shiver under that cold stare. He stepped toward her, but Dylan lifted the wand to stop him. Cole's eyes shifted back to Dylan. "Release her."

"You have no authority over me!" Dylan sneered. "I can still control you."

A slow and humorless smile spread across Cole's face as he lifted a hand, staring down at it in wonder. "For now. I have the power of those I have absorbed. You will only be able to control me for so long. Release them."

Dylan hesitated and stared at him. "What do you mean, 'for now'? I can control you! I have the ability."

"I am no longer just the creature. I now possess the abilities of the others. We will overcome this—and you," Cole assured him. Tabitha was aware of the strange, almost ethereal sound within his voice, as though he were speaking with an echo.

Dylan stared at him, his eyes wide, as he assessed the information.

Luc took advantage of the confusion. Before she could react, he pulled Tabitha through the door and down the hall, leaving the voices shouting behind them.

"Run!" Tristyn's voice cut through the din of the clash of metal and shouts of guards. Enforcements followed them down the hall.

Luc held her hand in his as he raced through the dark corridors, expending every ounce of energy. She sensed he was struggling as they ran. His breath was labored, and he stumbled every couple of steps. Footsteps approached behind them, and Luc detoured down a dark corridor, pressing them against the wall, as the guards passed.

*Are you all right?*

*I don't think I am completely healed. I can't breath.* He listened for sounds of pursuit.

*Let me help you.*

*Not yet. You will have an opportunity shortly.*

She felt the quiet pulse of his thoughts as he listened for sounds of pursuit. He grunted softly and led her out of the corridor and down to the right, deeper into the bowels of the manor. The basement twists and turns became a maze. Tabitha imagined them lost and wandering for days through the chasms beneath her father's estate.

"Do you know where you are going?" she hissed when Luc pressed himself against a darkened corner, his breath ragged as he struggled to continue.

He didn't respond. He struck off again, leading her around curves in the dark hallways, confusing her to the point where she had no idea where they were. Luc led her through another twist in the underbelly of the estate before they slipped into a dark room.

"What are we doing here?"

"Waiting."

"For what?"

Luc slid to the floor, his breathing labored. He put a hand to his chest. "All right, listen to me. We have to get out of here, and our timing has to be perfect. We need to journey out of here and stay one step ahead of them." He peered intently at her.

She stepped back. "What do you mean, stay one step ahead of them? Just what is your intention?"

"To draw Dylan away. We have to let him pursue us. He will throw everything behind catching us. He cannot afford to let you slip away from him. Your father will kill him. And he cannot afford to let me live," Luc explained quietly. "We have to draw him after us."

"And then what? Lead him, and he follows us... And then he, what? Gets bored? Decides it is too much work?"

Luc shook his head. "We lead him to a trap."

Tabitha stared, her eyes wide. "A trap? What trap?"

"The one waiting for him. But we have to lure him."

"But I don't know where we are going."

"I will tell you where to go. You just have to stay with me."

"Let me check you. Who healed you?" Tabitha was not sure she wanted to know the answer. Her mind refused to return to the image of that body on the cot. She was afraid to know who had taken Luc's place.

"I think you know."

She nodded. Tiny pain points once again pricked at her eyes as she slid her hands across Luc's chest, letting the warm healing energy flow. Luc started to protest, but she was already letting her fingers heat as she slid them across his chest. Her fingers slid inside his shirt as her consciousness slipped through him. The healing energy suddenly diverted and headed toward his heart. She released her cognizant hold and let it flow through him. Luc groaned, and she felt a slight tug and then a release over his heart. Something had been sticking into his chest, a tiny sliver between his ribs, resting against his heart. She felt the healing energy slide the obstruction away and out through the tiny pinhole it had made when it slid into him.

She extended a hand, and the sliver passed from him into her palm. Her other hand hovered over his chest; the healing energy knit the artery and muscle punctured when he had fallen from the sky. He released a long sigh. Tabitha allowed the energy to pass over him one last time, repairing anything that might have been missed.

Her hands cooled, and her eyes slowly opened. Luc lifted his head and glanced down at the object she had extracted. He smiled, and his color began to return.

"Feel better?" she asked.

"Yes." He sighed. "I am sorry."

She ducked her head and nodded. After a moment of silence, her voice emerged as a hoarse whisper. "I was wondering why the guards were all running around. They must have noticed he was missing."

"I was unconscious when they got me out of the room. They had already smuggled your grandfather out. They wanted to get us off the premises before coming back for you. When he saw me, your grandfather insisted on healing me. When I came to, he was leaning over me. He was gray, and his fangs were out, but he refused blood. He knew he was dying and asked us to leave him. He knew he could buy us some time if Dylan thought I was still in that room, and he knew he would not survive being removed. He was just too weak."

Tabitha turned her head and let tears slip along her eyelashes and quietly drop onto her folded hands. Luc lifted her chin so their eyes met in the gloomy room. "He saved my life for you."

"I know." Her voice was soft.

"Tabitha, he was too weak. I am sorry."

She shook her head and drew his mouth to hers. "He would be happy to know his sacrifice was not in vain. You lived. I could not have lost you both."

His kiss was quick and passionate. He drew back as she protested, her mouth following his for one more taste of his lips.

*We have to go.*

*Are they away? Tristyn and Alena?* She asked as she rose to her feet.

He shook his head and slid the door open. He peered around the corner. *Not yet. Once we draw Dylan after us, they will get Katie and leave. We need to be the ones Dylan follows.*

She followed Luc when he took off at a trot down through the maze of winding halls. As they approached an exit, the hall began to lighten. Luc threw himself against the door and grabbed her hand. With a silent whoosh, they stepped outside and disappeared.

# CHAPTER SIXTEEN

TABITHA GLANCED AROUND THE PATCH OF GREEN WITHIN a ring of trees. Luc stepped into the clearing with her. His grin was all she needed to see, and with a happy cry, she leaped into his arms.

"Not yet," he said softly against her hair. "We're out of the house, but our exit has set off the alarms. Not only is Dylan scrambling to track you, but your father is aware that you and I have left. We need to sit tight for a couple of minutes before we go."

She slipped out of his grip. "Where to next?"

She let Luc direct her to their next destination. With a deep breath, she stepped forward. Luc appeared next to her a moment later. She sent him a grimace and used their momentary break to stretch her neck and sore back. Luc let his thoughts extend back to check if they were being followed yet. He shook his head.

"We'll give it a couple of minutes and do the same thing. Once they start to track us, they will be moving quickly, so we'll have to pick up the pace. I'd like to remain a couple of jumps in front of them, so let's put a little more distance behind us before they catch up."

She nodded, and he again directed her haphazardly toward the north. With her limited geographic knowledge of the land, she could not say where they were, but she recognized that they were not following a direct path.

After two more leaps, Luc confirmed they were being followed. The triggers he had set at each stop were being tripped.

*Can they sense the triggers?* Tabitha asked as they stopped for a breath. She wiped sweat out of her eyes as she inhaled deeply, trying to slow her heart.

Luc shook his head as he reached out toward their next destination. *No, they dissolve when tripped. They will be gone before they have a chance to check.*

Once again, the scope of his abilities overwhelmed Tabitha. She began to understand why these people trained for years. Not only was mastering the abilities imperative, but the sheer range of things they could do was vast.

Luc nodded. She sighed with fatigue as she extended her thoughts and followed the path he laid out. She was about to step forward when his fingers slipped from her grasp. He began to shimmer.

"Luc!"

"Go! Go!" He began to solidify, and she watched ghost-like shapes seem to materialize around him.

He shoved her, and she quickly stepped toward their next destination. She held her breath for a second, and he was suddenly beside her. Before she could ask what had happened, he was directing her to the next stop and shoving her toward it. She tumbled toward their next step before she could catch her breath. The next two steps were the same. Tabitha was sweating with exertion. Her head pounded, her breath coming in frightened gasps. Luc appeared behind her with every step, but each time he appeared, he looked more wan and disheveled. She tried to cling to his arm, desperate to understand what was happening, but he would direct her mind and send her off so quickly she could do little more than step toward the next site.

After what seemed like an eternity, Luc appeared, his hands resting on bent knees as he tried to draw ragged breathes into his lungs.

"Luc, are you all right? Are they—"

"Yeah, they are right behind us, but we have gained a couple of steps. Now they are trying to keep up. They are not traveling in a pack. This will work to our advantage, as they will arrive in staggered numbers. Ready?"

She started to shake her head, but he was already sending the thought to her and pushing her to make the step. She stumbled as she arrived in yet another moonlit clearing, the cool breeze ruffling back her hair. The moments ticked by. Luc did not appear. Tabitha felt herself tense as the silence of the place engulfed her. Another minute passed, and Luc did not appear. Panic started to take hold.

*Luc?*

She felt his response, but it was vague and strained. She was trying to trace back from the last step to return when another mind was suddenly joined between them. The strength of this mind captured hers in a vice-like grip. Tabitha started to struggle, but the grip tightened, and she could detect the other mind's attempt to reach out to her. Everything Luc and Jules had been teaching her came crashing in as she desperately tried to find something in her limited arsenal to fight the intrusion.

She lifted her shields, capturing the other mind in a small and no doubt ineffective trap of her own. She was not confident that it would gain her freedom, but hopefully it would allow her a few minutes to find an escape route.

*Tabitha. Stop fighting me.*

*Bertòn!*

*Luc has linked me through to you. I am going to pull you to me. Stay focused on me and let me guide you.*

*Where is Luc? Is he all right?*

*He is connected here as well but preoccupied.*

*But...*

*Tabitha, follow me. We can only help Luc if we lead the people he is fighting to us. Let us help him.*

Tabitha nodded and focused on following Bertòn's mental nudge. The traveling was slow but the route was direct; they had to lead their followers north. As she struggled to follow Bertòn's guidance, she detected Luc's remote presence. The guidance from Bertòn was faint. Bertòn informed her as she made her way painfully and slowly along the landscape that he was not as strongly linked because the connection was flowing through Luc as a conduit.

*As long as you and I are connected, we know he is all right*, Bertòn informed her as she groaned through yet another step.

*But where is he?*

*He is behind you, holding them away from you until you can reach us*, Bertòn replied. His thoughts seemed distant, but Tabitha realized he was directing his energy toward leading her instead of responding to her questions.

Her strength was waning. Her concern for Luc seemed to triple with every leap she made that he did not join her. The trip became a blur of stepping, focusing, listening to Bertòn, and stepping. Repeat. There was no time for other thoughts to intrude into the streamlined focus on Bertòn's guidance and then the next steps.

She stepped through yet another guided journey to find herself in a small meadow dotted with large granite boulders and ringed with dense trees. Bertòn had cut off communication; Tabitha stood in the silent field alone, wondering what to do next. She extended a thought to Luc. In response, a large gray wolf leaped into the field out of thin air, as though he had jumped just as he envisioned his journey. He skidded to a stop and whirled to face her, his fur matted, blood coloring his shoulder.

*Luc? Are you all right?*

*Move! Now!* He turned, and Tabitha started to run, following as he loped across the meadow.

*Where are we go—*

A voice bellowed from behind her. "Halt!"

She spun around. Before she could react to the sudden influx of men racing into the meadow, Luc bolted past her, leaping for the throat of a man who lifted a long bow and aimed it at Tabitha. Tabitha screamed in terror when another man suddenly sank into a mountain lion shape and jumped onto Luc, rolling him off the potential shooter.

*Tabitha! To the sky! Now!*

She froze. The meadow continued to flood with men appearing from thin air. Suddenly, a low bellow sounded from the trees, and a volley of arrows flew into the middle of the emerging mass. Tabitha stumbled back, not sure how she had avoided being hit, searching frantically for Luc. Suddenly she was lifted to her feet from behind.

"You must leave now! Head north, just over that knoll. Sybille is waiting there!" Bertòn growled, shoving her behind him. Before she could respond, he dove forward, shifting into wolf shape and racing into the fray, accompanied by a mass of fighters who streamed from the trees behind her.

Tabitha snapped out of her frozen panic and turned to race across the meadow, desperately envisioning D'Noir as she did so, his glossy wings, his sharp eyes, his legs, feet, tail feathers, all deep ebony. With a cry, she threw her arms out and flung herself into crow shape, sweeping her arms down in a sudden, powerful surge. Her wings took hold of the wind, and she thrust herself up into the cool evening air as the meadow dropped away beneath her. She felt air hum beneath her body as an arrow slipped past, where her human back had been only seconds before. She pumped her wings furiously, gaining altitude and banking around the field, watching as the two throngs collided, some in animal shape, most human, long swords flashing in the moonlight. She searched for Luc and found him, still wrestling with the shape shifter who had become the mountain lion. The pair fought fiercely, teeth flashing, claws ripping through fur. Bertòn leaped into the fight and father and son in wolf shape circled the mountain lion, searching for the opportunity to distract him, working as a team to bring down the common enemy.

Tabitha shifted her focus away from the battle, desperate to watch but knowing that she was not yet above arrow range. She flew over the trees and looked north, over the knoll. She circled the clearing, searching for Sybille, seeing a legion of archers reloading their arrows and heading toward the meadow in lines. She spotted Sybille and headed down toward the tiny woman.

Sybille was talking with several men, directing them and their bows toward the southern end of the meadow. She was an impressive figure, wearing a snug vest, dark pants, and dark boots laced about her calves, twin blades strapped to her calves, her bow and quiver hanging down her back. Her tiny stature was superseded by the presence she commanded. She turned as the three men swept away and melted silently into the woods. Tabitha fluttered down, intending to change shape as she landed. She began to glide and place her feet on the earth, but the change as she landed propelled her forward, and she tumbled onto her belly and slid to a stop at Sybille's feet.

Tabitha pulled her face from the dirt and stared at Sybille's boot, which tapped in front of her. "I need to work on that."

Sybille chuckled and leaned down to assist her to her feet. "I would say so."

The small woman wiped the dirt off of Tabitha's cheeks, a warm smile on her lips as she cupped Tabitha's face. "I see you've learned to fly."

Tabitha felt her throat close at the woman's welcoming grin, and tears slid down her cheeks, fear and exhaustion finally exacting their toll. She nodded as she tried to hiccup back a sob.

Sybille smiled and wrapped her arms around her. "I missed you too. I have been so worried about you!"

Tabitha let the tears flood as she hung onto the little woman. Sybille let her cry and tugged her toward a large stone and gently lowered her on it. Tabitha gulped in air as she swallowed her tears. Sybille handed her a crock and Tabitha tugged the cork free and swallowed the cool water in grateful gulps. She used some of the water to wipe the dirt from her cheeks.

"Is Luc okay?" Tabitha asked.

Sybille glanced up and shrugged. "I haven't heard. They are fighting hard, but we have more people, and the archers will continue tormenting them."

"And what now? Did Tristyn and Alena get out?"

"You and Luc drew Dylan and his home guard away from the house. They followed you and left a small force back there. The plan was for Tristyn and Alena to get away with Katie and the other emissaries from St. Mikel before anyone realized they were missing."

"Did it work? Did they get away?"

Sybille inhaled deeply. "We know they got them out of the house, but we don't know where they are or how far they have traveled. Luc is the only one linked to Tristyn."

It looked like it would be a long night. She would not be able to rest until she knew Tristyn, Alena, and Katie were safe. Sybille led her toward a small knot of people waiting around a table in a small clearing set back from the battle. Peri stepped forward, a bow across her shoulder and two slim rapiers strapped to her thighs.

"Tabitha, thank the One God you have made it out safely. Did they follow you? Have Tristyn and Alena escaped?"

Tabitha shook her head. "I asked the same questions of Sybille. Luc was with me but we were so focused on our own journey that we didn't have time to check in with Tristyn."

Sybille glanced toward Peri. "Will you take Tabitha back to our camp? It's best that she remains safe until the fighting is over."

Tabitha shook her head. "Please, Sybille, I don't want to leave. I need to know Luc is all right. And he is the only way I will know if Katie is safe. I can't go now, I will go crazy."

Sybille smiled. "I understand. Our camp is only a short journey from here. Peri will guide you so that no one can follow you. We cannot let this battle be in vain if you are captured. Let Peri take you with her, so I will be able to tell Bertòn that you are safely away and guarded. Luc will want to know that."

Tabitha began to argue. "I don't want to be kept guarded and safe. I need to know that—"

Peri interrupted. "Tabitha, you are too valuable to be left within striking distance of the enemy. I am sorry. I know you wish to remain here, but those fighting will be more effective when you leave." Peri was already picking up a satchel and turning to go.

Tabitha made a face at Sybille, but her irritation dissipated when the tiny woman laughed. She turned to follow Peri but glanced over her shoulder. "I'll go. Please tell Luc to let me know he is okay"

"Diego is back at the camp. He can help us find out if anyone has heard from Tristyn. We will keep you well updated, I assure you." Peri told her.

Tabitha nodded and, with a sense of profound fatigue, stood to journey one more time. Peri smiled at her and took her hands. "Just relax, I will take you. I can feel your exhaustion. Just step with me."

With that, Peri stepped, and Tabitha lifted her feet to follow. The surroundings immediately shifted. Tabitha found herself in the midst of a large camp of round temporary structures set up in concentric circles around a main circular gathering area. As soon as she and Peri stepped into the clearing, a group of people who had been congregating around a large bonfire quickly raced toward them with questions and inquiries about loved ones. Tabitha felt herself tense and she clutched Peri in fear as the crowd around began to swell, closing in on her.

"Stop! They are fighting now!" Peri called above the din, pressing the surging people away from Tabitha. "*Step back! Give her room! She is exhausted! Let her be!* All of your questions will be answered, but she cannot answer to every one of you individually."

Peri shoved people away from Tabitha as the crowd continued to press forward, concern evident in their faces. The pulsating emotions of stress and tension threatened to engulf Tabitha.

"Cease this!" The voice was deep and commanding, and the crowd began to ease back. Marcus strode forward; people parted as he approached. "Word will be given to you all as we determine what is happening."

The crowd sullenly stepped away, melting back toward the central area, their murmured voices echoing the fear that emanated from them.

Marcus bowed his head to Tabitha. "Welcome. I apologize. People are concerned. We have limited their ability to reach out to loved ones. You see, it could be a deadly distraction during battle. Not to mention that the amount of energy pouring toward that one spot could pinpoint where our people have set their trap."

Tabitha nodded. For a people accustomed to being able to reach out to a loved one at any moment, having to curb that communication during a battle must be painful.

"Come. Let's find you someplace to rest and something to eat. You can fill me in about what you know. We are all anxious for news."

Tabitha followed Marcus toward a large rounded tent. She noticed posts in the ground leading to a wooden ring that supported a rounded roof. The cloth covering the frame seemed to shimmer with reflective colors. As a breeze ruffled the canvas, she saw the colors shift to reflect the scenery behind it. The top captured the deep blues of the twilight sky, and the sides shifted from the deep green of the woods behind it to the dark shades of the approaching evening. She stared in amazement as the canvas settled; the earth tones she had originally seen shifted to reflect the greenery behind it. There did not seem to be any magic associated with the color change. The fabric itself was almost a glimmer that captured and reflected the colors in the clearing.

Marcus stopped as a younger Caskan man approached. His expression was shy and he glanced at Tabitha with a tremulous smile. Tabitha tried to remember the face. Peri leaned in as Marcus spoke to the young man. "That is Luc's cousin, Tye. Tristyn's younger brother."

Tabitha smiled her thanks to Peri. She took the opportunity to again study the camp. It was a large site. Maybe thirty or perhaps forty tents were set up in circles around the main seating area. Some were larger, but most were small and set at the farthest points. As she took in the details of the encampment, she noticed that people were standing in small knots and groups, watching her curiously, their heads close in whispered discussions as she followed Peri toward the main tent. Her curiosity dried up in a wash of self-consciousness, and she dropped her eyes, wondering what these people thought about their families and loved ones doing battle in the glade not far away. As they fought, she stood in complete safety, having drawn the enemy to them.

Peri slid back the iridescent fabric, and Tabitha noted the myriad colors as the tent fabric took on the colors of the background. Her eyes quickly adjusted to the dim interior. A large fire crackled in the center. Otherwise, the tent was empty of people. Peri led her across to the far wall.

"I will get you something to eat and a change of clothes. I imagine you would like to freshen up before you speak to Marcus."

Tabitha nodded. "I would, but when I know Luc is safe."

"We are all worried. Let's get you fed and cleaned up. We will all know soon enough that they are well."

Peri led her through a back flap and around a corner to a small rounded tent tucked beneath a tall pine tree. Tabitha slid in past Peri after she opened the flap, barely noticing the warm and cozy interior. Peri left her with a final comment. "Come back to the main tent when you have cleaned up and rested. I will have some dinner warmed for you. We should know something by then. I will send word if we hear something before you join us."

Tabitha sank onto a pallet of warm, soft blankets. She glanced down at the temporary bed. For a moment, she wished she could crawl deep beneath the soft covers and sleep away the night and wake to find Luc curled safely beside her.

She sighed heavily and tried to catch her breath after the insanity of the past day. A single tear slid down her cheek, and she brushed it away in frustration. She had cried more in the past month than she had in her entire life. She slowly rose from the makeshift bed and stretched her neck and shoulders. With a resigned sigh, she wandered over to the curtain and tugged it back to reveal a tall tub of steaming water lit by a number of candles placed on nearby tall stools. A change of clean clothes and a fluffy towel hung from a tall rack standing by the tub.

As she began stripping out of her clothes, she noticed the blood on her shirt and the dark smudges of dirt across her pants. Her hands shook with fatigue as she slid the torn and dirty clothes from her body and climbed into the deep tub. It was not overly large, but the water was steaming hot. She let it slide over her and wash the smells of blood and dirt from her skin. Fear and worry bit at her belly as she scrubbed her skin and washed her hair, wishing she could rinse away the anxiety along with the dirt that had clung to her. She ducked her head one last time, rose from the steaming water, and grabbed the towel. She dried off and dragged free the clothes waiting for her on the hook. As she tugged the pants over her slim hips, she suddenly noticed a second set of clothes hanging on a hook behind hers. Men's clothes: a light soft shirt and dark trousers. She stopped dressing and lifted her fingers to the soft fabric of the shirt.

Luc. They had left clothes here for Luc as well.

She finished dressing and emerged from behind the curtain. The tent was round but not a perfect circle, made up of a number of flat panels of the same iridescent fabric. The interior was dark in the candlelight, but the fabric picked up the light and shifted to match the candles' warm glow. A snug pallet of warm blankets dominated the interior; the only other trappings in the place were the curtain to the bathing chamber and a small round table with two foldable wood stools tucked beneath it. Another hanging rack was tucked into the shadows beside the bathing chamber. She stepped closer and noticed an assortment of men and ladies' clothes hanging from it. Two pairs of soft boots, one for a smaller narrow woman's foot and the other made for a man's foot, were tucked beneath the rack.

She slid her fingers along the soft blankets of the bed and with a small smile realized that the tent had been set up for her and Luc. She felt her cheeks warm; she wondered how much his family knew of their relationship. For a wild moment, she imagined Luc arriving safely, the battle over, the two of them lying here together. The thought should have brought a warm smile to her face, but instead she felt melancholy overwhelm her. She sank onto the bed. How would she find the strength to leave him?

Her musings were interrupted by a soft voice outside the tent. A woman spoke to someone close by. Tabitha was startled to hear an answering voice from just outside the flap. She stood and opened the flap to find Tye standing outside the door, his back to the entrance of her tent. He turned as she emerged and Tabitha saw Peri approaching.

"They are on their way back. Come to the main tent with me, and we will hear what has happened."

# CHAPTER SEVENTEEN

TABITHA AND PERI TURNED TOWARD THE MAIN TENT. Tabitha was surprised when Tye fell into step behind her. She glanced back, and the younger man smiled at her, a slight blush tingeing his cheeks as he dropped his eyes from her gaze.

Peri glanced over, her sure and long strides eating the distance to the gathering area. She followed Tabitha's glance and nodded slightly. "He has been assigned to watch over you until Luc returns."

Tabitha felt her jaw tense. "After everything I have been through, it is hard to believe I need someone to 'watch over me'."

Peri shrugged and held the back entrance flap of the main tent for her. "You are much too valuable for us to not assign someone to watch you. In fact, it is only because Diego has had to join Sybille and bring back the wounded that it is Tye, not someone better trained."

Tye murmured a quiet comment to his sister-in-law in a language that Tabitha could not understand. Peri remained unruffled as she responded to him. "Then act like a man instead of a child. You know why your father did that."

He sniffed in disgust, but Peri shrugged at his disdain. "Take it up with him if you have a problem."

Tabitha wondered for a brief moment what they were arguing about, but the gathering crowd quickly banished any thought beside the status of the battle. She followed Peri through the crowd to where Marcus stood in the center of the tent. People reached out to touch her with brief and gentle caresses as she passed. She felt a chill pass through her body and pushed closer to Peri. The mass seemed to be closing in on her, their fingers reaching out with feather-like touches as she made her way through the crowd. She could detect the thoughts reaching out to her; amazement, awe, and a little fear swept over her from the people around her.

"Peri," she croaked when the crowd seemed to press on her, cutting her off from the one person she knew.

A deep bark parted the crowd from her. Tabitha felt her arm dragged forward as Peri snapped at the people pressing in on Tabitha.

"Stay close to me," Peri growled as she pushed her way through the growing throng. "Marcus!"

"People! Clear!" Marcus's deep gruff voice broke over the crowd. The mass began to melt away from her, and Tabitha found herself in a protective circle close behind Marcus, with Peri standing at her side and Tye close by the other side. Marcus turned to her. "Tabitha, sit yourself and remain nearby."

Tye tugged Tabitha to a spot behind where Marcus stood and nodded toward the floor. Pillows and blankets had been scattered in a semicircle around the huge fire. Tabitha lowered herself to the ground, tense and unsure of what was happening as the din of voices rose around her.

"What happened? Why was everyone crowding me?" Tabitha whispered.

Tye glanced back at the crowd of people as he lowered himself to one knee beside her. "Word has traveled fast about you being a healer. They are mystified and in awe. Everyone wants time with you. They are fascinated to see a healer." He smiled gently; his dark eyes warm as he leaned close. "You are the first any of us has ever met."

She swallowed and sank back onto a pillow. "How did they find out?"

He shrugged and leaned down to respond. She felt the warmth of his breath on her neck, and a shiver ran down her spine. "I am not sure. Only our family knew, and Marcus swore us all to secrecy. I do not know how people found out, but word traveled fast." He rested a hand on her shoulder, his mouth still uncomfortably close to her ear when he whispered, "Don't worry. I will hold them back from you."

Tabitha gently shrugged his hand off, uncomfortable about his proximity. "What of the others? The battle?"

"They are coming back now. We have suffered losses, and there are wounded. The others have either escaped or been killed."

"And Luc?"

Tye smiled wryly. "He is well, as is Bertòn."

"I can help with the wounded," Tabitha offered, anxious to be of assistance.

"Sit tight. Marcus will be addressing the group shortly. We can assess the need then." Tye advised.

Tabitha shifted her weight, uneasy with the growing crowd. She wished more than once that Marcus would get on with it already. Tye stayed close beside her, resting on one knee, his presence seeming to press on her. She leaned slightly away, trying to put some distance between herself and Luc's cousin. She scanned the crowd tentatively and saw the anxiety written on the faces as news spread of injuries and the battle-weary fighters returning. A young woman, attractive and intense, approached. She felt Tye tense.

Tabitha struggled to recognize her and suddenly recalled the young woman; she was introduced to her when she'd first arrived. *Mia. Tye's promised?* She remembered the young woman had dangled a charm at Luc, presenting herself as being promised. With a start, the pieces of her strange greeting fell together. A young man and woman exchanged tokens in a ceremony in which they promised to wed. Of course, Mia had been wearing Tye's token.

"Tye, what are you doing? Come sit with me," Mia demanded, assessing his close proximity beside Tabitha.

"Mia, I cannot. My father has asked that I stay with Tabitha until Luc returns," Tye stammered, his hands held out at his sides in a gesture of supplication.

"Well, that is hardly necessary in a roomful of people. I would guess that with Marcus just in front of her and Peri all but hanging on her, you are not also required. I need to get an update on my brother, and I want you with me." Mia's tone was resentful, the glance she sent Tabitha hardly warm.

"No, Mia. I am already in trouble with my father for listening to you last night. I need to stay with her." Tye's voice quavered, and Tabitha felt a pang over his discomfort.

Mia shook her head as she spun on her heel. "Come to me when you are done babysitting."

Before Tye could respond, she had melted into the throng of people gathering in the main tent.

"Tye, she's right. You don't have to stay here with me," Tabitha offered.

"Yes. I do," Tye retorted. "She will be fine. She can wait."

Tabitha started to answer, but commotion at the front of the tent quickly seized her attention. She stood as the front flap swept open and Luc and Bertòn swept in. Luc's clothes were torn; blood and dirt were intermingled on his skin. A long welt down his face was painfully red, and where his shirt was torn she saw another wound on his chest. Bertòn, his expression dire as he strode toward Marcus, had fared little better. Tabitha rose, but Tye gripped her shoulders. The room erupted into a myriad of voices and questions as more fighters strode into the tent.

Diego pushed his way through the crowd, shoving people aside as he hurried to reach Luc. Luc's eyes caught Tabitha's, but he turned as his cousin shouted his name. Luc turned to walk back toward Diego, and Bertòn snapped at the two men. Luc snarled a response. Marcus shoved his brawny frame toward the men. Suddenly Tabitha realized that Tye was restraining her from interfering in some argument between Luc and his father. Tabitha wriggled out of Tye's grip and tried to wind her way through the crowd to Luc.

As she approached, the heated voices grew louder. The group immediately following the men quieted as an angry volley of words shot between Luc and his father.

"Please explain to me what the issue is before you kill one another!" Marcus shouted over their voices.

Luc and Bertòn were locked in a heated debate. Diego answered. "Father, we cannot locate Tristyn, neither Luc nor I, and Luc tells us that Dylan was not among the fighters."

Tabitha gasped; her attempts at fighting her way through the crowd became more urgent. "Luc! Dylan was not with them?"

Luc turned to her as she made her way to his side, his jaw tightly clenched in anger and frustration. "No, dammit! Dylan was not among them. He would never have sent others to find you. Never." He turned to face Marcus. "Unless something more substantial had his attention."

Marcus's gaze switched from Luc to Bertòn. "And what would be more important than apprehending Tabitha? What could he have gone after that would placate Antoine more than locating his most recent treasure?"

Tabitha felt her face redden at the comment, but her embarrassment quickly evaporated. "Katie?" The color drained from her face

Luc nodded. "He would have pursued them because he knew you would go back for them. Choosing you, he would have lost the others, but he knows you will return for them."

Bertòn shook his head. "We don't know that. We have been unable to contact Tristyn. The rest is conjecture only."

"He would have followed us." Luc growled in frustration. "How could this have happened?"

"We don't know it happened yet!" Bertòn argued.

"It had to have! Tristyn would not have stopped communicating unless he was unable!" Luc swore.

Tabitha shook her head in confusion. "But how? Between the time we left and the time they followed us?"

"If he has Tristyn and Alena, possibly Katie, he has power to negotiate," Diego spat.

"We don't know that!" Bertòn grabbed at his son's shoulders, drawing a wince of pain from him. "We will find out what happened, but we cannot act on suspicions."

"They could be dead before we know what happened!" Luc's expression was fierce as he faced his elder. "There is more."

"What?" Marcus demanded.

Before Luc could comment, Bertòn interrupted. "No, Luc, this is not the time."

"Like hell it isn't!" Luc snapped at his father. "They need to know what we are fighting!"

Bertòn shook his head. "Marcus, this discussion must be held in private."

Marcus held up a hand and turned to Luc and Bertòn. "You two, eat and wash before you join us. I want you both clean, calm, and fed."

"But—" Luc began before Marcus turned and, with a single finger in the air, stopped him.

"Do as I say. I want you both fed and calm. You do me little good in a rage. We will have enough information to decide our next step." Marcus turned to gather his team and stopped to cast a commanding eye at Bertòn. "Both of you."

Bertòn's eyes held his brother's for a moment before he looked down with a nod of acquiescence. Marcus nodded and indicated Diego, Tye, Peri, and the other assorted members who had gathered at the center of the tent to follow him.

Tabitha glanced from father to son and saw the same stubborn and angry cast to their jaws as they each lifted a single fist and bumped wrists before separating.

*What was that?* Tabitha asked.

Luc turned and glanced sharply at her, anger still etched in his face. *What?*

*The wrist-bumping thing—what was that?*

He turned to face his father's retreating back and looked back at her with a grunt. His thoughts were obviously elsewhere. *It is a form of acquiescence. We have our arguments, but when someone can blow the top off a tree in a fit of temper, we must learn to recognize when we are losing control. The touching of wrists, a very vulnerable part of the body, is an agreement to disagree and walk away until such time that we can address the issue.* He glanced back at her. *Where can I wash?*

*Follow me.* She led him toward the tent that had been set aside for them. *I will find Sybille and assist with the wounded.*

He shook his head as he shoved the curtain aside and strode into the circular tent, his rage barely in check. *No, not yet.*

*Dammit, Luc! These people fought for me. They know I am a healer. I have to go and see if I can be of some use! Stop trying to protect me!* She stopped, hands on hips, furious at being coddled. She had gone from independent and self-sufficient to a place where she was constantly being hidden away and protected. How had this happened? *I can make my own decisions.*

As Luc was stripping off his shirt, he glanced at the tub of clean water. She felt the pulse of energy he sent to heat it.

His response was curt and abrupt. *You can make your own decisions when you have all the facts! And what do you mean, they know you are a healer?*

*Well, whose fault is that? You seemed determined to keep me ignorant back at my father's house, not trusting me with more than minute details! And now you criticize me for not having all the facts?* She felt her anger drain as she watched him tug off his boots and pants, kicking the soiled clothes from him. She turned away, not wanting the sight of him to again make her lose concentration. She pursed her lips in an effort to regain the thread of discussion and caught sight of his reflection in a tall mirror as he lowered himself into the steaming water, his shoulders and chest glistening in the candlelight. He sat back and rested his head against the rim of the tall tub.

*We did that for your protection. We needed you to be able to react as you did, impulsively and angry,* he commented. He then spoke out loud, his voice taking on a more tired edge. "How do they know you are a healer?"

"Oh, right," she stammered, half amused and half angry at herself for allowing her thoughts to veer so easily from their argument as soon as he took off his shirt.

He opened one eye and studied her. "Did you forget the question again?"

"Well, I would not have if you would stop stripping off your damn clothes every time we have an argument!" she growled, exasperated.

Her anger dissipated when he let out a low chuckle, the first she had heard in a while. She was relieved to know he was losing his anger. "I will remember that: when we fight, I will just take off my clothes. Fight over. I win."

She tugged the curtain back and slid it behind a hook and then sat on the bed; a sad smile curved her lips. "Well, in that case, I will continue to pick fights with you."

He opened both his eyes and faced her. His face mirrored her sorrow. For a moment, he played the game with her, the game where they pretended that she would not be leaving. "I look forward to it."

She tilted her head. "Tye told me that people know I am a healer. When I arrived, they were pressing at me, trying to touch me. I could feel them reaching for me. He told me that Marcus had kept it a secret among the family, but somehow it slipped out."

He grunted in response and slipped under the water, rinsing his hair and face. He came up and shook his hair from his face, wiping at his eyes.

"My father tells me that the injuries are not bad. We had two deaths; the rest will all recover."

"I could help with those," she insisted.

"Tabitha, can you use some patience? I want to find out what our plan is this night. If we can determine what is happening with Tristyn, Alena, and Katie and the wounded are brought safely to camp, I will help you. But I don't want either of us to be weakened should we need to move quickly."

She nodded, agreeing with his logic even though she bristled at being held at bay. With a sigh, she let herself lie back on the bed and try to relax. Katie was still out there, along with Tristyn and Alena. From what she had been able to gather, the other envoys sent to Windrift with Luc had been among the others fighting for her release. She could not guess how many of them were missing as well.

And, of course, there was Cole. She had not even taken the time to stop and consider what had happened to him. Her twin, and now he was some kind of a monster. It had been his voice she had heard coming from his body, but she understood that the creature now also inhabited his body. What that meant for Cole and his future, she had no idea. She could not drive herself insane by imaging the worst.

As fatigue tugged her deeper into the bed, she watched Luc rise from the tub, wrapping a towel around his lean hips. She admired the long, muscular body, and a slight smile curved her lips.

Luc dried off and slid into the clothes waiting for him. He was tugging on the soft boots when he noticed that Tabitha had quietly drifted off to sleep. He stopped and stared, his eyes trying to memorize every feature, from her tousled mane of hair to the dark lashes gently resting on her delicate cheekbones. Her lips were curled in a soft smile in her sleep, and he wondered when the last time he had seen her so relaxed had been. The weeks of stress had taken their toll on both of them. He slid the blanket up over her slender torso and resisted the urge to crawl into bed next to her. His own body screamed for rest.

With a resigned sigh, he turned from her and shoved the flap of the tent aside. He stepped out into the cool night air. Tye stood outside their tent, still watching over Tabitha. Luc felt a stab of annoyance but let it go.

Tye nodded when Luc clapped his shoulder. With a last resigned glance at the closed tent flap, Luc left his cousin on guard and headed over to the main tent to find some food and be updated on what Marcus had found out.

Two hours later, Luc sat cross-legged in front of the fire within the circle of Marcus's advisors. Four pairs of scouts had been dispatched in assorted animal shapes to locate the still-silent Tristyn and his team. Luc had picked at the dinner that Sybille had put in front of him. As the hours passed, even his usually stoic father began to shows signs of fatigue and worry. Sybille had retired, and Peri paced the tent, checking in with those sharing links with the scout teams and placing markers on an enlarged area map that floated in the air.

Marcus approached. Luc could detect the concern emanating from his uncle. He sighed, anticipating the impending discussion.

Marcus slowly sat next to his nephew. "You do not wish to heed my advice, I take it?" Marcus's rumbling, deep voice held a hint of amusement.

"I won't be able to sleep until I know if Tristyn and Alena are safe," Luc acknowledged.

"I know. My fear eats at me as well, but whether the news is the best or the worst, we must all be rested and strong to deal with whatever is coming our way. Should they be safely away and simply hiding, they will need us to be ready to receive and help them and then cover them as we all retreat north. If the news is that they are not safe, we must all be at our peak. As you are well aware, regardless of what our scouts find, Antoine and I are at war," Marcus said quietly. "The news you have shared is grave. I am not sure what to make of this information. I don't know what it means that Tabitha's brother has apparently assumed the creature within himself. You tell me they share his body. What does that mean?"

Luc shrugged. "We can ask Tabitha more when she wakes. She has been studying the Faye writings about the black elves. She knows as much as anyone at this time."

Marcus quietly snorted, amused. "This young half-Faye brought up in the human world seems to be setting our world askew."

Luc glanced at his uncle. "She can read the Faye scrolls. She understands the writing on them. What does that mean? Is it possible that Antoine is also Faye?"

"I don't know. It is possible, I suppose."

"You and Antoine are not at war; St. Mikel is at war with Chandolyn. We have dragged our entire state into this with us."

"And they have followed willingly. You know the truth of our people. You traveled with your fellow envoys. They wish peace but not at the price the governor of Chandolyn demands. The humans are our people as well. We cannot help the Plains tribes unless we know the truth about the trap that Antoine has laid." Marcus's words carried the sadness he felt about the impending civil war tearing the country apart.

"Did the other envoys get away? Do you know if they are safe?" Luc asked. His guilt at leaving his fellow St. Mikel companions in danger had weighed heavily on him.

"I have received word that one, Etienne, has escaped and is even now hiding at your Uncle Rhys's home. The other two were part of the team assisting Tristyn and Alena. As you are well aware, we have not yet heard word about their progress."

As Bertòn approached, Marcus nodded to him to join them. "I was just updating your son on what we know of his fellow envoys, as well as encouraging him to get some rest."

Bertòn gently rubbed his son's stiff shoulders. "Marcus has shared word that Rhys and Daniel are even now hiding Etienne."

Luc smiled at his father. "Yeah, he told me. She shall be well cared for in that household. I wish I had time to get to them. I miss them. They know what is at stake?"

"They do, and even though they live under the governance of Antoine, they will fight with us. I am not sure how long they will be safe there. I hope that Rhys gets out while it is still safe enough." His father responded.

"We can assist them," Marcus commented. "As well as any other human or Caskan who wishes to come forward and help."

Luc rubbed at his burning eyes. Bertòn leaned toward his son. "It is time you went to your bed. Get some rest. I promise you that we will wake you if any word comes."

"You are right. I need to regain my strength." Luc sighed, fatigue washing over him.

"You lost a lot of blood." Bertòn lifted a finger to the angry red welt running down Luc's face. "A few new injuries also sprouted during the battle, eh?"

Luc smiled, moving his face back from his father's touch; the sting of the long cut was still fresh. "Well, luckily, I have a healer at my disposal."

"Yes. Awaiting you in your bed, as a matter of fact." Bertòn's lifted a suggestive brow at his son and leaned back, wondering if Luc wanted to broach the subject.

"How is it that people found out she is a healer?" Luc stood, stretching his tired shoulders. His father and Marcus also rose.

Bertòn snorted and lowered his voice, waiting for Marcus to wander out of earshot. "Nothing is definitive, but I suspect your cousin's intended let the word out."

"Mia?" Luc's voice carried a note of disgust. "Why would she do that?"

Bertòn shrugged, turning his son toward the back flap and the tent he shared with Tabitha. "You and she were lovers, after all. She did not take it kindly when you returned to school rather than stay and promise to her. Common belief is that she has promised to Tye to get back at you."

"Get back at me? She knew I had no intention of promising her. I could not have dealt with her constant demands for attention. She knew that. Why would she think it would get back at me?" Luc seemed genuinely perplexed.

Bertòn laughed softly at his son's naïve response. "You expect me to be able to explain the mind of a woman?"

"Why Tye?"

"Because Tye worships you. He always has. He would have been an easy target; he would want to be like you," Bertòn pointed out.

"Including going after a former lover?"

"If it meant he would emulate you? And of course, Tye was quite taken to get the attention of such a sought-after woman," Bertòn commented.

Luc shook his head. "What a mess."

"And being almost part of the family, Tye would have shared with her what he knew about Tabitha. She would not have cared about Marcus's command if it meant the opportunity to be able to share gossip about your woman." Bertòn sighed. "Jealousy is an ugly thing."

"What would she have gained?"

"Who knows? Attention? It is what she craves." Bertòn slipped the flap open and the two stepped out into the night air.

Luc felt a slight chill; the late summer was starting to wane. The evenings were cooler. Exhaustion stripped his body of strength, and the cool air seeped into his bones. His father gently pushed Luc toward his tent as Bertòn turned to make his way to his sleeping wife.

"Get some rest. Worry is useless until we know more. Peri has promised to wake us both if there is any news."

Luc nodded and waved farewell to his father. Luc started when Tye's dark shape separated from the darkness.

"Sorry, Luc. Did not mean to surprise you."

Luc grunted, "Get some rest."

Before Tye turned to take his leave, his strained voice whispered from the dark. "Is there any news of Tristyn?"

"No, not yet, but we have searchers out, and they are linked to people here in camp. Peri is staying on it. She will wake us if there is news." Luc slipped through the tent flap with a mumbled "Good night" to his cousin.

Only a single candle remained lit. Luc saw Tabitha's long, dark hair spilling over her shoulder as she slept. He quickly brushed his teeth and slipped his clothes off. Blow-ing out the candle, he slid beneath the warm covers and took her into his arms.

Tabitha moved and turned to him, her voice husky with sleep. "Any word?"

Luc shook his head and buried his face in her dark mane. He inhaled the pleasant smell deeply, recognizing Sybille's shampoo. "Not yet. They will wake us if there is word."

She rolled over onto her back, and he propped his head up on one elbow, gazing down at her face, barely illuminated by the moonlight that penetrated the fabric of the tent.

"How long have I slept?" she murmured.

He shrugged. "A couple of hours."

She sighed. "And we still don't know anything? Where could they be?"

"Hiding, captured, or en route but keeping low. Tristyn may not trust someone who is along with them. It is possible he does not want someone to be aware of a link," Luc commented, trying to maintain his calm as he soothed her.

She grunted. "I should go see if I can help."

He shook his head and tightened his arms around her. "There is a whole host of people out there working on finding them. Just let them do what they do. Get some rest. A couple hours of sleep is not enough." He lowered his mouth to hers. As his lips gently brushed hers, he whispered, "Stay with me."

Tabitha's lips curved into a smile against his. "Well... when you put it that way..."

# CHAPTER EIGHTEEN

SUNLIGHT FILTERED THROUGH THE COLOR-SHIFTING tent in a yellow haze. Tabitha stretched and reached for Luc, only to find the other side of the bed empty. She sat up in disbelief and stared at the empty side of the bed, letting the soft blanket slide down to her waist.

She tugged the blanket up to hide her nakedness before huffing in irritation. "Seriously? Again? He left me again?"

Realizing that covering herself in the empty tent was futile, she threw the covers off and stomped into the bathing area, grumbling over finding herself once again alone in the morning.

*You had damn well better be missing this time,* she shot out to Luc. She directed an irritated thought toward heating the bath water. Misjudging her irritation, the water began to hiss and bubble like a theatric cauldron, and Tabitha swore again.

*Well, good morning... Will you be joining me for breakfast, or shall I send in a small animal for you to sacrifice?* Luc's warm voice sounded amused.

Tabitha concentrated on adding spring water that was magically pumped up from underground to douse the molten lava that was to be her bath. The water settled. She chose to ignore his sarcasm.

*You could have woken me instead of sneaking off. I am starting to get a complex about sleeping with you.*

She heard his faint chuckle. *Sleep? I don't recall getting a whole lot of sleep. I wanted to let you rest.*

*Don't try to charm your way out of this,* she growled, but a pleasant glow ran through her body. *You did it again... Stop putting me off focus. Do we have any news?*

*Yes. Get dressed and join me.*

Tabitha dressed and left their tent. She almost bumped into Tye as she emerged. "Oh, sorry. I did not expect you to be here."

"Well, when Luc is not with you, someone should be watching over you," he commented as he fell in step beside her.

Tabitha let the comment go but felt a familiar flash of irritation at being watched over. She tugged her damp hair up into a knot behind her head as she hurried toward the main tent. She entered through the back flap, ignoring Tye's offer to pull the flap back, and stepped in. It took a moment for her eyes to adjust to the dark interior.

"Good morning," Bertòn said, behind her.

Tabitha spun, startled. "Good morning. I was just looking for Luc."

"I trust you slept well?"

Did she detect a lewd tone in his question?

"Ah, yes, I was more tired than I thought." She chose to assume it was her imagination.

Bertòn nodded, but the slight twinkle in his eyes was unmistakable. "Well, I hope Luc let you get some of that much-needed rest and didn't keep you unduly roused."

Tabitha opened her mouth to respond. Color flooded her face. Was she seriously having a dialogue with the father of the man she had just spent the night with? And discussing it? Her jaw clacked shut, and she stammered a response as Bertòn led her to the far side of the fire, where Luc sat on a colorful rug, talking to Diego. Luc glanced up as she approached and smiled warmly, patting the floor next to him as he and Diego finished their discussion.

Diego smiled a welcome and rose to grab Marcus's attention as he passed. Tabitha sank to the floor and noticed that Bertòn's attention had been caught by another.

"Hey, beautiful, want some javé?"

She turned to Luc with a hiss. "Did you tell your father something about us and last night?"

Luc's brows rose in surprise. "Uhm…no. Should I have?"

"He was just asking me about last night, and… I mean, you know… He was acting like… Well…."

Luc shook his head, perplexed. "I am sorry, what is it you are trying to tell me?"

"Well, he was insinuating that maybe you and I… And that I should have rested…and…" She watched his face; it was obvious that her complete horror over Luc's father mentioning their night together did not seem to have fazed him even slightly. "Forget it. Just forget it. And yes, I do want some javé."

Luc rose in one graceful move. As Tabitha fumed over her apparently singular embarrassment, she glanced about the tent. For the first time, she noted the abundance of people gathered in small groups, working diligently and involved in quick, animated conversations around floating maps of the area. The room erupted with activity, and the buzz of voices created a steady stream of commotion. With a slight pang of embarrassment, she let go of her single-mindedness and realized that she had not yet even asked what had transpired.

Luc returned and handed her a cup of steaming javé before he lowered himself beside her again. "So I gather you didn't exactly wake in a pleasant mood?"

Tabitha let a small bubble of laughter escape before she sipped at the hot brew. "Why don't you stick around sometime and find out for yourself?"

"Yeah, well, not sure I am up for that." His face grew serious as he met her gaze. "They have been found. They are alive, but they have been captured."

Tabitha gasped and then took deep breaths, letting the news flow through her. A myriad of questions swirled, but she bit them back and nodded. "What do you know so far?"

"Dylan has them. They are about a hundred miles north of your father's house. He has not yet tried to take them back." He rose and pulled her up after him, heading toward a group of people who argued in front of a floating map. "Ladies, gentlemen, will you give us a few minutes so I can update Tabitha?"

The members of the small group departed shooting furtive and slightly awed glances at her as they drifted toward a table laden with food and huge canisters of hot javé. Tabitha watched them leave and turned back to Luc in amazement. "You just asked them to leave…"

"I did." He turned to her. "Look here, this is where we are." The map presented an aerial view of the area. Tabitha noticed she could see through it as it floated before her, as though it were hanging on an invisible sheet. She walked around it, and the view shifted as she walked, keeping in front of her as she tried to walk behind it.

"Wow… How do you…?" she started to ask before she caught Luc's exasperated expression. "Sorry."

"Do I have your attention? It is magic. We can summon a view of the land as big or as small as we like. It takes a great deal of energy so stay with me…" He shifted the view, and it rolled down as though he were simply tugging a map on rollers. "Here is your father's home." He rolled it back up and moved the image west. "And here is where we are. So they are fairly close to being right in between us."

He then expanded the image. Tabitha felt as though she were sliding into the image as it zoomed down to a campsite hidden among the trees. "And here is where he has them. He has been there since yesterday, and the scouts say he is making no move to leave. It looks as though everyone is alive. The only one in question is Tristyn. But Alena has been with him, and if he were dead, I don't think she would be tending him." He paused. "We have yet seen no signs of Katie."

Tabitha gasped. "Did they even get her out?"

Luc lifted a shoulder as he stared at the images. "We don't know."

"How close can you get?" Tabitha whispered.

"This is about it."

"And there are scouts out there?"

"Yes."

"Luc, Katie's time is very near. We don't know if she is with them?" Tabitha inhaled deeply.

Luc shook his head. "No, we don't, and that is not making any of this easier. We have to take into consideration that she is an unknown right now."

"We have to find her," Tabitha insisted, digging her fingers into his arm.

"We have to prioritize. Yes, finding Katie is on our agenda," Luc insisted, tugging her away from the map and signaling to the team that had been working there that they were finished.

Luc led her over to get some breakfast, showing her the different fruits and explaining the options on the table. Very little looked familiar, but she selected some fruit with little interest. She sat down to eat. Diego approached and spoke quietly to Luc. They moved away, intent on their conversation, as Tabitha popped a bright and juicy berry in her mouth. Her hunger satisfied, she rose to pour herself a fresh cup of javé and wandered over to Luc and Diego.

"Tabitha!" Diego smiled. "Would you mind joining us? We would like to ask you a couple of questions about the captors, as well as the prisoners."

Tabitha nodded, the word *prisoner* sending a chill down her spine. She sensed Luc standing protectively beside her. He grasped her hand as they followed Diego toward a group huddled around a map. This map, unlike the previous one they had studied, had a myriad of colors and flags attached to it. She was trying to figure out what that meant, but Marcus stood in the center of the group and captured her attention.

Diego and Peri stood with Bertòn. Marcus began to introduce her to the rest of the group. A gentleman stood, his elfish features familiar; Tabitha recognized him as the one who had given the blessing at the town meeting so many weeks ago. He introduced himself as Otro. He smiled deeply and thanked Tabitha for her help. Another tall Caskan, his deep ebony hair gently streaked with gray, stood and bowed elegantly to her. His name, Marcus told her, was Trak. He was a regional governor of Darford, a local region close by Calais. He explained that his region bordered the region where Dylan was holed up with his prisoners.

Tabitha sat and questions about what she knew about Cole and his capabilities began. Katie was included in the questions as well. Tabitha fought tears more than once; the questions brought home the fact that the captives were at Dylan's mercy. She told them what she had learned about Antoine and Dylan, as well as the rumors about Dylan's supposed involvement in the attacks along Chandolyn's border.

As she dredged up every memory and possibly inane fact she could remember, Tabitha felt the strain. Every bit of information was added to a list and logged. She felt vulnerable and stripped as they entered data and asked question after question. She knew that her information was necessary to discover a way to rescue them, but she found herself tensing as she divulged what she could recall from her stay at her father's estate. She fought the urge to run.

"Let's take a break," Luc suggested.

Marcus stood and gestured to the group. "Let's not be long. We do not yet know this man's intention for the people he has captured, and time is of the essence." He turned to Tabitha. "I know this has been difficult, but you have gotten closer to Antoine than any others that we know, and this information is invaluable."

Tabitha nodded, feeling dirty and less than proud of herself. She had no particular loyalty to her father after what he had done to her, but she was also less than enthusiastic to be regurgitating every incident and moment she could remember from her stay with him. She turned to find her way back to their tent, intent on finding a couple of minutes alone, when Marcus stopped her. "I apologize, but when we return, we need to know about your capabilities as well."

Tabitha froze. Luc had told her that it was considered a breach of etiquette to ask the Caskan about their abilities; she had hoped her own abilities would fall under that courtesy. "Why must you know that?"

Marcus smiled. "Because you will play into their rescue. As much as I would prefer you to remain safely here, I believe we will need you. In order for any plan to work, we must understand exactly what you are capable of. Should we base part of a plan on some ability you have not mastered, lives could be in jeopardy."

She nodded. "I understand. I don't particularly like it, but I understand."

"It is all I ask."

Tabitha fled the tent and shot down the path toward the tent she and Luc shared. She slipped through the flap and inhaled deeply, trying to still her racing nerves. She had no idea what they were planning, but she could not shake the feeling that by spouting every bit of information she knew, she had nailed down the ultimate betrayal.

She sank onto the bed and hung her head, the fear, stress, and insanity of the past weeks catching up with her. She sensed more than heard Luc come in. She did not have the energy to lift her head and face him.

"I just wanted a few minutes alone." Her voice was a thin whisper.

"I will leave if you prefer," he replied softly. "But we do not have time for you to fall apart right now."

She quickly lifted her head. "What makes you think I am falling apart?"

"Tabitha, we are all working on a plan to save them. Everyone in that tent's only thought is about finding a way to get them out of there. You do not have the luxury of withdrawing right now."

"I think I have earned the right to a few minutes to myself. I am, after all, sealing my fate with the one father I have ever known," she hissed, tears stinging her eyes as she glared at him.

"Ah. The only father you have known... The one who shot me? The one who gave you to a man you hated as a gift for his loyalty? He encouraged me to rape you, might I add?" he snapped back.

She shot from the bed. "It is not that simple! I am not saying he is a good father and not a monster, but I came over here a few weeks ago practically an orphan. I met my father. And now I am not only telling his enemies everything I learned about him, but I am also expected to divulge my own abilities." She combed her hair back from her face and threw her head back, gazing up at the ceiling as though the fluttering fabric held some answer. "Everything has happened so fast, I am just...overwhelmed."

"You did not seal his fate: he did." Luc's voice was level, and his even tone brought her off the ledge a step. She

turned to look at him. "And you also discovered two brothers and a grandfather. Fates now hang in the balance as we
decide what we can do to rescue the captives. And Katie as
well, if, the One God willing, she is still alive. I promise
you, once this is over and we have gotten them out of the
hands of your father and brother, I promise to let you just
crumble. But today, people need you to step up and help us
rescue them. This father that you have finally found will kill
every one of them without hesitation if we do not find a way
to get them away from him."

Tabitha rose to her feet. "Let's go."

They left to walk back toward the main tent. She commented softly as he held the flap open for her. "Eventually I
will take you up on that offer to fall apart."


Luc stepped from the main tent in the late afternoon and
stretched his shoulders. His cup of javé was cooling, and he
sent a thought to warm the liquid as he walked away from
the yellow semicircle of light before the tent toward the
shadows that crept over the camp. Frustration ate at him as
the plans for rescuing Tristyn and his team dragged on. The
endless drill of various possibilities drove him mad. He shot
glances every few seconds at the group huddled around Tabitha. He had tried to check on her through their link, only
to be intercepted by his father with a sharp reminder to get
back to work.

He had been sent from the group grilling Tabitha when
the endless stream of questions and digging began to erode
her patience. He had been less than gentle in his defense of
her, and Marcus had intervened and sent Luc to work with
another group working on extraction scenarios.

Now another day had slid away, though the plans were slowly coming together. Contingencies were polished and rehearsed, and each team was pulling the final strategy together to weave into the end outcome.

Another day.

Luc's breath exploded in a long hiss. He tried not to think about what the delay in rescuing them might cost his cousin and his team. Dylan was not known for his patience; Luc tried to keep his thoughts away from possible outcomes. Peri had been tirelessly monitoring the team of scouts and had assured him on numerous occasions that all was quiet at Dylan's camp. Finally, she too had been sent to get some rest. Diego, her replacement, had been less than patient with Luc's constant checking.

The team working with Tabitha had long since moved to another tent. Luc was very worried over what the more experienced Caskan were trying to get her to do in their effort to finalize a plan. He prayed on more than one occasion that someone on that team remembered that Tabitha was new to her abilities and could easily panic under pressure and forget any new skill they might be coaching her to do. For that matter, he thought with a wry smile, she might take out the whole damn camp in an overzealous fit of temper. In a scenario where she was used as bait, he was not sure who he was more concerned about, Tabitha or the offending team standing against her.

As if on cue, she came sauntering between the rows of tents toward him, a warm and welcoming smile curving her lips.

"Hey, stranger, what brings you out here?" Her voice was sultry, and he noticed the warm glow in her eyes as she approached him.

Something was not right. Tabitha in a fit of temper? Yes, he could recognize that. Smiling and engaging? Yes. Tabitha unsure or hesitant, her lower lip caught between white teeth as she fought insecurity? That he would recognize. Tabitha, wandering toward him with a seductive sway in her hips, a come-hither tilt to her head and a sexy grin? Nope, something was definitely up.

"Hey yourself." He could play along. "You almost done in there?"

She strutted toward him, her steps carefully measured, and for a moment he felt stalked.

She shrugged and continued her slow meander toward him, the moonlight reflecting in her hair as it was caught in a breeze. "For now."

Hmm... Something was not right. "You think you will be able to pull off the plan?"

Her laugh was low and sultry. She tilted her head toward him as she neared. She shook her head so her hair danced along her back as she slowly made a circuit around him, her eyes making a slow and detailed inventory of his body. "I am more interested in what you plan on pulling off in the near future."

His eyebrows shot up in surprise as he turned his head to watch her complete a slow path around him. "You are, huh?"

"I am," she said softly as she stopped in front of him, hands on hips. She looked up at him through eyes burning with intensity.

"Just what did you have in mind?" Caution to the wind—he was not one to slap the open hand of opportunity.

She gazed up at him, the breeze molding the top she wore to her body. "Why don't you come a little closer and I'll tell you."

Luc reached out to pull her into his arms, but as his fingers rose toward her, she suddenly melted in a sparkle of twinkling lights. Her delighted laugh echoed through his head as she vanished.

He snarled a curse and headed toward the main tent. He heard her answering giggle as he shoved open the tent flap. His father stood at the flap with a wide grin and turned toward Tabitha with an approving nod.

There she sat, among the group, her face tinged with red at her saucy behavior. When she caught his eye, she collapsed into helpless peals of laughter.

"Very funny," he croaked as his blood substantially cooled.

"She did excellent, Luc. Did you notice the hair and the clothes adjusting to the breeze? That was very good." Bertòn grinned proudly at his pupil.

"Yeah, nice job," Luc said drily, shaking his head at her. He turned from her to his father. "Why the seduction?"

"If she can fool you at that proximity, she can fool someone less familiar with her," Bertòn answered, his eyes fastened on Tabitha as she yawned, now trying to focus on what Otro was telling her.

"I don't want her close enough to have to fool Dylan at that proximity," Luc growled at his father.

Bertòn drew him away from circle of Caskans still coaching Tabitha, keeping his voice low. "None of us do. But you know as surely as I do that Dylan is waiting for a negotiation or an attack. As soon as we launch an attack, those we are trying to save will be killed. She is our only chance of trying to get to them before he can pull the lever on any defensive maneuver."

"And if he suspects? If he gets close?" Luc demanded.

"She will be far enough away so that he will be unable to reach her. She will be well protected," Bertòn assured his son. "She was able to project herself from her sleep well over two miles. She has had practice. Dylan has no way to know she has such capabilities. It is unheard of in a Caskan. And he considers her to be untrained." Bertòn shook his head, watching Tabitha talk quietly to the team around her. "Can you imagine what she would be capable of with training?"

"Well, since Dylan shares her lineage and has been trained, I would not be too quick to assume he will not know what she can do," Luc snapped.

"He has never shown such aptitude—"

Luc's voice was a low snarl. "Tabitha can read the Faye scrolls, which means there is a chance she may be full Faye, and if she is, then Dylan is as well. What makes you think he has by any means displayed his full aptitude? Would you have shown your abilities had the tables been reversed? Would you have made a spectacle of what you could do if you were the one vying for Antoine's attention? Would you let people as yet unknown to be allies know your aptitude?"

Bertòn stopped and stared at his son, concern etching narrow lines along his forehead. "I would not."

Luc shook his head. "He may be arrogant and he may be volatile, but he did not reach the position on Antoine's council by being stupid."

"She is our only hope for getting our people out alive. She is the only one Antoine would be willing to negotiate for," Bertòn whispered.

"And Dylan knows that. He knows we will not risk losing her. We had best be ready to move quickly," Luc hissed back as they approached the group.

"We will. We have no other choice."

Luc switched to their link as he approached the group, spoken words no longer a safe option. *And what of Katie? I have promised her we will find her.*

*There has been no sign. We cannot risk everyone else for one unknown. She may not still be alive.*

Luc let the conversation drop as he moved into the seat beside Tabitha, sliding an arm around her shoulders. Her welcoming smile was warm and dazzling, with a hint of shyness.

"Now *that* I recognize," he said softly against her ear as he nuzzled her neck.

She laughed and shifted away with a self-conscious grin. "You mean you didn't like my come-on?"

"I didn't say that! It was just not the woman I have come to know." His answering grin was suggestive. "Maybe we can find her later this evening and finish that discussion."

Tabitha blushed again. The gleam in her eye as she glanced at Luc spoke volumes.

# CHAPTER NINETEEN

DYLAN STOOD BY THE FIRE IN THE CENTER OF HIS CAMP. He perused the ring of tents one more time, looking for flaws in his defensive strategy. He knew he was being watched. He could feel the eyes of Luc's scouts on him as he moved through the camp, each step a study in positioning. Now he waited anxiously for his enemies to make their move. His own defensive team was out there as well, watching and waiting. His nerves were stretched taut as he prowled, wondering what the enemy had in mind and hoping, not for the first time, that he had thought through every possible potential plan. Every one of the leaders on his team had been sent to strategize about how they would go about attacking his camp. As he planned his defense, their plans were all taken into consideration. He had no intention of going back to his father empty-handed. He would hand over the prisoners as well as his sister and, if his luck held, a few others in shackles to further prove his worth to his father. Luc's head would be mounted on a spear before he went back to Antoine's estate.

Dylan slowly moved through the camp, letting the quiet settle his nerves. If it were him, he would plan a night attack. It was always best to let the darkness work to your advantage, not to mention the psychological advantage of emerging from the blackness. The embodiment of night-mares: the enemy slipping out of the darkness with intentions to use the victim's terror to further incite dread.

He chuckled at his own cleverness. His enemies, however, did not think as he did. They would emerge, ready to negotiate and trick, talking until his guard was down, all the while planning some elaborate charade to squirrel his prisoners away. His sister, he knew, would be among them. Luc was not a fool. He would understand that the only reason the prisoners were still alive was to use them to negotiate for her.

Antoine had been livid when Dylan told him of her escape and of his capture of the prisoners. He had not seen the logic behind the plan and had berated Dylan endlessly for letting Tabitha escape.

"Why? Why?" he had demanded. Why would Dylan have gone after the prisoners to secure a negotiation advantage when he could have simply followed her and Luc? Dylan had tried to make Antoine see that this plan was for the best because it would net more than just Tabitha and Luc. He could present Antoine with not only his wayward daughter but also her lover and potentially his family. Imagine, Dylan thought, if Marcus were fool enough to come himself. Marcus and Luc's father before his father in chains would be well worth the extra effort. He could, in theory, secure all of St. Mikel for Antoine in one attack.

His plan had the added benefit of blaming the attacks on Marcus' attempt to take Chandolyn under his own power. The explanation would be that Marcus had kidnapped Antoine's daughter and the battle had ensued to win her freedom. The black elf could be planted among Marcus's troops as a ploy to place blame on the north, thus enforcing the reason for Antoine's expansion to the north when the former leadership was killed in an attempt to invade Chandolyn. With no survivors, the remaining northern governances would have no choice but to swear fealty to Antoine.

This plan had no outcome but success. Dylan would not go back empty-handed. He would redeem himself. Of that, he had no doubt. The enemy was trying to get their loved ones back safely. They would use every trick they could think of to minimize casualties.

Dylan, however, did not share their concerns for life. He had only to supply one life. One healer. If he could bring back Tabitha alive after the loss of his grandfather, so be it. As long as he had a healer to return to Antoine, and perhaps a few traitorous bodies, he would be vindicated.

He stopped before the tent that held some of the prisoners. He heard the human woman quietly speaking to her still-comatose husband. He huffed at her stupidity. He would revive when and if Dylan chose for him to wake. Her constant crooning to the stiff body was annoying and, quite frankly, starting to be a little too cloying.

Let them try to find him. What a disappointment it would be for them when they attacked and found only the woman and her unconscious husband. He stood at the entrance of the tent, watching her sponge cool water on the man's wounds. What the hell good did she think that would do?

"You are a fool to cater to him like that. He'll not wake until I decide he will wake."

Alena tensed at the sound of his voice but did not turn toward the man leaning so casually at the tent doorway. "It is my time to waste."

"There are better uses for your time." His voice carried a low and deadly threat, and Alena felt a chill run down her spine.

"I prefer to remain with my husband." Her response was tart, and Dylan felt his temper flair ever so slightly.

"Face me when you speak to me, woman. I will not be ignored," he snarled.

Alena shrugged ever so slightly as she turned once again to the bowl of water, carefully squeezing the bloodied water back into the bowl and letting the cloth soak up fresh cool water. "You are nothing. I have no need to address you or give you my time."

Dylan stormed into the tent, his long strides devouring the space between them. He grabbed a handful of her hair before she could react and dragged her backwards, kicking and screaming, out of the tent.

He strode through the encampment, dragging her by the hair. She fought, unable to gain footing, stumbling on her knees behind him. He reached his tent and with a dramatic flourish threw open the flap and tossed her in. He glanced at the surrounding woods and smiled.

*Well, this should get their attention.*

He stepped in and dropped the tent flap behind him.

Alena resisted his efforts to make her scream, but Dylan was a patient and cruel man. The sounds of her eventual screams enhanced the enjoyment he got from using her body. He knew reports of her rape would quickly get to Luc, and he grinned as he took from the pretty blonde human what he wanted.

Luc clenched his jaw in fury. Peri put a restraining arm on his. "I would not have told you had I not thought you capable of controlling yourself." He nodded but did not respond. She turned his face to meet her dark eyes. "Don't make me restrain you."

Diego's eyes snapped with rage. He addressed Marcus. "We go tonight."

Marcus glanced at the team surrounding him. "We cannot let him goad us into action before we are fully prepared."

"They may not last until we are prepared!" Diego shouted.

"We will not risk additional lives. He knows what he is doing. He expects us to act rashly." Marcus felt pain for his daughter-in-law, but his words were ironclad. "We go through the plan one more time. If we are prepared, we move. If we find a flaw, we wait. I will not react to this. We determine our move, not him."

"I will go alone," Tye cried. "I will kill him!"

"No one moves until I give the command. No one," Marcus barked, and the protests subsided. "Now. One more time."

Bertòn raced toward the group, his eyes eager and alight. "Sybille is back."

Tabitha glanced up at Luc in surprise. *Where has Sybille been?*

Luc ignored her inquiry and leaped to his feet as his father approached. "And?"

"Let's go—you, me, and Marcus...now!"

Marcus gestured to the team staring in amazement at the three of them. "Back to work. Finalize those plans. With this development, we may yet be on the move tonight."

Peri and Tabitha exchanged startled looks. "What development?"

Peri shrugged. "I wish I knew."


Antoine swore again. His footsteps echoed through the halls. His voice bellowed for his staff to join him in his private conference room immediately.

Could Dylan be this stupid? To be caught at the border of Marcus's territory with prisoners and a small militia? Was he truly so arrogant as to not see the impending danger? Did he truly think that that they would hand Tabitha over and all would be forgotten?

He entered the conference room and stood staring at the map suspended on the wall. The fool was holed up north of his estate. With a monumental effort, he could salvage this, but it would mean outright war. If only Dylan had done as he was told and secured Tabitha and Luc, all of this could have quietly been managed. He could have found a way to smooth over Roane's disappearance and the loss of Katie. Cole alone was a less-than-credible testament on which to base a war. He could have managed this slip. But Dylan had captured them and was taunting Marcus's territory along the border with an armed retinue—there was little Antoine could do to forgo all-out war.

His only option would be to make sure this incident resulted in victory. The northern territory would be part of his alliance one way or another. Antoine preferred it had occurred through a more strategic and negotiated truce, not a forced attainment.

His thoughts were dark, but a plan was shaping within his mind when he heard the scrape of seats behind him as his counsel prepared to hear his thoughts.


Tabitha tossed again, a fitful sleep nagging at her as she fought for rest against a whirlwind of turbulent thoughts. Fear tugged her from sleep, and more than once her dreams haunted her with every possible outcome her subconscious could throw at her. She succumbed to fatigue. Dreams of the myriad pitfalls awaiting her as she tried to rescue her family and friends danced through her head. From the edges of her nightmares, a familiar distant voice seemed to call her name; she struggled to recognize it. In her dream, Tabitha was running over endless rows of grassy knolls. As she topped one, another would loom before her, like unending waves cascading onto a beach.

The voice continued to call her from beyond. As she struggled to reach it, she recognized her mother's voice. Panic engulfed her as she thrashed through sea grass that was suddenly growing taller around her. As she ran, she seemed to sink into the ground; she tripped and stumbled. The peaceful grassy knolls had become churning mounds of earth that rose up above her head and threatened to swallow her. With a cry, she dove forward and crashed to the ground as a mound of earth rose above her, blocking the blue sky.

She sat up with a horrified gasp, drawing air into her lungs, willing her heart to stop racing. She lifted a hand to sweep the hair from her eyes and cried out when a figure rose from the end of the bed.

"Hush, Tabitha," a woman's voice admonished. She slipped to the side of the bed and lit a single candle. "You will wake him."

Tabitha would have recognized that long mane of silvery hair anywhere. She gaped at her mother in astonishment. Doni sat at the end of the bed and lifted an elegant brow toward her daughter.

Tabitha's mouth opened and shut. As her astonishment turned to amazement and then to anger, she tried to regroup. She kicked the blankets off; Luc mumbled in his sleep and rolled onto his side. She glanced over at him and then back at her mother. "That is the least of my concerns! Where have you been?"

Doni met her daughter's eyes squarely. The directness of her gaze startled Tabitha. It was, as far as she could recall, the first time her mother had spoken to her eye to eye.

"Come with me. I will explain more." Doni stood and gestured beyond the tent.

Tabitha folded her arms and pursed her lips stubbornly. "Like hell. I am not going anywhere."

"You will come with me and we will end this now. Or you can dig your heels in, remain here, and lead these people to certain death," Doni responded with a shrug. "I am asking you not to wake your lover because I want you to leave with me, alone. And if he wakes, he will try to stop you. If he does not know until morning that you have left, we'll have time to try to get those people out and take you away from here with minimal bloodshed."

Tabitha quelled her embarrassment over her mother's mention of her lover. "You had better start explaining yourself. You cannot just to barge in here, wake me up in the middle of the night, and demand that I leave with you. We have all been working for two days to put together a rescue plan. I am not leaving with you." Tabitha stepped away from the bed, thankful for the short nightshirt she was wearing. This conversation with her mother would have been a little tougher had she been trying to wiggle into clothes under the blankets. She tugged one of the stools free and faced her mother, arms folded.

Doni watched her daughter with a small, amused smile. "Can we at the very least go out and speak." She glanced over her shoulder at Luc, resting fitfully, the blankets resting at his slim waist. "I do not wish to wake him. Once you have heard me out, you will need to come with me. If he is awake, he will try to sway you."

Tabitha stared at her mother, virtually a stranger to her. "I am afraid to trust you. Do you have any idea what has happened to your father? And to Cole? Not to mention Gwyn and Cole's girlfriend, Lena. You could have intervened earlier, before Alena was raped. Why should I trust you now? Why would I?"

"I know about my father. Sybille came to us and told me. She has also shared what she heard about what has happened to Cole. You need to come with me so we can understand what has transpired."

"I am not going with you. We have a whole—"

Doni cocked her head to the side in alarm. She stood quickly and reached for Tabitha's arm.

"Tabitha?" Tye's voice called from outside the tent.

Tabitha opened her mouth to respond, but her mother's hand grasped her elbow. She saw Luc lift his head and look in their direction as she disappeared.

Tabitha stumbled when her stool disappeared from under her. As her bottom hit the stone floor, she responded with an undignified huff. She gaped up at her mother standing beside her.

"I didn't even feel us move!"

Doni glanced down at her. "There is a difference in our abilities."

"Our abilities?"

"Yes, the Faye as opposed to the Caskan."

From the floor, Tabitha stared up at her. "Well, I wouldn't know, since you failed to mention that my father was a Caskan from a different world. What with me thinking I was human all those years, imagine my surprise!"

"Your father is not Caskan, and your sarcasm is not needed here," Doni snipped back.

Tabitha swallowed her hot retort when she suddenly realized that she had no idea where *here* was. She slowly pushed herself up from the cold flagstone floor and stared at the circular room surrounding her. The walls were mostly glass, and the single fire pit in the middle of the room sent a warm yellow glow dancing off the panes. A single glass door led outside but the darkness hid the view from her eyes. The room was comfortably furnished with elegant chairs and small round tables that held an assortment of glass jars and containers full of colorful liquids. The only apparent way in or out of the room was a set of stairs on one edge of the room that slid into darkness.

"Where are we?"

"At my home. With the Faye," Doni responded. "The exact *where* is immaterial to you, as you are unfamiliar with the land."

"I want to go back."

"Not yet. Please. Join me. We will discuss our terms."

Tabitha walked over and sat by the fire, wishing she had taken a moment to dress before their abrupt departure. "Could I go back and get some clothes?"

Doni shook her head. "You cannot. Had you left with me without stirring an alarm, you would have been able to dress. But you had to wake your lover—"

"His name is Luc. Luc! Please stop referring to him as 'my lover'," Tabitha snapped, hugging herself against the chill in the room.

"I am well aware of his name. I knew his mother, after all. He looks remarkably like his father."

"I have not yet told him that it was his mother's body back in Dark Hollow," Tabitha admitted. "We have been through so much that I can't find the words."

The aloof chill seemed to slip from Doni's face. "I can well understand that." They sat in silence for a moment before Doni lifted haunted eyes to her. "Tell me what happened to Cole."

Tabitha groaned and let her face drop to rest on her bent knees. "Oh God, how do I even start to tell you? It was horrible."

The tale tumbled out, beginning with hesitant, jerky words. Tabitha relayed what had transpired on the day Dylan had taken her down to the basement. Reliving the memory drove her to her feet. Doni watched quietly as Tabitha paced back and forth, the dark events again unfolding before her. She recalled every detail she could muster.

Tabitha sank down next to the fire. The emotion had sapped some of her nervous energy, and she felt drained and worn.

"Cole has become the black elf?"

Tabitha shrugged. "Or the black elf has become Cole. When he spoke, he demanded that Dylan release us, and his voice was weird. It was like he was speaking with more than once voice, like it was vibrating. I can't explain it. But when he stood, he responded to the silver stick that Dylan held against him, so I am not sure who is in control, Cole or the black elf."

Doni nodded. "I will need to share this with the others."

"Will we be able to get Cole away from it? How about Tristyn and Alena? Do you know if Katie got away?"

Doni lifted a hand. "Slow down. Let me speak to the others. A lot of things are happening here. Your main focus has to be getting home to Porta Negra."

Tabitha shook her head. "I won't leave until I know that they are all safe."

"You have no choice," Doni stated, cutting her off. "Regardless of what happens tonight and tomorrow, you must leave. Should Antoine get his hands on you, your fate will be as mine was: his prisoner. And he will shackle you here, as he did me. You've had a taste of his idea of family loyalty. He will do the same to you—a husband, children, and threats against those you love. And he will grow stronger because of what you can do for him between bearing children that he will give away and trading healing for fealty to him."

A bare glimmer of understanding dawned on Tabitha. "Is that what he did to you? Did he give Dylan away?"

Doni slowly nodded. "Yes."

"And then he threatened you with your father?"

"Yes, and Dylan as well. When Dylan was just a baby, he would threaten his life if I did not do what he demanded," Doni whispered, her eyes distant.

"And you stayed?"

"I had to. But I had a plan, and I had help." Doni stood. "Tabitha, someday, when this has blown over...when times are calmer, I promise to tell you everything." She laughed shortly, a brittle sound that ended like a hiccup. "It is funny. I have often thought of writing my memoirs for your eyes only. I thought, should something happen, I would want you to know the truth."

"I wish you had," Tabitha said quietly. "I have heard his version of your time here, but now you are sending me back without knowing yours."

Doni glanced at her. Tabitha marveled at her mother. Doni looked like a young girl, a young girl whose eyes stared back from the brink of some personal hell. The lack of wrinkles, the perfect features were not enough to offset her haunted eyes and the sadness that lurked there. For just a moment, Tabitha wondered if the truth was as simple as either parent's tales. She wondered if after her mother had revealed the whole tale, she would walk away feeling comforted that she did, in fact, know what had transpired.

"Someday," Doni whispered. "But not today. We must save them from Dylan and get you out of here."

Tabitha voiced the questions that gnawed at her. "Why must I go? If the Faye have the ability to help us and they have protected you, why can't I stay here with you? Why do I have to go back?"

Doni shook her head. "You cannot go with me, and I won't have you tied to this land's future. If he knows you are here, he will never stop looking for you."

"But what makes you think I am safe at home? I mean, if he has contacts over there, he can come after me and my family," Tabitha argued.

"No. He cannot. I will ensure he will not go after you," Doni said sadly. The darkness in her eyes seemed to engulf her, and Tabitha felt a cold finger of dread run up her spine.

"How?" Her voice came out in a croak. She also stood, staring at her mother. "What do you plan on doing that would make him agree to that?"

Doni turned back to her; her smile held a twinge of pain. "You will leave here tonight. You must. And you will take Katie and her baby with you."

"Katie?" Tabitha gasped. "She is alive? And her baby?"

"Yes. I delivered her son soon after we rescued her. She is fine, but she does not belong here. Take her back with you. Trude will take them in. She needs someone to care for when you go off to college," Doni responded. "Katie should stay on the island. She will be safe there."

"But how? On the island? I don't understand." Tabitha felt overwhelmed.

Doni lifted a hand, and the fire began to blaze. She lifted a glass carafe of javé and poured two steaming mugs. She handed one to Tabitha. "Dawn is only hours away. Marcus's team will wait for first light, and then they will proceed to try and rescue your friends. We must be ready to intercept them." She lifted the mug to her lips. Her face looked tired and sad. Tabitha held her breath, waiting for her mother to continue. "We have a lot to discuss...."

# CHAPTER TWENTY

THE EARLY MORNING FOG STILL GRIPPED THE LAND, BUT sunlight was slipping through the gray folds to dapple the mist with eerie golden highlights. Luc stood back, his thoughts dark, staring out at the wooded glen that would host the drama that would shortly unfold. Bertòn approached him silently and, without a word, handed him a steaming cup of javé. The two men waited as the commanders of the separate teams finalized their positions. Marcus moved through the ranks, quietly assessing and encouraging the people he might well have to ask to offer their lives in defense of their land.

"Perhaps she has convinced her to leave," Bertòn said quietly.

Luc let out an explosive breath before turning to his father, his jaw tight and his eyes snapping. "I pray she did, but Tabitha would not have snuck out in the middle of the night to save herself. I wish we knew what the hell they were doing."

Bertòn shrugged and cast a dark eye over the gathering of friends and family, nervously adjusting weapons and preparing for the upcoming battle. "They have committed to saving the prisoners. We will work with what we know. Dylan will have little to negotiate with once he loses them."

"And what then? We ask him to leave nicely?" Luc spat. "They steal her away in the dark of the night, without so much as waking me, leaving us to amend our plan—"

"Which included Tabitha to negotiate for the prisoners only," Bertòn pointed out. "Once the Faye let Sybille know that the prisoners are safe, Dylan is in direct violation of our covenants. We will ask for his surrender, to stand trial for his attack and the rape of Alena, among whatever other atrocities he committed upon our people during their imprisonment."

Luc had to swallow back a sharp retort and take a breath before responding. "And what makes you think that Dylan will surrender and that those he commands will disband without him?"

"Marcus's authority, plus the fact that they are on our land now. They have committed a grave offense against our people. Tristyn as well as both envoys have yet to be accounted for. He is holding hostages and wants to kidnap Antoine's daughter, who has come to Marcus seeking asylum. Antoine himself would be made to answer to the charges if she were taken against her will. They will see that they are in a political—"

"Bertòn, Luc," Diego interrupted. "Marcus wishes to see you. It seems we have lost contact with the Southern scout."

Alena heard Dylan hastily drawing on clothes. He cursed, demanding answers from the man who had entered the tent and woken him. She feigned sleep, drawing the blanket over her nakedness, but she was ignored. Dylan snarled questions at the man delivering what was obviously very dire news. Dylan stalked from the tent, leaving her alone for the first time in a day. After listening to the sound of his retreating feet, Alena leaped up and snatched her clothes, pulling them on as she raced for the tent doorway.

A guard passing by stopped her, but she stood her full height, staring him down and snarling in his face. "I am going back to my husband. If you want to stop me, you had damn well better plan on killing me."

The guard took in her battered face: one eye swollen shut, her lips bruised, one cheek carrying a deep purple swelling over the cheekbone. Her open eye snapped in fury, and he thought better of trying to stop her. With the slightest hesitation, he accompanied her to the prisoner's tent and stood outside as she entered.

She sank to the ground next to Tristyn and buried her face in his chest, fighting back sobs. Once she released tears, she knew she would crumble, and there was no time for that yet. Tristyn lay as she had left him, unmoving and unresponsive, but at least alive. She had not seen evidence of the other prisoners in days, but based on the commotion around the camp in these early morning hours it was obvious that something was transpiring.

The guard outside the tent was hailed. Alena heard the words "other prisoners." The guard's reply indicated the tent she was in. The flap swung open to admit a guard, followed by the other prisoners: the two St. Mikel envoys who had been accompanying them from Antoine's estate. The guard departed, leaving them tethered together.

"Are you all right? Both of you?" she asked quickly as she ran her hands along the ropes, checking to see if they were simply knotted or magically enforced.

The first of the envoys, Trey, nodded and lifted his bound wrists. "You won't be able to untie them. What has happened to you? Your face? Has he beaten you?"

Alena shrugged, ignoring the question. "I am all right. I fared better than Tristyn. He has not moved in days."

Trey shrugged, and Alena checked on the other envoy. "You are unharmed?"

The second, an older man from the northern territory of Galane, nodded. "We are fine. A little battered and bruised but mostly ignored."

"And Katie? Where is she?" Alena demanded.

The second of the two St. Mikel envoys shook his head. "Katie disappeared the first night. Haven't seen her since."

Alena looked around the tent, quickly assessing their position, already considering possible plans.

"All right… Well… we have to be—"

"By the One God! Look!"

They all turned horrified eyes to where Tristyn lay, still and comatose on the ground. Pale outlines of hands reached up from the ground and locked around his shoulders, hips, knees, and feet. Slowly, Tristyn began to sink into the ground.

Trey screamed, but Alena leaped over and quickly covered his mouth, hissing, "Stop! Remain quiet!"

"What is happening to him?" Trey moaned from behind her hand as he stared in horror. The body seeped into the earth, until all that remained was undisturbed dirt.

Alena smiled grimly. "We are being rescued." She glanced warily at the still tent flap. "And it is about time."

A dull headache pounded behind Tabitha's eyes. She and her mother had continued their discussion for hours, but the talk, tears, and shouts had still not answered all the questions that nagged her.

But it was a start. She wanted to know more, but the tiniest flicker of satisfaction glowed in her belly. Between her father, mother, and grandfather, she had begun to piece together the fragments of those stolen years into some degree of understanding. Her mother had been less than forthcoming about the lost years, glossing her responses with vague comments. Finally, after yet another bout of crying and frustrated shouting, her mother had admitted that there were still too many things she could not yet discuss. The pain was too intense. Then Doni had simply shut down.

Doni had admitted to sealing off the island with an intense net that no others with Caskan blood could cross. They spent long hours cross-legged beside the fire, facing one another, while Doni showed Tabitha the intricacies of her shield.

"You will need to form your own. Each of us leaves a distinct thought process behind when we set our guards. You will not be able to simply reinforce mine; you will need to cast your own in order to maintain the shield," Doni had explained.

"Well, why can't we simply do it together? Why do I have to build a whole new one?" Tabitha gave her mother a sidelong glance. "You are coming back with me, aren't you?"

Doni had waved off the question, and Tabitha was sidetracked when a group of Faye entered. She and Doni were herded down several flights of stairs to a large circular room filled with Faye milling about in small groups, strapping on weapons and conversing quietly among themselves. The energy level in the room was high. Tabitha felt her skin hum with the intensity of the power around her. Doni shepherded her over to a small table along the side and pressed her into a seat.

Tabitha glanced up, but Doni leaned in to speak quietly. "We will be moving soon. Stay here. We will tell you what to do."

Tabitha's thoughts swirled in chaos at the insanity that had occurred. People were planning and strategizing around her, and she was the dead center of the whole debacle. Luc's family had been planning on some kind of rebellion or confrontation with Antoine before she arrived. Antoine had been making plans for years to try to draw the three main regions of the Caskan land under one dominant ruler. Her mother and the Faye seemed to have a whole other objective, and here she sat, a pawn in the midst of it all. How had it happened? What if she had not arrived? What if these individual ventures had simply played out independently? How had she become a fulcrum in the midst of all of—

"Tabitha?" A familiar voice rumbled from the din.

"Kayle?"

The familiar fisherman from Porta Negra sauntered toward her from across the room. She stared in shock: *a fisherman from Porta Negra? Here?*

He smiled as he approached. He wore tall, laced leather boots with dark pants and a light shirt, open at the throat. The long broadsword strapped to his back caught her attention. He had not simply appeared here or slipped through a portal—he was with them.

"Kayle? What on earth are you doing here?"

He smiled and gestured for her to sit as he tugged a chair around across from her. He leaned on the back of the chair to accommodate the blade that hung below his waist. Doni spotted them together and started to hasten over, only to be gestured back by Kayle with a curt wave of his hand. He turned his light eyes to Tabitha. She tried desperately to reconcile the conflict behind the familiar face from Porta Negra suddenly appearing before her here. "I am from this land. I am of the Faye."

She stared, none of it registering. "But...but...you live in Porta Negra? You have always been on the island. How did you get there? And why?"

"I was there to help watch over you," he responded.

"Watch over me?" she sputtered.

He nodded. "I came to the island when your mother returned."

"How did you get past the net, the protection she placed over the island?"

"I helped her create it. No one with magical background could break through the barrier without our knowledge." He explained, "When your mother was with Antoine, she thought herself helpless against him. Once she realized she had the ability to control her destiny, and that she needed help, the Faye sent help to her." He paused. "I was that help. The Faye sent me to train her, to teach her to use her power to direct her life rather than remain a slave to him any longer. It would have been pointless for us to have saved her only for her to be vulnerable to capture once she was away." His gaze rested intently on Tabitha. "Do you understand what I am telling you?"

She was slightly taken aback. "Yes. So you went to help her escape from him?"

"I went to teach her to use her own abilities to escape herself. She needed to be able to protect herself." He spoke slowly. The familiar deep and gravelly voice seemed so out of place here. She expected him to say he had to get back to fix his boat motor, not remain and prepare for an all-out battle.

She pursed her lips as a thought occurred to her. "And what of me? Will I be sent back to the island with instructions to stay put and hide my head beneath the blankets, or will I be allowed to live my life? To go to college?"

His smile was slow. The lines around his mouth etched his cheeks with familiar wind-burned creases. "It is up to you. I will ask you to protect the island as your mother did. And then you have to make that decision for yourself. But know that as long as Antoine lives, he will be hunting for you. It would be best if you learn to protect yourself rather than need someone else to do so."

"And who will teach me that?" She inhaled with a deep longing as she released the next words. "Luc? Will he return with me?"

Kayle shrugged. "That is between you and him, but I guess that he will have his hands full with the damn civil war that Marcus and Antoine have created. And he is not of the Faye. Our powers are different, which would make it more difficult for Luc and his family to train you. You need to be trained by the Faye."

"Kayle, I think my father is a Faye. Do you know?"

Kayle gave a short, dry snicker as he stood. "Yes, your father is a full Faye."

Tabitha gasped. "Does he know? That means that Dylan is also full Faye!"

"I am being summoned. This is not the time for this long-overdue discussion."

Tabitha slowly nodded. "Will you be returning?"

"Looks like there won't be anything for me here. I will return for you when we are ready to move." He drifted off and melted into the crowd, leaving her perplexed.


Two hours later, the rising sun extended the slightest hint of gray along the horizon. Tabitha stared down at the hazy morning fog encasing the fields below her. The main room that they had gathered in had become a platform with a clear floor, revealing the field where the two Caskan forces would meet. Tabitha wondered if they had actually moved to the place from where they had been or if the meadow was being projected onto the floor, as though they were floating above it. Her curiosity, however, was not compelling enough for her to actually inquire. She was too tired to care enough to start the conversation. She huddled in a quiet area of the room, standing alone, clutching a steaming cup of javé in her chilly fingers. Her eyelids were scratchy from lack of sleep; adrenaline pumped tendrils of liquid anxiety through her body.

She felt a presence behind her and knew that Kayle approached. The shock of seeing him had begun to wane. She stared at the field below, still encased in fog, where Dylan and his warriors would meet against Luc and his family. The tall man behind her did not say a word, and the long silence quickly began to gnaw at her.

"Can you see them? The opposing forces?" His deep voice rumbled from his chest.

Tabitha shook her head. "The fog is too thick."

He lifted a finger to point to the far end of the field, his other hand resting on her shoulder. "Let me show you. Do not try and see through the fog with your eyes. Extend your vision along your senses." His long fingers gripped her shoulder, and with a shudder, she felt the power flow through him as he showed her how to see past what her physical eyes could see. She gasped as shapes began to sharpen before her; a large force gathered along the edge of a deep field.

"Is that Dylan?"

Kayle shook his head. "I am afraid not. It is Antoine, and he has brought a large retinue with him. How the hell he got this many warriors together and moved that fast, I cannot imagine. They must have already been nearby and ready."

"But where are Dylan and the prisoners?" she asked.

"Last night, the prisoners were taken out of Dylan's camp. Most of the relatively small troop he had with him is now incorporated into Antoine's army. The question is: where has Dylan gone?"

Tabitha turned to him. "Who cares? I hope he fell off the earth."

Kayle nodded briefly. "Agreed, but there remains the small issue of Cole being with him."

"What?"

"Yes, and that may cause a slight problem. Where is he taking his new weapon, and what will he do with him once he gets there?"

"Do you have any ideas?"

"No. But I have an idea who may know."

Tabitha gave him a sidelong glance. "Are you planning on sharing?"

"We have been focused on getting you away from Antoine and releasing the prisoners. At this point, we can safely leave Marcus and Antoine to the war they seem intent upon fighting," Kayle rumbled. He drew in a deep breath and lowered his voice. "We need to get that black elf out of Dylan's hands."

Tabitha whispered and gestured to Marcus's force gathered on the field below them. "And what price will they pay for my freedom?"

"The ultimate price, but this is not about you. This is about Antoine's desire to rule all of the governances. That is a Caskan war. The Faye need to be more concerned about the larger picture, and that is the black elf in our land," he commented softly. "It is imperative that we get you out of here. You are the key to the line of healers. Should you be lost, either through death or capture, the line will be lost. The future of these people will depend on someday being able to reinstitute the healers."

"They won't have a healer with me gone."

"In a war, neither side should have that advantage. With you in Antoine's hands, the scale tips in his favor."

"My mother was once in his control. I will not repeat her mistakes. I will not be his pawn," Tabitha countered.

The tall man remained quiet, and Tabitha wondered if he would respond. After a few moments, he drew in a deep breath. Words emerged, as though tugged from somewhere deep within him. "Your mother was never in his control. When she needed assistance, she received what she needed, but she was never out of control. The only control she lost was her own doing, and when she realized that, she was able to take steps to change her situation. She is of us, and it is because of her wishes that we will do what must be done this day."

Tabitha slowly let that sink in, knowing she would get no further clarification.

"What are you planning on negotiating with my father for my freedom?"

The slightest hint of sadness crept from his eyes to the twitch of his lips, enough to confirm that he would not answer her. Or that she would not like the response.

# CHAPTER TWENTY-ONE

TABITHA STOOD CAREFULLY HIDDEN AMONG THE SMALL army of Faye. The drama below began to unfold. She watched two small groups from each side meet in the center of the field, the fighters hanging back, awaiting a decision. She made out Luc's tall and lean shape and Marcus's more husky shape beside him, Peri and Otro standing with them. Marcus's force in the gray fog, with Diego's men lined up behind him, were little more than dark shadows encased in the steely gloom.

"What are we doing?" Tabitha whispered.

"We wait until the time is right. You are prepared for your part in this?" Doni asked without turning her head.

Tabitha swallowed at the enormity of her task. "When will we move?"

"Soon. Be patient. Timing is crucial."

They stood in silence, watching the figures below them, like live figures on a chessboard waiting for some surreal player to move them. The image shook her. She wondered if the Faye or yet another player would be the deciding factor in this deadly game.

"Tabitha, I understand you suspect you are full Faye?"

Tabitha's attention shot to her mother. "Yes. I can read the Faye scrolls. I mean, they tell me that I'd have to be full Faye in order to read the scrolls. And Kayle told me that my father is Faye."

Doni's eyes turned and gestured to the seats behind them. "Sit. It is time I told you the truth."

With a thudding heart, Tabitha turned toward the seats lined against the wall of the chamber. The clear view of the land below the floor was disconcerting. She stepped gingerly, as though expecting to drop through a hole in the sky with each step. The chair behind her looked as though it were floating; she gripped the armrests and lowered herself into it. To her surprise, her mother knelt before her, her hands gripping the seat as though to keep Tabitha from vaulting from it.

"Oh, this is not going to be good, is it?"

"Kayle is right, your father is a full Faye—"

"So Antoine is a Faye! Does he know?"

Doni shook her head and smiled. "Antoine is not Faye. Your father is full Faye."

"But wait. If Antoine is not full Faye, then how can... Oh." Tabitha stared at her mother in shocked silence. "Are you telling me that you... uhm... Oh."

"Yes," Doni answered, holding Tabitha's knees with her hands. "Antoine is not your father."

"Oh."

"Tabitha—"

Tabitha brushed her mother's hands from her knees and stood. The world around her seemed to spin crazily. Her rapid rise and the vertigo from movements on the ground under the floor beneath her sent her staggering. She grasped the back of the chair to keep from tumbling. "Antoine is not my father?"

"No."

"Then who?" Before Doni could answer, Tabitha lifted her eyes to Kayle, standing across the room, his arms crossed in front of his strong chest, his light eyes intent on the scenario beneath them. "Oh my God. He told me he went to help you find your way to escape from Antoine."

"Yes," Doni whispered. "Tabitha, I wish I had told you earlier."

Tabitha inhaled deeply as the reality of what she had suffered at Antoine's hands came crashing back. She felt her fingers sizzle. A blue sparkle began to shimmer along her fingertips and up her arms as rage mounted in her. "Earlier? Like before I went to him? You let me go to that maniac's house, thinking he was my father? I was trying to find some shred of connection. You knew what he was like, and you let me go to him?"

Doni stepped back and lifted her hands. "Tabitha, control yourself. You need to understand that what I did was for—"

"Are you kidding me?" Tabitha roared, the blue fire now crackling along her skin, engulfing her body. Her breath came in short, rapid spurts. Heat consumed her body as the hissing blue flame surrounded her. Her fury at full blast, she cursed and screamed at her mother. With a final shriek of temper, she extended her hands. The fiery bursts that exploded from her fingers sent chairs flying. The previously clear floor image of the ground below rippled and went black.

The room was silent except for Tabitha's breath hissing through her bared teeth. The explosion had left her weak and the anger that had consumed her dissipated with her outburst. After a moment, she lifted her eyes to her mother's.

Doni dropped her eyes and turned to Kayle, who was lying on his back, shaking his head as though to clear it. "Are you all right?"

Kayle took a moment to climb to his feet. "I was able to absorb the worst of it."

Tabitha swallowed back the tears that stung her throat. "I am sorry."

"You needn't be. Come with me. We have a few minutes to talk before we have to put this all into motion." He shook his hands and wiped his palms on his pants before giving her a wan smile. "You pack quite a punch."

Before she could respond, he put an arm around her shoulder and led her away from the stunned stares that followed her.

"They are all staring." Her voice was little more than a thin whisper.

"Even the Faye have never experienced power like this. They could all feel it building in you, and the amount of energy shocked them all," Kayle responded as he led her to a small sitting area around a cheery fire pit.

Tabitha took a seat and let fatigue wash through her. "I seem to be drawing attention wherever I go. I am an enigma to the Caskan, I am a freak back home, and even among the Faye I am some kind of mutant." Before he could respond, she lifted her eyes to his light gaze. Silver eyes, the same shade as hers, stared back at her. "Why didn't you tell me?"

Kayle leaned forward, his wrists on his knees, and returned her dazed stare with a calm one. "I wanted to tell you a hundred times, but I listened to your mother. She felt very strongly that the less you knew, the safer you would be. We were afraid that if those watching you knew you were a full Faye, you would be at a greater risk."

She sighed and looked at the toes of her soft boots, watching them as she tapped them together and apart. "You were so close. All my life. You were right there, and I didn't know it."

"I wanted to tell you that I was your father every day. I wanted to reach out to you. I watched you grow up from a distance for eighteen years." He exhaled loudly. "I was never fond of you dating Greg."

Tabitha let out a bubble of laughter. "No? Why was that? I thought coming from a fishing family, you would have liked him."

"He was never good enough for you."

"Well. It doesn't matter anymore anyway. As soon as he saw Luc change into a hawk and I told him I had similar abilities, I think that pretty much sent him running for the hills."

Kayle laughed softly and reached for a hand. "I will return with you. I will train you, as I trained your mother. I will help you control your power. Once you have it under control, you will be able to live as normal a life as you want."

She squeezed his fingers. "Thank you. Why is it that everyone seems to think that I have so much power? Where did I get it? Are you particularly powerful? Is my mother?"

"The Faye who lived before the Black Years were rumored to have much more power than the current Faye. We suspect that intermarrying weakened our abilities, and the illness that plagues our people also seems to have weakened us. We have not seen a twin born in many generations, and of course, you being a healer is a rarity in itself. Healers have enormous amounts of power and energy; they need it to regenerate cells and heal as they do. You are not only a full Faye but a healer *and* a twin. The elders suspect that as a twin, you gained more than your share of the power. Cole does not have any more ability than an average Caskan, even though he is full Faye.

"Tabitha, you may very well be the first in generations to hold the power of the ancient Faye."

She let his statement idea sink in, though the impact eluded her. "Kayle, what does all this mean?"

He shrugged a shoulder and released her fingers. "I do not know what it means. There are those who want you to remain here so we can test that power. There are those who want to make sure that you are mated to a full Faye, so that the power may be captured for future generations. We may be able to revitalize our abilities."

"Mated to a full Faye? Tested? My God, these people are no better than my father!" She spat and then with an apologetic grin corrected herself. "Sorry. I mean Antoine."

Kayle chuckled and poured her a cup of javé. "Your mother has fought every one of these Faye to ensure that you have the right to return to your own life. You are still a young girl. You have your whole life ahead of you and should have the right to choose the path you wish. You are not responsible for a world you never even knew existed."

Tabitha accepted the steaming mug and nodded.

Kayle poured himself a mug and sent her a sidelong glance. "Besides, you have marked your mate already. Regardless of what others may want for you, your wishes have been made known, and no one can dispute that. A healer's mark is a sacred thing to us."

Tabitha ducked her head to hide her blush, but Kayle seemed not to notice. He leaned back in the chair and propped his boots against the fire pit. She curled up on her chair and let the silence that seeped from him engulf her as she stared at the flames dancing before her.

Her energy began to resurge. She rested her head against the chair, knowing that the next few hours would play through this tribulation. She wondered, not for the first time, if she would have the strength to play her role in the drama.

Sleep crept up on her. After a brief respite from stress, Tabitha felt a nudge on her foot. Her eyes fluttered open and focused on the orange flames gamboling in the fire pit. She shook her head, attempting to clear the fog that clouded her mind. Kayle came into focus before her.

"You ready, Tabitha? It is time for us to move."

Panic clutched her belly, sweeping away the drowsy calm from her nap. She slid off her seat and shoved the mass of hair back from her face. She followed Kayle. Doni approached them, her eyes wary, but Tabitha slid her gaze away from her mother. There was too much depending on her performance to be caught up in the slow drip of information that Doni had been allotting.

A tall Faye approached, and Tabitha struggled to remember the woman's name. She had met her in the glade at Bertòn's home and the meeting with her mother, but her name escaped her.

"What's her name?" Tabitha whispered to Kayle.

"Larissa. She is one of the Faye leaders."

Larissa nodded elegantly to Tabitha in greeting. "Tabitha, we meet again."

Tabitha swallowed. Agitation chattered throughout her nerves as her impertinent attitude toward the woman on their first meeting came back to her. Of course, she had not known she was a leader of the Faye at the time. She mumbled a greeting. The woman's smile deepened before she turned to Kayle.

"You are leaving? You will be ready when the time comes?"

Kayle nodded, and Larissa turned to Tabitha. "You understand your part in the plan?"

"I do."

Larissa turned to go and glanced back over her shoulder. "I expect you will follow instructions? No heroics are required. You need only do what is required, and then I expect you to remove yourself from the situation. You are, after all, no fighter."

Tabitha felt a hot flush of anger at the veiled insult, but Kayle squeezed her arm and nodded to Larissa. He steered Tabitha away.

"You know, I am not sure I like that woman," Tabitha hissed under her breath.

Kayle chuckled softly. "I am sure you do not, but don't judge too harshly. You are, in fact, not a trained fighter, and you hold the key to quite a mystery about your abilities. You are too valuable to risk being killed in a battle."

"Well, if I am so damn powerful, why can't I just knock the shit out of Dylan with a well-aimed thunderbolt?" Tabitha snapped.

"Because we don't trust you not to also dislodge the eastern seaboard into the ocean," Kayle responded drily as he led her back to the main room.


Bertòn swore softly as he tried once again to locate the second and third scouts. "Where the hell are they?"

Sybille shook her head. She addressed the people linked to the scouts. "Nothing? No sign?"

The faces of those linked to the missing scouts were drawn and miserable. They shook their heads and then concentrated again on contacting their missing loved ones.

Diego approached, his face a mask of misery. "Our last scout has returned." Bertòn and Sybille turned to him. "He was able to slip away, but just barely."

The silence stretched. One of the women trying to contact a missing scout burst into tears. Bertòn gently placed a hand on her shoulder. He turned back to Diego. "Barely escaped from what?"

Diego inhaled deeply. "Antoine has brought a force up from the south. They seem to have arrived last night. We are surrounded."

Sybille turned to her husband. "It is time for me to go gather our reinforcements. I can leave before the noose tightens. If I delay, I may not be able to get past them."

Bertòn looked on the verge of refusing, but after a moment's hesitation he nodded and reached for her. His dark eyes stared into hers with urgent intensity. "Watch yourself. Be safe."

She lifted onto her tiptoes and placed her hands on his cheeks. After a quick but passionate kiss, she slipped out of his arms. She shifted into the shape of a fox even as the tent flap closed behind her.

Bertòn watched her go with a worried sigh and headed out to join his brother and son. Marcus stood with Luc, his face set in a dark scowl as he perused his gathering forces. Bertòn joined them. Luc glanced at his father and shifted his weight, indicating his impatience, and Peri shot him a warning glance.

"The rules have changed. Dylan has departed, the prisoner's fate is unknown, and Antoine has opted to join us here on the field. What do you say? Shall we see what our esteemed colleague of the south has to say? Until we hear from the Faye about the state of their rescue, we are at an impasse. We do not know what we are negotiating for," Marcus muttered.

Bertòn nodded. Before he could comment, two shapes materialized out of the shifting haze and began to solidify as they approached the group. They passed through sentries as though they were invisible. As the figures became more solid, Luc recognized the smaller of the two.

"Tabitha!" His father and uncle stopped him from approaching with hands upon his arms.

"Luc, the man with her. Who is that?"

Luc shook his head, bristling at the unknown tall stranger next to her.

*Tabitha, are you all right?*

*Yes, I am fine. Don't be worried; we have come with some news and help.*

The pair stopped before the Caskan men, and Kayle bowed his head respectfully to Marcus. Luc exchanged a quick glance with Tabitha, arching a brow at the anxious expression on her face. Her smile was quick and nervous. She slid next to him and grasped his hand.

*I hope you are ready for this!* She murmured to him.

# CHAPTER TWENTY-TWO

HOURS LATER, TABITHA STOOD AT THE END OF THE TABLE, nervously shifting her empty javé cup between her fingers as the round chamber began to slowly fill with the Faye. The large chamber with deep ebony walls reflected warm light from the series of lanterns situated in the walls. A large oval table and the surrounding chairs were the only things in the room except for the Faye milling about in small groups. Doni stood at the other end of the table, quietly directing the activities of the other Faye. The change in her mother baffled Tabitha; she could not figure out why her mother would be in an apparent position of leadership within the Faye. Her thoughts were interrupted as Larissa entered the room with a slight inclination of her head toward Tabitha. She approached Doni.

Tabitha spoke to Kayle, who stood behind her, his fingers locked on her shoulder. "Why does everyone seem to defer to my mother?"

Kayle glanced over to where Doni stood. "It may appear that way, but it is not quite deferment. Your mother will be the negotiator. She has been granted permission by our council to speak on behalf of the Faye."

"And what is happening now?"

"She is gathering those with whom we must negotiate."

"Where are they?"

Kayle's tight smile was grim. "Shortly, Tabitha. Be patient."

The room began to quiet. Doni pointed to a handful of Faye, who then took seats at the table. Several others were then selected and took places around the room. Those remaining once the heavy wooden doors were quietly shut drew into a circle within the large gap between the doors and the table.

The room became silent when those in the circle closed their eyes and slowed their breathing. The floor shimmered. Tabitha grabbed at the table when the floor seemed to drop beneath her feet. The patterned marble shifted to reveal the scene that seemed to float beneath them. Kayle chuckled softly and reached out to disengage her fingers from their clawed grip on the edge of the table. Tabitha let the sensation of vertigo pass. The floor remained solid when the scene below them shifted to a view of the field where Antoine and Marcus's forces stood ready to face off.

"It is time," Kayle whispered.

Tabitha held her breath in anticipation. She peered through the floor, searching to catch a glimpse of the people below, but the angle kept them obscured. Before she could ask Kayle a question, the air seemed to crackle with electricity, and a shape began to form in front of the doors.

"Oh my God..." Her breath escaped in a rush when Marcus suddenly appeared, followed by Bertòn. The amazement on their faces faded as the Faye herded them toward the table. With a final effort, the circle of Faye communally focused. The air seemed to shift and sizzle, and one more participant began to materialize. Antoine stepped into the room.

Antoine appeared at ease, his expression cool and aloof as he took stock of the members of the assemblage. Tabitha recognized the exact moment when he saw Doni. His cool facade crumbled; the myriad of emotions that cascaded across his face were a testimony to the feelings running through him. Tabitha could not have chosen one single sentiment to define his response to seeing Doni.

She tore her eyes from the pain and raw longing revealed on Antoine's face and noticed her mother's impassive expression. Barely a ripple of emotion passed over Doni's face as she watched the man she had once loved struggle to come to grips with her presence.

"Antoine, thank you for joining us." Doni's voice was cool.

"I do not recall being asked to join," Antoine responded.

"Be that as it may, I request that you please sit and allow us to review the matter at hand," Doni stated. She indicated the trio should take seats at the table. "Please, all of you. Let us sit and discuss…"

Antoine cut her off. "We were in the process of setting up negotiations. Why are the Faye suddenly interested in our administrative agenda?"

Marcus barked a short, dry laugh. "You failed to share that you brought a force up through my governance without my knowledge. This information would have been key to our negotiations."

"Had you not attacked my earlier representation, I would not have been leery to share such information," Antoine responded smoothly. "Your attack makes us believe your territory is potentially hostile, so I considered it prudent to keep our presence to a minimum until such time that we could determine your intentions."

Bertòn leaned forward and spoke in an amenable tone, but the snap of anger in his eyes belied any goodwill. "What were your original intentions in St. Mikel, may I inquire?"

"I understood my daughter had been kidnapped by your son," Antoine responded.

Tabitha shot to her feet. All eyes were upon her, but Kayle spoke before she could bellow a retort.

"We will remain quiet on this point. It is not the intention of our council to address your current adversities but rather to find an amiable and hopefully peaceful resolution."

"No, we do not! We want to scratch…" Kayle shushed Tabitha and pushed her down in her seat; her eyes snapped in fury. As her temper cooled, she caught sight of Bertòn hiding a grin behind his hand as he coughed lightly.

Doni stood. "Kayle is correct. The Faye are not concerned about your internal warring, but the fact remains that your two governances have come to fight over two of the Faye. That is what has caused us to intercede. Do you all agree to this neutral forum?"

"We do," Marcus acknowledged.

"We do not!" Antoine stood. "It is obvious that you have your own agenda. Marcus is sided with the Faye, seeing as his nephew is her lover."

Tabitha rolled her eyes. "Does everyone have to keep saying that?"

Doni lifted a hand to quiet her. "We are here as an impartial—"

"Impartial?" Antoine scoffed. "Hardly! You have clearly sided with Marcus—you have come to me on his behalf."

"We have simply removed the prisoners from your son, seeing as their care was... shall we say, less than gentle?" Doni countered.

Antoine snapped. "That lie is formulated to further encourage the Faye to take up arms against Chandolyn. It's based upon fabricated claims. Those people were under my protection—"

"Your protection?" Bertòn rose to his feet. "You call raping my niece *protection*?"

"Rape?" Antoine repeated.

Marcus nodded. "Our scouts and seers witnessed Dylan dragging my son's wife from her tent and into his own."

Antoine shrugged. "Again, you have no proof of what transpired between them and whether it was of a nonconsensual sexual nature."

As Bertòn and Marcus's faces revealed their outrage, Doni lifted a hand. "Perhaps we should ask her?"

With a graceful wave of her hand, the wall to the right of the room began to waver. The darkness began to gradually lighten until it dissolved to reveal another room. Alena stood next to a bed, Tristyn lying motionless in it. The two envoys captured in the rescue attempt stood with Alena.

"Where is Katie?" Tabitha whispered to Kayle.

"Katie is being kept hidden with the baby. We are not sure if Antoine is aware that she is alive, so best to keep her concealed," Kayle murmured.

Tabitha watched Doni approach Alena. Alena's eyes had caught sight of Marcus and Bertòn; her face revealed her relief, but her eyes remained cautious. Doni and Alena spoke quietly. Antoine took his seat, waiting for their return with barely disguised disgust.

As Doni returned to the table, Antoine leaned back in his seat. "Regardless of what the human female says, what makes you the judge of my son's actions?"

"You mean the atrocities he has committed against our race, as well as others?" Doni asked.

"You say 'atrocities' as though you know his deeds for a fact. What brings us here, however, are negotiations between St. Mikel and Chandolyn. St. Mikel incited a war by attacking a legion of my men passing across their lands. Let's say we start with Marcus's actions."

Marcus leaned forward in his seat. "Is this to be a true forum to discuss our differences? If so, I suggest we list offenses. Starting with why you have two armed war parties on St. Mikel land, as well as an armed guard on St. Mikel citizens."

"What were your son and his wife doing in Windrift? Stealing away Chandolyn citizens in the dead of night? Secreting away a healer, who also happens to be a Chandolyn citizen, not to mention that your nephew took advantage of and then kidnapped my daughter," Antoine responded curtly.

Tabitha felt Kayle's iron will pressing upon her as she struggled against leaping up and screaming at the audacity of Antoine's comment. Taking advantage of her? When Antoine had given her to Luc as a reward! Kidnapping? Antoine had held her prisoner and threatened her with worse if she attempted to leave again. As Kayle's will kept her silently in her seat, Tabitha clenched her teeth in frustration.

She was aware of a seam of sweat along her brow as she fought his control. Suddenly, with a quick glance at Kayle, she felt more than a little mortified to realize that her struggle was barely even taxing his energy.

Doni lifted a hand between the two arguing men. "Regardless of who did what to whom, we are not here to hash out your political grievances. I am more concerned about the lives of those you kept prisoner and the release of my daughter to return home. If we can find a suitable agreement that results in Antoine abandoning St. Mikel and leaving without the hostages and Marcus swearing that he will accompany my daughter to the portal to return home, we can—"

"Where is your father?" Antoine demanded, cutting her off.

"He is none of your concern," Doni responded.

"He *is* my concern. A citizen of my jurisdiction, he was under my protection. He is also a healer, as we all are well aware. I will not leave without him."

Marcus stood. "I will not leave this place until I am assured that Dylan will be held accountable for his crimes."

Doni sighed. "I don't think you both understand that we are not here to determine who is at fault. Once we have released you both to your prospective regions, you can begin the war that you both seem determined to engage in. I am only concerned about returning the hostages."

"Your father is no longer your concern. He became my responsibility when you abandoned him," Antoine responded.

"I did not abandon him. He is my father, and Faye, for that matter." Doni barely flicked a glance at Antoine before returning her attention to the assemblage.

He was not, however, prepared to let it go that easily. "When you kidnapped our children you did abandon him, and he may be Faye, but the Faye were most certainly unconcerned about his welfare. He has been under my care for eighteen years. I would like to have him placed back under my care."

Doni's eyes snapped. "My father was murdered under your care."

"What? That is ridiculous!" Antoine's face revealed his shock.

"Oh? Shall I have Tabitha explain what happened to him?"

"Are you seriously going to accuse me of murdering your father?" He shoved an accusatory finger at Marcus. "His son and wife stole onto my property. How can you assume your father was not killed during some ill-fated attempt to kidnap him?"

Doni sent Tabitha a nod and a warning glare to keep her temper in check.

Tabitha responded quietly. "I was there when the black elf took my grandfather's life."

Antoine's face began to slowly redden. Tabitha watched him swallow and clench and unclench his fingers. His eyes narrowed dangerously. Kayle met his glare with cool regard. A moment of tense silence slid by before Antoine spoke. "Just what is it that you are accusing me of?"

"We are well aware of Dylan's crimes to your people. We chose to ignore them. But it seems not all of those attacks were Dylan's doing." Kayle's words were deliberate. Antoine's dark eyes snapped at Kayle, who ignored him and continued. "You have made very dangerous alliances. Should you opt to continue on this path, we will be forced to intervene for the good of our world. You know all too well that the appetites of those you feed will not be satisfied when their numbers increase."

Antoine stared at Kayle, his jaw tight. With apparent calm, he responded. "Again, I ask just what it is you accuse me of."

Larissa lifted a hand and spoke. "We will release you, and we will release your troops, but you must discontinue this alliance with the dark ones. We must eradicate the few you have foolishly allowed into our land. The portal must be closed and never reopened. Will you agree to this?"

Marcus's face was red with fury. He clenched his fists against the tabletop. Doni lifted a hand to calm him and request his patience.

Tabitha noticed Doni's eyes narrowing as all eyes turned to Larissa.. "And...you will hand over your son." She swept her hand toward Antoine. "A life for a life."

Antoine choked and stood to face the Faye leader. "I had no intention of harming Roane, only seeing to his care through the remainder of his life. You, on the other hand, do not have the same intention for my son."

Larissa nodded sagely. "We would repay him with the same treatment he has given his victims. We intend no bodily harm, but through a series of mental interventions we would allow him to experience the terror, anguish, and physical pain his victims experienced."

Antoine shook his head and assumed his seat. "I will not allow the Faye to judge what they avow has occurred. You do not have proof of any wrongdoing."

Kayle rose. "We are certain of Dylan's attacks on the outlying villages, and what is more…" He paused. Larissa stood as well. Their eyes met, and she nodded for him to proceed. "We have agreed not to pursue those allegations, which shall be reviewed by your Caskan peers. We have agreed to not police the Caskan people. However, you, Antoine, made a fatal mistake in your choice of partner."

Antoine stood. "I wish to go. I will take my son and daughter with me. I will leave your prisoners, who I believe to be criminals in my governance due to their actions, but I will not leave here without my children."

"No. You will leave alone with your troops, and you will turn over your son, as well as the black elf," Larissa insisted. "Your only child is your eldest. New information has recently surfaced to negate your paternity of Doni's two younger children. As such, you have no right to them or their lives."

Tabitha gasped at Larisssa's cold and heartless way of informing Antoine. Despite his behavior, she could not help but feel a twinge of compassion for him. A shock wave rippled over his face, and the open confusion written in agonizing pain across his face was almost too difficult for her to bear. Tabitha looked at Doni and saw the cool gaze that Doni returned to her. Her mother's eyes shifted uncomfortably, and Doni swallowed, trying to maintain her aloof pose.

"Is this true?" Antoine queried in a ragged whisper.

"I hardly think this is the time to discuss—"

His deep bark cut her off. "Is. It. True?"

Doni met his gaze, her chin defiantly tilted, but her expression lost some of its calm facade in the face of Antoine's agony. "It is. Cole and Tabitha are not your children."

He looked away.

Tabitha looked down to give him privacy. She noticed that Larissa wore a triumphant smirk. Tabitha glanced up. From the set of Kayle's jaw, she suspected that he too had witnessed Larissa's expression.

"Antoine, where is Dylan?" Larissa pressed.

Antoine turned haunted eyes to the woman, his mouth twisted in an angry scowl. "You wish me to tell you that? I owe you nothing." He stood. "I will return with my troops to Chandolyn, but I agree to no other of your terms."

Larissa, refusing to back down, leaned forward, her eyes direct as she stared Antoine down. "You have no ability to leave this place until we release you. You will depart, but not until you tell us where your son is and where the black elf is."

"Release me. If you wish to punish Dylan, I cannot stop you. It seems he has become a liability to me. But I do not know where he is at this time. You will have to use your own resources to find him," Antoine sneered. "As for my partnership with the black elf... This is an endeavor started by Dylan in an attempt learn their capabilities and control efforts—"

*Bullshit*, Tabitha thought. She kept her thoughts to herself as Antoine continued.

"It is my understanding that Dylan has already disposed of the black elf. It seems to have grown beyond his ability to

control it. I demanded he cease and desist his experimenta-
tion. The black elf has been removed from our world."

Faye voices erupted. Even Larissa's attempts to quiet the
clamor proved ineffective. Kayle's voice cut through the up-
roar. "What has he done with it?"

Antoine shrugged, his face once again assuming a dis-
dainful, aloof cast. "I told you, he is sending it from this
world. It will no longer be a threat to us." His dark eyes
snapped toward Tabitha; she noticed the slightest hint of a
smirk. "The creature will be someone else's problem."

Tabitha groaned and rose, her eyes reflecting the horror
stabbing her heart. "I know where Dylan is heading!"

Kayle nodded in response, and the two of them disappeared from the chamber.

# CHAPTER TWENTY-THREE

TABITHA FELT HERSELF DROP BACK INTO HER BODY. LUC was leaning over her, a grin sparkling from his blue eyes. "Welcome back."

Kayle groaned as he rolled off the sofa. His hands went briefly to his head. Then he turned to grin at Tabitha. "Nicely done. I believe they had no idea we had been separated and were not physically there."

Luc helped Tabitha sit up. Her head spun as she re-acclimated to her body. Luc leaned over to peer closely into her eyes. "You all right? Your strength good?"

She nodded and inhaled deeply. "It got easier when I got used to holding both of our images." She turned to Kayle. "Were you separating or letting me carry us both?"

"I had separated and let you give me that extra power that made me look solid. Larissa told me that she could not tell that we were separated," Kayle commented as he rubbed the kink out of his neck.

Tabitha let Luc rub the tingling from her arms. "Well, your hands on my shoulder made it pretty easy to keep us both fully solid. I am not sure I could have done it without that contact."

"Did you discover where Dylan went?" Luc asked.

Kayle glanced over sharply. "Tabitha, you said you knew where he was headed before you released. Where are they?"

"My God, he is taking the creature in Cole's body to the portal. He is going to send it to my world."

"What?" Luc demanded. "The portal?"

Tabitha briefly recapped the meeting for Luc, finishing with Antoine's last comments. "He said that the creature was already growing beyond Dylan's control. He said he demanded that Dylan send it where it would no longer be a threat to our world, and then he stared right at me. He is sending it through the portal, where it can now wreak havoc on my world."

Kayle shook his head. "Dammit. We need to stop him, and we need to get that black elf away from him."

"Can you journey? I can do it for you," Luc offered as he stood.

Tabitha nodded, and the three of them left their tent and ran toward the main tent. Peri and Diego were waiting for them when they burst inside. Tabitha and Kayle quickly relayed the details of the meeting, as well as Tabitha's belief that Dylan was heading for the portal with Cole.

Peri glanced at Luc. "Did you tell your father where you think Dylan is headed?"

"I told him with our link as soon as Tabitha told me. We have to get there before Dylan does. We can't let him release that black elf into another world. Cole seemed to have some control of it, but we don't know how much."

"Agreed. Your father will let Sybille know where we are headed. Let's go." Peri turned to Diego. "I will grab a handful or warriors. We will let you know what we find. You can bring Katie along to the portal once we have placed Dylan under arrest."

Diego nodded, but before he could comment, Tye stepped forward. "I want to come."

Peri shook her head and reached for her pair of rapiers. "I won't have you on this team. You don't listen to orders, and you respond too emotionally."

Tye shook his head, red faced. "I will. I promise. I can't stand what he did to Tristyn and Alena."

Peri strapped on her blades and glanced up at Tye. "That is the reason you cannot come with us. Those are not your words. Those words coming from your lips are Mia's."

Tye stared at her, open mouthed and enraged.

Diego handed Luc his sword and snapped at his younger brother. "The intention must be true, Tye, not just empty words to impress your intended bride. You need to grow up."

Tye turned without a word and stalked out of the tent. Luc glanced at Diego with a raised eyebrow; Diego simply shrugged. "A lot of things are going on with him, and they all have Mia's name on them. We will get to the bottom of it when this is over. I don't have time for his tantrums right now."

Diego and Peri accompanied Kayle to the armory tent to find him a weapon. Luc led Tabitha outside. Tabitha felt as though her skin was vibrating with nervous energy. She clung to Luc's hand in an effort to keep her control. Her power seemed to be rippling under the surface of her awareness. She recognized that in the past few days of forcing herself to push her abilities, new abilities seemed to be opening at an alarming rate. Raw power swam through her blood; her fingers tingled with need to use the magic that pushed and prodded, as though searching for an outlet from her skin.

"Let's go meet the team and end this," Luc said with a rough growl as he led her toward the team that waited for them. "Once Peri and Kayle are back, we will head for the portal and hope to beat Dylan there. I am not sure what we will do if the creature has already been released to your world."

"By the 'creature', you mean my brother." Tabitha's voice held a snippy edge.

"You will have to face the fact that the creature has taken over your brother's body," Luc responded.

"Cole is still in there. You heard him."

"I heard Cole's voice."

"That *was* Cole—and he *is* in there. He told Dylan to release us. I don't know how much control he has."

Luc shook his head. "Regardless of how much control he has, the creature will need to feed. From what you told me about your research, the more the creature feeds, the more it requires. I am not sure Cole will be able to restrain it from taking what it needs from yet another victim."

Tabitha swallowed back a retort. She realized that although she did not like them, Luc's words were true.

The birds flew over the open field with an abandon that set Tabitha's heart thumping. The urge to change into her crow shape and join them as they frolicked through the gusts and billows of wind was strong, and she could see the same wistful longing in Luc's eyes before he turned back to

Kayle. Tabitha let the others discuss strategy as she caught her breath after the journey to the field that held the portal. The black stone on the chain around her neck seemed to hum with familiarity. Was it sensing the nearby portal?

There were eight in their group, including Tabitha, Luc, Kayle, Peri, and four other Caskan whom she had met briefly before beginning to journey to the portal. Peri had them cast a field around them that Tabitha thought made them invisible until Peri explained that the net around them simply reflected their surroundings.

"If we actually became invisible to the eye, we would easily be sensed from the power we would be expending," Peri explained. With a smile added, "You have to adjust to the fact that we use six senses in this world rather than five. Remember that anything we do can be easily detected so if we intend to remain hidden, we must remain hidden from all of the senses."

"Speaking of which... Tabitha, you need to raise your shields. You are humming so loudly that I am surprised you haven't drawn them to us," Kayle commented.

Tabitha brought her shields up and leaned back against a large white boulder that was absorbing the afternoon sunlight. Although the air was warm, Tabitha felt chilled after the days' excitement. The sun heated the rock; she closed her eyes to let that warmth infuse her and melt away the chill that crept deep into her core. She ignored the voices around her while the group waited for Dylan to arrive and let her energy levels replenish.

She sensed more than heard him approach. She opened one lazy eye when Luc leaned above her on the rock. "Does Dylan have access to a stone for the portal?"

She nodded. "I would imagine he has my fath—I mean, Antoine's rock. Antoine showed me his when I first arrived. Dylan might have that."

Luc cursed and turned back to the others.

The afternoon had begun to wane, and the group had become quiet and restive as they waited. Tabitha began to doubt her belief that Dylan was in fact coming to this portal. What if she were wrong? Had she just assumed this was where Dylan was headed?

Her musings were interrupted by the creak and groan of wheels traveling the grassy slopes. Tabitha sat up; the others stood at the edge of their protective barrier and watched the entourage approach. Tabitha's fingers dug into Luc's arms when the rolling cage came into view. She craned for a better view of Cole.

"I can see him, he's in the cage," she whispered to Luc.

Luc grunted but did not respond. He reached for his sword, glancing at Kayle and Peri as they did the same. "You ready?"

Kayle shook his head. "Wait until they are closer. I don't want them to have time to scatter. I want to see how many people Dylan has with him. Speaking of which, where is Dylan?"

Tabitha's eyes swept the oncoming group and realized with a gut-wrenching twinge that Dylan did not seem to be among them. "Where is he?"

Before anyone could respond, Peri tilted her head, as though listening. Tabitha detected a faint stirring of energy. With amazement, she realized that she was capturing the energy from a link between two Caskans. The ability to recognize this seemed to leap out at her, and she could barely contain her grin of delight.

Her pleasure was dampened when Peri groaned. She turned to the others. "Diego just reached out to me. Katie and the baby are missing."

"What? How did that happen? Who was watching them?" Kayle demanded.

Peri clenched her teeth in anger. "By the One God, Tye was watching her! He wanted to try and redeem himself. Diego discovered him, unconscious."

"Where would Katie have gone?" Luc asked.

Tabitha shrugged. "The baby is only a few days old, and she does not know the area. I cannot believe that she would have willingly gone anywhere."

Kayle growled low in his throat as he watched the procession approach the portal. "I think we just might know where Dylan has disappeared to."

Tabitha groaned. "Oh my God, you mean that Dylan might have Katie?"

"If he thinks that the child may be a healer, he would try to get to it." Peri watched the procession approach the portal. "We have no choice but to get that black elf away from them first. Then we need to go after Dylan."

Tabitha snarled in frustration. "How did Dylan know that Katie was alive and had delivered her baby? He has seemed to be one step ahead of us all the time! It is like he knows what we are doing— What?"

Tabitha realized that Peri's face was set in an angry scowl. "Katie is not the only one missing."

"Who else is missing?" Tabitha asked.

Luc watched Peri as awareness dawned upon him. "Mia is missing as well, isn't she?"

Tabitha looked back and forth between them, confused. "You mean Tye's fiancé? Dylan took her too?"

Luc let out an explosive groan. "She has been using Tye all along for information, hasn't she?"

Peri turned to give Kayle a quick synopsis of the situation. As Peri described Tye and Mia, it began to dawn on Tabitha what had happened. "Are you telling me that Mia helped Dylan and betrayed us?"

Peri shrugged. "We don't know that for sure. We will need to find out more when Tye wakes, but yes, it does look that way."

Tabitha cursed, drawing a raised eyebrow from Kayle. She almost laughed at the comical expression on his face at her choice of language. "I am over eighteen, *Dad*."

Her sarcasm drew a short laugh from him before he turned back to the others. "It looks to me like the only option is to proceed with our original plan. We cannot let them release that creature into the other world. We need to contain it. Let's do what we came to do. Then we will need to figure out how to get Katie and her baby away from Dylan."

When Tabitha stood, the slim blade that Kayle had given her knocked against the rock. It clattered and hit her leg with a sharp *snap*. She let out a short cry of pain. Luc stopped her, amusement in his eyes. He knelt down and drew the shorter lanyard around the lower part of her thigh and secured it to her leg.

She gave him a rueful glance, and he chuckled and re-minded her, *You were the one who got upset when one of the Faye commented that you are no fighter.*

*I know, but no one wants to be told they're a wimp. I can fight,* she retorted, walking stiffly with her attached blade. *And Kayle gave me this, assuming I would have to fight, right?*

*I think Kayle gave it to you in the event that you need protec-tion,* Luc responded. *I am not so sure you should be using a blade, but Kayle seems to think it is a good idea.*

Tabitha grinned at him. *I won't cut off my own hand.*

He nodded but looked less than convinced.

She and Luc approached the entourage making its way toward the portal. Peri shot a glance around to the group and lifted her hand, warning that their protective shield was about to drop.

The collective guard around the gray cage came to a roll-ing halt and turned in surprise at the eight Caskans that suddenly appeared.

Peri strode forward and hailed them. "What business do you have on St. Mikel territory?"

One of the guards strode forward to meet her. "I have not been made aware that we could not pass within each other's borders without harassment."

Peri lifted a sardonic brow and raised a single blade to point to the gray cage. The top of the enclosure was barely visible behind the group of guards who had clustered before it. "Of course, but you must admit that the sight of you roll-ing a prisoner through our territory may solicit a few ques-tions."

The guard pursed his lips and cast a glance over at the cage. "I can assure you, the prisoner is being dealt with and will not be any threat to you or anyone within your boundaries in a very short time."

"Do you intend to kill him on our soil?'

The guard looked shocked. "Of course not."

"Then how is it that you are so sure he will not be a threat?"

"We are transporting him to a portal and allowing him to return to his own world." The guard's voice was confident; he waved his cohorts to proceed.

"Halt!" Peri demanded. "I have not yet released you to proceed."

"What authority do you have to stop us?" the man challenged.

Peri lifted her blade and reached for the second rapier, drawing them together before her, the steel crossed, her intention clear. "I speak for Marcus DesChamps of St. Mikel. I am his spokesperson, and I will determine when it is safe for you to continue."

"How do I know your words are true?"

Kayle strode toward the line of guards gathered before the cage. "If you truly have no ill intention, then you won't mind me seeing the prisoner."

The guard, caught by his own cleverness, hesitated before responding. "The prisoner is not your concern. I assure you that upon his release into the portal, he will be unable to return."

Kayle stopped when two of the guards approached, swords drawn in warning. Kayle waved one man aside, but the second guard, nervous and anxious, lunged forward, drawing a warning shout from Peri. The meadow erupted in a maelstrom of flashing swords and clanging steel. Tabitha had known a battle was possible but was unprepared for the mayhem that ensued around her. Luc grabbed her and shoved her behind him. She stumbled and dropped to her knees. One of the guards who had accosted Kayle fell beside her, blood spurting from his throat. She screamed and rolled away. Luc planted his legs on either side of her as he swung a powerful stroke at an attacker.

Another body hit the ground, and Tabitha swallowed back the panic that threatened to immobilize her. There was no safe place in a battle for someone who couldn't even draw a blade, never mind fight. She saw the edge of the cage holding Cole from the corner of her eye and with a focused thought, she closed her eyes and journeyed over to it. She slit her eyes open and found herself kneeling on the ground beside it.

Cole sat in the cage, his knees drawn to his chest, his head down. He lifted his eyes in surprise when he noticed Tabitha kneeling and clutching the bars. His pale hair was knotted and disheveled, and his eyes, the same shade as hers, seemed to radiate a haunted dull glow.

"Cole, are you all right?"

"Tabitha, what are you doing here?" Cole demanded, his eyes darting to the fighting.

"We've come to get you away from Dylan. Do you know he plans to let you loose in my world?" she hissed, pressing herself against the cage as two fighters trampled past.

"I don't know what he plans to do with me, but I have my suspicions." He shook his head with a doleful smile. "He and I don't talk much."

Before she could comment, he eyed her fingers on the bars. "Tabitha, I am not fully in control of this monster. I am not sure you should be so close. It needs to feed. I am not sure I can keep it from you. Did you ever learn to shape the crow?"

"Crow? Yes."

"Get into your shape. It won't bother you in a shape that small. Its appetite has grown. It won't go for smaller animals any longer," Cole reported.

Tabitha shifted into her crow shape and fluttered to the top of the cage, her eyes seeking out Luc. She saw him almost immediately, fighting intensely. Small cuts and bloody lacerations crossed his shoulder and along his jaw. The battle in the meadow raged; Tabitha's mouth grew dry when she realized that the St. Mikel Caskan seemed to be outnumbered. She caught sight of Peri fighting ruthlessly with her twin blades. Kayle was dragging a second attacker off Luc. They turned to fight back to back, holding off several of Dylan's guards at once. Her heart sank as she saw two more guards come out of nowhere to join the skirmish; their numbers were multiplying, overtaking Luc, Kayle, Peri and the remaining two St. Mikel fighters.

# CHAPTER TWENTY-FOUR

As Tabitha watched the battle with a pounding heart, her panic swelled into a foreboding sense of dread. Dylan's guards appeared in the meadow in twos and threes, joining the fight, outnumbering her companions. She scanned the area, frantically seeking a way to help, to do something. She marshaled her powers, trying to find some way to improve the odds, but terror held her at bay.

"Tabitha, look! Who is that?" Cole gripped the bars, his interest in the battle increasing.

She peered through the mass of fighting bodies, trying to see what he was talking about. A man seemed to emerge from the ground between Peri and one of her attackers, a broadsword in hand. Peri's astonishment at this development was obvious even from Tabitha's vantage point. More figures seemed to emerge from the ground, placing themselves between Dylan's guards and the St. Mikel Caskan. The numbers tipped toward the St. Mikel group as more new participants emerged, men and women alike, weapons glinting in the fading sunlight.

Kayle and Luc stopped fighting and watched their attackers being overtaken by the mysterious new warriors. Luc bent and leaned his hands on his knees, panting, his sword in his hand, watching in amazement.

Tabitha watched as the newest arrivals fought, quickly overrunning Dylan's guards. Soon the remainder of Dylan's guards ran for the edge of the field and journeyed out of sight. As she was lifting her wings to flutter to the ground, she felt her crow body grasped in a pair of strong hands. She was able to let out a startled *caw* before she was tugged off the top of the cage.

She heard Luc cry out to her, but before she could react, Cole's arm shot from between the bars to squeeze the guard's throat between strong fingers. The guard's eyes widened as he was dragged bodily over to face Cole. Tabitha flew from the man's released grip and changed shape as Luc raced toward her, pulling her into his arms. She clung to him and buried her face in his shoulder, not willing to turn and see what Cole would do to the guard. She was fairly certain about what would happen next. She could not bring herself to watch another succumb to the ravenous appetite of the creature.

"Are you all right?" Luc asked against her hair.

She lifted her face to him. "Are you? I saw some wounds—"

"Not Now. Look!" He gestured to a pair of figures walking across the meadow toward them.

"Sybille?" Tabitha cried out as the little woman approached. Her brows knit in confusion. "Darko? Is that you?"

"You know each other?" Sybille grinned at them as she approached.

Tabitha turned to the Northern Faye. "Thank you."

Darko smiled. "You are very welcome, pretty lady. I told you when we met in Windrift that I would assist you when the time came. You promised me assistance with finding the substance that Edgar Lee Donn discovered. For that, I owe you."

Luc hovered in anxious attendance behind her. Tabitha sensed some intensely jealous vibes coming from Luc. She swallowed her amusement and introduced Darko to Luc. As the battle-weary Caskans approached, she also introduced him to Peri and Kayle.

Peri commented. "We owe you our thanks. We were quickly becoming outnumbered."

"I am glad we could help." Darko acknowledged and then glanced at Tabitha. "Let us see to our wounded. I ask only that if our healer assists any wounded, I be permitted to witness it. None of my people have ever seen a healer."

Luc glanced at her with a raised eyebrow. She shrugged and followed Sybille to check on the injured. Her next two hours were spent healing first the worst and then the lesser of the injuries. Luc stood nearby, offering his blood as needed. Sybille hovered close, offering support. Darko watched intently, asking questions as Tabitha worked. She felt her energy drain, and her responses became shorter as her focus began to waver. Finally, she turned to look for Kayle, but Luc shrugged. Kayle had disappeared while she worked. She turned to Luc and lifted tired arms toward the lacerations across his body. He gripped her hands before she started.

*Are you sure you are up for this?*

She grinned at him, showing him a quick flash of sharp teeth. *I need you healed enough to be able to give me some strength.*

When his wounds were healed, Tabitha self-consciously succumbed to the need for blood. Luc sat back against a large rock, and she slid into his lap. She could not have said how long it was before she released her mouth from Luc's throat, her energy replenished and her fangs receded. Luc glanced down and she gave him a smile, pressing her lips quickly to his before she climbed off his lap and pulled him up.

They made their way over to join Peri, Sybille, and Darko near Cole's cage. Darko was watching Tabitha's twin with interest, his dark eyes glancing between the caged man and the guard lying dead on the ground.

"Can we do anything to help my brother?" Tabitha asked Darko as they approached.

Darko's eyes were lit with curiosity. "Your brother? I was under the impression Dylan was your brother."

"He is my older brother. Cole is my twin."

Darko glanced between them, amazement evident in his expression. "Twins? Truly? I had not known Faye could have twins anymore."

Tabitha indicated Cole. "I don't think you are the only one to be surprised."

"And did you uncover the mystery behind your Faye blood?" Darko asked.

Tabitha felt her face redden slightly as she nodded. "Uhm, yes. It seems both of my parents are full Faye."

Her comment piqued Cole's interest, and his head snapped up. "What?"

She turned to Cole. "Cole, it seems our mother is quite a master at keeping secrets. Kayle, one of the Faye who was here fighting, is a fisherman from my home island in the other world. I recently found out he is not only a full Faye but that he is the one who helped our mother tune her powers so she could escape." She paused. Not knowing how else to say it, she blurted out her final statement. "It seems he is our father, not Antoine."

Cole was obviously perplexed. His gaze shot between Tabitha and Darko. Cole's eyes held a wild expression, and it was Luc to whom he turned. "Is she serious?"

Luc lifted a shoulder. "Apparently so."

Cole exhaled.

Darko watched this exchange with interest. "So the host of the black elf is a full Faye."

"Will that make a difference?" Tabitha asked.

"I don't know," he commented, his expression thoughtful. "But it may help. I would like to take him north with me. We will try and find a way to help him."

Tabitha glanced among the faces around her: none of them offered an answer. It became apparent that the decision would be hers and Cole's. "Can I speak with him alone, please?"

The people in the group nodded and began to quietly disperse. Some headed over to the small group of Dylan's guards sitting on the ground, the Northern Faye standing guard.

Tabitha turned back to Cole, her fingers gripping the silver bars encaging him. "Cole, what can I do to help you? Do you want to go north with Darko? Please, tell me how to help you."

Cole's glowing eyes, luminescent in the late afternoon sunlight, held a deep sadness. "I don't know how to answer that. I don't know what to do about having this thing in me. I don't feel all that different, but I am," he struggled with the words, "not alone." He stared at her and then shook his head, a deep sigh escaping him. "I can only control so much, although I am trying to discover a way to get more control. The more the black elf feeds, the more control I lose." Tabitha leaned closer to hear his muted words and noticed for the first time that his raised voice seemed to share the quality she had heard when the black elf had taken over his body. It sounded as though more than one voice was passing through his lips.

"Cole. Are there others in there with you?" She was almost afraid of his answer.

His eyes met hers. After a moment, he slowly nodded. "They are here, but not like me." His voice cracked, and he dropped his face to his hands. The anguish poured from him, and Tabitha was startled by the intensity of his pain as it engulfed her. "They are like shades, whispering to me, haunting me. I cannot sleep. I cannot shut off their voices or their pain. They are stuck here, watching the horror of this thing as it engulfs more and more. They will remain in this half-alive and half-dead place until the creature is destroyed."

"Gwyn?"

He nodded. "Gwyn too."

"Why did he kill her? Why would Dylan have let it kill her?" Tabitha asked.

"Dylan did not allow it. The creature escaped. It tracked her because she had been meeting with others who were hunting the creature. The creature sought her out because she had been in touch with the Northern Faye," Cole admitted. "Once the creature became part of me, its thoughts are mine."

Tabitha gasped. "Northern Faye? Darko?"

"Yes." Cole glanced at the guards behind her and dropped his voice again. "They sensed the creature when Antoine had the portal opened. They hunted it, and it knows."

"But why the Northern Faye? They came to me to ask me to help them find out how to destroy it," Tabitha admitted.

"Yes. They know how to contain it, and it fears them. I am not sure what else they can do, but the creature seems to think they are a threat."

Tabitha gestured to the bars. "This stuff, do you know what it is?"

"I only know I cannot approach it. It won't kill me, but I cannot touch it or be near it."

"Cole, do you know how to kill it?"

He shook his head. "I only know that the more it feeds, the more it will control my physical body and the less I will be able to control it."

"So this is what Dylan was after? To have the creature take him over?"

Cole snorted. "Dylan thought that with the power of the creature, he would be invincible. He wanted to be the host so he would be able to wreak havoc and no one would be able to stop him. I am assuming he was unaware that the creature would gain more control as it continued to gain strength."

Luc slid up behind her. Tabitha sensed the others approaching.

"Cole, do you know where Dylan is?" Tabitha hissed.

Cole glanced at her and nodded. "He has Katie. He took her from the St. Mikel camp. They have already crossed into the portal. He has taken her back to your home. He intends to wait for you there."

Tabitha dropped her head in her hands, a long groan escaping her. "Oh God, no! Will he kill her?"

Cole shrugged and lowered himself to sit in the cage, his knees drawn to his chest. "I don't know what he plans. I just know he was heading for the portal. The guards were supposed to be bringing me along to meet him. The only other thing I overheard was some description of a house or something, and some woman named Trude."

Tabitha's stomach clenched. She released the bars and turned to Luc. "We have to go there. Do you know where Kayle went?"

He shook his head and offered a guess. "Maybe back to tell the Faye what is happening?"

She turned to Darko. "You won't kill him, will you?"

He shook his head. "No, with the creature's ability to manifest itself and solidify as it feeds, the host cannot easily be killed. The question is can we separate them? Or can we kill the creature and save your brother?"

Cole said, "I would rather die than live like this."

Tabitha turned to Darko. "Promise me you will take care of him?"

Darko nodded. "I promise we will do everything in our power for him. You will research Edgar Lee Donn and that symbol I showed you?" He slid a long gray wand from his sleeve. Cole slid back at the sight of it. Darko turned to Tabitha. "Your mother sent this along. It is the same material as the bars. It will keep him contained but not kill him."

Tabitha turned to Cole. "I will find a way to help you. I promise."

Cole extended his hand and then withdrew it. "If you can't find a way to help me, find a way to kill me and release us all."

With a last glance, Darko gave her a grave nod of farewell, and the Northern Faye gathered around the cage. They laid their hands along the bottom of it, and the entire group journeyed their way out of the field.

# CHAPTER TWENTY-FIVE

EVENING HAD SET IN. THE SKY TURNED DUSKY PURPLE AS Tabitha and Luc made their way through Dark Hollow. Tabitha could sense the familiar sights and scents of home, but the changes in her life since leaving Porta Negra made her feel as though she were watching home movies of someone else's life. Deep pangs of loneliness cut at her emotions. She wondered if she would ever adapt to this duality.

Tabitha glanced up at Luc's broad shoulders as he stepped over the weeds and onto the pavement in front of her. If they were able to get this figured out and return Dylan to the Faye, how would she ever say good-bye to Luc?

She shoved the gloomy thought aside and focused on the challenge before them. The last time they were here, she had brought him to see her world while she had come to search for her mother. This time, she needed to find a way to get Dylan out of her world. Her stomach clutched with worry as she imagined Dylan believing he would not need Katie any longer.

They approached the house with tentative steps. Tabitha felt the sweep of a searching mind as they approached.

*Did you feel that? Was that Dylan?*

*Yes. Keep your shields up. Let's go,* Luc responded. *Change into your crow shape.*

Tabitha let her body pour itself into her crow shape. Luc was already taking flight; her crow instincts reacted with a shot of fear at the proximity of his hawk shape. She ignored them and she let her wings drive her into the air, following him.

Tabitha detected muffled shouts as they approached the house. Luc banked over the trees and she followed suit, casting an eye toward Trude's house. The higher tree peaks blocked her view, and she swept her wings to ease around them for a better view.

The porch came into sight, and Luc's sharp warning echoed in her mind. He kept to the treetops, avoiding detection.

*He won't be looking for us up here*, she snapped back.

*Of course he will. He knows I can shape a hawk, and I guess he has put the clues together as to how you could have gotten out. He knew we had a crow in our room,* Luc responded as he alighted on a wide pine branch overlooking the back of the house.

*I think you are giving him too much credit.*

*And you are not giving him enough,* Luc retorted. *Look. There they are.*

Tabitha landed next to him on the branch, craning her neck to see through the pine boughs. Katie and Trude sat in chairs on the back porch, their eyes watching warily as Dylan paced back and forth before them. Their voices floated up to the pair of birds huddled behind the deep green branches, but the words were hard to make out. Luc nodded, and they hopped down a couple of branches, keeping themselves hidden in the relative safety of the pine boughs.

"Where is he?" Dylan's angry shout assailed them.

Katie leaned forward and snarled in fury. "I'm not telling you anything!"

Dylan's hand swept back and caught her across the mouth. Katie rocked back, but her arms remained attached to the chair arms, obviously fastened in some way.

*Luc, where is the baby?*

*I don't know. Judging from Dylan's tirade, it sounds like neither does he.*

Trude's voice reached them, begging Dylan to stop, but he lifted a hand in warning to the older woman.

*If he lays a hand on her, I will destroy him,* Tabitha growled.

Dylan lifted his pistol and placed the muzzle against Katie's forehead. Between clenched teeth, he growled, "For. The. Last. Time. Where did you hide my son?"

Katie met his glare with a stony challenge in her eyes. "Go ahead and kill me, and then you will never know where he is."

Dylan's lips pursed in a scowl before his face became more thoughtful. "Well, I may not be able to kill you, but I can most certainly kill her." Dylan turned the gun toward Trude's head. Tabitha saw the color drain from the older woman's face.

Voices came from the driveway. Tabitha watched as Dylan quickly slid the gun into his waistband and turned to see who approached. Mia stalked around the corner of the house towing Kayle behind her. Kayle's face was a mask of confusion as he regarded the two hostages.

"Who is that?" Dylan demanded.

Mia shoved Kayle up the stairs, the slim blade in her hand pressed against his spine. "I found him approaching the house. He said he is a fisherman from town, stopping by to see the old woman."

Dylan's scowl deepened. "Why would you bring him here?"

"He was coming anyway!" Mia snapped, her tone defensive, as she shoved the larger man toward another chair. "What is the harm of one more human?"

Dylan growled a response and gestured with his chin for Kayle to sit.

Kayle took the seat and put his hands up in surrender as Mia leveled the blade at his face. "Trude, what the hell is going on here? I was just going to deliver some fish. Who are these people?"

Mia slid the blade closer and demanded his silence. She waved her fingers around his wrists, securing them to the chair.

*Oh my God, they have Kayle! He must have followed us over here. Why would he let her grab him?*

*As a Faye, he could have easily overpowered Mia. I suspect he is trying to get a closer assessment of what is going on. We need to be ready to move, but not until we know we can safely protect Katie and your aunt,* Luc responded.

*Do you think there are more of them?*

*I wish I knew. I can't sense anymore, but they could be shielding, as we are.*

Tabitha turned her attention back to the porch, her nerves tense. Kayle tried to defuse Dylan, only to be threatened into silence with the gun.

Dylan turned back to Katie and again demanded to know where she had hid the baby. At her continued silence, he turned to Mia in frustration. "She was only alone for a couple of minutes before I came back through the portal with you. She could not have gone far. Go back to the portal and look again. He has to be somewhere nearby!"

Mia nodded and headed back toward Dark Hollow. Tabitha could feel Luc's attention shifting. *So Dylan left Katie to go back and get Mia. Katie must have used that opportunity to hide the baby.*

*Luc. He is only an infant. He cannot stay alone for long.*

*Agreed. Tabitha, I will stay here to help Kayle get Dylan away from these two. Head into Dark Hollow and see if you can find the baby.*

Tabitha sent him a quick acknowledgment and took off from their protective branch, glad to have something productive to do.

Luc's warning rang in her head as she flew over the treetops. *Watch out for Mia. She can be dangerous.*

*Are more of your ex-lovers going to be out there trying to kill me?* Tabitha could only sense his response but laughed at his obvious derision.

Tabitha cautiously remained hidden by the foliage during the short flight, her shields tight and solid against Mia or any other Caskan who might be lurking in the gloom. The summer air was still hot but the dark gloom of Dark Hollow brought the temperature down quickly. As she maneuvered through the dense growth, Tabitha felt as though she had slid into a cool mist.

She flew past the portal and extended her senses over the lush growth, looking for any sign of the child. If Katie had been able to get away from Dylan, it would have only been for a couple of minutes. Which direction would she have taken? Would she have run deeper into the swamp or toward the road? A few minutes was not much time to find a safe hiding spot for a newborn. Tabitha shuddered at the thought of Katie having to hide the baby in the undergrowth of Dark Hollow. She must have been convinced that Dylan was more of a threat than hiding her baby in the swampy vegetation.

Flying concealed became more difficult. Tabitha dodged branches and slid among the leafy canopy concealing the earth. Human instincts fought with crow instincts; she tried to shove branches from her face instead of trusting her natural crow ability to dodge the foliage, but her concern over the baby overrode everything else.

A dark shape appeared on the ground below. Tabitha saw Mia stomping along the trail, using her blade to cut through underbrush as she searched for the baby. Tabitha felt a groan of fear bubble up within her as she watched the girl slashing; she prayed Mia would not locate the child before Tabitha could.

She winged toward the portal and began to fly in a circle, trying to determine how far Katie could have gotten. Moving in concentric circles, she watched the ground closely for a spot that would hide an infant. Of course, the swampy green floor was full of places that Katie could have concealed the baby.

Tabitha paused on a branch as she thought this through for a moment. Katie would have had only a matter of minutes to run. The thought of hiding a tiny baby in a dark swampy forest would cause any mother to panic. Why couldn't they hear him now? Would an infant abandoned in the woods remain quiet?

No, something was not right. Katie would have protected that baby with her life; she knew Dylan wanted him alive. She would not have risked something happening to the baby alone in the woods.

So, with only a couple of minutes, where would Katie have believed the baby would be safe enough to leave? Where would she feel that the baby would be protected if by chance the mother was unable to come back for him?

Something was not making sense.

Tabitha landed in the foliage on a branch and watched as Mia hacked her way through the underbrush, passing beneath the tree where Tabitha hid.

No, Tabitha was sure the child was not hidden in Dark Hollow. Katie had not known Trude or where Tabitha lived. Even had she enough time, she would not have been able to make it all the way there. Where would she have left the baby?

A slow suspicion began to dawn on her as she watched Mia tromp around the corner. Tabitha took to the sky and dodged branches, making her way over the treetops. She was pretty certain she knew where that baby might be— there was one place to check.

Flying above the treetops, the island was spread beneath her. Tabitha felt the warm summer breeze beneath her wings as she raced toward her destination. Her spirit rose; the salty air and familiar scents of home boosted her courage. Dylan was in her territory now, and she knew that she had the advantage. She began to descend toward the familiar neighborhood. Her aunt's house came into sight. The urge to change shape and race into Aunt Ellen's arms and be comforted surged within her, but she knew that she had to get back quickly.

She circled the house and floated on the gentle air currents, drifting toward the ground. Her crow feet hit the back deck, and Tabitha hopped along, catching sight of herself in the reflection from the glass sliding doors. Her ebony wings reflected the evening sun with a midnight blue sheen, and her dark crow eyes glittered with interest as she hopped over near the door. The screen was open, and Tabitha heard voices within. Her heart raced at the familiar sound of Aunt Ellen and Callie's voices. They cooed, and with a chuckle like a quiet caw, Tabitha recognized her aunt's high-pitched speaking-to-baby voice. Tabitha saw that she carried a tiny bundle wrapped in a blanket.

The front door slammed, and Roni trotted into the room, dumping her backpack on the floor. She approached her mother.

"Hey! Whose baby?"

Ellen smiled at her younger daughter and shifted the baby into Callie's eagerly waiting arms. "I am not sure. Kayle dropped him off and asked us to watch him for a few minutes. He said he would be right back and explain everything."

Tabitha turned to the edge of the deck and let her wings lift her toward the sky.

*Luc, I found the baby.*

*Is he all right? Where is he?*

*Kayle took him to my family. They have him now.* She circled and headed back toward Trude's house.

*Kayle? How did he find him?*

*I don't think he followed us over here. I think he ran over as soon as the fighting was over. He may have been waiting for them. I think Katie may have given the baby to him.*

*You coming back?*

*Yes. Is everything all right?*

*Dylan is starting to lose control. He is getting wild, and Katie won't give him any information. I may have to intervene.* Luc's tone was grim.

*Wait for me to get there!*

The contentment from seeing her family evaporated, and panic engulfed her. She thrust her wings hard as she raced for Trude's house. The sun began to sink toward the ocean as her speed intensified. She sent repeated silent prayers for their safety. The dazzling sunlight reflecting on the ocean blinded her as she flew for the familiar shape of home.

As she flew over the house, her fear escalated when angry shouts from the back deck assailed her. She sought Luc among the pine branches and headed for the safety of the trees before Luc's warning echoed through her head.

*Look out!*

Before she could react, a gunshot blast rang through her brain. Terror gripped her as her body twisted in midair, knocked off course by the bullet that sped past her and clipped her wing feathers. She raced for Luc and saw him sweep from his hiding, flying toward her.

*Luc! No!*

*Tabitha, get into the trees!* His voice was an urgent shout in her brain. He flew beneath her, inserting himself between her and Dylan's bullets.

"Get down here, you cowards! I see you!" Dylan shouted.

*Tabitha, get into the trees. Let me take care of this!* Luc circled beneath her, urging her toward the relative safety the deep pines offered. She sped for the pines, sparing a glance below as she did.

Kayle had leaped to his feet and was wrestling the blade from Mia's hands while Dylan shouted for them to come down, the gun in his hand aimed up at them. Tabitha turned her attention toward the pines before Dylan's taunt froze her blood.

"Tabitha, I give you until the count of three—"

*Tabitha, no. Don't listen to him!* Luc's voice cut in above Dylan's shout.

Tabitha turned to see Dylan standing with his gun pointed at Trude's head. Trude's face was a mask of terror, and Tabitha turned before she could think. She knew deep inside that she would do anything to wipe that look of dread off of her elderly aunt's face.

Kayle was still fighting with Mia. The pair had tumbled off the side of the deck, blood wrapping them in a slippery sheen. Luc tried to fly in front of her, but Tabitha ignored his warning and dove straight down. She was changing shape even as Luc lunged, talons toward Dylan, intent on slamming the gun from his hands. She felt her feet touch the ground in front of Trude. Katie screamed, and the explosion rang in Tabitha's ears.

She marveled for a split second that she had finally been able to land and change on her feet before the shock of the impact sent her spinning past Trude and crashing to the ground. The world spinning before her eyes, she watched Luc leap onto Dylan, the momentum from his flight as he changed shape driving them both to the ground. Trude's cries rang in her ears, and her chest burned with a searing pain. Tabitha struggled to draw a breath. She observed the older woman's feet struggling as Trude tried to disengage from the chair.

Katie's screams were the last thing Tabitha heard before darkness overtook her.

# CHAPTER TWENTY-SIX

WARMTH INFUSED TABITHA'S BODY. THE DARKNESS became a soft glow that seemed to hover above her chest. Hot pressure had replaced the pain; she listened as her chest pumped her breath in and out. She seemed to have no control over her body and allowed herself to float in a lethargic dreamless state.

The slow thump of her heart and the dull hiss of her breath consumed her awareness. No other consciousness interrupted her languid drifting; her entire world seemed about blood flowing through her veins and simply existing.

Blood.

Pain.

Slowly awareness began to awaken; memories of pain, of blood spurting through her fingers and Luc's frantic ministrations, came in a rush. The darkness that had engulfed her had been pierced with pain tearing through her. She felt as though she were drowning; she coughed and struggled for breath. The memories pushed her to swim frantically toward the surface of awareness, shoving the cocoon of oblivion beneath her as she struggled to wake.

The cocoon tightened, and a warm, familiar sensation overwhelmed her. She felt her hair being gently stroked back from her burning face, heard a soothing voice telling her all would be well. The smell and touch of a mother tenderly caring for her child allowed Tabitha to slowly sink back beneath the cocoon, back into the simple darkness that took with it all of the pain and fear.

As she began to emerge into the present, light pierced Tabitha's eyes. She heard the indistinct murmur of voices around her and felt a light touch infused with warmth on her arm. Her head felt as though it weighed hundreds of pounds, and the effort required to roll it and look around seemed too monumental. She closed her eyes and let the world settle back into place. Heaviness began to slowly seep from her limbs. The murmurs became more distinctive as cognizance shook the last dregs of drowsiness away.

"Tabitha?"

She recognized Doni's voice and opened her eyes to see her mother smiling down at her. "You feeling better?"

Tabitha nodded and inhaled deeply, feeling strength begin to ebb into her muscles. "Where am I?"

"Back in the Caskan camp."

As the memories of her last conscious moments came crashing back, she gasped, her hands reaching for her chest. She craned her neck and looked down at her exposed chest. Pink lines were slowly receding, as though the skin had just finished knitting together. She felt no pain. Her skin felt warm and whole under her exploring fingers. She rested on her elbows, and a hand helped support her. She looked over to see Luc watching her, concern etched across his face.

"Hey."

She smiled at him, reaching out a hand to touch the welts and bruises on his face. "What happened? Did Dylan do that to you?"

Before he could respond, Tabitha became acutely aware she was laying bare-chested with both Luc and her mother in the room. She struggled to rise, looking around frantically for a shirt. Doni chuckled and tugged a clean shirt from the rack behind her. Tabitha felt heat rise in her face before concern over Luc's injuries dominated her thoughts, releasing her embarrassment.

Luc stroked her cheek. "I'm fine, Tabitha. Your mother has promised to fix the worst of it when she regains her strength. We needed to make sure you were alive first."

She glanced over to see Kayle entering the tent. "Tabitha, you are doing better, I take it?"

"Yes. What happened? Did anyone get hurt? Where is Dylan?"

Doni sat on the edge of her bed and nodded. "Luc subdued Dylan. He and Kayle brought him and Mia back. Katie and her baby are fine and are with Trude. And you, it seems, saved Trude's life."

"The baby is back with Katie?"

"Yes, they are all safe. Luc got you back here just in time," Doni said. She turned to Luc. "Let me take care of your injuries, and then I will leave you two."

Tabitha scooted off to the side and watched her mother settle Luc on the bed she had abandoned. Her hands began to heat as she noticed that he held his arm at an awkward angle. The cuts and bruises she had originally observed seemed to have multiplied as he climbed onto the bed. Doni tugged Tabitha to the side and settled her into a seat.

"Let me take care of him. You are still too weak."

Kayle leaned back against the tent post and watched the procedure with hooded eyes. Tabitha glanced at him and saw his red welts fading; she had to assume that Doni had healed his wounds. She returned her attention to her mother and watched as she slowly slid her hands over Luc's body, a silvery blue glowing on her hands. Her eyes closed, Doni let the healing energy slip along the wounds. Tabitha watched, fascinated, as Luc's skin began to knit beneath her mother's fingers, blood easing back into his body. Bones appeared to slide beneath her palms and settle back to full strength.

Luc's eyes were half opened and she rose and walked over to see him, a smile curling his lips as he watched her. Although he seemed conscious, her mother passed her fingers over his eyes and the lids dropped. Doni focused attention on his torso. Tabitha watched; Luc's ribs seemed to ripple beneath Doni's palms.

Doni's eyes opened, and she glanced at Tabitha. She beckoned her and then moved her left fingers to Luc's forehead. She hovered her glowing right fingers along Tabitha's temple. Tabitha felt the warmth of her mother's touch and could sense the connection flowing between her mother's fingers and Luc's quiet body on the cot. A sudden sharp mental wrench made Tabitha stagger back a couple of steps.

"What did you do?" Tabitha demanded, her hands on her head. Something was different—missing—but she could not identify what felt wrong.

Doni's hands began to lose their glow. Almost as an afterthought, she reached for Luc's throat and with an almost sensuous stroke ran the tips of her glowing fingers along the scar Tabitha had left on his throat after the first time she had healed. Tabitha opened her mouth to protest but quelled her objection. Her desire to keep that mark on him seemed selfish.

Doni's brows pulled together in the briefest frown. She ran her fingers over Luc's scar a second and third time. Despite her attempts, the skin refused to heal; Tabitha's mark remained.

Doni let the remaining healing energy slide from her fingers before she turned to Kayle with a pale and drawn expression. Tabitha caught the briefest sight of her mother's fangs before Kayle wrapped her in his arms. His palm supporting her head, he directed her mouth to his throat. Her mother's arms wrapped around Kayle's middle. Tabitha observed the tremor in her fingers, recognizing all too well the weakness that engulfed a healer after a difficult healing. Kayle's mouth tightened as Doni's mouth fastened on his neck. His face was close to her hair; he spoke to Doni in a gentle murmur.

Tabitha turned away, awkward about witnessing the tenderness between the two. She turned her attention back to Luc and slid her fingers along his jaw, wiping her mother's sleep suggestion away. Luc's eyes opened, and he glanced over at her, a slow smile curving his lips.

"Feeling better?"

He slid his hands along his arms and ribs and nodded. He sat up, glancing down at his dirty, bloody and torn shirt. "Yes. Much."

She turned and saw Kayle slowly step back, his hands still on Doni's hips to keep her steady. Tabitha could not shake the feeling that something was not quite right. She reached out to Luc but found nothing but the echo of dead space. She gasped.

She tried again, but the only sound was a hollow emptiness that rattled through her brain. Luc did not even glance up. He had not felt her attempt to reach out to him. She turned back to her mother. "What did you do?"

Doni stepped from Kayle's embrace and glanced between them. "I broke your link. I placed it there when you were both children, and now I've broken it. If you are going home to pursue your life, the life you have planned and saved for, then the last thing you need are any ties here."

Tabitha stared at her, her mouth open. "You had no right to break that link."

Doni ignored her and turned to Luc. "Did your father tell you about your mother? The truth?"

Luc slowly nodded. "He did. When we returned to camp from Antoine's."

Doni seemed to struggle. She inhaled deeply and dropped her head, her face filled with sorrow. "I am so sorry. She lost her life helping me escape with Tabitha. I can never express the loss I feel. I miss her every day."

Luc nodded, his head bowed, but said nothing; his eyes were distant.

Doni and Kayle held hands and moved toward the tent flap. They exited, leaving Luc and Tabitha alone.

Tabitha broke the silence. "You knew? About your mother?"

"Yes, my father briefly told me. He has promised to tell me more of what he knows. I don't think it has sunk in yet," he admitted. "I am not sure how I feel about it, but I never knew her. I am proud of her bravery, but the truth is, Sybille is the only mother I've ever known. I guess when it all quiets down, my father and I will talk again."

Tabitha slowly sank next to him on the bed. "I am sorry I did not tell you. I wanted to, but we were always involved in such craziness that I never found a few peaceful minutes to tell you what my mother had told me."

Luc shrugged. He tossed the bloody shirt to the ground before rising to find a clean one on the rack behind her. "It was not your secret. I suspect we have only scratched the surface of all the secrets. You have discovered a million secrets that your family kept from you. I am not sure you have actually found the truth of some of them."

Tabitha nodded silently.

Luc lifted her chin to meet his gaze. "What will you do now, knowing that your family has kept secrets and lied to you?"

"I don't know." She felt silent tears begin to spill from her eyes. "So much has happened. I just cannot seem to grasp it all."

Luc lifted her to her feet and slid his arms around her, pulling her close. "You need to go home, you know that? I want nothing more than for you to stay here with me, but the war has just begun, and I can't guarantee your safety."

Tears rolled in earnest as she wrapped her arms around his shoulders. "I don't want to leave you. Come with me."

His response revealed a brief hint of amusement. "I have no place in your world. My place is here, helping my family and my people against Antoine's desire to rule our world. We don't know if he has more black elves or what he has promised to those alliances he has built. His reach is deep in our land, and we need to know if the other governances are aligned with Chandolyn or not."

Tabitha nodded against his chest. Silence expanded as they stood torso to torso. The loss of their link was still too raw for Tabitha to imagine. Her voice was barely a whisper. "What about us?"

Luc tightened his arms around her, and she felt his cheek rest against her temple. He did not respond for a long time. When he spoke she felt the words rumble softly from his chest. "My world is falling apart. You are the last of the line of healers. You need to train and learn how to control your power."

"And then?"

She felt him lift a single shoulder and drop it. He did not reply for some moments. "Maybe when you have gained control over your power, maybe if you find the solution that allows us to eradicate the black elves...maybe then you will return? I don't know."

Her eyes met his. "And how long will that take?"

His lips lifted in a sad shadow of a smile. "Months. Years. A lifetime. I wish I knew. But when you do, come find me."

Lifting herself on her toes, she tugged his mouth down to hers, silencing any further discussion.

They spent the evening in the main tent sharing a meal with Luc's family and Doni and Kayle, surrounded by the clamor of laughter and discussion. The food offered Tabitha little flavor. Luc's company stole all of her attention. She could not help but drink in every nuance, as though she would be able to replay the sensations in the future to savor when she was alone.

She caught him glancing at her more than once, his eyes were intense as they traced her features. There was always a gentle hand on a knee or fingertips skimmed along an arm. The moon rose high in the sky, and Tabitha prayed that for once time would slow to a crawl.

Tabitha took a small respite from watching Luc when she noticed her mother talking to Marcus and Bertòn near the exit. Kayle's face was solemn and drawn when he rose and walked to the tent flap, turning to wait for Doni. With a solemn nod to both men, Doni turned to Tabitha and beckoned her. They left the tent together.

Tabitha rose and, after a quick word with Luc, headed outside to join Doni and Kayle. Kayle waited tensely under a nearby tree with a black scowl across his usually stoic face. Doni waved her over, slid her arm through Tabitha's, and led her to a moonlit field at a slow and meandering pace. The sounds of the Caskans enjoying the evening in the tent faded as they walked.

Tabitha was the first to break the silence. "Where is Dylan?"

"He is with the Faye. Marcus will be responsible for punishing Mia. The Faye will reprimand Dylan, and then he will be turned over to my care," Doni explained.

Tabitha felt her chest tighten. She pursed her lips, hesitant to ask the question that hung in the air. "You are not returning with me, are you?"

Doni's silence grew. The wind whispered in the treetops, and the moon lit the field in a drizzle of pale light. Doni slipped her arm from Tabitha's and stopped beside a ring of stones that huddled in a small indent in the field. She gestured for Tabitha to sit and perched on one of the dark boulders. Tabitha climbed over a rock and lowered herself across from her mother.

Tabitha found her voice. "Where is it that you are going to be after Dylan is released to your care? Will you be staying with the Faye?" The question was like tugging a scab from a wound. Her only desire was to get through the worst of what her mother wanted to tell her.

Doni's head shook back and forth in a slow arc, her eyes focused over Tabitha's head. She bit her lip, and then words began to emerge. "No, I will not be staying with the Faye. When I tell you what I am about to say, I don't want to hear any more arguing. I have fought enough these past weeks to last a lifetime." She leveled her gaze on Tabitha. "You know that everything that has transpired in the past weeks has not been without its risks? There were confessions to be made. The plain truth is, Tabitha, that the charges that were leveled against Antoine cannot all be proven."

"What does that mean? He won't be punished for what he has done? He will have—"

Doni interrupted what promised to become a tirade with a single hand in the air. "Let me finish, Tabitha. Antoine will have his own demons to slay, but the Faye will not police his actions. That is up to his peers in governance, not the Faye. We will, however, be taking action against Dylan for his crimes. Should he survive, he will be released to me. I will be with Antoine."

Tabitha leaped up, amazement and horror clashing. She cried out, "What? How can you?"

"Antoine will not relent in his efforts to get you back under his control. Until you are fully trained, he will always be right there, somehow trying to drag you back to be his personal healer." Doni stood and placed her hands on Tabitha's shoulders. "I have bargained my freedom in exchange for yours. He has promised to relinquish any further attempts to hold you as long as I return with him."

"You can't do this. You can't go back there." Tabitha whispered, her voice harsh.

Doni answered gently. "I am not the same girl he once controlled. I am not sure he knows what he is gaining in this bargain, but he'll have some surprises if he thinks I will meekly submit. I will be carefully monitoring Antoine. I can keep an eye on him as well as Dylan, and I will keep the Faye informed of his activities. You can safely return to your life. He has made this bargain based on emotion only. He has not thought through how he plans to control a full Faye." Doni's expression revealed an odd blend of smugness and fear that Tabitha could not decipher.

"What makes you think he will allow you to 'watch over' him?" Tabitha blurted. Her raw emotions were stretched over her worn-thin skin; the thought of abandoning her mother to go back to Antoine knotted her stomach. "Why can't you just come back with me, help me from there? Kayle has promised to train me. He will make sure I am strong enough to take on whatever Antoine can throw at me. You cannot go back to him now—after everything."

Doni dropped her head, her white sheaf of hair falling forward, concealing her face. Tabitha, holding her breath, watched her mother struggle to find an explanation. Before Doni responded, Tabitha asked, "And what does Kayle think of this? How long have you been planning this? He told me that there was no reason for him to stay here, so he must have known you had no intention to return."

Doni did not respond. Tabitha unconsciously rose on her feet, in tears, cajoling and begging to understand what would possess her mother to give away her freedom. Guilt began to crush her chest. She finally fell silent and dropped back onto the rock. "How can you do this? I cannot live with knowing you are sacrificing everything for my safety."

"I am not only doing this for your safety. Antoine has experienced only a setback. Once he regroups, there will be little to stop him. He will never allow this single episode to impede his progress. He will continue his plans, which are deeply and well sown. This will not stop his plans—they are well underway," Doni replied. She reached over to touch Tabitha's cheek.

"But you admitted that the Faye will not police him or punish him. In that case, why is one of their own going in there?" Tabitha retorted, pulling away from her mother's gentle stroke.

"The Faye will not allow the black elves to enter this world. I can monitor Antoine's actions. Should he cross any other lines, we will be ready to take action. He can strive for power, but we will not let him impact our world," Doni responded, still calm. Tabitha's emotions, however, churned. "Besides, who else would a mother sacrifice herself for if not her own child?"

The tears began to slip down her cheeks, and Tabitha swept them away impatiently. "You have already sacrificed so much for me."

Doni shrugged and stood, gently leading Tabitha from the ring of stones toward the main tent. "Tomorrow morning, you will return home. Hone your powers, because those in this world who know where you are will never let you rest. With Kayle's help, place protection around the island, and watch over Katie and the baby."

They stood outside the main tent; the cool night breeze fluttered their hair. Kayle separated from the shadows and silently took a protective spot behind Doni. Mother and daughter stood silently, the din from within the main tent trickling out and washing over them. Doni gathered Tabitha to her chest, hugging her close.

"This is not good-bye," Doni whispered. And then, with barely a sound, she was gone.

As Tabitha reentered the tent, the clamor of the Caskan gathering ran ragged fingers along her raw nerves. Tears threatened to spill from her eyes; the revelry surrounding her crushed her resigned mood. She gasped, suddenly short of oxygen, but before she could panic, Luc's arms were sliding around her, pulling her close to his warm body.

She knew his smell, the feel of his body. His very essence seemed to envelop her in warmth and calm. His body protected her from the tent full of people as he steered her toward the back tent flap. He led her outside into the cool night air.

The darkness and silence were balm to her taut nerves. She kept her arms wrapped tightly around his waist. Her head pressed against his chest, she heard the quiet rumble of his question but not his words. She felt devastated over the loss of their link, but after the turmoil of the past days, it seemed as though she could barely process the fact that her mother had severed it.

She heard the smile in his voice as he repeated his question. "Do you want to take a walk? Get some air?"

She lifted her head to meet his eyes and shook her head. "I want to be with you. I just want you to myself for as long as I can have you."

His head dropped to meet her lips. Later, she could barely remember the last steps to their tent.

The morning sky was painted in her prettiest hues, soft violets blending into the pale orangey tints that seemed to melt into the deep blue of the remaining night sky. Tabitha stood on the back deck of Trude's house, watching the same sky, the same sun just beginning to peek out above the velvety carpet of ocean waves, tears flowing down her face in earnest. She had just been standing beneath those same rays as they began to spread over Caska. She had watched the golden hues illuminate the clear blue of Luc's eyes as he held her for the last time.

Their last night had been a mixture of desperate, wild lovemaking followed by tears and slow, soft caresses that awoke deep yearnings. Her fingers had slid over his skin, memorizing the contours of muscle and the planes of his flat belly. She had thrilled to the feel of his shoulders, the shape of his chest, the way his jaw felt beneath her lips. They had been awake all night, talking, laughing, weeping, lying relaxed and warm in a tangle of naked limbs, awaiting the single touch that would enflame them again.

How can a single night be classified as the very best and the very worst? The pain of their parting capered along the edges of the pleasure of just being together—the simplicity of the other's company, the beauty of their bodies merging without further expectations. Her body was still trembling from the last time she had felt him deep within her, their sundering farewell looming in the near future. She could still feel the trembling deep within her, the rough texture of his unshaven chin scraping along her throat, the feel of his lips in a deep and passionate embrace that consumed her essence and left her empty but sated.

Saying good-bye had been the hardest single moment of her life. The night sky had begun to slightly brighten when Marcus swept her into a bear hug, promising her his aid, should she ever need it. Diego and Peri had been there; wishing her luck; Alena had hugged her in a teary embrace. She promised to kiss Cyra for her and give Tristyn, who was still too weak to accompany them, her best. Tabitha felt hot tears sting her eyes as Bertòn gathered her close, his voice a hoarse whisper that she could barely hear over her gasping tears. Then Sybille had pulled her into her tight grip, her small arms wrapped tightly about Tabitha as she whispered that she should enjoy her life and be true to herself.

She was empty of everything except rasping sobs when his family moved back. Luc's arms were around her, his lips pressed to her temple while she bawled on his shoulder. She had promised herself to maintain her composure and leave with dignity, but she clung to him, begging him to not send her back. Luc lifted his hands and pulled his gold token from around his neck and slid it over her head. With trembling fingers, she had removed her own silver chain and slipped it around his neck. His voice was choked with emotion and their final kiss had seared through her soul. She pulled herself from his arms, stumbling in a daze, until the flaming ring of the portal swallowed her. Then she found herself, on her knees, alone, sobbing on the ground of Dark Hollow.

Her tears began to dry, and Tabitha squared her shoulders. The sun had now made her glorious appearance. The deep ebony of the waves began to turn silver-gray; the white foam caps glistened in the brilliant morning light. Tabitha gripped the deck railing and glanced down to see the long blade still strapped to her thigh. She smiled to herself.

The same girl had not returned to Porta Negra. Her mother was right. In the same way that her mother was no longer the frightened girl who had escaped Antoine, Tabitha was not the scared teen hiding behind anonymity. She was a full Faye among humans, and she would never bow her head in fear again.

She could sense Kayle's power simmering in the west, toward Horseneck Beach, where his bungalow was tucked down by the piers. She inhaled deeply, and the tiny sound of an infant wailing slipped from the house to where she stood.

Her nephew was awake and looking for breakfast. Her mouth twisted into a slight smile when she heard Trude's voice calling to Katie and offering help. Katie shouted back some inane comment. Tabitha chuckled at the thought that these hard-headed, loud women had found each other within the shreds of the debacle.

Tabitha felt the slightest twinge of power singing along her skin as she lifted her fingers and inhaled the ocean air deeply into her lungs. With a long stretch, her body exhausted from lack of sleep but pleasantly sated from a night with her lover, Tabitha turned toward the door.

Today, she would catch up on some rest. Tomorrow promised to be a whole new day. A lot could happen in a day.

# EPILOGUE

ICE TAPPED ON THE WINDOWPANES OF THE DOCTOR'S waiting room. The chilly wind whipping back and forth swept the flags in front of the hospital and sent people's scarves swinging wildly around them. Tabitha lifted a hand toward the chilled windowpane and watched as the warmth of her skin affixed a gray silhouette of her hand on the glass.

She had been waiting for nearly an hour; it had taken well over a month to even get the appointment, so she was willing to wait. She'd had no idea how difficult it was to simply get on a physician's calendar for a routine visit. She just needed thirty minutes of the famous pediatric doctor's time. She knew she would be able to convince him, at the very least, that she had the ability to help some of his patients: the most critically ill children, those without hope. She could help.

On her last night with Luc, they had discussed her desire to heal without becoming a spectacle. Luc had nuzzled her neck and suggested she simply identify a small part of the population she could help that would mean the most to her. Upon her return from Caska, it had not taken her long to figure out which population segment to target. After several weeks of research, she found the best physician to target. Dr. Lawrence Golding at Dana Farber was a renowned pediatric cancer physician with a history of trying new, industry-challenging methods to treat his most critically affected patients.

Tabitha was about to offer him a fairly new and very enigmatic new treatment for cancer patients. She could not save the world, but she could help a small population. So here she stood, in December, waiting to offer her services. He might throw her out, thinking she was insane, but if she had judged him right, he would at least hear her out. With a little luck, he would let her show him what she can do.

The three months since her return had been a whirlwind of change in her life. Her mother had not returned, leaving Trude and Tabitha to find ways to explain Doni's absence. Tabitha found herself becoming adept at lying. To her shame, she had to accept that in a small way she was now no better than the accusations she had leveled at Trude. Now *she* was becoming the keeper of the secrets. Trude still owed her a long discussion about how she had gotten involved and her Caskan connection, but that had yet to happen. Tabitha found, after having made the decision to get on with her life, she could not bring herself to sit through the whole story. Her nerves were still too raw and her emotions too sensitive to look beneath the surface and face the pain that still bubbled beneath her skin.

She and Callie had stayed up an entire night as Tabitha had gone over the entire experience. Callie had sat and listened and let Tabitha cry, laugh and share every detail of her months in Caska. She was the only one that she had spoken to about Luc and once the dawn had risen the next morning, Tabitha had slipped the experiences away into a place where she could come to terms with what had happened. Her only allowance was his gold token that still nestled against her chest beneath her sweater.

School had been a welcome distraction from the heartache. Three months had flown by. The college workload along with part-time waitressing was enough to keep her focus firmly on the here and now instead of her loss of Luc. She thought of him daily, but she could not yet savor those memories without pain slipping between the cracks in her facade.

Kayle was renting an apartment in Boston, allowing her easier access to training without having to head back to the island. His friendship had proved to be a welcome balm, and she found herself looking forward to their weekly meetings. She called him often to just grab dinner or a cup of coffee; they both seemed to find some solace in their new relationship. Her own pain had been in the forefront, but she recognized that Kayle was also struggling with the loss of Doni.

Tabitha had been more than surprised to find that he still traveled to Caska with messages and updates as needed. She had yet to ask about Luc, and Kayle had not offered the information. To her surprise and joy, he informed her that Doni had sent D'Noir to Bertòn for care. Knowing her old crow friend was safely tucked in with Luc and his family was perhaps a small matter, but she cherished that bit of information when sadness crept up on her.

Kayle had also updated her on the FBI's investigation of Victoria Ristucci. Upon their return, Kayle had called his friend, Sergeant Donaldson of the Porta Negra police department. He and Tabitha had shared the information about pregnant girls being enticed over to Caska and kept there against their will. Victoria Ristucci disappeared before being questioned and had as of yet not been located.

Tabitha returned to Porta Negra briefly for Thanksgiving. She had to admit, the bond between Trude and Katie was a welcome outcome. Katie had found an openhearted home, and Trude had found someone to care for. The baby was growing quickly, and Tabitha delighted in her little nephew, although she could see Dylan in the dark eyes and brows. Katie was a wonderful mother, and little Dillon thrived in his new home. Tabitha had to laugh at the memory of her first day home, when Katie whispered that she had come to the conclusion that they had not been in New York.

The nurse called her name, and Tabitha turned from the window, squared her shoulders, and followed the young woman wearing festive scrubs. She could almost feel her fingers tingle with the need to heal and wondered if she was responding to the illnesses behind the closed doors of the hallway. The healing energy was anxious to escape. Tabitha felt the slightest hint of a smile. If escape was what her power needed, she had come to the right place. The thought of helping families devastated by illness boosted her spirits.

She found herself grinning back at the silly Christmas elf decoration hanging on the office door as she entered. A tiny elf sat prettily on a wrapped Christmas gift; with its pointed ears and long dark hair, it looked so much like Sybille that Tabitha could only smile. She winked at the impish little decoration and let the door close behind her.

*The End*